A TRYST WITH

MAHAKAAL

THE GHOST WHO NEVER DIED

TILAK DUTTA

First published in November 2019 by

Becomeshakespeare.com

Wordit Content De sign & Editing Services Pvt Ltd
Unit - 26, Building A -1, Nr Wadala RTO,
Wadala (East), Mumbai 400037, India
T: +91 8080226699

Cover Illustration: based on an Original Photograph of the Tso Moriri Lake taken by the Author in 2006. Secondary material includes photos taken by Guillermo Ferla and Chuttersnap on Unsplash.

Many references about 'Santji' aka Bhagwanji (Gumnami Baba) used or quoted in this book have been taken from the work 'Oi Mohamanob Ashe' by Charnik (revised and unabridged version 2010) published by Jayasree Prakashan Kolkata, with the kind permission of Shri Bijoy Nag.

ISBN - 978-93-88942-83-6

Disclaimer
This is a work of fiction. Names, characters, businesses, places, events, locales, and incidents are either the products of the author's imagination or used in a fictitious manner. Any resemblance to actual persons, living or dead, or actual events is purely coincidental. All the hand drawn maps are indicative and the Author makes no claims to the accuracy of these maps. They are only meant to be aids for the reader to follow the respective war scenario narratives.

Dedicated to the memory of
my late parents Gayatri Dutta and Nripendra Lal Dutta

Also to Kumar Gandharva and Nikhil Banerjee
whose music first awakened the seeker in me

'I am inscrutable' - Mahakaal

'Nobody can write my life because
it has not been on the surface for man to see' - Sri Aurobindo

CONTENTS

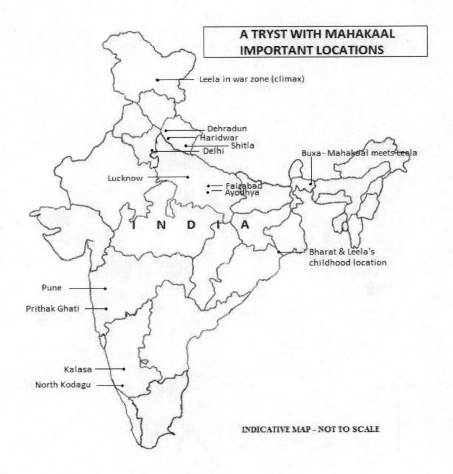

A TRYST WITH MAHAKAAL
IMPORTANT LOCATIONS

Leela in war zone (climax)

Dehradun
Haridwar
Shitla
Delhi

Buxa - Mahakaal meets Leela

Lucknow

Faizabad
Ayodhya

I N D I A

Bharat & Leela's
childhood location

Pune

Prithak Ghati

Kalasa

North Kodagu

INDICATIVE MAP - NOT TO SCALE

CHARACTER GUIDE FOR "A TRYST WITH MAHAKAAL"

BISWAS FAMILY
SHIV BISWAS, [Rebel Indian National Army or INA]. Elder Son of Rai Bahadur Biswas.
MAHADEV (MADA) BISWAS, [British Army]. Younger Son of Rai Bahadur Biswas.
SARASWATI [INA], Shiv's wife
ANURADHA (Anu), Shiv and Saraswati's daughter
RAJEN is Shiv and Saraswati's son, given in adoption to MADA
RAJEN married twice. Second wife EMMA.
LEELA BISWAS, Rajen and Emma's daughter.
BHARAT BISWAS, Anu's son twenty years senior to his cousin Leela
URVASHI, Bharat's wife
SACHIN, Bharat and Urvashi's son
ADITYA BASU, Leela's ex-fiancée
Gen. ARJUN PONAPPA and his wife CHITRA are linked to the BISWAS family

PRITHAK GHATI : Key residents
Birbal Kaka [Sarpanch]
Dr Ms. (Mancrop) Manchanda, Head of the "Integrated Medical Center"
Rudolph Weiss, German Engineer
P.C. Hindre, inventor
Makhonlal Ghosh [Machenda], ex trade union leader
Col. Satinder Singh {HELI SIR}, ex Ordinance engineer.

Members of Bharat Biswas's household
Kaushalya
Sonichari
Puran Singh
Firdaus
Kalia

Political TRIAD opposing Bharat Biswas
Sobha Singh Gujral
Prabhat Aiyar
R. Subramaniam

Bharat Biswas's college mates leading the DETOX movement
Avinash
Brijesh
Rajshekhar Rao
Srinivasan

PART ONE

LEELA

ONE

Leela had driven through heavy tourist traffic from Haldwani to Shitla in her rented car. Now, as she took a break to gaze at the Himalayan peaks bathed in the soft amber rays of the rising sun, she braced herself for her meeting ahead with Aditya.

It was in Shitla that they had met for the first time, on a rescue mission to find Leela's cousin Bharat who had gone missing during a trek. The first sight she had of Aditya was that of a ruggedly handsome man, heaving and panting as he climbed with Bharat's unconscious body on his back. Despite this heavy load, Aditya had still stopped to smile at the birds that scattered from their nests, shrieking in alarm. This was a moment which was embedded forever in Leela's memory.

Now that smile was long gone. An inherited burden on Aditya's shoulders had replaced his serene demeanour with worry lines. However, despite his humble, middle-class background, Leela knew that he would never abandon his search for a Buddha 'Image' which was certain to destroy him. Her own family had several members afflicted by similar dogmatic attitudes, especially 'hang-ups' about Netaji Subhas Chandra Bose and the INA (Indian National Army) who had fought the British during the Second World War. These had nearly ruined them as a household.

Leela had sworn not to spend her life with such obsessions. She knew the time had come for a straight 'yes or no' confrontation with Aditya.

An hour later, she parked her car carefully over a narrow culvert at the end of the ridge road. She quickly tied her long, dark brown tresses in a low bun accentuating her high cheek bones. Despite her trepidation, she looked ethereal and irradiant.

She could see Aditya standing below on the cliff edge, his hair ruffled gently by the breeze. He looked up towards her, their eyes meeting. A faint shadow of his old smile returned but it was tired and laboured.

Leela climbed down slowly, almost praying that he would agree to let go of this obsession which was devouring him. In her heart though, she knew the answer already. His face told her what she did not want to hear.

They stood facing each other.

Then she whispered, 'Yes?'

Aditya looked into her eyes for a long time. His expression tore her apart, as the dreaded 'No' manifested as a faint headshake.

Leela closed her eyes for a moment to stop the tears that were forming. They ran down her cheeks anyway.

Through her tears, she saw Aditya stepping forward to hold her. Yet another gesture; a tender embrace in sorrow... only to open a chapter which was bound to end in the same way?

Fearful of his touch that could induce her to change her mind yet again, she turned her back on him and fled from the clearing.

Aditya stood transfixed, his extended arm frozen in mid gesture.

It was over.

Aditya heard the car being reversed and then moving away. After some time he lost awareness of his immediate surroundings. Numb with pain, he did not know how long he stood there. Finally, only a solitary Buddha figure pervaded his consciousness and remained there as a constant soothing deity.

Leela sped down the NH 9 in a daze, without the usual stops at scenic spots which marked such long drives for her. Right through her long drive there were frantic messages on her mobile from her kin and close friends, who were all anxious about her imminent schism with Aditya.

A speeding bike zipped past her and also over a roadside pup, leaving it to die a slow death. In the past, Leela had always performed a rescue act as well as hauled up such offenders. She had streamed umpteen such incidents live on the social media and had a crusader's streak in such matters. But now she was herself a wounded animal in shock moving through a crowded urban forest in a state of complete stupor.

Nine hours later at the Delhi Airport she tapped the SEND option on her mobile: 'It's over. Topic closed.'

TWO

Leela's flight to Imphal took off in time. Her British friend Martin was in India with some friends for a visit to the World War II Cemetery in Kohima. They had already visited the INA memorial in Moirang in Manipur, and Leela planned to meet them directly after participating in a rally and seminar in Imphal.

As Leela reclined her seat for the long flight, she remained tormented by the memory of Adi's pained face in parting. Earlier she had wanted to call off this trip, but now she sorely needed such a diversion to overcome her trauma.

Her family situation was also another area of recurring friction. She sometimes wondered if there is indeed free will as well as rebirth, why was she 'freeborn' into such a divided and *obsessed* family? How she hated this one word!

Her granduncle Mahadev Biswas (Mada) was the scion of a disciplined Rai Bahadur's joint family which was loyal to the British. He joined the British Indian Army very early and rose rapidly through the ranks as a commissioned officer to finally retire as a Lieutenant General in the 1970s.

Everything was going well for the family when Mada's elder brother, Shiv, who was looking after the family's business interests in Burma, turned against the British Raj. One day without any warning, he donated the entire family assets in Burma to the Indian Independence League. Later he joined the Indian National Army (INA) in 1943 with his wife Saraswati, after being inspired by Subhas Chandra Bose's clarion call for joining the freedom struggle. Saraswati also enrolled her minor son Rajen in the Bal Sena, which was the first batch of children mobilized by the INA for disciplining into future model citizens.

Shiv trained in the INA volunteers spy school at Thingangyun (Burma) and was dropped near Sangyu by parachute in late 1943 to organize support bases among the tribes in Nagaland and Manipur for the planned invasion of India by the Japanese and INA forces.

The brothers fought on different sides of the divide, Mahadev in the Battle of Kohima and Shiv in Imphal. Mahadev, then a young recruit in the British Indian Army, was injured early in the battle and was helped by locals to reach safety.

On the Imphal front Shiv fought bravely, inflicting numerous casualties on the British forces. He was injured and unconscious when he was captured by them. At this time, Saraswati was stationed in Monywa (Jalan Ipoh camp). She had to retreat to Burma with the main INA forces, where she was taken into custody by the British army in Rangoon.

Shiv was later tried and sentenced to death, which was commuted to life imprisonment.

In course of time, Saraswati was released from prison and regained the custody of her infant son Rajen, who had earlier been handed over to the Biswas family by the British. Shiv himself was finally pardoned and released just after the Indian 'independence' was effected in August 1947.

The family extracted a cruel price for his deeds. Shiv came back with multiple injuries from torture in the Andaman jail and was unable to work. He was persuaded to legally give up his seven-year-old son Rajen in adoption to the childless Mahadev.

While Shiv and Mada respected each other as soldiers, there was a strict, unwritten rule in the family that there would be no discussion between them about World War II, the partition of India, and lastly Subhas Bose or the INA.

Eventually Shiv and Saraswati settled on a small farm on the Bengal-Orissa border with several other INA veterans. They had another child, a girl whom they named Annapurna or Anu. Many years later, Annapurna came back to them as a young widow with a baby boy. Anu's son grew up to be Leela's eventual mentor and closest relative, Bharat.

Mahadev went on to adopt a progressive lifestyle. He educated Rajen accordingly in the upper crust mould at the Doon School and St. Stephen's College. Rajen was encouraged to have constant interaction with the Indian National Congress Party bigwigs and the suave civil servants steeped in the Lutyens culture. Homes in New Delhi, Dehradun and Pune; memberships in all the elite clubs; shooting wildlife till India wore the protectionist fig leaf; ultimately retired life at the Pune Club… this was the way their life panned out. At home they all conversed in English and the occasional Bengali, but there was little else to bind them to their roots.

Shiv and Saraswati's life was a financially painful existence borne with good cheer. They farmed their small plot and Shiv, who had earned a law degree before joining the family business in Burma, provided pro-bono legal help to all and sundry. Annapurna taught in the nearby town school. While they all knew English well, they read Bengali literature and literary works of other languages translated into Bengali.

Rajen's first marriage with a General's daughter ended in a divorce. His second marriage was to Emma from a British-Pakistani family in UK. *Leela was born within a year in 1985.* After four years of enjoying the opulence and glitter of high life in chaperoned India, Emma began to push frantically for her own space and identity. But Rajen's ambition to expand his business empire and to outsmart his Industrialist rivals consumed all his time. Leela and Emma were completely left to the care of domestic helps.

Emma gradually grew disenchanted with her privileged life in India. Eventually she eloped with a Brazilian aristocrat whom she met while holidaying with Rajen in the Bahamas. Leela was left behind with Rajen, while Emma legally relinquished her rights to Leela's custody.

Saraswati and later Annapurna took over Leela's upbringing with a distraught Mahadev's consent. Rajen protested vehemently, but Mada realized it was better that she grew up in touch with the soil, rather than surrounded by domestic helps at Rajen's home.

Leela had a wonderful childhood on the farm in Bengal. Saraswati (Sarasdida) and Anu Mashi slowly filled her with the legends and facets of Indian history she was not aware of till then – very different from the convent educated stereotypes which would invade her life later. Bharat, who was her senior by over twenty years, played the role of mentor during his trips home from work.

And then it happened – an inevitable fallout of the fault lines that ran deep in the family. Leela was visiting her father and granduncle in Delhi and a big party was in full swing. She overheard some VIPs criticizing Bharat's views about the political economy and the role of Subhas Bose. This was a period when Bharat had defied the unspoken family rule by initiating public debates on Subhas Bose, bringing him into conflict with Communist intellectuals and the established Congress Party circles.

Even as a little girl, Leela had a ferocious energy and an instinctive choice for words which could perforate the most hardened adult armour. She launched into a fierce diatribe against all those who were speaking ill about Bharat. The offended guests left hurriedly, politely advising Rajen to control his daughter before it was too late.

An emergency family meeting was held. Rajen accused Shiv and Saraswati of indoctrinating Leela with the legacy of a loser, Subhas Bose, and especially his INA who had primarily joined the Japanese as traitors to the Indian Army to escape Japanese torture. He would not allow her to be brainwashed by Bharat with his outmoded, hare-brained views.

But Saraswati and Anu defied the menfolk and were not willing to change the way Leela's 'nationalistic' home education was shaping up, uninfluenced by the British legacy which still dominated school education.

Within a week, Leela was packed off to a reputed boarding school in North India. Bullying by deriding schoolmates followed soon after, since she stood out like a sore thumb. The contrast in education between the convent school and her local town school in Bengal and her training at home; the constant teasing by her schoolmates about her rural upbringing and attitudes; her initial opposition to popular kitsch tastes and her sudden exposure to television and later to the Internet; the glitzy malls and new role models from the west… all these made her grow up as a fractured personality, dreading the loneliness that was her wont throughout her school days; seeking a role model in real life and finding none.

Leela ran away twice from her hostel to be with Saraswati and Bharat, only to be apprehended and dragged back by Rajen amidst explosive situations at home. Finally, she was packed off to UK when she turned sixteen. When she later dropped out of her doctoral studies and switched to a course in Gerontology, Anu Mashi understood that concern for her own elders was behind this decision.

A few years later, when Aditya entered Leela's life, Anu Mashi was certain that he was *the* level-headed individual who would bring out the best in her. But this was not to be. Leela soon discovered an obsessive legacy which Aditya's dying father had left for him to fulfill – the search for a mythical Buddha image. Every year Adi would vanish in an expedition to some Buddhist region in the world, armed with new leads and sponsored by a core group of Japanese admirers, only to return empty-handed in deep dejection. For weeks thereafter he would behave like a terminal patient, with no will to live, sexually passive and dysfunctional. Each time Leela would nurse him back to normalcy.

This was an addictive illness she could not fight any more, nor live with for the rest of her life.

THREE

All through Leela's journey from the Imphal airport to the Circuit House where her stay was arranged, she could see signs of tension in the town. There were banners asking the government to throw out the refugees from Myanmar who had poured in for several months. Leela's own NGO was involved with helping such refugees settle into makeshift Camps, which were already under rampant attacks from groups opposed to the Govt's refugee resettlement policies.

There were intelligence reports that Pakistan's ISI (Inter-Services Intelligence) agents backed by extremist Islamic organisations in Bangladesh had infiltrated various trouble spots in a huge arc from Mizoram to Siliguri. Their fresh recruits had already secretly penetrated the new refugees to foment trouble in this entire area. Some state politicians were even discreetly encouraging such refugees – the usual vote bank. For this reason, Leela herself had spoken out against giving resident rights to these refugees.

In this volatile situation, the organizers of the two rallies supporting the refugees on humanitarian grounds were receiving daily death threats from the regional militant outfits. The young volunteers were all tired and scared.

Two days into her exhausting work at the new refugee camps in inclement weather, Leela's personal trauma was dwarfed by the sheer pain on evidence everywhere. After their ordeal in getting to India, the hapless refugees were now huddled under small tents, terrified by sporadic attacks from locals who resented their presence. She was glad that her team could offer some real relief.

Finally, she boarded the Rajdhani Express train from Tinsukia to New Alipurduar. When Leela stepped into the hotel lobby with her baggage, Martin was waiting with a lady friend in tow. He spun Leela around and lifted her in a bear hug while some guests in this small town looked on with a sense of affront. The proverbial Brit stiff upper lip was curled up in his usual grin.

'Trust the little lady to keep us waiting.'

'The little lady asks to be put down.'

Martin was a tall, lanky man with a perpetual smile which often threatened to go out of proportion. He quickly put Leela down and turned to his equally tall companion. 'My partner Elena. A Putinskie commie.'

Elena quietly shook hands with Leela and exchanged a Namaste too. 'I'm just as commie as Mart is native Somalian.'

Martin made a funny face and bounced up and down.

Leela said with a grin, 'I'll check in, but where are the others from your group?'

'They're resting. Fagged out by the humidity. But our tour was terrific. Kohima, Tawang, a cruise on the Brahmaputra – couldn't get enough of it in such a short time.'

Elena added, 'Most of us got emotional at the INA memorial…'

Leela had checked in and she was told her room was being readied. She paused after taking her key. '*You* got emotional? I don't get it.'

Martin said, 'Thereby hangs a tale. It…'

Elena interrupted, 'That can wait. Leela, we take rest. No tale.'

Leela said, 'Mart, I see that your tail is up. But I'll go with Elena. I'm a bit tired too. Maybe over dinner?'

'Okey dokey. See you in a few hours.'

As Leela took the stairs to her room, Elena's words played back in her mind. Why would a Russian woman get emotional at the INA Memorial? When she tucked herself into bed for an unscheduled siesta, this thought kept pricking her mind.

She was awakened by the hotel phone. Her mobile was switched off, and though she had told the hotel staff that she would not take calls, obviously someone in this small hotel had goofed up.

It was Martin. 'We are all waiting honey. It's time for dinner. And my tail is down.'

Leela realized with a start that for the first time in ages, she had in fact overslept. She mumbled an apology and quickly changed into an informal dress to make herself presentable. As she rushed down and entered the dimly lit dining hall, the entire group stood up to welcome her. She folded her hands in a simple Namaste.

Martin beckoned her near him. Patting the chair next to him, he said, 'So here we are at last. Let's do the who's who…'

Leela said, 'I already know about all of you, courtesy Martin and the net.'

One of the members, Hidayat, smiled at her and said, '*Nomoshkaar. Adaab.* Leela Didi, we have forty-nine members in this online group started by Lin and me,' He stopped to identify Lin who nodded back, 'but the five of us were the only ones who stuck to the idea of making this trip.'

They were all sipping drinks of their choice and as soon as she sat down, the waiter approached Leela. She asked for some fresh green tea from the nearby Darjeeling gardens. It was almost immediately served. Taking a sip, she looked up and asked, 'I'm still intrigued. How did such a disparate group get together and come here?'

Martin tapped the table twice for attention and turned to Leela. 'Knowing your impatience, I will spell out our agenda face up right now. We're here because each one of us has an elder or foster parent who had something to do with the battles fought in Kohima and Imphal.' He took a long swig at his beer and continued, 'Or they were somehow involved with the mystery surrounding the fate of your famous leader, Subhas Chandra Bose. Simply put, our present lives have been deeply impacted by inherited enigmas.'

He noticed Leela sighing deeply in a gesture of *déjà vu* and shook his finger at her playfully. Meanwhile, dinner was served.

Leela turned to Elena, 'I know that Mart has contrarian views about the role of the British in India, but I am curious why *you* got emotional at Kohima.'

Elena spoke with some effort. 'In 1949 my grandfather was with your Leader Subhas Bose in gulag, where he hear true facts about Kohima war. Actually this story – how say in English... roundabout, circuited?'

Martin smiled while nodding, 'The word is circuitous. It started with me meeting Yugo in Tokyo for a conference on macrobiotics and cancer prevention. We got talking about the ills of society, and all the whys for stress and cancer. Me about Britain and our angst, and him about his 'Jap' variation. Soon we got personal and discovered that our grandfathers, in fact two cousins from both sides, had fought each other here in India near Kohima.'

Yugo said impassively, 'His granduncle has a memorial plaque on a grave in Shillong, where he died shortly after the war. My grandfather: no sign, no bones. Only family memory and military records.'

Martin added, 'And then ....'

He took out a coin and dropped it into his glass. 'One of the pennies, the first of them, fell into place. We unearthed the fact that we both had inherited a baffling legacy. Each of us had to unravel the mysterious stories told by our elders...'

Yugo warmed up, 'For example my granduncle. He survived the

same battle and returned with injuries. As long as he was alive, he was in torment about the fate of his senior, one of our most famous Generals, Gen. Shidei, who was supposed to have perished in Taipei in a plane crash with your own war hero Netaji Subhas Bose.'

Leela leaned back in her chair, her face set. 'The way I see it, each of you seems to have some legacy from the World War II, which was fought over seventy years ago. Instead of moving on...'

Hidayat said, 'Once you know the links, as a morally sensitive person...'

Leela said, 'Sorry. No offence meant, but I'm really tired and I don't want any of this history digging.'

There was a sudden pause, as Leela's tone caught the gathering off guard. Lin shifted uneasily in his chair.

Martin frowned at her. 'You don't want? Even if it has a lot to do with India's condition today or the fate of Subhas Bose?'

Leela shook her head emphatically. 'Even so. Digging up the past has never been my idea of doing something to address the horrors around us,' she paused as Martin's lips formed the word INA as a hint to her several times, 'Yes Mart, especially if this is about Subhas Bose, the INA, *who did what* seventy years ago. I have had enough of this since I was a child. Today, it is a dead issue and no one gives a damn. So please excuse me friends. Maybe we can talk about something different tomorrow night at the tea garden. By the way, Mart, thanks for making this trip possible. Looking forward to seeing how my tea is made.'

Leela beckoned a hovering waiter and asked for a finger bowl to wash her hands. Martin and Hidayat looked crestfallen, while the others maintained an impassive front.

Hidayat said, 'Didi, I am sure if you had heard a bit more of the links, you would...'

'I am sure I would not,' Leela cut in, 'I don't intend to be rude, but please forgive my inability to participate.'

Martin's smile was back, as he inclined his head. 'Forgiven. Only for now.'

Back in her room, Leela lay down but sleep refused to come. She had always avoided such discussions as toxic but somehow, somewhere an inner bell always rang. The past was always there weighing heavily on her present, on each mangled path she walked. It was calling out from under her feet, crying to be de-weeded and then discarded.

She had just met five people who were all concerned with their present being impacted by a corrosive past dumped on them. Aditya had gone down that path, as had her grandfather Shivdadu. She wanted to be free of all this. Life was so stressful even without such willed burdens. Aditya's agonized face came back to haunt her almost every day.

The fact was that there were no historical figures who inspired her in today's world. They seemed so distant and dusty.

Leela gave up on sleep and got up to check her baggage for the next morning. Then she wrapped a thin shawl around her and sat down on the recliner on the balcony. Alipurduar was still a lovely place.

When she awoke, it was almost time to leave. Martin called out to her to hurry. She ran out and boarded her bus, which was full of passengers. When they were leaving the hotel compound, she saw a security Police Inspector talking to some armed constables and bus drivers near a police jeep. They were meant to provide security cover for an incoming bus full of activists who had campaigned against ethnic violence in the refugee camps.

As the bus moved on, the other passengers either opted for a small nap or dabbed at their mobiles. A few co-passengers were young tourists and they seemed to be in better spirits; chatting, snacking, taking selfies, singing loud songs. To top that, the bus driver would not turn down his loud CD player despite several requests.

It started raining, first as a slight drizzle and then in sheets. She thought about the discussion from the previous evening and wondered what had inspired them all in this mission. Maybe for Hidayat it was his family's involvement in the INA. But Yugo? Elena? Lin was from China and Netaji Subhas Bose would be 'oh, so far away' for him. What was his motivation?

And Martin, for whose elders Subhas Bose had been a sworn enemy? Why was he in it? Was there some feeling of guilt which was working in him? Martin often spoke of the millions of enslaved Indian labour whom the British had used to create their wealth; the deliberate famines that were engineered in Orissa, Guntur and Bengal to push the crushed Indian masses into indentured slavery or the British Indian Army. Martin was also vocal about the lesser known British 'concentration camps' during both the world wars. He said that Churchill was an equal if not greater war criminal than Hitler, and the sooner the Brits accepted this, the better. She dozed off thinking these thoughts.

She was suddenly awakened by the sound of a tremendous explosion, followed by screams of terror from the passengers. Before she could gather her wits, the sound of an approaching mob could be heard. The windshield glass had shattered and injured people in the first two rows, but there was no time to attend to them. Gunfire was heard.

The driver brought the bus to a screeching halt and jumped out, followed by the conductor. While scampering away, they beseeched the passengers to run for their lives.

Leela and her friends got off from the back door after the other passengers, and started running. Short bursts of gunfire and shouts of 'Kill the bastards!' could be heard close by. She tried to follow Yugo but was distracted by the sight of a big group of lungi-clad men who were running towards a group of college girls. The boys accompanying them were desperately trying to call for help from their cell phones, but it was apparent that there was no network coverage. The attackers had chosen their spot well.

As the first attackers caught up with them, the college boys cowered and fell on their knees. This got them no sympathy from the goons who beat them soundly with thick lathis (sticks). Some other miscreants lunged forward towards the terrified girls.

Martin broke away from his own group and ran towards them. Elena screamed at him to turn back and made to follow him, but Hidayat and Lin pulled her back while shouting at Martin to stop and return.

The college girls huddled against a thick wall of stunted trees about a hundred metres away. Martin picked up a stick on the way, and he had his hunting knife ready too.

A second, bigger bunch of miscreants headed towards Leela's group. Hidayat pulled out a gun from somewhere and fired in the air, warning the assailants. Yugo took up an imposing, attacking posture, while the others formed a group around him. This made the attackers pause for a moment.

In that instant Leela found herself running towards Martin without heeding the warning shouts. Martin had almost reached the girls when the first group of miscreants confronted him. He fended off two of them with his knife. The girls took courage and ran towards Yugo's group. They had almost crossed Leela when someone shot Martin in the head from behind. He slumped forward without a sound.

Leela had reached these attackers by now. She caught the solitary gunman in a vice grip and twisted his arm to make him drop his weapon. As the screaming man fell over, the enraged attackers started chasing her, shouting death threats and expletives. They cut off the return path to her group.

One of the leaders suddenly recognised her and shouted, '*This* is that bitch Leela Biswas. Cut her down!'

In the meantime, Yugo and Hidayat swiftly shifted everyone behind another clump of trees which were bordering a cluster of rocks. Lin clambered atop these rocks to block off attempts to surround them. The rest of the group hid among the trees. Hidayat was firmly holding back Elena to prevent her from leaving the group and reaching Martin. He shouted a warning in Bengali to the attackers that they were armed and would shoot to kill.

Leela had no way of returning to her companions, as two different groups now converged to chase her. She started running through the thick undergrowth, her waterproof rucksack still clinging to her back. She was trained to do this in the Himalayan jungles, so her pursuers found it tough to keep pace.

However, one of them hurled a metal pole at her. It slammed into her knee, making her stumble and fall awkwardly into a watering hole almost fifteen feet below a ledge. She screamed in pain. Her pursuers shouted with glee at having almost nailed their prey.

Leela scrambled to her feet and continued running in a hobble. She fell several times, as her pursuers gained ground rapidly. Moving painfully through slushy mud, Leela found herself on the edge of a small, fast flowing river. She jumped in and started swimming furiously. A couple of shots were fired, but she was clear.

As she neared the opposite bank, she could hear the shouts of her predators approaching. Two boats appeared from the western side of the river, each with about five armed men shouting at each other to hasten and catch their prey.

Leela clambered onto the river bank. Immediately a searing pain shot through her right leg. She could barely pull herself to the base of a large banyan tree, where she collapsed in a breathless heap with the rucksack still on her back. She looked around for something with which to defend herself. There was nothing, not even a rock. She felt around the rucksack and realised there was nothing inside that could help her now.

Her predators reached the river bank. They disembarked and ran a few steps till they spotted Leela lying at the base of the tree on the high bank. *No one paid any attention to some trees which started swaying.* They huddled and had a frantic ad lib discussion about whether Leela might have a hidden weapon. One of them even fired a shot which hit the bark of the tree behind her. They soon realized that she only had a small stone in her hand.

There was a collective yelp of victory as one of them shouted, 'She is trapped!'. Her attackers mounted the bank, whooping with delight at having got their prey. One of their leaders even exposed his intent of sexual assault by lifting his lungi and displaying his erect member. His fellow attackers chortled, 'First we all take turns – and then the slaughter.'

A stranger appeared behind Leela. She did not see him directly at first, and only realized someone else was there behind her from the startled reaction of her pursuers. 'Motherfuckers, a sadhu has come!'

A voice said with tremendous power, *'Jao!'*

Leela got a jolt and looked back. She saw a tall, powerfully built bearded old man. He commanded again in his deep, booming voice, 'Bhago! (Scram)'

Some of the attackers took a step back. A voice commanded, 'Shoot this oldie.'

A gunman drew his weapon.

At that very moment a huge elephant suddenly emerged from the swaying trees and trumpeted in anger. To Leela, in her painful and exhausted state, *the scene appeared and sounded ghostly and surreal.*

The lone tusker charged. That was enough for the entire gang to take flight, screaming in terror that demons have appeared to kill them. They rushed into their boats and started rowing furiously in the turbulent river.

One of them refused to give up without a fight and raised his gun to fire. The boat was rocking aggressively and his shots went wide off target. Then it tilted over and capsized. Leela saw one gunman being grabbed by a mugger crocodile and pulled under water. This added further to the panic and chaos, as the mob screamed to the gods ad lib to save them. Soon they disappeared from sight around the bend in the river.

The elephant turned around. For a moment Leela thought that it would attack the old man. But instead it trumpeted once before vanishing in the jungle. All the other sounds gradually faded away as suddenly as it had all started.

The jungle was peaceful again. A solitary woodpecker pecked away. Crickets hummed in the background. The rain drops drummed on the puddles and the forest frogs continued their orchestra. It was as if nothing had happened.

The old man came forward. When Leela looked into his eyes for the first time, she was completely overwhelmed, transfixed by a tremendous wave of love and benediction. Tears started flowing down her eyes. She was not aware of her bodily sensations, just a feeling of utter peace.

When the old man spoke, his voice now had such gentle softness, that sobs broke out again from her throat.

'*Utho, Maa.* (Arise, mother),' he said.

Leela fainted from pain and exhaustion. The last memory she had was of being gently lifted and carried by this man.

FOUR

The police jeep which had left Alipurduar about thirty minutes after the bus, heard the sound of firing echoing through the trees. They speeded up after failing to connect with the crew of the ill-fated bus. While parking their jeep at some distance from the ambush site, they heard another burst of gunfire. The Inspector immediately sent a wireless message to be relayed that he needed urgent reinforcements. There were only eight men with him. They started to snake their way towards the direction where the shots were coming from.

The first sight which met them was of a group of miscreants looting the abandoned luggage of the passengers in the damaged bus. These men scattered after being fired upon.

One policeman saw some men trying to disrobe Martin's body. A short gunfight ensued in which one of them was injured. He was taken into custody.

As the police neared the rocky area sheltering Yugo's group, it became evident that the attackers had completely surrounded the victims. A minute later and they would have reached the top of the rocks to open fire indiscriminately. The Inspector fired a warning shot and shouted at them to surrender. The hoodlums climbed down and returned fire but when firing ensued from another direction by the second group of policemen, they panicked and started running away.

As soon as the all clear was given, Elena rushed towards Martin's body, with the others on her heels. The weeping and hysterical college girls were escorted back by the Inspector. They refused to talk to their boyfriends, who were also limping back to the bus.

Elena sat next to Martin's body, weeping inconsolably. The others surrounded her in silence. The sound of sporadic gunfire could still be heard, as the police forces pursued the different splinter groups.

The Inspector knew they might be attacked again, once the miscreants realised that the police 'force' had just a handful of men. He quickly moved everyone into the stalled bus. Fortunately, two armed police contingents soon arrived from the nearest police station, as well as a number of forest guards. They fanned out immediately in pursuit of the mob, which had escaped into the wild in the pouring rain.

The bus crew were still missing. Two police men were deputed to drive the bus after loading the luggage which lay scattered and wet on the road. Leela's friends were ushered separately into a large police vehicle along with Martin's body.

The media crews had already started arriving and were trying to get 'breaking news' bytes from the victims and the police. One of the reporters spoke into the camera in pouring rain. 'It needs to be asked as to how the state government, which had several explicit intelligence warnings about such attacks, chose to disregard them. The police say that the culprits are possibly from the same groups that are creating violence within refugee camps in the North-East. Their target was actually a busload of activists who had recently campaigned against them in the north-east. These hooligans used explosives and firearms to attack an identical Volvo bus that was carrying local tourists and International guests. It appears that a bunch of college students from Kolkata were mistaken for the activists. You can see the ill-fated bus behind me with these students and other passengers.'

The reporter gestured towards the police jeeps and added, 'The miscreants have killed British national Martin Cameron, when he tried to save some young women from being assaulted. Moreover, the well-known personality Leela Biswas was also on this bus and is now missing. She has been quite vocal recently on the NE refugee crisis. The police say that these criminals have chased her into the forest. This is certain to bring major International condemnation for the government's inept handling of the entire refugee resettlement issue.'

Another reporter was shouting into a different camera, 'No cell coverage, no police outposts within an hour's drive – the spot was well chosen. In fact we have news coming in that local factions owing covert allegiance to the ruling party here have already claimed credit for this heinous attack.'

More such live coverages went on air. The news reached Mada and Rajen within a few minutes, as also the rest of Leela's family and friends. A flurry of calls followed to the high-ups. The media had already arrived outside their residences as well as Leela's Pune apartment to elicit her neighbours' reactions. Rajen himself was shaken, but could not help remarking on the phone to his sister Anu that 'this girl will never leave them in peace'.

A similar clip was watched by Gayatri, Aditya's mother, which showed the British Prime Minister condemning the attack in strong language. This was followed by the news that Martin's aged father had suffered a heart attack and was in a critical condition. A couple of British politicians announced that they were flying to India with Martin's brother to bring back his body. This news feed closed with the reference that Martin was Leela's family friend, and that she was missing.

Gayatri turned to find Aditya standing behind her and watching the news. His face was pale and the shock was palpable. Before she could speak, he turned sharply and left the room.

Gayatri paused for a while and then followed him. As she had expected, he had locked himself in his mini museum. She knocked twice and called his name without getting any response. Then she sighed and walked away.

FIVE

Leela was awakened by the familiar smell of *khichri* being cooked. She realized that she was lying in a dark hut. The space was damp and smelt of fungus.

She tried to get up, but the severe pain in her right leg made her gasp in agony. She looked around and saw that her rucksack was standing in a corner. There was a solitary candle burning on a broken plate. She spotted a metal, old-fashioned trunk in the corner, on top of which was a travelling bag and a couple of books. There was a pair of canvas shoes too. The rest of the hut appeared bare. The sound and smell of cooking was in fact coming from outside.

Feeling her body, she touched a big swelling on her right leg below the knee, where her attacker's metal rod had hit her. It was already bandaged. In fact her benefactor had completely undressed her and eased her into a shirt and lungi. Further, he had wrapped her in a thin but warm Rajasthani blanket, a *rajai*, the kind one hardly sees in stores anymore.

Leela dragged herself to her feet and opened her Patagonia rucksack. Miraculously, despite the dip in the river, her Notepad and mobile phone were spick and dry inside the additional protective casing. She turned them on but there was no network coverage.

A clean dhoti and a man's vest were kept neatly stacked near her rucksack. Most of her clothes had been left behind in her luggage on the bus, or had she taken out that travel case and dropped it somewhere in those desperate moments? She could not remember. The set she had been wearing along with the shoes were set out to dry, no doubt by her benefactor. All she had here was one set of clothes for an emergency, and these were a bit moist too.

Emptying her bag, she found a pair of rubber sandals was also there, hastily put in by her at the last minute this morning. As she put these on and took a step to go out, the searing pain made her emit a sharp cry. The sound of the cooking stopped for a moment and then resumed again. No one came to her aid.

She wrapped the thin blanket around her for warmth and hobbled outside. The light blinded her for a moment. There was still a steady drizzle. She could not make out how far she was from the site where she had fainted.

The hut itself seemed very old and rundown. In fact it was built onto a damaged tree trunk. She could hear the roar of a river far away. The jungle was very thick on one side. She even spotted some orchids and browallias growing in the wild. The colours were exquisite.

The continued sound of cooking brought her back to her benefactor. She was yet to see him, so she followed the sound to behind the hut and the tree. The old man was cooking on a kerosene stove with his back to her. He had just taken off a pressure cooker from the flame. The hissing sound had stopped, while the enticing aroma of *khichri* pervaded the air. Without turning to face her, he said in Hindi, 'Wait till I attend to the fracture.'

The gentle loving tone and the measured words left Leela with a feeling of utmost trust. It was almost impossible for her to believe that the same person had confronted the ten assailants armed only with his stentorian voice.

Then he turned to face her. The eyes. It was first the eyes that held her in thrall. The love flowing from his voice was only an echo of the benediction which burst forth with a hypnotic glow from his eyes. She suddenly felt like a trusting child before a parent, without any sense of shame. This was a stranger and yet...!

She could not tell his age. Somehow, he looked familiar. He was bald in the front with flowing locks behind and as already noticed by her, he had a tall and powerfully built body. He was wearing a simple cream *fatua*, the indigenous cotton vest worn by locals, and a pair of white cotton trousers with rubber shoes. He walked past her and then turned and nodded at her. She pulled the blanket tightly around her and followed him.

When she turned the corner, he was nowhere to be seen. She looked everywhere but there was no sign of the man. Surprisingly, not even for a moment did she feel unnerved or scared. She called out 'hello' several times but there was no answer.

She peeped inside the hut again. The candle had been put out, but when? By whom? There was no wind or even breeze. She could not spot footprints in the soft mud near the hut. Her leg was aching and she sat down on the threshold of the hut.

'Come and sit here.' The voice made her start. Leela prided herself in being a fearless person but now this man was standing just behind her with a flat, heavy tree trunk and an assortment of wild fruits and leaves in his hands, and she had not even heard him approach.

'Where... how did you vanish and appear just like that?'

The man did not answer her and gestured that she must sit down on the tree trunk which he had just put down.

Leela grew defiant. 'First you tell me how you disappeared!'

The man looked into her eyes. Leela stopped speaking. She had to. Suddenly the desire to know how he did the vanishing act, to understand it in rational terms, just dropped from her mind. It was as it was. He had gone. Now he was back. And she was only there to witness.

Leela sat down quietly on the tree trunk. Again, questions started forming in her mind. How could he have carried such a massive tree trunk so easily? He appeared well built, but the trunk was perhaps more

35

than the weight of two grown men.

He went back to the stove and after a while, came back towards her with a metal cooking pot. There was some concoction which he had been boiling. She waited patiently till he ground the different leaves on a small stone grinder…the partly dry ones from the forest which he had just brought, and the cooked leaves separately. He made two fine pastes.

'Please let me help.'

The man looked up at her for a brief moment. That was all. Once again the look translated into the clearest possible message in her mind. 'You have no role. Sit still and calm your mind.'

Instead of her usual bout of self-righteous anger, Leela was again amazed at her own response. It was as if she was observing her own body dispassionately as a witness. She found herself actually grateful and happy that her injury was being tended to by someone whom she trusted.

The man put the first paste around her swelling and then dressed it with some broad leaves. Then he put a very thin layer of the second paste on the outer surface of these leaves and used another huge leaf to wrap this. The whole thing was secured by a forest vine. He swiftly smeared a greater part of the second paste behind her head, above the nape of her neck, and pressed those points for a while. Then he gestured silently that she should not touch this. It was all done with minimum fuss and in quick time.

She found that he had even fashioned two crude supports for her leg, which he slipped under her armpit. Both the contraptions were too long, so they were cut to fit her by using a *daao*, a local axe. Once this was done, he gestured to her to use them for moving around.

Leela found herself asking in Hindi, 'You don't want to speak. But I want to thank you from my heart for saving me.'

The silence continued.

'At least tell me how I should address you? What is your name?'

The man stood erect, looking at her in the eye. There was a long pause that she found almost unbearable. Just when she thought he would not answer, he spoke in an even tone, 'I am Mahakaal.'

A small group of British citizens landed in Kolkata airport along with James Cameron, Martin's brother. They were besieged by an impatient media crowd, security officers and MEA (Ministry of External Affairs) personnel. James was silent and ignored all requests for a statement. Just before getting into the waiting security car, he turned around and spoke into the cameras, 'My brother is gone but those at the top must be held accountable and not just some foot soldiers who fired the shots.'

The paramilitary forces had by now fanned out deep into the jungles to find Leela and the absconding attackers. All the other missing persons had been located.

But there was no sign of Leela, nor could anyone provide any leads. There was immense political pressure from New Delhi on the Special Investigative Team (SIT) to deliver results. Some locals expressed apprehension that she had been kidnapped by criminals. Others spoke of the chances of her having been swept away by flash floods.

Mada and Rajen were relentlessly pushing for a breakthrough. Rajen rushed to Kolkata and offered monetary rewards to anyone with information about Leela. The SIT even screened a radius of sixty km via satellite to track any movement or human presence.

From the arrested attackers' confessions, a couple of hard-core local political leaders were soon apprehended. They cracked under intense interrogation coupled with third degree and admitted that they had expected to corner and attack all the volunteers including Leela, who were campaigning for helping the various refugee settlements.

There were two 'squads' assigned to this task. They soon realized that the wrong bus had been targeted, but one amongst them recognised Leela Biswas and they turned their focus on her.

Within forty-eight hours, the SIT together with the paramilitary forces was able to round up all the members of these two squads who were in hiding. One of them admitted to having fired at Martin, but he said he had no intent to kill, but solely to immobilize him. They were only having some 'fun' with the college girls, he said, and Martin was coming towards them 'aggressively'.

The arrested men revealed the names of senior politicians who had actually planned and instigated the attack. A fierce debate broke out on the media and a couple of cases were filed, demanding the arrest of these politicians. There was a clamour in Parliament that the state government should resign. The named politicians immediately applied for anticipatory bail and denied all allegations made by the arrested assailants.

For the first time, the investigators let out to the press that they were being told a most outrageous tale by the culprits. The accused men had admitted to having chased Leela across a river in boats and cornering her, when an old man, a 'devil' in their description, with a flowing grey beard and red eyes (!) had appeared. At his command, a number of elephants had charged at them. Other wild animals could also be heard. When they tried to escape in terror, one boat with five people was overturned and pulled away by giant crocodiles. All the beasts appeared to be under the spell of this so-called devil dressed as a sadhu.

The broadcast of this account with its subtitles created further outrage among the political class, Leela's family and most viewers. Both Elena and Yugo were interviewed and they said that for the police to have even taken cognizance of such a ridiculous story showed which way the investigation was heading.

Under great pressure, the state government assigned the case to a new crack team. Friends and families of the missing miscreants were interviewed and they all denied any knowledge about the whereabouts of the five missing men. Despite this, the SIT somehow extracted testimonies that these men were possibly holding Leela hostage somewhere.

In the meantime, divers were able to recover the half-eaten bodies of three men, confirming the alligator angle. It was for the first time that such an attack was reported in this stretch of the river. Wildlife experts had a grand time on television dissecting croc behaviour, that mugger crocodiles could be populating the small tributaries from Bengal merging with the Brahmaputra. However, two of the five attackers remained missing.

It was now a week and Leela's case continued being covered as frontline news by almost all news channels. The sleuths asserted that it was a case of kidnapping for ransom or political hostage swapping. However, no such demands came in. Despite extensive questioning of the locals in and near the forest, no one appeared to have seen or heard of an old man with a flowing beard.

On the sixth day after Leela disappeared, the sleuths had to eat crow a second time. The bodies of the two missing men were found thirty km downstream in a badly decomposed state, when the river had ebbed and calmed down. They too had been mauled by crocodiles.

With intense public badgering following Martin's killing refusing to die down, the DSP and two top police officers were transferred and the state Home Minister offered to resign.

Aditya had spent much of this trying period in his museum, having hardly eaten or slept. Gayatri came with a food tray and knocked on the museum's door. He could not deny her and let her in. She stood there quietly while he went to a corner to pour himself a drink. Then he slumped down and rested against a Yakshi image, his eyes fixed on the ceiling. Gayatri sighed and silently left the room.

SIX

Leela had now spent a week deep in the forest, in constant communion with this man who called himself 'Mahakaal'. Who was he? What was his surname? What on earth was he doing in this deep, remote jungle? The man would not answer but only smile and close his eyes.

Only once he reacted, when he suggested with a wide smile that in line with the brevity of speech adopted by the present generations, she could address him as 'MK'. But she could hardly ever bring herself to address him in this manner.

In these seven days, the rains never really let up. She remained cut off, and the river nearby was still in spate. She limped to its edge a few times, using her crude crutches. Was this the same river which she had crossed? One could not be sure. It seemed to be much wider now. When asked, Mahakaal would remain silent. All he said was that she would be able to go back to her world at the appropriate time: not before, not after.

Her existence was rooted in simple monotony, often vitiated by the memory of Martin being shot before her eyes. Mahakaal spoke to her in Hindi and sometimes in English. He tended to her injury twice a day. She surrendered to what she thought was a crude, primitive way to treat a fracture, but now marvelled at how swiftly she was recovering.

Soon, she became aware that a day in these jungles had several distinct rhythms. The forest here was alive in intangible ways, and no experience from her extensive treks in the Himalayan ranges was comparable to this. She wondered why. Was it because the day for her began at pre-dawn, watching MK sitting in meditation outside the hut? At night, he slept on the floor on a thin *dhurrie*, while allowing her to use a very old camping mattress. During the day he sometimes meditated on the small mud porch at the hut's entry, barely escaping the rain. At other times, he would do his *dhyana* sitting under a big tree, with the rain pouring down his torso. He always dried himself with a spare *gamcha* after he was done. How this cotton towel dried, if at all it did, she had no clue.

He would often be gone for hours and would come back with new or strange vegetation and roots for cooking. He seemed to have the barest supply of cooking oil and usually steamed the food in a bamboo steamer of a kind she had seen in Manipur. Only a few items were lightly stirred in mustard oil in a *degchi*. In each instance, the food was delicious.

Leela had not known where to relieve herself and on the very first day, Mahakaal showed her a kind of pit formation at a short distance. He told her in English, 'Cover your excreta with soil and leaves.' So she would now hobble each day on her 'crutches' to the pit, and once she was done, she covered it up as instructed. For washing up, there was an old aluminium bucket and mug always filled with river water.

What she thought would be a boring, temporal existence, revealed itself to be a gateway to a new world. The thing that struck her was her calm acceptance of the way things were. She became aware that something was happening within her, which was catalytic.

From the second day onwards, she started jotting down notes in her laptop till the battery died out. Then she started scribbling with a pencil on the notebook that was always there with her. These notes and memoirs would return to her in sudden therapeutic waves in the future days and months, always coming at the most unexpected moments. And each time these flashbacks would be accompanied by the vision of MK standing or sitting quietly without as much as a glance towards her.

Many old musical experiences came back to her, note by note, made incredibly alive by unfolding at the appropriate time of the day. These were full live recitals of past great masters whom she had heard long ago, which would manifest in her mind as if she was actually hearing

41

the musicians playing live behind an invisible curtain. All the '*bhaar*' and crossover ragas which she loved would emerge from somewhere inside her and retire again into that vast consciousness after the last note was played or sung.

She watched with great joy when at different times of the day, a number of birds perched themselves on Mahakaal while he meditated. They nuzzled his bald head and chirped while he remained still. Whenever he opened his eyes, not one bird attempted to escape. He stretched out his palm and some of them would hop onto it and remain there till he closed his fist and then they flitted away. Quite often a wild cat lay asleep close by, completely at peace in the presence of humans.

There was a dog which soon appeared and always loitered around Mahakaal. One day she witnessed how this dog and a leopard faced off, and then each walked their own way.

Once she asked Mahakaal, 'Why you are here? Is this your permanent place for *dhyana?*'

At first he never answered. Three hours later, after they had their lunch, he suddenly observed, 'I am only passing by. Neither this nor any other place is my permanent abode. Nothing is permanent.'

Leela asked, 'Then how do you know the animals and birds here? That elephant, even the birds that...'

Mahakaal laughed. After a while he said, 'You want to know them? You can. Just learn to trust fully and you can communicate with them.'

'But you commanded that elephant!' protested Leela.

Mahakaal corrected her. 'No I did not. The grosser elements that were pursuing you had vitiated the energies in the forest. The elephant had already sensed this negative energy. I simply transmitted the same to the other sentient species around. They all responded.'

'Huh? But I saw a crocodile seizing one man, so how can anyone pass or transmit any energy to even crocodiles? They are cold-blooded creatures.'

'To them I radiated nothing, though it is possible to transmit energies to every form – even this rock. Your attackers' own feelings of terror attracted the crocodiles, and then they manifested to seize their prey.'

'I don't...I can't follow. How can this be possible? Are Mugger crocodiles even found in this river normally?'

He did not answer and walked away.

A couple of days later, when they were sitting quietly, Mahakaal commented, 'The weather will clear in about three days.'

Leela asked, 'How do you know that?'

Mahakaal spoke slowly with gravity, pausing between sentences and waiting for his words to sink in. 'The birds, the forest, all existence communicates. When you experience the oneness with nature, you will know her hints because you too are a part of the same consciousness.'

'But why am I separate? I never wanted to be.'

'By upbringing. Habit. These are layers or blindfolds which have developed over your inner transmitter. Right now you are like a single band radio, while so many other bands can be tapped into.'

'Upbringing? In what way?'

'As a toddler you were utterly trustful. Now you are careful, even fearful. So these other channels have closed. The moment you become trustfully aware, the ability to sense all the waves will gradually return.'

'I have spent years in the Himalayas and never felt like I do now. Why?'

'Because you were still the same Leela there.'

'You even know my name?'

'I *know* you,' said Mahakaal with a smile. 'In the Himalayas too you were separate. Here, that separateness has dropped a bit. You have let go and life has allowed you a glimpse of your true energies. When you go back to your urban life, either these energies will vanish again, or you will drop the blindfolds more and more. It is all in your hands.'

Very often Mahakaal's silences forced Leela to ask questions, many of which he would not answer. But later, astonishingly, the answers formed in her mind with such blinding clarity that she was dumbfounded. It was as if this man had entered her mind and was answering her directly.

Her questions came in torrents: 'Who are you? How do you sustain yourself? You appear well educated, so are you a modern healer or what?'

His answers came in wafts:

'I am a pilgrim who will not speak about his past.

'I am passing through here.

'I do not sustain myself, existence sustains me. I only align myself in gratitude with this mother energy and wherever I go, my sustenance appears effortlessly. Would you think of this as a coincidence or a miracle? No, this is benediction.

'Sometimes I heal people I meet; at other times I have different tasks. Right now it is you; tomorrow it is someone or something else. It could also be a group, a generation, a nation. Nature heals her wounds using me as the doer.'

Leela recalled the last sequence. She had frowned and asked, 'How can you, a solitary person, heal a group or an entire people... let alone a nation?'

Mahakaal had laughed and replied, 'It is not for me to do or decide. There is a conscious energy force which uses me as its extension to perform these things.'

Once Leela had asked, 'So, are you a sadhu, an ascetic? What were you earlier?' And Mahakaal had replied, 'I am neither of them. My karma is as a *Yodha Sanyasi*.' Leela had wondered, '*Yodha*?' He had answered, 'Yes, I am like a simple foot soldier of the divine mother energy, the force which permeates every cell of my mortal coil; which

44

drives me. More than this I cannot say. My past life carries no meaning. I am dead to my past.'

At another time, he had amazed her by suddenly naming the political forces who had engineered the attack on her. He said more such incidents would follow, leading to a catharsis. He knew the nation's path ahead. It had to pay a price to self-correct its total abdication of dharma. When she asked him to elaborate, his silent smile returned.

After the first three days of incessant rains, Leela was getting worried about her clothes that would not dry. She then found an old but clean sari stacked neatly near her head when she awoke. She asked him from where he got this. Once again, there was no answer.

At one point, Leela had complained, 'Why don't you change things and help remove miseries?'

Mahakaal had answered, 'I can guide but not live others' karma. Each person has to do this personally. No outsourcing.' Leela had laughed heartily on hearing the English word 'outsourcing' among a host of Hindi words from a modern mendicant. He had also laughed like a child, and this was another side to the man which became pronounced later.

On the sixth day of her stay, he had suddenly remarked that she and others of her generation were all paying dearly for accumulated negative karma. Her own family was also resolving past karmic equations, through reincarnation. Leela had strongly objected.

Mahakaal continued that if Leela dug deep and with doggedness, she would learn of how India's fate as a nation had been sealed by secret understandings revolving around the Transfer of Power Agreement (T.O.P) in 1947 between Britain and the new Indian State.

Then he laughingly uttered a few seemingly nonsensical childish rhymes, gently waving his hands like a music conductor cutting through the air.

'Geee aaaand...Deee ,

DOT Fiveee Fourrr,'

Then he waved his hand diagonally,
'Slash...Fiveee Nineee...
'then we slash again...
siiiix twooo —
'then we Slash again...
siiiix naaaine...
'then came the little Dash —
followed by E and three Roman I's...
where the Bracket jumped in
to enclose M for movement —
& — A for what I am doing now...Activity...
and then the Bracket closed.'

'Did you get it? This is your language, right?'

Leela had been giggling like a little girl, and she shook her head foolishly, 'Nooo!'

Mahakaal had joked that she was from the 'slash and tag' generation, and then he made slashing and dotting gestures again, while uttering syllables like in a nursery rhyme recitation: '...*hindaa// jindaa// dot dot//jogadeem//jigdum// dot dot...*'

He proceeded to rattle off a few more. When she put up her hands in helpless laughter, he remarked that these were like baby alphabets which could give her starting insight into *which* part of a hidden past was impacting her present today. Even though she was confused, she wrote them down painstakingly in her notebook.

He expounded with a childlike smile, 'I behave in a chaotic manner, not worrying about what is right speech or wrong. That is why I sometimes give trouble to others — bawl like a new born; gurgle like a child; scream like a disobedient boy; imitate elders like teenagers do; become a twenty-year-old and behave like an aged intellectual; cross into age forty and speak with "maturity"; become eighty and shake my head in sage advice; become two hundred and make pronouncements like a *Jagat Pita;* become two thousand and merge with the eternal hymns; touch five thousand years and roar like Mahakaal. That is my release in this phenomenal world.'

Mahakaal's ability to predict high velocity winds when not a leaf was stirring was another amazing feat. She was equally astounded when he predicted that helicopters would be looking for her in under an hour. He laughed off her query as to why they could not see this hut? He said something about human bodies being both transmitters and receivers of the subtlest frequencies at the same time. He mentioned how most of mankind had shut down almost all receiving antennae and were transmitting their flawed, stress-filled energy waves. He even gave her a quick rundown of how to interpret the calls and messages from the many birds that came and sat around him.

Finally the rains tapered off. Mahakaal said that she would have to leave soon, since her injury had healed enough and the rivers would be navigable. However, he could not accompany her as he had other 'tasks' to do. She would need to walk patiently and with least stress to her injured foot.

Leela awoke at the crack of dawn on the eighth day to find the dog at her feet, nudging her. Her belongings were packed and Mahakaal was waiting patiently at the door. Leela felt the pain of parting like never before. Even separating from Aditya did not compare. She found that she could not stop her tears from streaming down. She did not want to go back. Her overwhelming desire was to remain at his feet, to sing, to experience and 'see' in a different way.

She bent to touch Mahakaal's feet. This was a gesture that she had not performed for ages with strangers. He pulled her up and looked her in the eye with an unforgettable loving gaze.

'It will be a lonely and tortuous path. But always remember that I will be with you. Always.'

Leela opened her mouth to speak, but no words escaped. The dog nudged her to move. She picked up her backpack and shuffled out on the crutches. She had no idea which way to go. The dog came back to her barking. Then again it ran ahead, signalling her to follow. She put her chin up and turned to walk ahead. Perhaps she would never see Mahakaal again?

She glanced back to find him following her. This time he was wearing his dark glasses.

As they entered a faint trail in the forest, there was only the massive forest around them with its typical sounds. Raindrops were still falling off the overhanging trees, and her 'guide dog' was sniffing its way ahead. It was a long and slow walk punctuated by several halts to ease the mild pain in her leg. There were times when they had to clear the path with an axe.

The dog eventually guided them to a riverbed, different from the one that she crossed a week ago. She was surprised to find that a boat awaited her. There was no one around. The boat itself had not been used for quite some time and was covered with patches of moss, but it seemed usable. Mahakaal helped her to get into it and then stepped away.

As if reading her mind, he spoke, 'Ma, we will meet again when the time is right.'

This was not the first time he had used the Bengali endearment 'Ma' for her. Was he a Bengali, because only *they* used such an expression for daughters? Or was he just familiar with the language because he had lived in Bengal for some time?

But now it was time to say goodbye and not ask questions.

When she hesitated to start her journey, the dog jumped in and started barking loudly. She smiled at herself. This untrained dog seemed to have more native intelligence than many urban dogs, including her own pet – Bima. He seemed to be a clairvoyant. Or was he also a reincarnation of someone?

She chuckled and started rowing. After a while, she turned again to find that Mahakaal was no longer to be seen.

The river proved quite easy to navigate. Once she docked on the other bank, the dog jumped into the river and swam back. She waited till she saw him clamber onto the bank and disappear from her view. Later, in the coming months, she would remember his licks each morning and his soft nose nuzzling her.

She stepped off the boat. There was a faint trail ahead. Slowly, she started walking. The forest was now getting thinner, and she felt sad that she had to leave it and enter the urban jungle.

SEVEN

After almost two hours of a tedious walk, she found herself on the edge of a village road. Her leg was hurting again. She inserted her spare battery in her cell phone but it was still unable to connect.

Then she saw a lone cyclist coming her way. The man went past her with a casual glance, and then braked abruptly. He pedalled back furiously and came face to face with Leela, his mouth open wide in shock. He suddenly broke into a huge grin. 'Leela – *tumi* Leela, *haa?*'

The man was friendly and not overbearing, but this first touch with a human being after her days spent with Mahakaal was like a sharp incision into her being. She composed herself and nodded silently.

The man looked around and then patted the rear saddle on his cycle. Half an hour later, they were at the highway. She still had some cash in her bag and offered this to him, but the cyclist would have none of it. Instead, he furiously waved down the next bus which was a local 'mini passenger' travelling to the next town. He climbed into the driver's cabin and whispered to the bus conductor about his prized guest.

But the driver refused to take Leela on board. 'You have gone mad. The "Mamas" (police) will tear us apart. First we'll call them.'

The conductor called the police, and the disgruntled passengers were informed about the special situation leading to a delay. The air buzzed with excitement. Many people, especially ladies, came up to peer into Leela's face and whisper among themselves. The 'Mamas' were on their way, informed a jubilant conductor.

Leela found that her mobile had a network signal at last. She called Anu Mashi, but the number was switched off. Then she gritted her teeth and called Mada. She could barely recognize the voice at the other end. This was not his assured, authoritarian tone, but a hoarse whisper. 'Leelaaa? Is that you Lili?'

'Yes Mada,' whispered back Leela. For some time there was silence, while she could hear the domestics screaming in the background. One of them, Pushpa, came on the line. 'Where are you, child?' And then Mada's voice came back, still quivering with emotion, 'Are you safe? Where the hell are you?'

Leela replied calmly. 'Mada, I'm OK now. I think I am somewhere near Jayanti village, where…'

She was interrupted by screaming sirens as two police jeeps and a mobike raced into sight. Leela mumbled, 'Police have just come. I'll connect later.'

'Wait, let me handle that…' roared Mada, but she disconnected.

For the next few hours, her life was a horror that she had to endure somehow. The police picked up the hapless cyclist for questioning and took her to the nearby police outpost, where they advised her to switch off her mobile. She anxiously asked about Elena and the rest of the group. She was told they had been moved to Kolkata for the time being. Everyone was safe.

From the police station, she was immediately escorted to the nearest Railway Hospital on the road to Alipurduar, where a senior doctor examined the injuries on her leg and did a thorough check-up of physical indicators. She was asked about any sexual assault but she denied any such harm and refused permission to be examined for the same.

A senior team of sleuths arrived from Kolkata. Media persons started arriving in hordes. The town had rarely seen such high speed VIP activity. Only one Senior Superintendent of Police (SSP) was permitted inside the hospital and he waited with an angry look in the senior doctor's office while the doctor himself finished his check-up. After the examination, Leela got to her feet and followed the doctor to his office where the SSP sat in wait. The doctor started writing his report, and then looked up at SSP Rakshit.

'Barring some superficial bruises, Leelaji has one major injury — this.' He tapped the sore spot on her right leg, 'A fracture from a violent impact from some blunt object. She is lucky that it is a stable fracture and not an open or spiral fracture. But it is healing well. We will now do a cast.'

'Fracture? Healing on its own?' The SSP's eyebrows shot up as he turned to question Leela.

'Sir, please. You can speak to her after a few minutes. Let me do my job now.' The doctor was smiling, but he was already irritated.

'Yes Leelaji? How did you get this fracture?' asked the doctor.

Leela spoke with a resigned, flat voice, 'I was hit with full force by a metal rod thrown by the people chasing me. I saw it when I fell.'

'Who tended to you? How was this treated?' asked the doctor, gesturing at the wound.

'I was rescued by a stranger, an old man. He later dressed my injury with pastes he made from forest plants. I have no notion what these were. He dressed it twice a day for as long as I was there. And he fashioned this support which I used till now.'

The SSP turned to look at her sharply at the mention of the old man.

The doctor picked up the crude crutches and nodded, 'A village tribal?'

'No, an educated type but he seemed to know the forest plants very well.'

The doctor nodded again silently as the nurses swiftly put Leela's leg in a cast. He completed jotting down his initial report, asking questions all the while, 'Forest plants? Jari booti? Hmmm. And what was your diet? What did you eat?'

'He cooked every day. He had a pressure cooker and…'

'Pressure cooker in a deep forest? Hmmm. Cooked what?'

'Simple things. Rice, dal, vegetables…I mean greens which I can't identify, which he brought from the forest.'

The SSP asked in a gruff voice, 'Don't follow. Was this a home in the forest that stocked supplies?'

'A simple mud hut. That's it.'

The doctor glared at the SSP and then turned back to Leela. 'Greens from the deep forest? And did he use any oil?'

'Yes. He would fetch wild plants including fruits. He steamed the greens in some kind of bamboo steamer. He also used mustard oil very sparingly in a *degchi* for frying sometimes.'

'This gentleman tended to you very well. I am really curious if he used tobacco plants for the medication, or what he made you eat. It is almost as if these contained bone morphogenetic proteins, though I cannot imagine any such treatment in a deep forest!' The doctor finished writing his report and gave it for typing. He continued, 'Medically I can't see any problems. Your fracture is healing fine. In my experience, it is remarkable that you could recover so much in a week, even after subjecting the leg to strain when you returned. We will of course await your pathological report. Now you rest after SSP Saheb is done with you.'

As the doctor walked away, the SSP stopped whispering on his mobile and switched it to silent mode. He leaned forward, 'Madam, I'm…'

'I'm not Madam. You can call me Leela.'

'OK Leela Madam…'

'No!' Leela cut in sternly.

The SSP stopped smiling. 'Ok Leelaji, I am Benoy Rakshit, SSP Siliguri. We would like to know in brief the true account of where you were, how you were freed, how you came back on your own – all the details.'

'True account? That's what I just gave, and you heard it.'

'Come on Madam – Oh sorry, Leelaji!' The SSP started laughing helplessly at his faux pas, 'Some old man in the forest with a pressure cooker and bamboo steamer! He feeds you fresh food and dresses your fracture like an expert. No one will believe this.'

'What others believe is irrelevant. These are the facts, whether you like it or not.'

'Ok, are you telling me that a hut like this with human activity would have been missed by satellite scanning?'

'Looks like. Yes.'

'The whole story appears suspect. To start with, the accused assailants say that they chased you through the forest till you reached a river. How did you cross? They say you swam in that river with a high current… is this version correct?'

'I am a trained swimmer and diver. I have swum in Himalayan rivers with grade four rapids.'

'And then they cornered you on the other bank and an old man appeared from nowhere. Now, how could this old man chase away a fully armed gang of killers?'

'I don't know. I was lying injured and half conscious. But he did confront them…'

'With elephants? A wildlife brigade?'

'I saw only one elephant. And it charged at the men on its own –

that is what I remember.'

'So that they rowed away and got eaten by crocodiles!'

'I had a glimpse of a man falling over and a crocodile jumping up to seize him.'

'There was no firing? No one fired at the old man? By the way, does he have a name?'

'Someone had fired at me just after I had collapsed. Then I heard one or two shots being fired later, but the man... I mean Mahakaal or MK, was not hit.'

'Mahakaal?' Rakshit frowned deeply. 'Now I've heard this name earlier. That was his name? No surname?'

'No. He said this was his present name, and that as a sanyasi, he was dead to his past.'

'Ok good. Sanyasi. Did he prevent you from calling for help, to protect his dead past?'

Leela waved her index finger at Rakshit. 'Please don't be sarcastic about someone you don't know. He did not prevent me from doing anything. I could not walk. There was no network. In fact I tried almost every day, several times.'

'You could not walk. But this man could have helped you, escorted you to human habitation, knowing you were cut off from contact, yes?'

'No, I do not think so. We were marooned. I presume this spot is hedged between two rivers, and both were in spate for long. When I could row across, I came.'

'You know rowing?'

'Yes.'

'And then? But first...this man...what was the name – Mahakaal. So he brought you to a boat?'

'Strictly speaking – No. He *did* accompany me, but it was a dog that brought me to the boat, though the river looked different from the one which I had initially crossed.'

'Just a minute. A dog brought you means? A trained guide dog? This Sanyasi has trained pet dogs too?'

'No, it just appeared there after two days. I never asked if the dog was trained or whether it belonged to him, but it brought us to this river bank.'

'Now why didn't this kind soul bother to bring you back personally to the mainland, especially with your injury? Anybody could have attacked you again.'

Leela stared at the SSP with a clear gaze. 'He told me he had other tasks to attend to, and that he knew I would find my way to safety.'

Rakshit stared back at Leela. She could sense that he was getting exasperated. His jaws had started working furiously and his right leg was conducting a steady tremble. Leela remarked, 'Do you have a liver problem?'

'What?' Rakshit was incredulous. 'How do you know – Leelaji! Don't try to divert please. Tell me the real facts.' Leela opened her mouth to speak but he stopped her with an open palm stop signal, 'You were held captive by a gang. Yes? And you don't want to tell us what you went through.'

'No, not true.'

'We understand your trauma, but trust me. Tell us everything. If you don't cooperate, your captors will never be convicted.'

'No! There were no captors.' The sharp military tone from Leela made Rakshit wince. The smile disappeared from his face. The doctor came running, as well as a nurse and a security guard.

'What are you doing, Sir! The patient needs rest. I am requesting you to please leave for now. You can do all your questioning after we release her.'

'No need for that,' Leela continued in her combative tone, 'I will not add a word to what I said earlier. You are entitled to believe or doubt. I don't care. *This* is the exact truth. An old man saved me, fed me, nursed me and arranged to guide me back to human contact, all so that I have to face an ugly world that thinks I am a liar. That's it. Period.'

Rakshit got up. His practiced smile was back in place. 'Ok you rest. We'll talk later.'

He walked out. Soon Leela could hear his voice on the mobile, 'But Sir, she is not talking! Who will buy this crazy story of an old man?'

'I believe you, Leelaji,' said the doctor in a reverential tone, 'You have a healthy glow which can only come from a positive experience. Not from captivity or trauma. Sounds incredible, but…'

Leela smiled and limped back to the bed. The others left the room and a dim blue light came on. She waited for a while and then checked her mobile out of habit, only to thrust it away in disgust.

She closed her eyes. Mahakaal's magical voice kept echoing in her head. Sometimes Adi's face and voice also faded in and out. She wanted so much to share all this with him. Her fingers fed his number several times on her mobile, but she recalled his face and could not think of opening the wounds again. Slowly, she dozed off as the injection she was given started to work.

In Dehradun, Aditya had just finished working out. This was a very modest home and typical of his middle-class background. His 'Mini Museum' had been built and attached later to this small house with donations from a group of Korean and Japanese followers who had great admiration for his knowledge of Buddhist artefacts and restorations of the same.

After he had towelled himself, he found a chit under the door from his mother. 'Check on the news. Now.'

He went to the study-cum-media room adjoining his bedroom. Gayatri was already sitting there sporting a big smile, with the TV running. He turned and saw Leela's face on the screen as she was being taken inside the hospital. He remained frozen in the same posture till his mother got up and guided him to a chair. She watched as his body slowly relaxed and settled back in the sofa.

Two hours later, Gayatri retired for a siesta. Aditya had been hoping for a call, but none came. It was past nine pm. He called Leela's number without any hesitation and got a 'switched off' message. He would never learn that Leela had dithered about calling him just fifteen minutes earlier, before falling asleep.

EIGHT

Leela was awakened by a nurse who brought her dinner. There were two envelopes on the tray. One was a message from Mada via the IG (Inspector General), Police Kolkata. 'Waiting for your return. The police tell me that you are not cooperating. Don't be difficult. Tell them all you know. Please understand that this is now a major political scandal, so they can't release you till you have given a *full* statement.'

Leela sighed and pushed the note away. The second envelope contained the printout of an email sent by Anu Mashi to the Police headquarters in Kolkata. It said, 'Tell them what you want to. Then come soon. We are waiting.' It was signed by her and Shivdadu.

As she was slipping it back into the envelope, she saw a postscript from her cousin, Bharat: 'Relax. This will pass.' After ages, it was her dearest Bharat Bhai writing to her. He must have been visiting Anu Mashi when this was sent. Leela smiled and felt good.

She found hundreds of messages waiting on her mobile, and chose to open only the one from a close friend, Ishita, who summarized the full story of what the media had been circulating till now: the main and parallel leads, Martin's death and subsequent arrests, the visit of British politicians, many other press links etc. Leela went through them all.

She paused and then typed a reply. 'Can't forget Martin. Hurts like mad. Overall, arrested chaps speaking truth. Old man buggered them. No idea how. Spent a week under his care. Marooned. Life changed forever. FOREVER. He is from another planet! Has access to mysterious knowledge, hidden political info which I can't fathom as yet. Cops hounding me. Don't believe me.'

A TRYST WITH MAHAKAAL

When she closed her eyes, Mahakaal manifested in her mind's eye, looking at her with his gentle glow. She fell asleep with his voice ringing in her ears.

When she awoke again, it was morning. Even from inside her locked room, she could hear a buzz. She got up and walked on her new cast and crutches to peep out of a window. The hospital premises outside were teeming with people: Reporters, TV crews, doctors, several jeeps flying banners of different political hues, a mass of curious onlookers… whew!

By the time she was through with her breakfast with nurses peeping into the room to check on her every five minutes, the buzz outside had almost become a rumble, louder than ever. She was about to get up and peep out, when the hospital administrator came in. The noise also entered like an angry, impending storm.

'Madam, have you finished breakfast?' he asked.

Leela nodded, so he continued, 'The police are waiting and…'

He was cut short.

'No thank you, I will go home now.'

The man was stumped. He swallowed, scowled and closed the door. The rumble was pressed back, waiting to sweep in again. Within a minute, the door opened and Rakshit, along with two other senior officers in uniform trooped in.

'Madam, I mean Leelaji – please meet Mr Kainthola and Mr Natarajan, members of the SIT who are now handling the entire investigation. I have given them my report that you are not cooperating.'

Leela did not answer initially. Instead she shook the proffered hands from the SIT Officers. Then she turned to Rakshit, 'Not cooperating? How? After failing to protect us, allowing my friend to be killed in a pre-meditated attack…'

'Leelaji, please listen.'

60

'…which has been sponsored covertly by local political leaders, now you talk of cooperation?'

'So you don't want to talk anymore,' Natarajan spoke slowly, munching his words and fixing her in stare.

'No, I have said what I have to.'

Natarajan suddenly shouted at her, 'But you are fine with sharing secret info with the entire world, except us!'

'Sorry, I don't get it.'

Kainthola cut in. 'The person who saved you is some political entity who has changed your life. Yours is a typical "Stockholm syndrome" reaction. Can you deny this?'

Leela was puzzled, and she showed it.

Rakshit smiled and rubbed it in, 'Leelaji, even now I am requesting, please cooperate. The net is flooded by your own version of events.'

'Can I?' asked Leela as she fiddled with her mobile. The officers nodded. She found that Ishita had let her down. She had first spread the word that Leela needed help from friends. Then she had posted Leela's message on several forums on Facebook and Twitter. It had now gone viral on the net. Leela looked up calmly.

'But my account only corroborates what I had told you earlier. My personal feelings about my benefactor can hardly be relevant to your inquiry.'

Kainthola leaned forward. 'You mentioned to your friend about "mysterious knowledge, hidden political info" and…'

'Officer, I myself did not understand him, as you can see from the same message that you are quoting. This man told me that he was only passing through that area. He hardly spoke. I did not see any books or gadgets; he was more like a mendicant.'

'Mendi…what?'

'Like a sadhu; an ascetic. Many such people carry supplies like kerosene stove, rice, dals, and a few clothes. You would meet these types anywhere in India.'

Natarajan boomed again, '*Hidden political info*! Leelaji, answer the question.'

Leela leaned back and took a deep breath, 'Well, just once he mentioned that India was still suffering some kind of political cancer due to buried state secrets going back to the partition of the country.'

The officers exchanged glances. Rakshit quipped, 'What was his name... something Mahakaal, and you call him MK, right?'

Leela nodded. Rakshit turned to the officers, 'Sir, any match?'

Kainthola shook his head, 'Can't recall, but I have heard that name somewhere. In any case, Mahakaal is a common word.'

Natarajan kept staring at Leela, 'Is that all he told you?'

'I was talking about what is usually taught in our classrooms about events in the 1940s and 50s, about World War II, India's partition etc. That is when he made this comment. I tend to avoid digging into the distant past, but here the context was my trip to Imphal, the present refugee crisis and its roots. There was no further talk, but I was wondering what this sanyasi could have meant.'

'Sir, nowadays these sadhus know more politics than our politicians...' Rakshit ventured, only to be silenced by a stern look from Natarajan.

'Leelaji, did this man mention where he stays, or where he was going?' Kainthola asked.

'I asked. He said he has no fixed place and keeps moving from location to location.'

'Doing what? I mean how does he sustain? Did he tell you?'

'Uh huh. No idea. He hardly talked. Did not answer many of my questions, and reacted only when he wanted to.'

Natarajan turned to Leela. 'Leelaji I'm sorry but we need to take you to the site, if you can trace your way. We really need to find this Mahakaal for probing all links to this crime.'

'But why? This man saved my life, so what can he have to do with the attack? Plus, don't you already have the culprits? Ask them who is behind all this.'

Kainthola pulled his chair closer to Leela and whispered to her in a conspiratorial manner, 'Leelaji please understand. We are under great pressure from the government. The media has roasted us for failing to find you in a week despite satellite tracking and local intelligence. We can't explain how this hut or hideout, *jo bhi hain*, escaped detection. We need to know if there is something behind this man. It all sounds so incredible.'

'You are free to go thereafter,' Natarajan quipped.

'I am free to go anytime,' Leela said in a sharp riposte, 'Now I need to rest. I have no desire to go back to that place, just so that you find and harass my benefactor.'

The officers exchanged looks. Rakshit was quick to respond, 'Why should we harass?'

'You know, you sound like the so-called scientists who stumble upon a rare species in a deep forest, take possession, conduct tests, put a radio collar National Geographic style – all in the name of preservation. My benefactor troubles you because he doesn't fit into your "plausibility" landscape…SO…so let's get him. And you want *me* to help?'

'Leelaji, we just need to complete our investigation. We took the accused men to the area but could not locate the exact spot where they cornered you. Maybe you can lead us there, so that we can nail the attackers.'

Natarajan seconded Kainthola, 'We need to find your saviour and use his testimony to get a conviction for the culprits.'

'His testimony?'

'Yes of course, as a key witness and participant. Or else our case is weakened. These accused will not get convicted. What they admit in the police station may not stand legal scrutiny. Is that what you want?'

Leela could not bear the thought of Mahakaal being questioned by cops or brought to a court. She closed her eyes. 'I will go home now. I need rest. Leave me alone.'

Rakshit beckoned to the others. There was a short pause, and then the men left the room. Natarajan started making a call from his mobile.

They were back in an hour with a triumphant look on their faces. The District Magistrate had passed an order that Leela could be taken to the 'attack site' if accompanied by a doctor and with minimal stress. They showed the order to her.

Next, Natarajan held out his mobile to Leela. It was a call from Mada. She did not take it and started limping to her own mobile. She found it was vibrating anyway. This was from Shivdadu. He spoke in his slow, laboured drawl, 'Lili, I know what is happening now. If you don't go along with them and cooperate, they will ultimately get you back from Pune. Just finish it. This is *not* an ego thing.'

Before Leela could respond, the call went dead. She peeped from her corner and found that the men were huddled together. Natarajan was still talking animatedly on his mobile, perhaps to Mada.

'Shall we go now?'

The officers whipped around in amazement. Rakshit found his voice. 'With us?'

'With you.'

The men looked as if they had just won a lottery. Only Natarajan remained impassive.

NINE

Retracing her way proved to be a mixed bag for Leela. The first step involved meeting the hapless cyclist who had helped her. The man's toothless smile had vanished, replaced by a terrified look and dried tears. He fell at Leela's feet and blabbered about his innocence.

'This is exactly why I wanted to opt out,' said Leela in a biting tone, 'I can't believe that you people can do this to an innocent man who...'

'Leelaji, please listen.'

'...who actually helped me reach the road-head? Please let him go.' Leela's tone was slowly getting to 'injurious' levels.

'We have only questioned him.' said Rakshit in an apologetic tone.

'I know very well what your questioning the poor means!'

The officers conferred and the man was told to leave, on condition he would not abscond and would appear as witness later. Leela told Rakshit that they would have to compensate him for his troubles, or else she would do this herself. Rakshit quickly agreed and pressed some money into the man's hands. He returned the same fearfully and fell at Leela's feet again in gratitude, before a constable brought his cycle and he wheeled away.

From a certain point, the police jeep could not go forward and they had to move on foot. The SIT had organized that she would be taken in a makeshift *palki* (palanquin), so that she did not have to walk in the forest. They reached the point where the boat she had used had been found by the police, and then they crossed the river by a speedboat.

Leela's navigating instincts were still intact. She managed to trace her path back to the river bed where she had made her landing after being chased. It was already over a week and even though they did not hope to find much, they located at least two well preserved footprints of a large elephant and traces of elephant dung on the muddy bank. The rains had washed away all traces of the many men who had landed by boats and clambered ashore to follow her. A bullet was found embedded in the bark of the tree under which she had collapsed in exhaustion. Now at least they found a proof that this was where Leela had been cornered.

Almost an hour later they finally reached the clearing where Leela had stayed. Leela's heart was pounding as she got off the *Palki* and looked around. There was no hut now, only the old huge tree trunk around which it had been put up. A pile of old bricks and mud lay scattered. Someone had pulled it down. There was no sign of any human presence. Even the place where Mahakaal had cooked was covered with mud and small shoots of wild growth.

It was as if no one had been there for months.

Finally, Kainthola spoke out in a frustrated tone, 'Leelaji, please tell us the truth. No one has been here. There is nothing!'

Leela suddenly uttered a small shriek and hobbled to the pit where she had performed her morning ablutions. She looked down and found that the 'evidence' was still there in plenty, albeit covered with caked mud and leaves. 'This is where my benefactor had advised me to relieve myself. Maybe he used the same pit too. If you doubt me, go ahead and test the shit.'

Rakshit could not believe his ears and whispered an expletive under his breath.

Natarajan issued instructions to the forensic team who gingerly collected 'samples'. One of the local villagers from across the river who was accompanying the police shook his head. 'We have never seen or known someone to stay so deep in the forest. Some migrant tribals may have built a seasonal hut for collecting roots and honey. But a Sadhu? That too with a pressure cooker and supplies? Never.'

Another local remarked, 'Tribals make homes only with mud, cow dung, chopped straw, stones... but never bricks.'

A third local said, 'There is an abandoned temple some two km from here. Maybe someone brought bricks from there?'

Rakshit said, 'We'll check it out. Has anyone rounded up tribals who usually pass through here for collecting honey?'

A local Inspector replied, 'Yes sir, we have tracked all the typical communities who pass through these parts. They collect wild fruits, honey, herbs. No one has been here recently, and none has seen a sadhu or a hut.'

'Are you done with me?' asked Leela.

'Presently yes. If we need your inputs later on, we will get in touch,' replied Kainthola.

Rakshit walked up and shook her hand, 'You will be airlifted to Kolkata airport immediately. The press is also waiting to speak to you. If you don't want to interact with them, we will take you right up to the aircraft and you will be home by tonight. We have alerted the Maharashtra Police about handling the situation in Pune once you reach there.'

Leela said, 'Ok, my thanks to everyone here. Let's go right away.'

She declined to get into the *palki* again and started walking on her crutches towards the speed boat. Natarajan overtook her and said, 'When we put up the accused for trial, you would be our key witness. We have confessions from the people who attacked the bus and also killed your friend Martin Cameron. I am sure you would like to see justice being done.'

Leela nodded in silence. Then she hobbled to the boat and was helped in by Rakshit.

Bagdogra airport was teeming with reporters, many from local newspapers. They were all young and aggressive. Everyone wanted a quote based on the odd bits they had already gleaned from their 'inside sources' in the police and the Railway Hospital.

'Were you in the custody of Don Nakul Ranjan?'

'Madam, would you say the person who saved you was a powerful tantrik? Do you believe these things?'

Leela smiled and walked on, but the barrage continued.

'Leelaji, please. Is it true that there were others with this old man, and you don't want to admit that? Did your family pay a ransom?'

Leela turned and answered that one. 'I have nothing to hide. No, there was no one else.'

'You now believe in Babas and supernatural events?'

Leela was pushing ahead to the security check. It was a very small airport, and a lot of policemen and local staff had also gathered to watch the 'fun'. She turned for the last time. 'No one has asked me what I felt about Martin Cameron being shot, while trying to save some women. You just want your piece of flesh for "breaking news"?'

A chorus of voices broke out in ad lib protest.

Leela said firmly, 'I don't pander to scavengers.'

By the time she reached Pune, the media had put out mixed reports about her Bagdogra airport quotes. The reportage conveyed widespread anger that she was arrogant and that there was more to her story than some old man saviour, which needed investigation. But it brought the focus back on the attack near the Buxa reserve, and the state government's alleged covert support to the lumpens behind it.

Mada called her several times but she excused herself saying she needed some rest. Rajen had come to receive her at the Pune Airport, but the high security had whisked her away from a side exit to avoid the media, without bothering to inform him. So now he drove down to her apartment with a big flower bouquet and her pet Bima in tow.

There was a sizeable crowd of curious onlookers blocking the way into the apartment complex, with a couple of Leela's neighbours talking animatedly to reporters. Rajen pushed their concerns politely aside and walked into the lift with Bima barking loudly behind him in excitement. He was quickly let in by Leela's domestic help Asha. He held Leela in a tight embrace, weeping tears of relief. Leela declined to speak about her experience for now and promised to meet him again soon. In any case Bima was hyper after this long hiatus and would not allow them to talk. Leela could feel Rajen's anguish as a father, but to talk to him in brief about Mahakaal now was certain to be a disaster.

Leela hugged him back again when he left, and the doorbell immediately rang to announce the next visitors who would keep coming for over a week to express concern at her ordeal. Rajen had put a guard on duty in front of her door for the night to ensure that no one rings the bell after nine pm. His daughter needed sleep. Asha too promised to stay the night, despite protests from Leela.

She again hesitated to contact Aditya to share her condition. When she did call, his phone was switched off.

Very few of the visitors believed Leela's narration of her experience and thought that she was hiding something, as was being given out 24x7 by the news channels and state politicians in Bengal. She recalled Mahakaal's words, 'To manipulate and control the masses in this digital age is child's play for scheming politicians who understand the baser human psyche. Do what you have to and don't look for results.'

The 'nonsense' rhymes sung by Mahakaal now came to her mind.

The scene replayed vividly in her mind. Leela had started laughing at his rhymes. Immediately, MK had turned the narrative on its head by stating that Leela's ability to laugh at herself had been impaired by a vitiated past which could trace its present moral rot to a great betrayal during the 1940s. These were exemplified by secret deals governing the nation's birth which could be glimpsed – *only glimpsed* – in the 'real' Transfer of Power (T.O.P) documents and other deals not open to public scrutiny.

There were several such 'rhymes' or alpha numerical codes, and now she rushed to her backpack to get the notebook. When Leela had been examined and her baggage checked by the police, she had worried that someone would find out. Luckily, no one had laid an eye on the scribbled jottings in her scrap book.

Now she took a good look at them. MK immediately appeared in her mind's eye, 'These are only the first steps of a process which will lead you from the outer to the inner realm.'

Leela had cut in, 'But wait a minute. How did you access such info?' He had laughed and stretched out his hand with his *three* fingers held out. Then he had brought them inward to his eyes in a back and forth movement. 'Simple perception. I can see them.'

Leela now stretched out two fingers and brought them to her eyes in a mimicking action. Bima glanced at her and went back to sleep. She smiled at the memory and closed her eyes, asking herself aloud, 'But who will believe the perception of a man whose quotes I cannot authenticate, or prove that he exists?'

MK's voice echoed in her mind, 'No one. But they will have to believe the content. Quoting these "slash and tag" codes will get you the attention you need.'

'Let's get cracking,' She said to herself and sat down with pen and paper, ready for a long night. She struggled to put the first one uttered by Mahakaal in place. It finally read: GD.54/59/62/69 - EIII(M&A). What on earth did this mean?'

After another thirty minutes, she thought she had the next three in place. The second one read: 46/47/49 - LEM (GANJ) KHIMAL.

Mahakaal had remarked that there were binaries involved in his 'alphabets' which were twins in reality. The next two read: 48(50)/PINA - JNVP(GG) and 48/LMED/POW/INA/PN.

The next morning she called Mada. He eagerly picked up the phone. 'I'll be over this afternoon,' Leela said and heard his sigh of relief as she hung up.

TEN

Mada strode towards her with an alacrity which belied his age. His heavy-set features were twitching with emotion. He embraced her without a word and kissed her brow. When she opened her mouth to speak, he put his index finger on her lips and walked her inside. Leela noticed that his fingers were trembling much more than usual.

Once inside, Mada presided over an elaborate lunch. No talking was encouraged. Bima was off to play with the domestics. He would peep in once in a while to see if Leela was OK.

Later, as always they settled with dessert in the garden. Leela kept her crutches aside and checked if anyone was around. Then she leaned forward. 'Mada, no one should be able to overhear our talk.'

'Oh? Then – the pond?'

'Ya, Ok.'

Mada called out to the domestics, 'We are at the pond. No calls.'

He walked slowly, leaning on his stick, with Leela supporting his other arm around her slender shoulders, while propelling herself with the crutch under her right arm. They reached the corner of the plot. There was a mini lily pond there. Goldfish peeped out now and then from among the leaves. A tall wall with a barbed wire topped barricade lay just beyond.

Leela asked, 'While we're here, keep a person on the back gate so no one eavesdrops.'

'Child, are you telling me the nuclear password?' said Mada, scowling deeply.

Leela smiled, 'Yes. Passwords for releasing buried secrets, dark energies.'

Mada's frown deepened. He ordered the security, 'Raghuvir, put someone on duty at the back gate while we are here.' Immediately, Raghuvir swivelled his gun to one side and opened the back gate to step out himself.

Mada turned back to face Leela and said angrily in a hurried drawl, 'I'm losing patience. What the hell is going on? Were you really cut off and had no means of contact, or was that a cover for something?'

Leela leaned back and closed her eyes for a moment. Mahakaal appeared in her inner eye. Cover for something?

Mada broke into her reverie. 'You're smiling?! No dodging. Just tell me. Ok, did someone harm you? Blackmail you? Did *any* harm come your way?'

Leela shook her head, tossed her hair back and leaned forward. 'Every word you heard on the media quoting me is true. I would have been killed but for this old man.'

'Ok, but who the hell is he? How could an unarmed old man neutralize an armed, killer gang? No one believes this part.'

'But it is the exact truth. I have no clue as to who he was and how he did it. No clue at all. Others' beliefs don't change the fact that he existed, exists.'

'But how? SSP Rakshit tells me that his team found not a shred of evidence that a man had lived or been on that location! No standing structure, no footprints, objects, leftovers from the cooking which he did for you – nothing! Only some excreta which you pointed out, which I trust raised Rakshit's hackles.' Mada allowed a chuckle to cross his face, 'Now we have shrinks on the job, saying it could have been a mass delusion.'

'Oh ho! So now both me and ten odd attackers were deluded,' Leela shrugged, 'And we dreamt up an old man in that state? Your cops gave them third degree, but the delusion ghost does not leave yet, yes?'

She paused and then laid her palms out, 'It is as it is. The bullet

73

lodged in the tree there can't be wished away. Plus I am sure if they do a DNA test on the faeces, they'll have the results that two of us were there as I said.'

'But then who was he? Was he a doctor? He treated your fracture like an expert.'

'Blank. He spoke seldom. Gave no hints. Often never replied to my questions.'

'His name?'

'Mahakaal. He told me in good humour that I could call him MK.'

'Huh? What kind of a name is that? No surname?'

'He said as a sanyasi he was dead to his past, and right now he was Mahakaal. He spoke excellent English and Hindi, which many sadhus can anyway. He also knew Bengali or maybe he is a Bengali. But Mada...,' She paused as he opened his mouth to speak. She was astonished at how possessive she felt about 'MK'. She did not want to share him with anyone.

'But Mada what?'

'He simply changed my life. Without effort or persuasion. Just by being what he is.'

Mada's eyebrows shot up and then settled again. He was now both intrigued and alert. 'He, HE changed your life? In seven days? Somehow I can't see someone changing you at all, let alone in a week.'

'He did nothing to change me. But just being with him in that forest, seeing the way he was integrated with every speck of life around him, his intimate knowledge about the forest...'

'This sounds quite vague to me.'

'You touch him on any topic,' said Leela, snapping her fingers, 'ANY. And if he agreed to speak – either at that moment; or three days later at *his* chosen moment, suddenly you found yourself in a limitless universe.'

It was obvious that the 'Army no nonsense' stance was showing up on Mada's face, and he was getting worked up. He controlled himself and rested his chin on his stick, his eyes narrowing with an impatient condescending look.

'Pithy utterances on various subjects, such as cuisines worldwide…'

'This sadhu has savoured international cuisines?!'

'Yes Mada. Then, he always used just a few words – it could be about ship building, marine life, undiscovered minerals, music and its efficacy, black holes…'

'Black holes? This man talks of black holes?!'

'Infinite power in a vacuum.'

'Ok, Ok, I think I get the drift. This is some super learned person, an outcast from modern society.'

'Mada, I believe unexplained circumstances brought me to this man. One of the topics he stressed upon was the impact of the events leading to our Dominion Status in 1947 on our family. Most intriguing was that he seemed to know you and Shivdadu.'

Mada burst out, 'Are you telling me that this old fogey even knows our family?'

'Yes. How, he would not tell.'

He slapped his hand down on his stick, 'Explain that.'

'Once, he briefly told me of the events leading to Shivdadu and you being on different sides during the Kohima and Imphal battles. He said that you later went along with our leading politicians' betrayal of the real heroes of the freedom struggle... Now sit down.' Leela scolded Mada, who had stood up in anger and then promptly sat down with a muffled obscenity.

'Man needs to be shot! Who the bloody hell is this ghost to tell you such nonsense? What can he know about that period? Maybe he was not even born at that time.'

'His age? No idea. Though sometimes he spoke of events as if he was present there in the 1940s.'

'Is he as old as me? And HE fought off this mob? Holy crap! We better find him and give him a real medal – if this is true.'

'He looked around sixty. Seventy at most.'

'Then he was not even born in the 1940s. What rubbish!'

Leela disregarded Mada's protests and carried on, 'He said that *you* were aware of the fact that over ninety per cent of the commissioned officers in the armed forces at that time had great regard for the INA.' She paused when Mada slammed his fist on the bench in anger. Then she continued, 'If you don't want to listen, well then, it's better I leave.'

'So bloody hell what? Does it make me and other officers who fought under the British flag – traitors, unpatriotic? Nonsense! We were all soldiers and we all fought honourably, whether INA or us. Just because we were in the Army doesn't mean we all wanted British rule. Many of us fought because it was our occupation.'

'True. But it's what happened later. I read up on my Kindle this morning, linking some references to what this man spoke about. Once the long suppressed news of the INA's attack on Britain in North East India broke in public, and especially after the Naval Ratings mutiny in 1946 *inspired by Subhas Bose and the INA*, the British panicked and decided to exit India.'

'Damn it, I know all that. You are talking about events from my youth when you were not even born!'

Leela remained impassive and focused, 'Mada, please note that this was the first serious mass revolt in the armed forces after the 1857 Indian rebellion against the British. And yet, though the Naval Mutiny was followed by the RIAF (Royal Indian Air Force) and the Jabalpur Army Signals Mutinies in 1946, all our leading Politicians betrayed them and let them down without an iota of support: Patel, Gandhi, Nehru – the whole lot! Most Congress politicians wore the 'support INA robe' to fool the public and win the elections. However, after 1947, these brave INA men were dumped ruthlessly and never re-inducted again into the Army, except on 'de novo' commission. A few were offered openings in other areas. Even Pakistan treated them better and took them back in their army – not us! They were ditched...'

'I repeat: most of the army was nationalist, but they fought to fulfill their duties; feed their families. And don't trumpet about the INA, which many POW's joined solely to escape Jap torture.'

Leela went on relentlessly, '... ditched in their own country India, Mada. Condemned to an existence of penury. Like your own brother Shiv. That also meant a blank out and falsification of the history we are taught in school – wait, I am not done,' Leela cut off Mada's protests and continued, 'There would be no mention of the INA or Subhas Bose in army offices; no plaques or photos. Blanked out by your heroes, PM Nehru and so on – I see their huge busts still standing in your Hallway. You went along with the outright falsehood that we got our Dominion Status *solely* through "*Ahimsa*"! This is what MK meant. Now, how many of you including your seniors resigned or protested this betrayal of Subhas Bose – at that time – ten years later – even fifty years later?'

Mada roared, 'I will not be made to feel guilty. I had neither the authority to challenge this...'

'Nor the will, nor that thing which we call conscience. You went along with the people who sold the country. In fact you prospered under the looters who milked this country for six decades and brought in horrors such as the Emergency. *You* made sure that Baba became the amoral monster that he is today, while your own brother and his family rotted away.'

Mada's face was not a pretty sight at all. He raised his stick and then staggered for balance. As Leela got up and rushed to offer him support, he angrily thrust her away and fell in the process.

Raghuvir came running from near the back gate. As he helped

Mada to his feet, he told Leela in a rough tone, 'Be careful. He is not balanced anymore.'

Mada was panting heavily after he was made to sit down. He glared at Raghuvir, who resumed his duty at his post. Leela sat quietly, waiting for the tempest to fade away. Then she got up. 'Mada, I better go. You need rest.'

'Sit down!' roared Mada.

Leela remained standing, 'No Mada. I always end up reopening old wounds. If I can't help… Mada?'

The old man was weeping. Leela had never seen him cry or even break, not even in the most traumatic moments when his wife died. 'Lili, I *am* that culprit,' the words just slowly and painfully tumbled out between pauses, 'The monster who buried his honour. I can cheat the whole world, Rajen can drown his conscience in drink, but I can't hide from you.' He looked up at her, 'What can I do to undo it at least one bit. I will rot in hell anyway.'

Leela bent down and embraced him. He shook with his bouts of sobbing. She spoke gently while caressing his brow, 'Mada, that you accept it is enough.'

Leela held him close while he whispered again between deep sighs, 'It haunts me. What can I do now?'

Leela slowly made him lean back in his chair. 'There *is* something you can do, but it may mean a battle bigger than any you have ever fought.'

Mada's poise returned, along with the hint of a proud soldier's smile, 'Try me.'

Leela went back to her handbag and fished out her notebook, taking care that her back was towards Raghuvir, who was watching. She bent down again to Mada and whispered in his ear, 'Shortly before I left the place, something strange happened. Mahakaal was in a jovial mood and he recited some apparently nonsensical rhymes along with hash and dot gestures, referring to our "hashtag" generation as he called it. Maybe three or four times. Then he turned serious and said that these, I think he said codes... or was it first alphabets, would make me understand how all the issues which impact my present are linked to a past which I could look into. I had jotted them down. I don't know what these are. They resemble file numbers or codes. Can you help me find out more?'

Mada's eyebrows shot up. 'Are you suggesting this old fogey gave you some riddles that in turn revealed file numbers – FILE NUMBERS! This has to be some spy posing as a sadhu. What have you got into?'

Leela withdrew her hand. She slipped the notebook back in her handbag, picked up her crutches and started walking away. Mada pulled himself to his feet and staggered to overtake her. 'No, don't go like that.'

'I'll manage on my own.'

All the entreaties of Mada failed to hold her back. She whistled for Bima, who came bouncing to join her. Driving back, she smiled bitterly that she could have become so worked up about Mahakaal being called a 'spy'.

Three hours later when she was quietly reading, the doorbell rang. It was Mada. It was apparent that he was in deep stress. The driver stood just behind him with a worried face. Leela ushered him in and gestured to the driver to be around, while Bima welcomed Mada by nosing his hand.

They sat in silence for a while, sipping tea. Not a word was exchanged. Then he spoke in a gruff, contrite voice, 'I'm sorry.'

'You don't have to be. After all this is only some spy,' said Leela.

'No. It was my ego. No spy would know or care about Shiv and me, save and nurture you in a forest, and then give you…what was that he gave – codes, passwords or what?' said Mada.

'Maybe. But he only said that these could reveal a hidden betrayal around the Transfer of Power in 1947, and in this are cloistered the seeds of our present rot: moral, political, you name it. He sang these number-letter combinations almost as nonsense nursery rhymes.'

'But did he suggest that you should learn all this from… from some confidential files?'

'No. He thought it unlikely that I would make much headway, but he said the very act of probing would bring alive the entire ethos since the last seventy years with a new relevance for me today.'

'Give them to me, these codes of yours. Or at least show me.'

'Sure?' probed Leela.

'I just said so. I'm always sure,' said Mada with his trademark patriarchal tone.

Leela smiled and he smiled back like a child, even giving her a wink. She fetched her handbag and gave him the notebook which she had taken out some time ago. 'I'll copy the number and letter combinations for you. I'll be making another copy for myself and hiding this notepad in a safe place.'

Mada looked at her with a raised eyebrow. 'You've been watching spy thrillers.'

The Lt. General took the notepad and jotted down the details on a paper provided by Leela. His fingers were trembling, but he held firm. Then Leela made another copy and went to hide the notepad. All this while, Mada was staring at the content.

Leela's mobile was vibrating on a nearby table. She checked it and found several missed calls and messages from the Police HQ and the Pune Police Commissioner's Office. They were awaiting her confirmation for a session with the police sketching expert.

'The Police HQ wants me to come for their sketching session to describe MK. At some point I will also have to fly to Kolkata to identify the accused in a TIP (Test identification Parade). What a charade! They know the whodunit chaps very well,' said Leela.

'It *is* a charade,' said Mada, getting up while pushing down on his cane, 'What they really want is your old man, the fly in the ointment.'

'I will go and get it over with tomorrow,' said Leela.

Mada turned at the door and held up his fist holding the paper. 'Let me see what I can do with this. It looks strange to me: maybe file numbers, maybe not. I mean why would anyone oblige? They will all ask: What's in it for them or for me? Why am I interested?'

'Thank you for helping out, but naming me or MK will only create trouble,' said Leela, adding softly, 'You don't have to do this.'

Mada stared at her. Then his crooked smile appeared again. He winked and stomped out with his walking stick. Bima cocked one eye open, yawned and went back to sleep.

ELEVEN

The next day found Leela at the Pune Police HQ. The forensic artist patiently made one portrait after another, while throwing suggestions and queries at her. He was soft spoken and drew her into a free flowing description of the various situations with Mahakaal.

At the end of an hour, he beckoned to her to see the results. Senior Superintendent of Police (SSP) Arolkar also came in to watch this part of the exercise. He remarked, 'Leelaji, we also have the SketchCop FACETTE Face Design System Software, but we rely more on our artist.'

There was no doubt that the artist was very talented. At least two sketches out of the four prototypes made bore resemblance to Mahakaal. When Leela pointed out the discrepancies, the artist drew over the sketches and promised to have the final copies ready by the next day.

'So *this* old man held off the attackers?' SSP Arolkar's very tone and look gave him away, in that he doubted Leela's version. She did not react and walked back to her car on her crutches.

By the weekend, the highway attack, Martin's death and Leela's story were relegated to second string news or discontinued. A few local Bengali and Pune newspapers continued giving updates and a few fringe elements persisted in posting on these stories on blogs and social networking sites, but in general, the public interest plummeted.

It was almost 10 pm on Saturday when a call came twice from an unknown number. Leela took the call the second time, but it was cut. A message followed from the same number. It was Mada. 'Meet me at 5.30 am at the Osho Teerth when I take my walk.' Leela frowned. She could not recall Mada being so secretive about anything.

At pre-dawn, Bima was delighted to be up at his favourite time. Leela bundled him into the car and drove to a lane just adjacent to the park. While she got out and secured Bima on a leash, a scooter pulled up next to her car and a couple got off for their morning walk.

Leela found Mada waiting in a shaded corner of the park. They walked together in unison silently for three rounds, with Raghuvir a few steps behind.

Leela could sense that Mada was tense and alert. Sure enough, he soon chose an open part of the park where usually a lot of morning walkers did freehand exercises. It was the worst place for any private conversation, but Mada guided Leela there. 'There are already two people on your tail.'

'My tail? Where?' said Leela in a low voice, 'I can't see anyone.'

'You won't. These two who are coming this way.' Mada whispered.

Leela's eyes widened in disbelief. This was the middle-aged couple who had parked their scooter next to her car. They were walking and flexing their arms like any other normal couple here.

'Can't be.' said Leela.

'I can spot them a mile away,' said Mada. 'Raghu, track them.'

'This is impossible!' said Leela indignantly, 'Overnight I am on radar – and you too? For what?'

'Now just walk me to my car and get in. Do that normally, as if you are seeing me off,' said Mada in the same low voice, 'Don't ask any questions here.'

They took two more slow rounds. The other couple was always ahead of them, varying their pace so that they were within sniffing distance from Leela. Bima was growling at them from time to time, underlining Mada's opinion.

Then Mada reached his car, with Leela and Raghu in tow. Raghu produced a flask and poured two glasses of the fresh vegetable juice with which Mada started his day. Once the glasses were poured, Leela moved into the car with him, as the couple walked past.

'Now you really are on the radar for the Intelligence officials,' said Mada gravely, 'These codes you gave me, they are the numbers for some kind of files – no, actually not even that. These are NOT typical files at all. They don't show any originating department or the trail as to where they were created, only year numbers and a special code which nobody except a handful of privy people can perhaps decode. The existence of these codes which indicate secret documents, has been under cover with all Governments till date.'

'But why? What's the gravy in there?'

'I can only guess. Most likely these codes pertain to the Transfer of Power in 1947-9, the real deal that holds details about the secret terms under which the Dominion Status was granted by Britain to India. There could be other deals too which are secret and legally impacting the core of our existence – even today,' emphasized Mada while tapping his index finger on his thigh, 'Yes, even today. This is what a retired Union Cabinet Minister told me, who had a vague idea about what it could all mean. Similar response from a current PMO top man, who fends off any attempts via RTI (Right to Information) to uncover anything related to this.'

'But Mada, why should you or I be under surveillance?'

'Look here. Indians are the world champions for snooping on others, as well as hiding secrets. The FBI could take lessons from our guys. So when I present a chit like this, any ruling junta will panic. How did you and now me, know this detail?' Mada said gravely. Then he posed, 'Have you deciphered other such codes too?'

Leela nodded silently.

'The Cabinet Minister told me that there is no mainstream politician alive who will dare touch these issues connected with the code numbers on your slip. Among those at the very top that came to know anything after taking oath, none has had the balls to do anything, especially since they find no political benefits to extract – only trouble.' Mada tapped his stick on the car floor, 'They suspected me – *me*! So I took the straight path. I told them about your saviour.'

'How could you do that!'

'You never told me that this was about exposing the *Ravanas* of yesteryear who had played *Rama*,' said Mada with a stuck smile, 'Have you left the notepad you showed me at home somewhere?'

Leela looked into Mada's eyes. 'Yes, but it's safe. I have a paper with all the codes in my handbag with me.'

Mada smiled back and then patted her head. 'Just head home... no wait.' He rolled his window down and Raghu was there to take instructions, 'Raghu, escort Lili to her car.'

As Leela made to step out, Mada clasped her hand tightly. 'Drop it Lili. It serves no purpose. I don't know what you've got into, who this man *really* is, and what past he wants to connect to your present. But I...I am bloody uneasy. No good.'

Leela smiled, 'Would you back off from a promise made to someone who saved you?'

They looked silently at each other. Mada's face was masked in pain and worry. Leela bent down and squeezed his hand. 'Don't worry. I'll be careful. If MK has put me into something, he must know how to get me out if needed.'

Raghuvir walked Leela and Bima to her car. While she was fixing Bima to the car's rear seat harness lock, Raghu quickly looked over the car's interiors with his trained eyes and waved her off. Hardly a lane later, she spotted the same couple drinking tea at a roadside stall. The lady had a jogger's headset on, and was nodding with her eyes closed. Leela smiled and drove on.

At home, she was not one bit surprised to find that a window near the front door was ajar. This was a window that remained shut at all times. To someone strolling through her flat, it would look undisturbed but she could see that her typical hiding places had all been screened. She was thankful that she had carried the paper on her. The flat otherwise looked in order. The original chit was exactly where she had left it, tucked inside the false sole of her hiking boot. The intruders had done their work professionally except for the window remaining open, which meant that they had exited just when she was on her way up. On checking with the guard, she found that all three surveillance cameras in that part of the apartment building had been disabled, and the security staff never got wind of this.

Asha came in and went about her work. Leela made herself some toast and 'desi' eggs and sat down with a cup of herbal tea. Just as she was taking her last sip, the doorbell rang. The Pune Police team arrived with the final drawings made by the forensic artist. They wanted her confirmation about the accuracy of the sketches.

Leela was impressed. Indeed this artist was very good. He had almost perfectly created MK's likeness. She tapped two of the drawings and observed, 'Yes, these two seem to be quite close.'

While the team exchanged knowing looks, Asha came in with tea and biscuits. Bima was growling outside, being secured on the kitchen balcony. SSP Arolkar bit into a biscuit and said, 'We have already run these sketches through our entire data base. They were also flashed to every single *thana* in Bengal, Bihar, Jharkhand; even Nepal and Bangladesh databases, by prior arrangement. There is great pressure on us to identify your benefactor,' Arolkar emphasized the word *great*. 'Around thirty nebulous matches came up. These were all identified and rejected, since the people matched were in other locations on the days in question.'

'Why are you after this man?' Leela asked, her eyes flashing, 'He saved me. Maybe that is a crime?'

'No Leelaji, it's not that...'

'None of the *real* bigwigs behind the planning and execution of this attack have been caught yet. Their names, addresses, backers, all these are known. And here you are, sending out alerts even internationally, for an old man who helped me. Isn't that perverse?'

Arolkar took his time to sip his tea. 'Frankly, we need him. Otherwise no one believes this story, that an unarmed man could scare away a full gang of killers. Now their lawyer is cleverly changing their admission of guilt, which goes along with your own narration, by arguing that this was done under police duress.'

'Ahaaa! That means I spun a tale? If the accused don't support my version, is it falsified? A good friend of mine is dead, five of the culprits themselves were killed and there are people who actually think that I spun a tale?'

Arolkar looked at her impassively, 'Yes Leelaji, unless — hear me out…unless it is corroborated by a second source. This old man.'

'If you don't believe me, why are you here?' Leela was up on her crutches, 'Why waste time?'

'Please sit down. For once, see it from our point of view,' said Arolkar, while another officer quickly refilled the SSP's tea cup from the pot.

'You are chased by almost twenty people, out of whom ten odd men get into two boats and follow you across a river. Your version, yes?'

Leela did not answer and kept staring at Arolkar.

'Their version too. Then, an old man scares them off. They claim that elephants charged at them. You say: single elephant. OK. And then they say five chaps are drowned when their boat capsized in panic and then crocodiles attacked them.'

'So far the versions are matching. But you stay in that location for over seven days. You have a major fracture. Yet, when you are back, what do we find? Your fracture is healing and tended to. You are well fed and healthy. In a place with no edible vegetation, not one tiny outlet providing supplies, this man sustains you for over a whole week.

'Again, when the Bengal SIT goes there, what do *they* find? No standing hut, no signs of fresh habitation, no evidence of human living whatsoever. Only your excreta, and that of someone else, who could also be someone holding you captive in a tent stocked with supplies. No wonder the accused are now changing their version.'

'Can you enlighten me why I would make all this up?' said Leela.

Arolkar went on without answering, 'And now above all, your sole witness has evaporated. What we are thinking now is: You were under the custody of people who were part of this gang, and that the boat capsized by accident. So there was no surreal attack at all.'

Leela took a deep breath. 'Maybe I was also a part of the plan to attack this bus and kill Martin! Tell you what, go tell your seniors: if they can't get it up, don't blame their wives.'

'Please control yourself!'

Leela's voice went into whiplash mode, 'This SIT is just a bunch of incompetent morons. Now that you don't have any clues, or don't have the guts to follow the ones you found, you think I am in cahoots with some spy. You put a tail on me, raid my flat...'

Arolkar stood up. His men looked very upset. 'What the hell are you talking about?'

'Don't pretend that you don't know. Please leave. I don't have anything more for you.'

Leela hobbled to the door and held it open. Bima had been growling for long. Now he started barking. The men trooped out with sullen faces. Then SSP Arolkar turned back, 'One last point Leelaji. In case that interests you. After such an exhaustive search, we did find one approximate match for these two sketches.'

There was a brief silence as Leela and the SSP stared at each other. Then she yielded and walked back to her chair. Arolkar followed, but kept standing. He continued, 'And that match too cannot be traced.'

Leela smiled bitterly, 'That was only to be expected, right?'

'Cannot be traced...' replied Arolkar with a grave look on his face, 'because these sketches resemble a man who almost no one ever saw, and who supposedly died in 1985.'

Leela controlled her urge to burst out laughing. 'Died in 1985? And then?'

Arolkar chose to sit down. He seemed to like the biscuits, and picked up one. 'Leelaji, there was a mysterious Baba in Uttar Pradesh, who never gave *darshan* to anyone and who spoke to rare visitors from behind a curtain.'

Leela spoke in a tired voice, 'Baba? Arolkarji, I am allergic to Fakirs, Babas, Maulvis and their likes. So then?'

'Only a handful ever saw him directly. A couple of imagined sketches were made from their descriptions.'

'Like the forensic ones you have shown me?'

'No, no. These were made by an illustrator in 2001 and not by our trained composite artistes, who only did some touch up. Take a look.'

He handed a sketch to Leela. She looked. Immediately she could sense that perhaps this was Mahakaal, but not so much because of an exact resemblance. Instead, an acute and overpowering sense of 'Yes! Yes!' overcame her. Mahakaal had looked like a younger version or 'relative' of the person visualized in this sketch.

'*Hai naa miltaa jhultaa?* You think it is him, don't you?' Arolkar's voice was triumphant.

Leela spoke in a bare whisper, 'Yes.'

Arolkar saw the look on her face and stretched his hands above his head in a languid manner, while his smile grew a tad wider. His next sentence took her breath away. 'This man in the imagined sketch, I repeat *imagined,* is still a mystery. Because he was known as Gumnami Baba of Faizabad. You may have heard about him in the media – that he could have been Netaji Subhas Bose living in secrecy.'

Leela started laughing loudly, which made some of the cops standing just outside to peep in. Then she slumped back in her sofa and looked up at Arolkar, 'Whichever thread I get connected to...does it *have* to always end up with Netaji – INA – and now this Baba?'

Arolkar did not smile in answer.

'So I actually met a dead person who grew a few decades younger in appearance?' said Leela, 'You called my earlier story crazy. Now what would you call this?'

The SSP and his team bade her goodbye and left. She absentmindedly waved them out.

And then she remembered.

She started flipping through a pile of magazine clippings and found what she was looking for. SSP Arolkar had tried to trap her! She had been shown a computer generated sketch which had in fact used a photo of Subhas Bose as the base. Arolkar's gifted artist had only touched it up to fool her. So the SIT was trying to prove that she had approved Netaji's sketch as Mahakaal, because she had been indoctrinated as a child by her INA elders.

But damn it, there was a resemblance! Uncanny, but true. How could this be so?

Slowly, Leela became aware that there was a new essence in the room. It was very distinct. She looked everywhere, but could not locate the source. When she stepped outside the flat, it disappeared. She came back and sat still. Very gradually, the essence became more and more pronounced till she remembered.

One day Mahakaal had brought an exquisite forest flower which had already matured and bent over in the rain. It had this specific fragrance. Then he had said that when she needed to be reassured in a situation of stress, she would know of his presence by this typical fragrance.

Bima, who had been edgy all morning, started sniffing around and then sat at her feet quietly. He nuzzled at her toes and even rolled over on his back, asking to be tickled. His relaxed mood quickly transferred itself to her. She let go of her doubting faculties. The essence was real. That was all. How did it matter if MK looked like some Gumnami Baba who was rumoured to be Netaji?

TWELVE

The next morning Leela drove directly to Rajen's home without notice. She was sure he would be there since he had almost withdrawn himself from the day-to-day management of his many enterprises, some of which were not doing well.

There was no preamble. No sooner had she entered his sprawling living room, he accosted her from his sofa, 'Mamon, I thought you were today's woman, but all of a sudden you become a grave digger?'

Rajen had just finished a very late lunch and was in an expansive mood.

'Baba, will you or won't you?' asked Leela with an exaggerated smile.

'Will I what?'

'You know what. You also know the strings better than anyone else. You wear all the political hats when it suits you: breakfast with the socialists, lunch with Congis, tea with the commies, and now of course Dinner – in fact correction! Now all the main meals with the Chaddis. All the others are *Chai paani.*'

Rajen started laughing uproariously.

'So please doff the right hat to my cause. After all I'm your own daughter – hopefully?'

Rajen made a mock gesture to hit her. '*Maarbo!* Now tell me.'

'Baba, you already know everything. Yes, there was an old man who saved me, more remarkable than any person that I have ever met. He showed me a different reality. Now don't compare him with all these gurus you have around you.'

Rajen poured himself a drink. 'No, I won't take offence. Someone who can have this kind of impact on you has to be very special. But now, what's the problem?'

Leela waved her index finger, 'The Police can't find him. What's more, they found only one thread – to a Ghost.'

Rajen broke into another bout of laughter. 'Ghost? Ha Ha! The ghost of Netaji. But maybe I understand. You, brought up on this INA thing by Anu and Ma and seeing the departed hero's photo nailed to the cross – sorry to the wall – right through your childhood; now you have shaped the likeness of this ghost to Netaji.'

'Not true.'

Rajen downed another gulp and said in an impassive voice, 'What do you want from me? Produce your Netaji or your old man alive?'

Leela put her hands on his shoulders and peered into his face. 'Yes or no?'

'Yes or no what?' Rajen shot back, 'Ok tell me what you want. I'll really enquire. Mada told me that you jotted down some strange nursery rhymes which your old man uttered in jest? Ok...wait, let me write on a pad, or you write.'

Saying that, he pushed himself up with her help and fetched a notepad. Leela hesitated, and then she wrote down the same two codes which she had given to Mada. She decided against revealing any of the other rhymes or codes.

Rajen stared at the chit with a deep frown. Then he looked up and said, 'Ok, This remains top secret. I will give it a real shot.'

Leela added, 'If anyone asks about the source, just say your daughter got these from "researchers" examining documents such as India's Transfer of Power or the Government of India Act 1935 and so on.'

Rajen shot to his feet, as he assumed his sombre public stance, 'Now run along, I have appointments coming up.'

This was more than Leela had bargained for. She waved a goodbye and left the room as Rajen stretched for his mobile.

It did not take Leela long to realize that her father could not help her beyond a point. He got her appointments with top officials at the MEA (Ministry of External Affairs, India), the MHA (Ministry of Home Affairs, India) and even the PMO (Prime Minister's Office), all at lightning speed. After six weeks of meeting such people including two senior ministers, Leela found that she was not getting anywhere. Most of them told her that someone had played a practical joke on her. Others wanted to know who were these 'researchers' who were wasting Leela's and also their time?

A few ventured to tell her off the cuff that her codes 'could' perhaps pertain to files about the Transfer of Power (T.O.P) and Netaji Subhas Chandra Bose which were not even part of government records. They told her that normally such files, if they existed, were accessible only by the PM. In the larger interests of the country, usually such information would not be released in the public domain.

Leela herself short listed and met an assortment of people who mattered on the subject: retired bureaucrats, veteran politicians inimical to her father or the present regime, ace civil servants who had worked under the British, renowned historians and so on.

What most of them said basically was that her inquest was only creating paranoia and adding to the Internet trash about the T.O.P documents, such as India being on lease for ninety nine years, which was without any substance. Especially scathing were acerbic historians who deemed themselves to be the last word on such issues.

After a few weeks, a senior Minister personally called Rajen at night and pointedly asked who was guiding Leela. The Minister told him: 'Can you ever think that any ruling politician would commit hara-kiri over a *thanda* (dead) issue like the T.O.P files, which presently brings no political dividend of any kind? In any case, almost all these documents have already been *officially* released by the FCO (Foreign and Commonwealth Office) in UK, and there is no timeline as yet for the one remaining classified document.'

But he had heard 'unofficially' that Leela had mentioned codes to documents which are so highly secretive that even their names cannot be divulged. Some could indeed be linked to Netaji's fate, but how did she know such a code? There was in fact an internal inquiry to find out if there had been some security breach at the highest level. 'Leela is suspected to have been in captivity in a forest with anti-national elements. We have decided to keep her under 24 x 7 surveillance for now.'

Rajen analysed all other similar confidential feedback which he had received and had a handwritten note dropped in Leela's mailbox: '*Stop this grave digging ASAP. The "REAL" T.O.P info which your old man may have hinted at, will never be put out in the public domain, and it is connected at the navel with the disappearance and fate of Netaji Subhas Bose. Given our family's INA History, you are suspected of harboring a typical agenda, and no one believes the "old man in the forest" trigger for your queries. Mamon, now shut shop and resume normal life. I can't do more. Nor can anyone else.*'

Rajen ended up spending more time in his temple room, performing special pujas to clear the dark clouds and evil planets from Leela's life.

Confirming his fears, early one morning Leela was quite taken aback to find both Kainthola and Natarajan at her door, along with Arolkar. She was driven to the Police HQ and thoroughly grilled about how she got the two codes, and why she had not mentioned the same when she had given her statement in Jayanti and in the Railway Hospital Alipurduar. Her explanation that she initially thought this was some joke from MK did not wash with them. Why had she probed the same *now* through her family? She told them this was an afterthought and ran through the whole sequence again and again, but they still suspected her. Before her lawyer could step in, she agreed to a Lie Detector test, where she came clean.

Soon thereafter, the Police SIT admitted that they were examining 'other possibilities', since the old man as their key witness was yet to be found. Even the lawyers for the accused now took the line that their clients had cooked up the old man theory to escape 'third degree'. On the other hand, there was the bullet found in the tree near where Leela had collapsed, as well as the crocodile eaten bodies of five of the accused. So these loopholes continued as a mystery around Leela's disappearance.

She stuck to the facts about being under the care of an old man, but gradually her version found fewer and fewer takers even among her friends. It was concluded that she had been in the custody of a Master Spy group in a tent, and with her recent inquest into the T.O.P files, this theory got a boost. But no motive for her captors could be established.

THIRTEEN

Two days later, a weary Leela went to Delhi and took the Dehradun Shatabdi to see Shivdadu. Once again, she left Bima with Rajen. Ever since her break up with Aditya and the attack on her in the Buxa Reserve, both Shiv and Anu had been expressing their desire to see her. She too wanted to meet them.

Both father and daughter were waiting for her at the entry to their tiny two-roomed cottage. Shivdadu was bent over slightly, and his movements were very slow and impaired after the torture he had suffered in the Andaman jail. Anu Mashi was her natural bouncy self, supporting Shivdadu and smiling away all their worries. But when Leela looked closer, the sadness and strain on both their faces hit her hard. They embraced her and shed tears of joy.

The next hour was spent in bliss, saying hello to all the poor souls who lived on the tiny farm, worked on it and consumed much of its bounty. This was followed by a heavenly meal served on old stone plates. The greens were all organic produce from the farm.

Then, once they were rested and had aired their concerns about the attack and Leela's stay in the forest, Anu Mashi suddenly asked her about what she had gotten into. Apparently Mada had called her from an unknown number and after briefing her about Leela, he had asked her to talk Leela out of this 'mission'.

Leela said, 'Is that what you want?'

Anu began speaking, 'Well, we always thought that you don't want to look back, and now suddenly…'

'No!' The sudden, forceful interjection from Shivdadu jolted them all into silence. Coming from a man who hardly spoke, this was like a cannon shot. He was sitting on his ancient planter's chair, looking fixedly into a distance. When Leela attempted to talk, he held up his hand for silence. Anu proceeded to work in the kitchen, from where she signalled to Leela to keep quiet.

Then Shiv spoke again in a slow, halting refrain, 'No matter what they throw at you, don't give up. For the sake of so many unknown Indreni Thapas, Rasammah Bhupalans, Shangara Singhs, Meenachi Perumals... ordinary people who gave up not just all their belongings but often their lives when they fought for the INA – for what? Tell me. We survived by eating lingra grass or nothing at all for weeks... so that you all live in freedom. Yet, we pass each day in ignorance, not knowing that we remain secretly enslaved.'

'Enslaved, Dadu?'

Shiv went back to his silent mode. Then Anu spoke in her matter-of-fact way, 'Ma would make notes after some of Baba's INA colleagues visited. These included a few INA seniors who had made peace with the political bigwigs at that time,' she continued kneading the dough for the evening meal, 'They had been rewarded and all had prospered. Once, one of them who had become an Ambassador abroad, dropped hints that we were still tied by several secret agreements which impacted our very existence as a nation. The British offered a "take it or leave it" gamble. Our leaders signed on the dotted line. The partition and killings, these were systematically allowed to happen.'

Leela shook her head, 'This is a crazy, fringe view.'

'Keep quiet about things you know nothing about!' said Shivdadu sharply. Leela was quite taken aback by the aggression in the old man.

'Baba, let her be. When your own generation or even the next ones chose not to speak up, why blame this generation? They don't know, that's all,' said Anu, 'Thousands of unarmed INA POWs were executed by the British in Nilganj and Jhikargacha, just like the Polish

98

officers who were killed in Katyn, Poland on Stalin's orders. This is far more than the Jallianwala Bagh killings and yet, many such horrific deeds remain hidden in files. Our politicians wanted power at any cost.'

Leela was already getting irritated that the topic was going back to the past. 'Mashi, this is only speculation.'

Anu said, 'You want the true facts, but I don't expect real declassification to happen.'

Shivdadu shook his head from side to side: 'Declassification? Huh! What do these activists do? Press "LIKE" buttons on mobiles. Sign petitions online. *Nothing* will change.'

He suddenly tried to get up, doubling over and coughing in the process. His face was marked with pain. Anu and Leela tried to help him, but he waved them off. 'Convenient to bury Netaji in a crash or in Siberia. Because... we continue celebrating the falsehood that we got freedom mainly through *Ahimsa!* How many want to know the truth today?'

Leela spoke in a resigned voice, 'Dadu, the main files remain hidden. That's what I found. The ruling party has played the game the same way as the past regimes, only given it a smart spin.'

'Good you can see that,' said Anu.

'People are fed up and Netaji is a boring, distant topic for them. That's why there is no major movement backing the declassification of these secret files.'

'But what is this link between Netaji and this sadhu you met?' asked Anu.

'None that I know. The top police bosses tell me that Mahakaal, as described by me, looks a lot like this computer generated sketch of Gumnami Baba which is based on Subhas Bose's photo. Now this unseen Baba, even if he was Subhas Bose, died in 1985. How can he resurface more than thirty years later looking a lot younger? I met a ghost?'

'But he was real, this man,' remarked Shiv.

'Absolutely. And so are the strange rhymes he had uttered in jest, where bingo – I seem to have struck pay dirt,' said Leela.

A wacky smile appeared on Shiv's face, 'Rhymes? But where are *my* rhymes?'

Saliva slowly started drooling out of a corner of his mouth, and Anu was quick to wipe this off. The silence grew awkward. Then his look became distant. Anu whispered, 'Leave him alone. He has gone into his shell.'

Leela nodded and gestured with her hands that she was going out and would be back for the evening meal. She proceeded to meet a couple of school friends in a nearby coffee shop. They avoided all talk of what had happened with her and enjoyed reliving old memories.

Once she was back home, Anu Mashi lovingly prepared hot *phulkas* which they had with *dal* and delicious *alu-gobi* from the farm's organic produce. Shiv had already had his dinner and was now staring into the distance. There was the barest hint of a tear, and then he closed his eyes. Leela got up and sat near him with a sigh.

Shiv started exercising his neck. Then he turned to her with an impish grin and muttered:

'Bho bhon bhon, Sho shon shon, bhappa bhappa bho...

...Hirat jabo Kabul jabo, marte hobe chho.'

Leela jumped up with a shriek. Anu too came running, her mouth wide open in astonishment. This was one of Shiv's self composed nonsense rhymes which were an integral part of Leela's childhood. She grabbed his hands and implored, 'Dadu, recite that "Pook Pook" poem please!'

Shiv's mood changed again, as his voice came in a hoarse whisper, 'Your father, my own son Rajen, could find out more about these codes. Could.'

Leela's face fell. She replied in a strained voice, 'Baba tried. But he reached nowhere. He says that the real info about the Transfer of Power files, which Mahakaal may have hinted at, will never be put out in the public domain. That it is linked to the disappearance and fate of Subhas Bose.'

Anu sighed and went back to the kitchen. Shiv's eyes were still closed, while he continued. 'And my grandson Bharat has withdrawn from the battlefield of life. He should have done this task, which now you, a woman, have to...'

Leela exclaimed in exasperation, 'Dadu, I can handle this. It's not fair that others are distressed because I have to pay my debts to Mahakaal.'

'Truth bites.' Shiv spoke even as he kept on nodding from side to side. 'They will always find excuses to turn down someone, who is not even a journalist, asking for information which has been kept from us. This option to demand the real T.O.P was there from 1950 onwards. But we allowed it to be buried. Wilfully.'

Anu Mashi entered the room wiping her hands. 'Baba, someone from this manipulated, wired-up generation will fight and unearth this truth. You watch.'

A bitter smile crossed Shiv's face. 'We're watching. Not fantasizing.'

He broke into a really severe bout of coughing. Leela immediately eased him back into his bed. Anu quickly fetched the nebulizer and made Shiv inhale it for some time. He fell asleep after that.

Leela sat on a garden chair outside with a cup of tea. The lower Himalayan foothills were silhouetted by the glistening moonlight, and the gurgling stream nearby soothed her frayed nerves. After many years, today she had heard Shiv's nonsense rhymes and her elders views about Netaji and the freedom struggle. This was a central theme during her growing years in Bengal.

What she still remembered the most were the special occasions when the entire Biswas family and some villagers including the farmhands would put on costumes and enact patriotic plays written by Shiv. The household had their main store in the attic, which held a sense of mystery for Leela because this was where Shiv kept many trunks including those holding costumes for his plays. Saraswati would stitch these costumes from discarded garments. Leela waited with bated breath when these were brought down and opened, and the different costumes tumbled out one by one. The audiences were mostly the farmhands' families.

There were also Shiv's original poems which he would read from time to time, some of which her cousin Bharat would set to song and even lull her to sleep with. When the Santhals (local tribals) had their special dance festivals, Shiv would usually recite Leela's favourite poem. This was an admixture of Bengali, Hindi and Santhali hunting folklore, where the 'Pook Pook' conveyed gunshot sounds made by Santhal hunters:

'*Chol Shikaar kori bon mei dhuri,*
Duto khorgosh shojaaru boraa pokhhi mari,
Aare Saat noli chaali,
Aare pook pook pook,
Baadhone porechhe boraho bolihaari.'

Later, Saraswati would fire her mind by telling her innumerable stories of India's glorious past. These stories would flow throughout the day, beginning with the bathing sessions near the rivulet or the farm well.

All three, Saraswati, Shiv and Anu, told Leela about a hidden history of India, quite in line with what she had heard again in Dehradun today. They spoke about India's decline from the world's richest and most influential nation to one of the poorest. Much of the finance for the entire Industrial revolution in the West largely came through rampant extraction from India. The East India Company, which was the world's first multinational, resorted to every trick in the book to swindle, pilfer and finally slaughter millions of Indians to enable this loot and establish their dominance. Leela's elders explained that the Company planned the destruction of Indian Industry which had been the world leader till then, to turn us into servile beggars. They bought over politicians in Britain and made the Crown favour them with naval support and money.

The Mughals had settled in India and not exported their riches back to their homeland, but the Europeans created a system to suck out India's wealth and impoverish her beyond belief. The elders told Leela about the holocaust in Bengal in 1942, and several ones earlier, when famines were triggered by Britain and were entirely man-made so that our wealth could be extracted and indentured labour could service their empire abroad. Then there were the mass executions following the failed 1857 revolt against the East India Company, a sordid history that stretched right up to the large-scale killings of INA soldiers in captivity in Nilganj etc. These were all hushed up.

Saraswati often gave Leela such key lessons during her meals in the kitchen. One of the biggest frauds perpetrated by the politicians post 1947 was making the gullible public swallow Gandhi as the person who brought India her freedom *by non-violent means,* which was utterly false. Saras opined that Gandhi was imported from South Africa and actually nurtured by the British to divert the real freedom movement. The middle class found it fashionable to wear the Gandhi cap and Kharau (Sandals), rather than face bullets. The genuine freedom fighters such as Rani Abbakka Chowta who was martyred by the Portuguese; Bagha Jatin, Udham Singh, Alluri Sitarama Raju and so many others were all ruthlessly killed, and most of this history was never taught in schools and colleges.

Shivdadu told her that this is why Netaji Subhas Bose was considered the Number One enemy of the British Empire. He challenged the falsehoods which were being taught under British Rule as well as the servile vision sold by Gandhi and the coterie under him. Netaji was a leader with a detailed ground plan of how to rebuild the nation from scratch after expelling the British. *His vision was inclusive and not clouded by communal or caste divisions.* His INA commanders and cabinet members were Muslims and Hindus in equal measure who were willing to die for him. Shiv and Saraswati had personally experienced how all castes and communities lived and ate together under the same flag when they fought the British as inspired INA soldiers. This was part of the history which was obliterated from Indian education syllabi.

More than the martyred freedom fighters, Bharat himself laid much more emphasis on telling her about the *rishis*, philosophers, scientists, the gifted artisans, the pioneers in the visual and performing arts – all of whom had made the country the dominant and wealthiest world power. He emphasized that many of them had lived their outstanding lives and passed away without making any claims to greatness. As Leela became more demanding in her quest for knowledge, it was Bharat who opened up each facet with the details stored in his incredible memory. This had created major problems for her after she left Bengal, mostly in her convent boarding school with other students and her teachers. Rajen was hard put to explain the source of his firebrand daughter's 'knowledge'.

Leela had often wondered as to where these traditions had gone now and why had people around become so different from those described. Saraswati had replied, 'We allowed our social order to be corrupted, from a balanced society to one deeply divided by caste and power privileges. Thus, we weakened ourselves and became the decrepit society we see around us.'

Leela's reverie went into a slow fade-out. The quietude on this Dehradun farm had to contend with several distant farmhouses blaring some midnight sit-com. Even at this late hour, she could also hear mobile ringtones and people talking loudly.

She sighed and got up. Her world was one which had little interest in India's 'true' history, to which her elders still remained committed. This was a distant dream which she could never make her own. It had been a futile quest to know some hidden truth which Mahakaal had mandated to her. Her father was right. Perhaps it was time to let go, but she could not. She still had to pay her debt to Mahakaal.

FOURTEEN

As time passed, Leela started struggling to hold on to what she had heard in the forest. She concentrated on her work with the old age homes her organisation was associated with. These were spread across the country and even though she did not have to visit them all, there was a mighty load of correspondence she had to attend to, especially after such a long gap. Whenever her thoughts went back to the week spent with Mahakaal and she started getting despondent, his visage and words played back in her mind, giving her fresh courage.

While the dust was settling on this, the Biswas family – Leela, Rajen and Mada, had a get together for the latter's birthday. Leela looked off colour and left within a few minutes, citing a headache. Rajen shared his latest experiences involving her with Mada, and they also spoke to Shiv and Anu on the phone. They all agreed that Leela had to be guided out of her quagmire. There was a feeling that her 'addiction' to this old man in the forest could be a fallout of her painful separation from Aditya. She needed help. Since she was alienated from her erstwhile mentor Bharat, only one other person could persuade Leela to switch course.

Mada picked up his mobile and called General Arjun Ponappa.

Gen. Ponappa (MVC) was a highly decorated soldier who had just retired. From his ex-colleagues to currently serving senior Defence officers and active politicians, all held him in the highest esteem. He occasionally appeared on TV shows and Panel discussions. Invariably, his rasping voice, razor sharp analysis and fearless comments put all the other participants in the shade. It was widely believed that but for his iconoclastic streak, he may have become the Chief of the Army Staff

(COAS). He was still supremely fit and often trekked to remote places. Bharat and Leela had accompanied him on a number of such treks, and they all had wonderful memories of those times.

The childless Ponappas were very fond of Leela and kept track of everything that was going on in her life till the time she vanished after the highway attack. So when Mada called Gen. Ponappa and told him about Leela's obstinacy in following leads from an untraceable old man, the General was all fire and brimstone. Leela, following some old Looney? Impossible!

When he was told that the police artist's composite sketch was tallying with a hoary Baba who purportedly passed away in 1985, Arjun Ponappa erupted, 'Where the hell is Bharat? Ask him to lay off.'

Mada was puzzled, 'Bharat? Tiger, he has no contact with Lili for years. In fact we are shocked at his apathy towards his little sister whom he loved more dearly than anyone else.'

Rajen, who had been trying to catch the drift of the talk, now took the mobile from Mada's hand and put it on speakerphone mode.

Arjun was emphatic. 'Nah Sir. I can't swallow that. I'm sure they have been in touch.'

'No way Tiger. We know,' said Mada.

'By phone, SMS, email…how would you all know if she had contact or not?' asked Arjun.

Rajen could not hold himself, 'But even if they had contact, what does that have to do with Lili's obsession?'

'Sir, everything.' said Arjun firmly, 'Leave it to me. I will sort this out.'

'Wah mere sher! Just the balm we needed,' said Mada in a relieved tone.

The next morning, Leela was woken by Bima's barking. Someone was at her door. It was six am, and for an autumn morning, this meant it was still not quite light outside. She peeped through the keyhole and could not believe her eyes. It was Gen. Arjun Ponappa. No wonder the security had not alerted her. They knew him and no one would question him. But there was no smile on his face.

She opened the door, still feeling groggy. He stood at the entry, leaning on his military staff and fixing her in a stare. Leela welcomed him in with a hug. He waited till Bima had greeted him and strolled away. Then he walked in and cryptically asked, 'Lili, answer me straight. This man you met in the forest – and who is supposed to resemble this "dead Gumnami Baba" – rather Subhas Bose; has Bharat been feeding you his Encyclopaedia on this Baba?'

Leela stared at him in disbelief, by now completely jolted out of her grogginess. 'Pony uncle, what *is* all this?'

'Yes or No?'

Leela snapped back in the same tone, 'NO!'

'He has not mentioned this subject to you at all?'

'Bharat Bhai has not mentioned *anything* in the last few years. We have not met, neither has he called after that Buxa attack. I only saw his postscript on an email sent by Shivdadu after I came back from the forest,' said Leela, staring back, 'He has vanished from my life. Maybe his affections for me have also vanished.'

The General's shoulders suddenly dropped, 'Damned that I am wrong footed like this!'

'Wrong footed?' posed Lili as she quickly dusted the sofa.

Gen. Ponappa sat down and patted a seat next to him for her to sit down. It was an affectionate gesture, but one would think that the room already belonged to him, and Lili was visiting. He waited for a few seconds before carrying on, 'In fact this is one mother of all coincidences. We'll talk, damn it we have to talk, but *after* you meet your brother,' said the General with a sombre look.

'I called Bhai and left a message; dropped him an email too. Haven't got a reply as yet,' said Leela, as she poured out the tea from a flask which she had kept for herself.

'So after you talk to him, I'll be waiting for you,' said Arjun with his head tilted to one side. 'My place. Piping hot food. Real wrestling. No holds barred. Either you come out in one piece. Or me. Done?'

Leela smiled for the first time. This was a man who always gave her tremendous energy. After Arjun left, she ruminated over his words. As a legendary quizzard, Bharat may have picked up data about some 'Gumnami Baba', but like her he had always been distant from any Babas. Gen. Ponappa had slipped big time.

FIFTEEN

Meanwhile, the accused who had shot Martin mysteriously died in prison. The rest of the indicted persons who were behind bars for the highway attack on Leela and her friends were granted bail due to lack of credible evidence. They were still charged on a separate count for having chased Leela and attacking innocent bus passengers, but the main charge of a murderous assault on Leela did not sustain. The death of five people who were eaten by alligators was explained as a rowing accident. Leela's testimony was attributed to her disturbed mental state while suffering from a 'Stockholm syndrome'. The clinching factor was that there was no corroboration regarding the existence of any old sadhu in that region.

Following an uproar, the government said that it would consider appealing this verdict.

Nothing seemed to help Leela come out of her low down state. All her activities paled before her certitude that a different reality *was* there for her to live and experience. There was a man in flesh and blood who had opened up this reality for her to imbibe, and he was somewhere out there.

At this point, Ishita asked her if she would be interested in accompanying her family to the Kumbh Mela, as a complete change to her usual routine. Normally Leela had no interest at all in religious events. The Kumbh Mela and stories of the mammoth crowds and the 'cleansing of a lifetime of sins' had always put her off.

So she was quite astonished to experience a sudden intense surge of interest for attending the event. She did not reply for a few seconds and then said 'Yes' to her own surprise. Ishita's family was delighted.

Leela shifted Bima to her regular dog shelter. Next, she called Mada to inform him of her plans. She learnt that her father Rajen too was attending the event with his guru.

They travelled by AC 2 Tier. The train was packed with devotees. From soothsayers to jeans clad and mobile wielding youth to curious foreigners – their devout energy was simply overwhelming. They all 'dug' Kumbh.

Ishita's family had their own fun with their 'time pass' routines of playing cards, singing devout songs, eating non-stop and tending to the screaming toddlers. Leela now wondered what weird impulse had made her volunteer for the trip.

Once they arrived at the 'Dwarkanath Guest House', they went for the *Shahi Snan* or the cleansing bath in the river. Leela had no chance to remember her discomfort. Pushed and jostled by the unbelievable crowds and volunteers, deafened by the loudspeakers, amazed by the diversity of people, colours, flavours around… Leela surrendered and enjoyed soaking in the 'real India'.

They had their meal in the comfort of the guest house. Later, Leela decided to take a stroll through the crowds again. She wanted to see the *Shivirs* (tents), while the others rested. She knew how to get back to the guest house on her own anyway.

She had read about the feeding of the devout, by the devout. These were usually saints who rarely if ever left their seats of meditation in the Himalayas, or other remote spots scattered over India. Some came to the Kumbh Mela just once in thirty to forty years. Many were Naga Sadhus, many others were unknown. The belief was that if a pilgrim fed such 'elevated' souls with devotion and no expectations, then they would receive tremendous blessings.

Leela had just passed the venue of a media attended conclave, when she saw Rajen's driver. She peeped in and could spot her father's current Guru Somaswami on the dais. This is precisely where she did not want to be.

She finally reached a venue where meals were cooked by the volunteers and served to the rarely seen souls who graced the Kumbh. Though she had gorged on a sumptuous meal earlier, she felt hungry again. If only she could be there, being served simple food with such love and devotion! She laughed at her own thought.

With a wide smile on her lips, Leela turned to look at another section of the tent. And then she froze.

At the far end, about a hundred meters away, she spotted a figure in dhoti and a tunic who had finished his meal and was getting up. An old lady serving him had just picked up the disposable leaf plate, while the man put up his hand in a gesture of thanks and benediction. As he lowered his hand, Leela was hit by a tremendous jolt.

It was Mahakaal.

She opened her mouth to shout his name, but no words came.

Mahakaal turned back and started moving out to join the ever flowing crowds. Leela found her voice. Just when he had disappeared from sight, she screamed, 'Baba, Baba!'

A number of people looked up startled. Several volunteers came running, looking suitably concerned. But Leela pushed past them and started running towards where MK had been sitting. This caused consternation in the gathering.

Volunteers ran after her and finally caught up with her near the spot where MK had disappeared. Some reprimanded her for creating a hullabaloo, while others asked her about her trauma. She could only mumble, 'I just saw a sadhu whom I knew earlier. But I can't find him anymore in this huge assembly.'

An elderly man told her knowingly, 'We understand. But if a spiritual person has forsaken his earlier identity and gone away, you should not try and contact him.'

Leela had no patience for such homilies. She tore herself away from the surrounding crowd and started looking frantically all over this vast area, leaving the others shaking their heads in pity. By now tears were streaming down her face. At every turn she was stopped by concerned people, asking her what the problem was. All she could mutter was that she had lost someone.

After almost an hour of frantic running around and searching, Leela suddenly slumped and sat down in despair on a vacant chair. An old couple came by, and she chose to get up and offer her seat. The lady saw the tears in Leela's eyes and held her hand, asking in her local dialect about what was paining her. Leela touched her forehead to this old lady's hand and turned away.

Once again, something caught her attention far away. In the milling crowds, for just a few moments, she saw the familiar figure in a dhoti and tunic.

It was Mahakaal. Alone.

In that split second, Leela was engulfed by such a wave of raw energy that she could hardly stand. Before she could react, the figure was engulfed by the multitudes. This time she chose not to run or chase him.

Soon he reappeared again. He was looking at her directly. He held up his hand in blessing and as an assurance. Next he put his hand on his heart and held it up again, smiling all the while.

Then he was gone.

Leela walked rapidly to the spot. Mahakaal was nowhere to be seen. He did not want to reveal himself or meet her yet. She had to accept this with grace, *but she could not.*

She returned to the guest house. Ishita's family was shocked to see her traumatized, tear stricken face. She politely brushed aside their concern and proceeded to her room to wash her face.

As soon as she entered, she was once again engulfed by the typical forest flower smell.

113

A TRYST WITH MAHAKAAL

She sat there in a trance, as all her anxieties gradually faded away. She realized that she immediately needed to take a break to come to terms with her Mahakaal experience. Then she washed up, quickly packed her baggage and stepped out to the waiting family to announce that she was going back to Pune. She parried their objections and thanked them again and again for bringing her to the Kumbh Mela. She did not utter a word about her experience, or why she wanted to leave.

A chartered car was organized at considerable expense, which Leela paid for immediately. Two male members from Ishita's family offered to escort her, but she declined and left right away.

Ishita was by now very worried about Leela. She called up Rajen, who in turn messaged the cab number to the state Director General of Police (DGP). Leela was surprised to find two senior police officers waiting in a jeep at a traffic signal. They brusquely told her that they had instructions to oversee her safe journey. The jeep followed her cab to the local airport.

At the airport, Leela found another person waiting with an air ticket for a hopping flight to Pune. This was remarkable for a period when all flights and trains were overbooked months ago.

Leela asked herself why she should take this offer. Her father was again in the frame. She declined the ticket and asked the car driver to instead drop her at the bus depot. She bought an open ticket and boarded the bus scheduled for Delhi. She was sure that she was being tailed.

When the bus driver stopped for a while to get some *paan* during a halt and some more passengers were getting in, she quickly got off unnoticed at the last minute by wrapping herself in a non-descript shawl, making sure her face was covered. She was determined to be alone and not 'looked after' by relatives or friends, but she could not figure out how to shake off them off.

Just then, she got a call on her mobile which made her pause in disbelief. It was from Bharat Bhai. She took it but could not speak.

She heard his warm tone after years. He simply said, 'Come over. I am waiting.'

Click. The call was over. Her brother had reached out to her at last.

Now she knew how to dodge her father and the others. They could never guess that she would make a detour to meet Bharat, from whom she was known to be estranged for many years. Her various organisations' work was on auto pilot mode and would go on undisturbed. She only had to call her trusted lawyer, so that she could be informed about her court hearing for the Buxa attack case. The lawyer would never reveal her whereabouts even under threat. This was exactly the break she needed to muse over her experience with Mahakaal.

For a moment Leela thought about Bima, but she knew that he was safe for the time being in her trusted dog shelter. She messaged Mada, Rajen and Anu Mashi that she was taking a break at an unknown place with a friend and they should not worry for her. She would return once she was fully rested and recovered. For good measure, she dropped old fashioned postcards stating the same to all three of her relatives so that they did not think that she had been kidnapped again! Then she disabled the location services of her phone and switched it off. She hadn't felt this free in a long time.

Finally, she withdrew cash from a nearby ATM and called her lawyer from a public booth. The latter would inform the police officer assigned to Leela's trial about her absence and could act as the contact point if there was a need.

She took a train to Satara, the nearest railway station to where her brother stayed in Maharashtra. There was just a heady thought which kept playing in her mind: 'Yesssss! My beloved Bhai has reached out to me again.'

PART TWO

BHARAT BISWAS & PRITHAK GHATI

SIXTEEN

Bharat Biswas was a prodigy. Born to Annapurna when she was just seventeen, Bharat was brought up on the farm in Bengal under the watchful eye of Shivdadu and Saraswati. His father's family had quickly given up all responsibilities after his father's premature death and Annapurna raised her beloved son with her maiden surname.

He was only twenty when he completed his study of civil engineering at IIT Kanpur. In an unusual change of heart, he wanted to pursue medicine too. He was about two years elder to most in his group in Maulana Azad Medical College (MAMC) in Delhi but he turned out to be the most popular student. Despite his incredibly busy schedule, he still made time to pursue his interest in Indian classical music by making periodic visits to a little known, reclusive *Dhrupad* master.

By this time Bharat's fame as a quiz expert and debating genius had already spread to many educational institutions across India, so much so that many competing college teams would withdraw from a quiz contest if they knew that Bharat was participating. It was a given that he would turn to politics, and his friends were later disappointed when he did not turn his oratory skills to fulfil that end.

Besides this, Bharat was a rage in the college canteens from his IIT and MAMC days because of his wonderful singing abilities. Students, interns and residents alike would sit around the tables and listen enthralled while he sang classical-based songs, one after the other. The Canteen Managers fixed a special rate for him, since students did not want to leave when he was singing and the orders piled up. But he never participated in contests or TV shows. He said, 'I enjoy. You all enjoy.'

While he was in Kanpur, most batch mates became his admirers and remained his lifelong friends. Amazingly, his most steadfast friendships developed with students who held the in-fashion 'left' intellectual position, though it was diametrically opposite to his views which were quickly identified as 'ultra right', an absolute rarity at that time. It was quite another thing that many of the same leftist friends would immigrate to USA and other western countries and go on to positions of high influence. Most of the financial support for his start-ups later came from these friends who believed in his genius.

A similar story followed with the friends from MAMC in New Delhi. The tremendous energy that he brought to everything he did without any anger or pettiness towards others who stood on opposite platforms in their life choices; his harbouring genuine affection for them; this was the key to his great popularity among his fellow students both in IIT and MAMC. At that stage, Rajen too was bedazzled by Bharat and forecast that he would undo all the idiocy and impractical choices made by the previous generations in their family. On the other hand, having grown up without a father and in really difficult financial circumstances, he was given to bouts of withdrawal and depression.

He met Urvashi during a national inter college quiz fest. Both were in their late teens. Till then, he had been considered to be apathetic to women despite being much sought after in college. This had made him the butt of healthy jokes until Urvashi enthralled him. He soon found out that she was rebelling against her rich family by slumming in a lesser known Delhi college. Both of them were mavericks in their own lives journeys. They were soon in a relationship that was passionate and tumultuous. Urvashi was amorous by inclination at that time. When Bharat stumbled upon one of her 'affairs' by accident, she regretfully told him, 'I *am* a bitch Bharat. Just drop me.' But they stuck together despite the lows and highs, while she struggled to complete her education and defied her conservative family by taking up a job at a five star hotel in Delhi.

It was during this period that Urvashi first sensed a change in him, which was not some typical mood swing. He had just joined medical college and she asked him if he was unnerved by the work load there, but he promptly denied this. She too was under constant stress due to her estranged family and tough work situation. Finally they split for real and Urvashi vanished somewhere. By then many others also observed that Bharat had undergone a major transformation. This, at least for the world at large, was attributed to his broken relationship with Urvashi, but nobody knew the real story.

After studying these two mammoth courses of engineering and medicine, Bharat shifted to Kumaon to work on a construction site for a dam. He loved design work. This had to go hand in hand with his medical profession, and how he balanced the two was a great wonder.

He started a small clinic with subsidized treatment for the poor and also enrolled himself in a correspondence course in economics from a popular open university. Alongside, to earn something, he wrote various human interest stories for a few newspapers and magazines based in Delhi. Soon enough, these articles acquired a devoted readership. He gradually progressed from an occasional feature writer to travelogue writer to even writing articles on economics. By the time he was twenty-six he was a rising star, a maverick who could not be ignored by the ruling intellectual circles.

This was the Bharat who was Leela's hero. His visits to the family farm in Bengal were full of frolic, games as well as learning for Leela during the five years she stayed there. At this time, he was also just finishing his correspondence course in economics, and discovered that the course material was not enough to satiate his thirst. On his next trip to Kolkata, he explored his favourite old book shops on College Street as well as public libraries and studied many treatises not mentioned in his college syllabi.

This led to a new series of articles written by him, which was published by a major daily. These articles coincided with India's precarious Balance of Payments crisis, when the country was almost bankrupt. The government was being urged to embrace 'Economic reforms' by the IMF (International Monetary Front), and the ruling alliance embraced these with gusto under their New Economic Policy (NEP).

Bharat took the past and present threads and projected step by step how some of these policies would negatively impact the nation over the next twenty-five years or more. He predicted that unless people grew self reliant and compelled the Executive to sustain high standards for the basic pillars of governance, the rot could worsen with each generation. He also enumerated ingenious tactics which the disenchanted public could use to confront corrupt governments in a stand-off via well connected mass movements.

The articles created a furore. Furious political parties of all hues, especially the ruling Congress and the Communists tore into him, often citing his lack of a formal college degree in economics as a sufficient reason why he should not be taken seriously. Many from the intellectual circles questioned the newspaper proprietors during informal get-togethers as to how some 'fly-by-night ex-quizzard', a total greenhorn and 'petty contractor' to boot, had the audacity to question what top-rated economists and even Nobel laureates had opined in the field.

By the time the seventh article was published, the series was cancelled. Bharat refused to issue a rejoinder. He had withdrawn from the debating field long ago and would not speak on the burgeoning private TV news channels in 'panel discussions'. Instead, he gradually faded himself out of public attention for good, much to the consternation of his friends.

Many years later, when Leela learnt of his 'fadeout' from her elders, she was shocked. She thought of him as a coward who had withdrawn from life's challenges, despite being so gifted and equipped to combat these on his own terms.

From this point onwards, Bharat insisted on confining his project choices as a civil engineer to the countryside, thus confounding his family and friends, since he had many lucrative opportunities open to him in urban India. He declined to explain his bias, except to repeat succinctly that this suited his temperament. His first such project was in rural Bengal, which ultimately became the first of many projects he left midway in disgust due to the rampant corruption that he encountered.

In the meantime, the ultra left communist gangs had started dictating the way life moved in Shiv's village in Bengal and neighbouring areas of Orissa. Despite his frail health, Shiv stood up to the communist party cadres who were tyrannizing the residents. After several face offs, they warned that he would be liquidated like any other petty bourgeois if he kept parroting his reactionary mentor, *Quisling* Subhas Bose.

Ex-INA friends who had settled in Dehradun urged the Biswas family to shift there. Moreover, Bharat had signed on a project in the nearby Assi Ganga region for creating a model village. This was the trigger for Shiv to reluctantly leave his farm in Bengal and shift to the Doon valley to a farmhouse owned by a fellow ex-INA soldier.

However Bharat's scheme near Assi Ganga ran into trouble when powerful landlords started sabotaging all his efforts to overhaul the civic system. Further, once he opened up his inexpensive model clinic for poor patients, he had several altercations with the local doctors and corrupt government health officials since he was seen as a threat to their machinations. When he spoke up against 'non-existent' projects such as fake dams which had been floated by local politicians to gobble up state and central grants, he received overnight death threats from rogue contractors and criminal elements.

He soon proceeded to a new location in Karnataka, where a few other friends were planning a similar project. This area was near the temple town of Kalasa. Like his previous models in Bengal and Assi Ganga, he started with the idea of being energy-sufficient. Biogas; latest low-cost solar panels; model windmills; small hydro energy set-ups linked to the Bhadra river – these were the cornerstones of his start-up Energy Centre. He knew that Solar and wind energy had major disadvantages, being neither truly green nor clean, but simply being independent of the severely deficient State power grid was a huge plus.

However, soon the first signs of trouble began. Sometimes Maoist rebels from nearby Sringeri would drop in at night in Bharat's model farm to seek food and overnight shelter. He would not ask them any questions, and they never bothered him. He was arrested for doing this. He stated emphatically in a Karnataka court that he never asked someone for his or her antecedents before giving a hungry person nutriment and refuge overnight. The court acquitted him of all charges and the Police there also sent him a public apology.

Nonetheless, after this incident his problems multiplied. When he proposed to install a waste disposal system to handle local waste, the Panchayat insisted that such a scheme should obtain the approval of the corrupt Government Officers who were used to their 'cut'. It was a battle of wits and Bharat waded into it with gusto.

SEVENTEEN

1998. One night, Urvashi reappeared dramatically in Bharat's life. He did not ask her any questions about her past or where she had gone. They lived together blissfully for a year before she became pregnant. That was when they got married.

Bharat was now experiencing the best period of his life. Even though there were problems, the Kalasa project was nonetheless going on well, with support from the grateful native residents. After Sachin was born, Urvashi had turned vegetarian and was slowly getting into a personal space where she wanted solitude. She was a loving mother to her small child, but Bharat could sense some deep torment within her about her past. She would not ventilate, and he did not want to press her.

That proved to be a very costly mistake. One evening, a car appeared in the Valley with four occupants who were trying to track her down. Somehow the news reached Urvashi before Bharat. She left a sealed envelope for him and drove out in an old, dusty Premier Padmini which was only kept as a standby.

She never returned that night. Bharat read the note and rushed to the police, who were not so cooperative after his past run-ins with them for having allowed Maoists to sleep overnight at his farm. The note was almost resigned and suicidal: *'My dearest, if I don't come back, take care of Sachin. And forgive me, for I have only brought you trouble and misery. I tried! Oh dear God, I honestly tried, but my past will not let go of me. If there is a rebirth, I would want to come back to you, right from the first sight, the first touch. I love you too much.'*

The next day at noon, the police were at Bharat's door. They had found two cars which had fallen into a deep ravine after a crash. All the occupants were dead, among them Urvashi.

The initial inquiry found that she had lived with and later married an expatriate doctor living in London. They had divorced later due to irreconcilable differences, but she had shamed him in the media by exposing the shady dealings of his powerful family. When she flew back home to India, her own family in India had also disowned her.

Finally she tracked down Bharat near Kalasa. It was after four years of blissful marriage that the assassins sent by her ex-husband to 'settle scores' finally found her. The police inquiry revealed that the assassins had threatened to kill Bharat and Sachin if she did not fall in line.

Typically, Urvashi never fell in line.

For the first time Bharat stepped into a phase of alcoholism and disinterest in life. He let go of all his schemes and wandered around the forests near Kudremukh in a disoriented state. The media continued to put out small news clips about him – Mada's grandson and Rajen's nephew, 'a one-time genius who had now gone to seed'.

Anu rushed to Karnataka after Urvashi's death to look after her grandchild, but after a few visits she found it impossible to manage both her ailing parents in Dehradun and her visits to far-off Kalasa. Some project members and a handful of research scientists somehow kept the Kalasa set-up running. Bharat also got much needed help from a couple of ladies from the scientists' families who volunteered to look after his infant child.

After another of his aimless treks in Uttaranchal, Bharat suddenly returned as a transformed and charged-up man. His friends ascribed his mercurial change of mood to his 'eccentric and maverick' nature. He stopped drinking and plunged into life like a new-born. He assured Anu that he could manage Sachin on his own.

When he returned to work, their set-up near Kalasa was facing an artificial labour shortage and daily acts of sabotage. Bharat came to know that all their troubles were instigated by a local 'Wellness Guru', who probably saw Bharat's growing presence as a future threat to his own plans to dominate the small place. Bharat's sponsor friends had political clout in Karnataka and wanted to take on this guru, but Bharat said that he was not here to fight people. Maybe this too was not his place.

In 2005 just before Sachin turned five, Bharat shifted to Prithu Ghati in Maharashtra, where the Sarpanch extended a *carte blanche* to him with a ten year period of no interference to implement his self sustaining vision. The intermediary was Shivanna, whom Bharat had earlier helped to escape the debt trap in Andhra Pradesh. Several loyal friends from Canada and Germany also agreed with his new vision about what could work, and provided support in different stages.

The Panchayat with its wizened Sarpanch 'Birbal Kaka' backed Bharat all the way when he worked on two key areas: education and health, mainly for the unorganized sector. One of his idealistic college mates set up a school where books, uniforms, meals, and fees were all provided free of cost. It grew in leaps and bounds and graduated more than six hundred children from Prithu Ghati and surrounding villages. This was Bharat's first success.

After a while, there was an influx of a most unusual mix of people: A couple of retired Europeans from an Indo-German venture near Pirangut; holistic healers; artistes; agro-horticultural experts; a few scientists experimenting with new techniques including using microbes which could even treat plastic waste; entrepreneurs manufacturing small medical appliances and so on.

All these initiatives boosted the economy of the whole region. There came about new dwellings with radical designs and the use of local material sourced at site. The corrupt and unimaginative local politicians and government functionaries could not understand how this was happening in such a remote area. Several attempts were made by them to make life difficult for Bharat's team, but they failed in the face of formidable support for his plans from the aggressive villagers. Bharat's peers, both in India and abroad, also pitched in by pulling strings where it mattered.

Bharat's biggest success was on the health front. His holistic treatments, while keeping the core allopathic option fully intact, were a major success. This led to the establishment of an Integrated Medical Centre headed by a retired Professor of Medicine, Dr Manchanda, who became known as Dr Mancrop due to her eccentric views. Devoted doctors from various disciplines including Allopathy, Ayurveda, Acupuncture, variations of reflexology, homoeopathy – all collaborated under one roof. They treated each patient with the best option or combination specific to that case, while tracking the progress of the patient within a fully scientific, evidence-based approach. Costs were kept as low as possible, depending on the economic status of the patients. Within two years this Centre became one of the calling cards of the village and patients came from far off places to avail treatment.

A couple of years down the line, Bharat convinced the residents to abandon refined sugar and switch to organic sweeteners such as jaggery. This initiative was revolutionary and took a lot of persuasion to succeed.

In due course Prithu Ghati became known as Prithak Ghati (PG), often lampooned as 'Pagla Ghati' (Crazy Valley).

Prithak Ghati enjoyed only mixed success initially for all these path-breaking efforts. Some initiatives or innovations utterly failed due to unsuitability to the region, or they flopped at the concept level, or lastly because of steep input costs. Bharat wanted free flow of technology, but not at the cost of balance and self-reliance. He opined that both were possible in co-existence.

Occasionally some youth from the village who worked in cities ran up debts to finance their spending habits on goods which they could hardly afford. But when they came home to ask for financial support, Bharat was unforgiving. He told their elders: 'Self correction, yes. Permanent crutch, no.'

Prithak Ghati was not very far from the erstwhile areas of Maoist influence. Some local youth who became resentful towards Bharat, now invited Maoists from the DKSZC (Dandakaranya Special Zonal Committee) faction to infiltrate their area again. These ultras were more aggressive than the Karnataka cadres whom Bharat had encountered earlier.

Initially the Reds hesitated to enter PG when they learnt that Bharat had fought in the past to free oppressed tribals held in jails without trial. But he was eventually hectored by a 'faction' of the Maoists. Some local politicians even insinuated that Bharat was a closet Maoist supporter. Birbal Kaka fought back on his behalf. He testified before the police that when the Maoists came to extort money from the farmers, Bharat stood up to them despite being threatened at the point of a gun to his head.

The political intimidation stopped since there was no real case, but there was always political pressure on the police to put Bharat behind the bars. In the hue and cry, the Reds kept away and reverted to their traditional stronghold some two hundred km away.

But it was ironical that after Bharat actually shifted to the area, the much desired reunion with Leela did not quite pan out the way Bharat had envisaged. Her initial visits to Prithak Ghati ended in rancour each time. Leela drove here only rarely to spend quality time with Sachin. Bharat was her greatest let-down and she spared nothing to let him know that.

EIGHTEEN

After getting down at the Satara station, Leela boarded the early morning bus for Prithak Ghati. She got a vantage seat behind the driver. As the landscape changed from the many sporadic buildings, mobile towers and billboards to the gently undulating landscapes leading to Wai, she pondered over when and how she had lost touch with Bharat.

She had little contact with him during her years spent abroad for her higher education, except the sporadic letters which did not carry much information. Following her return to India in 2009, it had been a frenetic period of non-stop activity to set up the first four Senior Citizen cum Old Age Care Centres. She had borrowed the start-up capital from Angel Investors to get the Centres up and running.

In time, her various ideas including that of affluent senior citizens supporting abandoned orphans became a super success. Many such citizens who wanted to live independently had shifted into her complexes and devoted time and money for the upkeep of such destitute children with professional help at hand. Later, she also extended the idea to animal adoption as a therapy for lonely old patients who needed psychiatric help to get over their depression. Furthermore, Leela also ploughed back earnings from these affluent clients towards subsidizing the large number of old and infirm inmates from poor households who needed constant aftercare and could not afford such homes.

During this entire period, she only heard bits and pieces about Bharat from Mada and Rajen, who were mostly dismissive of his efforts as yet another of his eccentric ventures. Her last visit to Prithak Ghati was almost seven years ago, when Sachin was still in school, and the village had not yet acquired its special character which she subsequently read about.

As the bus lurched and twisted on the bends going up towards Prithak Ghati, Leela recalled the first time when she actually rediscovered Bharat's views. This was in 2015, when three of Bharat's unpublished articles from his turbulent days were first uploaded on the internet by an admirer. The uploads had created a big commotion on the social media, and Leela was surprised to get a link on Whatsapp from a shared source. Bharat Bhai, and back in the public arena by default – Ahem! She had gone through them word by word and had marvelled at his prophetic vision. What a pity that he had wasted himself away in this remote part of India.

NINETEEN

Leela got off the local bus on the outskirts of Prithak Ghati (PG). An e-rickshaw was at hand to take her to Bharat's place. She had been to Prithak Ghati long ago, when the town was hardly developed. Now it had changed beyond recognition. It was in an undulating valley with both hills and farmlands, and the giant Deccan Plateau mountains towering behind them.

The talkative rickshaw driver started educating her. Their Panchayat had decreed that not a drop of water was to be wasted, since the changing weather pattern here usually had a drought year followed by an excess rainfall year. There were water harvesting systems of all kinds – bunds, covered canals and extensive use of drip irrigation. There was a water budget, and depending on the water availability, each year the Panchayat decided on a cropping pattern to direct which crops should best be grown.

Following the Tembhurni model, four-feet-deep soak pits were made behind each rural dwelling, which had sand and gravel under cement pipes to do away with open drains and the mosquito menace. The entire Town waste was treated in a Waste Treatment set-up where wax worms converted any plastic into bio waste. Every housing cluster had locally designed toilets, and PG was open defecation free. This was a remarkably clean village town deep down to its bowels.

The rickshaw driver left her at a Laterite stone house merged into the forest, which had all kinds of gourds and pumpkin creepers growing over it. The gate had a plaque with their family name Biswas, as well as the surnames of all the farmhands staying there.

She walked down the short rustic driveway and reached a veranda with cane chairs in two settings. Someone had placed a bunch of Rajnigandha flowers in a vase and the scent was delightful. Depositing her suitcase and bag there, she went through a long corridor to reach an inner courtyard with a tulsi plant in the centre. There were three other smaller mud huts on the plot, probably for the workers, all of which faced this courtyard.

As she walked around the property, she could see that Bharat had included almost all their favourite activities from the original Bengal farmstead in this habitat. Two farmhands, Kaushalya and Sonichari, were cleaning the cowshed and feeding a bull, along with the two humped cows and a couple of small calves. Kaushalya recognised Leela and hastened to greet her with folded hands. Bharat was away to look at a patient.

Kaushalya accompanied Leela to the bird-feeding square, which was alive with a great assortment of visitors. Lapwings that were on the verge of extinction jostled with the common sparrow and wild pigeons, picking grains put in feeding huts tied to tree branches. Two yellow footed green pigeons were frolicking in a stone bird bath placed at the side, sprinkling water all over. Leela was glad to see a lot of sparrows here which had almost disappeared from the cities.

The loyal crows outnumbered the rest. Kaushalya told her that if a hawk tried to steal the baby chicks, the crows would create a tremendous racket and also attack the intruder. The commotion would usually attract some farm member to drive off the bird of prey.

The bird-feeding place was cordoned off from the dogs that lived within Bharat's farm. They guarded against the jackals who would try to steal the poultry. Kaushalya informed Leela that once a leopard had entered and carried off one of the dogs, but now that they had the numbers to live as a pack, the dogs were not so vulnerable any more.

In so many ways, this Habitat reminded her of the farm in Bengal. This is why she had come here anyway, to revitalize herself with those memories.

A farmhand Firdaus brought her a hot mug of herbal tea and left quickly. While she was sipping the tea, she continued with her round at a leisurely gait, as once again her childhood enveloped her in its inchoate and protective sheath.

She reached the granary where cereals were pounded and recalled being woken on that Bengal farm by the sound of rice husk being sieved. When she reached the pen with several roosters and hens, she 'saw' a little Leela running at the crack of dawn to check for new eggs under the hens as they cackled angrily and stalked off.

She chuckled as she passed the toilet block. What a relief that these were not small holes in a concrete floor on a raised platform. In Bengal, Leela always had the dreadful feeling that she would fall through such a hole into the drum of excreta! Shiv and Saras had insisted on cleaning this night soil themselves, whereas it was traditionally done by lower caste labour. They had even begun to train her to do this before she was whisked away by Rajen. Unlike that Bengal farm, here there was no smell whatsoever of night soil manure or fungus, despite Prithak Ghati being in a high rainfall zone.

Bharat had even established an apiary and a centre for collecting honey. Leela recalled the apiary which she would pass along with Saraswati and Anu Mashi on their way to a small rivulet for their daily bath. While returning home, she would be joined by her playmates from the farmhands' families. Leela always took the lead in climbing mango trees and stealing the fruit.

Here in PG, there were plenty of lemon, guava and jamun trees. And jack fruit too! Leela stopped to inhale the heavenly smell. The sound of tin drums being beaten played back in her mind, as she recalled the elephant herds that would invade the Bengal farm, intoxicated by the jackfruit smell. Locals would beat such tin drums and light fires to scare the pachyderms away. What an adventure!

Needless to say, Bharat was her partner in all these adventures whenever he was home, though he was almost twenty years her senior. He joined her for skipping, hide and seek – even gulli danda and *keeth keeth*, the typical male preserves that she insisted on invading.

She entered the huge mud kitchen to see what all had come in from the PG farm – and stopped short. Just like her Bengal days, here too the kitchen was stalked by many cats and delightful kittens, while the farm produce was being sorted out.

She recalled the gentle arguments that broke out when Bharat deposited vegetables from the Bengal farm in the kitchen. Saraswati would say that even vegetables have life and feelings, so one should ask forgiveness from them before cutting and eating them. Leela found this very funny. Bharat would argue back that with life having the central reality of atrophy affecting all physical objects, eating anything in essential moderation was basically the guiding principle, and not a moral albatross around the tongue.

After making her round Leela sat on a cane chair outside, wrapped in a shawl. It was so pleasant here, unlike the great heat in Bengal which was burnt into her memory. During his periodic visits, Rajen was always complaining about the weather and preferred to stay in a palatial house belonging to a local politician. He would have Leela brought to the stately Hall, which had three electric fans. However, when the electricity failed, a domestic help would sit and pull at a rope which swung a massive overhead draped carpet to create a manual fan. Leela would shoo the man away and often pull at this rope till her hands ached or till Rajen caught her and had the rope taken away.

With the onset of summer, there would also be fun-filled interactive sessions where the women of the house would undress and make Leela 'pop' their *ghamachees* (small eruptions of prickly heat) which invariably appeared on their upper arms and back. She would prick them open one by one with a 'pop' sound, using small seashells. This would be followed by a saltwater bath which would burn these eruptions.

Leela's thoughts were halted by a short and sudden shower. Ambling out, she saw that the small water channel outside Bharat's habitat was overflowing. But here there were no small fish which she could catch with *gamchas* (thin cotton towels), to be brought home and cooked fresh. Instead, she was surprised to find two paper boats stuck among the pebbles and caked mud. Had some other young Leela and Bharat made and floated these boats? She nudged the boats and off they went.

She went back to her chair and sat in silence for a while, savouring the ending passages from the first 'rain dance Suite' for the day. Pheasant crows, koyels and Parakeets were all rendering their celebratory birdsongs. The crows were drying themselves in silence, while a couple of crested Mynahs had flown in from the forest to sit on the shrubs in the courtyard.

She whispered to herself, 'There is no bigger intoxication than life.'

TWENTY

Leela was now feeling tired after her long winding journey from the Kumbh site, even though she had slept on the train. After a bath, she had a simple early lunch, which a girl from the kitchen laid out for her on the verandah facing the inner courtyard.

It was almost dusk and there was still no sign of Bharat. For a moment, the sound and smells of cooking invited her to peep again into the mud house kitchen. She was transported to her days with Mahakaal, when he would cook.

Then she sat down on a recliner. This too was a throwback to the days in Bengal, when Shivdadu would sit on his planter's chair and tell her his amazing stories. But right now, it was Mahakaal who stood before her with a vast forest behind him. His pithy words and responses to her questions enveloped her as she leaned back on the recliner and dozed off in her tired state.

She seemed to hear a song from her childhood, a part of her dream. This was something that Bharat would sing for her to put her to sleep.

She half opened her eyes. Someone had lit an overhead lamp near her. The soft lullaby continued. She looked around and saw a slim figure sitting in the darkness and singing. As he leaned forward, the light from the lamp fell on Bharat's face.

She got up with a start. He opened his arms wide and she ran into his embrace. When she looked into his eyes, there was the unusual glint of tears from her stoic brother. In that one instant, the entire recrimination and resentment in Leela was swept away. This was her first hero, her maverick brother Bharat, the same as he had always been.

Shining crystal clear eyes, tousled and slightly curly hair, a compact and gaunt figure: he looked the same as when she had seen him last.

A wonderful dinner followed. Farm-fresh vegetables; her favourite *patodi rasa bhaji* which was very mildly spiced on Bharat's instructions; aromatic organic rice and fresh chapattis with a slice of delicious lemon from a hybrid lemon tree. Leela was reminded of the food made and served with love by Saraswati over twenty years ago.

While they all helped in cleaning and wiping the dishes, Bharat asked Leela about Bima. 'How I am missing him,' she sighed, 'I know he's Ok in the shelter but...'

Bharat proposed, 'Give me a signed authorization form with the receipt for Bima's pick-up right now. Puran Singh goes to Pune tomorrow for some work, and he can easily pick up Bima from the kennel. No one from Mada or Rajen Mama's households knows Puran, so they can't track you by checking on his signature.'

'Good idea, but is he savvy with dogs? Bima has never seen him, right?' Leela sounded anxious.

'He's a magician when it comes to animals. Don't worry.'

Leela smiled gratefully. 'I feel a heel that I can't do this myself, but the minute the word gets around that I am here with you, the urban chaos will track me and keep bothering us.'

'Urban chaos? You mean your NGO people?'

'No, first the Police. Maybe I am still under surveillance following the Buxa incident. Then there are friends who can't desist from posting on social media. People still call me after the bus attack. I need a real break from all this,' said Leela.

Bharat grinned. 'I know about the surveillance part and every other detail about your experience from Ma. But I'm alerting you that your one dedicated fan is coming in tomorrow. He has plenty to ask you and he won't take no for an answer.'

'Sachin?' said Leela.

Bharat nodded. 'Yes. He has a long holiday coming up. You're his surprise. He has a permanent search keyed up on his mobile for anything you do.'

'What a waste,' said Leela, 'Are *you* OK with him using a mobile for...'

'I'm OK with anything, provided he can take full responsibility. Sachin often tests himself to see if he can live without a mobile for an indefinite period.'

Leela was looking intently at Bharat's face, which was glowing and completely relaxed. 'Bhai, I was wrong about you. You look really enlightened.'

Bharat made a mock gesture of hitting her. Leela shook her head. 'No really. I've met too many spiritual shopkeepers, part of an entire industry of "being enlightened" – and mostly their effort shows. And here you are. Effortless.'

Bharat's face became serious, and his stress lines showed up for the first time, 'No Lili. At peace, yes. Enlightened, no way. Too many questions that I have no inkling about. Anyhow, I'll get along now.'

'But I want to talk till morning, like we used to.'

'Lili, I've had a long and hard drive, so better tomorrow. You've had an even longer journey – taxi, train and then bus, so off you go to bed. Or should I sing?'

Leela squealed with delight and jumped up, 'Yes, yeees! Just two lines Bhai. Pleassssse!'

Within five minutes she was tucked into bed. Bharat cleared his throat and started singing a folk song he would sing to lull Sachin to sleep. He held her hand and caressed her head from the brow to the nape. Leela felt her tears of release come, but soon she went out like a light. Bharat stayed like that for a while. Then, he got up and walked out on his tiptoes into the dark night. He could see the outline of the mountains and the promise they always held for him of a coming dawn.

TWENTY ONE

The morning was even more beautiful here than Leela had experienced seven years ago. Winter was around the corner, with the forest sweat merging into the autumn fog. The barun (varna) and other deciduous trees were shedding their leaves in anticipation. For Leela, this was a slowing down and resting one's roots before the inevitable spring.

After a solitary breakfast, Leela put on her dark glasses and went for a brisk walk towards the main town, but she forgot to call for a rickshaw from Bharat's habitat. Then she saw a house hidden behind a few thickets. A group of dogs from there came running towards her. She was startled, but a single whistle made them scramble back inside the house.

There was a white foreigner sitting in the front yard, repairing what looked like a motorized thresher. The man was silver haired and balding. He stood up, rubbing his face with a hand towel, and spoke in a guttural voice, 'Namaste. Sorry for commotion.'

'That's Ok. I am used to it,' Leela smiled back.' All your dogs?'

'Yes, I look after.' The accent was distinctly Austro-German. 'You visit here? Bharat's guest?'

'His sister. Cousin.'

The man dropped his gadgets, pulled off his gloves and strode out in his boots. Leela shook his outstretched hand, 'Ah so, ah so! The sister I am waiting to meet.'

'You stay here?'

'*Entschuldigung*, my name is Rudolph. You are Leela. Ich weiss.' He was still shaking her hand vigorously. 'Yes, I stay here alone for last six years. *Rentner* – retired. India is now my land.'

'My dog will arrive later today, and then maybe he makes friends here,' said Leela.

'Not here with you?'

'No, I didn't come here from home, so Puran Singh has gone today to pick up Bima from Pune.'

Rudolph produced an all knowing smile, 'You here secretly?'

Leela made a thumbs up sign. 'Yes, you guessed right. I am here to take some rest but I don't want any attention for Bharat Bhai or myself. Please don't share my presence here with anyone else.'

He waved her concern away. They talked a bit about his experiences in PG. She soon deduced that he was one of the technical experts whose typical German discipline and last mile detailing had contributed to the village's success in a major way.

She requested him to call for a rickshaw. After twenty minutes she was dropped where the sloping road entered the main cluster of houses. She ambled along, soaking in the good cheer which was evident on just about every face that she passed.

Suddenly there was a shout and fast paced footsteps behind her back. Before she could fully turn around, she had been lifted into the air.

It was Sachin. How he had grown since she had seen him last! Lanky, curly hair, first signs of a moustache – he looked extremely sharp, but perhaps more like his mother than his gaunt father. His eyes though were very much his father's. Sharp and crystal clear.

Sachin's first question was typical of his mental state, 'Hope you're not leaving soon.'

Leela playfully shook her head from side to side alternated with nods, while Sachin shouted: 'Noooo!' A number of bystanders were distracted by this small commotion.

He had a small suitcase and rucksack with him, so Leela cut short her walk and they decided to climb all the way back to Bharat's home. Looking closer at the young boy, Leela sensed a certain sadness in him, but Sachin proved quite adept at guarding his inner vault.

Bharat welcomed his son with a quick hug, but he had to leave soon for another medical case. Leela had heard about the great relationship between Bharat and his son, yet instinctively she felt something was missing. As soon as Bharat was called away, Sachin's exuberance appeared subdued for a very brief while, only to reappear with some effort on his part. This was either loneliness or a feeling of having been forsaken. She could not tell so soon. But it was unmistakable.

Sachin seemed to read her thoughts, 'Arre Lishi, I am not grumpy.' He had combined Leela's pet name of Lili and *Pishi* (father's sister) and produced 'Lishi' as his very own name for her. 'Just that sometimes I wish Baba and I could spend some more time together. You know, my friends often come here to play games with him, like "String".'

'What's this String thing?'

'A simple deductive process. I'll tell you about it later.'

Leela had heard that Sachin was very quiet, but right now he overwhelmed her with his non-stop talk. His interests ranged from acoustics to oceanography and astrophysics. Eclectic, but very well informed. Well, if Bharat had been such a legendary quizzard in his time, Sachin was at least a chip of the old block. Apparently he had also worked with a government cybercrime unit as part of a project from his school to ward off cyber-attacks on government installations. This was an area in which he was considered a prodigy.

Bharat did not return for lunch, but Bima did. He was so happy to be with Leela and Sachin that he even dropped his innate aggression against the dogs in the compound. In fact he became a part of the pack in no time, and his tail was performing an unflagging dance.

Leela meanwhile was having a frothy time. She joined the ladies for a leisurely bath under the open sky in the enclosed space near the well. There was nothing demure about the working women as they freely rubbed her and played around, giggling and screaming like small children. Later when they came out, Bima came running and splashed water on them, making them all rush inside.

Sachin was his usual self during lunch, asking the ladies about the many residents in town. He licked his plate clean and clicked his tongue to show his appreciation for the wonderful meal prepared in his honour. Both of them then carried off the bowls of moong dal halwa and went to Leela's room. Sachin plonked down on the bed and said, 'Lishi, you will never get to meet as many,' He dabbed the air with his fingers, '... so called weirdoes anywhere else as here. Right from Mancrop Aunty, to Machenda, to Windmill Sir – that's Pavan Chakki Sir...'

'Heyyy! One at a time please.'

'That's why I come here during every break, even when Baba is on tour. Not one person fits into a slot. All wild flower types. If you want, I can start you on a round of Prithak Ghati today itself.'

'Do that,' said Bharat from the door.

Leela and Sachin spoke together, 'Back already?'

Bharat eased himself into an arm chair with his bowl of halwa. 'Lili, when you go around, observe without being judgmental. There's no second place like this.'

Leela leaned back and asked, 'Did you invite some of these people here or... how did all this work out?'

'Well, the first few knew me personally and came here one by one. It was only a trickle. Then it became a flow, including people who probably came here out of a curiosity to confirm that I was rotting in some hell hole – and then got hooked!' chuckled Bharat.

Leela whistled, 'Wow. But Bhai, why here?'

'A clean, ordered civic life enmeshed with nature. A sense of relief in getting away from the urban chaos. Uninterrupted power supply. Above all – operating without any external pressures...'

Bharat had finished his dessert. He came and gave Leela a warm hug and tousled her hair, like he would do when they were younger. Sachin's hair too received some deft finger intimacy. In a moment he was gone to attend to another patient.

When she was alone in the guest room and the lights were out, Mahakaal appeared yet again in her mind. Try as she might to put the Buxa attack and her time spent with MK behind her, he was omnipresent everywhere. He was now 'telling' her that she had something vital to learn during her stay in Prithak Ghati. What could it be?

TWENTY TWO

Sachin and Leela went for a long stroll around town. Leela had her dark glasses on. Sachin had instructions to introduce her as a relative named Lishi. Bima was very happy to tag along.

Sachin insisted that Leela should try some snacks near the town square. It is here that they ran into a few other residents at a very quaint eatery.

There was PC Hindre, better known as Pavan Chakki (PC) or 'Windmill uncle'. This was a man who had many simple inventions to his credit, including solar cookers fashioned out of discarded Dish antennas, bullock carts which generated power, and so on. He had recently invited a teenaged inventor to experiment with a new windmill model based on 'maglev' technology in Prithak Ghati, and this was typical of his attitude of encouraging cutting edge inexpensive innovations.

His comrade was Col. Satinder Singh, addressed as 'Heli Sir' by the young crowd. His one strange habit was to emit sudden shouts of 'Halla Hoo!' He had been a specialist in maintaining high altitude attack Choppers used in the Trans Himalayan Region by the Indian Army. After retirement he had developed a new flow battery design to store power. This ex-Ordinance engineer would not let even a pin go waste, so he complemented PC Hindre's thinking of 'zero wastage' to a T.

Their idea was to push the local start-ups to create consumer durables many of which were meant to last for a lifetime with systematic maintenance, thus running counter to the prevalent 'use and throw' manufacturing dictums. These included borewell scanners with cameras and solar sensors to control water usage – and so on.

First PC Hindre shook hands with Leela and graciously pulled up extra chairs for the guests to join their table, while Col Satinder Singh (Heli Sir) greeted Sachin and Leela with his typical, 'Hallo Hoo. Aao ji, welcome.'

Heli Sir was one of the first settlers here. After some small talk, he confessed that initially he himself had tried to ride roughshod over the strict discipline that the Panchayat was enforcing to achieve a unique civic standard. He wanted to have his way on waste disposal, and to enforce his demand to have a butcher's shop on the main road.

PC uncle provided them the context. He told Leela that once the village had started generating a steady growth pattern, some local politicians became very upset when the Panchayat (Panch) did not support any group. So they hatched a plan to bring in several poor Muslim families as new residents in Prithak Ghati and have them create trouble. These families became unwitting pawns for these political leaders and insisted on opening an abattoir in Prithak Ghati, disobeying all the rules and civic strictures that had been put in place by the Panch after much effort. A brief spell of violence broke out. The police were called in and false charges were filed against the Sarpanch as well as Bharat. The matter was finally resolved when a supportive IAS Officer stepped in and spoke to the politicians and the families concerned.

Heli Sir quipped that to harass the Panchayat, these politicians had now proposed a Development Plan (DP) which included a sanction for an Industrial zone just beyond the village boundary. They were demanding a new road to run through the town for access. The residents from Prithak Ghati had gone to court and taken a stay, but incidents kept cropping up to create trouble.

While Heli Sir was talking to Leela and Sachin about these episodes, they failed to notice a couple of jeeps descending the loops into the village. Leela could spot from far that they were from the fourth estate. She cursed her luck that almost on the heels of her arrival in PG, there were press people hanging around.

She quickly excused herself from her hosts and beckoned to

146

Sachin They briskly crossed the street and paused to see the action from under a shaded sit out, while Bima was delighted to sniff around.

The vehicles rounded a bend and crawled to a halt where PC Hindre and Heli Sir were seated. One scribe and his driver got down. A second driver too got off later and proceeded to a spot just behind the eatery. He wanted to pee.

He was brought to his senses by a roar from Heli Sir, 'Halla hoo! Oi! It's written in Marathi that urinating in public places is forbidden. There's a toilet facility a little ahead.'

The driver was typically hard-boiled. He lifted his small finger, smiled sweetly and started unzipping his trouser. Both PC Hindre and Heli Sir were up in a flash and surrounded the nonplussed man. This time Heli Sir produced his commando tone, '*Aandar honaa hai tho bol.* Want to get behind the bars?'

Two young men came running from the jeeps. They scolded the driver, who stalked off muttering under his breath. Heli Sir turned to the first scribe, 'Are you Press chaps?'

'Yes Sir, Sorry for…' said the first scribe.

'You should know what to expect here in Prithak Ghati. There are proper places for travellers to freshen up and do this.' He showed his small finger.

'Sir, can you guide us to Mr. Bharat Biswas's place?'

'Sure,' said Heli Sir, 'Is he expecting you?'

'No Sir. But we hope to meet him, as well as the Panchayat members and do a story.'

'*Aree* suddenly *kyo bhai*? We are fine being little known.'

Another scribe stepped forward and shook hands with him. 'Sir, I am Jagat from the Pinnacle and this is Aman from Max News. We want to do a combined TV-Print documentary on Bharat Biswas. Post demonetization and GST, and now the recent economic crisis, there has been a lot of fresh interest in his old articles that had been uploaded a couple of years back. Our Editor thinks it's worth a good feature, if not a series.'

'And?' PC Hindre queried, 'You expect Bharat bhai to give you bytes?'

'Why not Sir? *Nahin denge kyaa?*'

'Try.' said Heli Sir, 'This is a man who has turned his back on public exposure.'

'Sir, this is no ordinary interest. Today the junta is so disillusioned with the leaders and intellectual class that suddenly they are feeling that maybe there is a hidden hero here.'

'*Yeh lo,*' exclaimed PC Hindre, 'A man who has left all that behind and keeps zero social presence – now he is to become a popular Hero?'

'If Bharatji comes on record, *that* will be our scoop. We want to interview you both and many other residents too. *Kya aap baad mein time denge?*'

Heli Sir replied, 'We are ex defence personnel, so expect us to speak direct.'

'Note right away that we live under constant external threat,' said PC Hindre. 'People want to ruin this place, do like your driver wanted to do, pee and shit all over the place. They claim that's their birthright – *saale ek kaan ke neeche!*'

As the media team started driving out, the first scribe leaned out and asked, 'Sir, is it true that Prithak Ghati is designed in a special way and geared against a nuclear attack... I mean an attack on a city which cripples the system in a large radius, like...,' He looked at his notes, 'like this EMP thing?'

Hindre answered guardedly, 'We don't know about that possibility but yes, we have a regular drill on what to do in such a crisis. It also goes with Bharat bhai's idea of being ever ready to live with the barest minimum. It is better you ask him directly.'

TWENTY THREE

Leela and Sachin walked through the woods to reach a clearing where Sachin was embraced by his friends who had gathered there. They were all passing through PG after their last day in school. Leela was quite curious about Bharat conducting some 'sessions' with these youth, especially since it was well known that he hardly spoke.

The students appeared very well informed. They were already throwing non-stop questions at Bharat about their concerns, many of them aggressive in their tenor, but he kept his composure till they calmed down. Bima too settled down, munching a long chew stick and watching the proceedings.

Bharat resumed: 'You asked: Why are you restless? Why do you need cell-phones, gadgets, thousands of ways to pass time? Why must time be passed?'

They exchanged glances and made faces.

Bharat: 'Shall we pull the *string* more? Anyone?'

Shanta: 'For me, it's like I can't stop craving activity.'

Bharat: 'So you think you are riding life, but really life as you define it is riding you. From day one, you've been put on this auto elevator which goes on and on. You can't get off on your own.'

Reena: 'Coz we're scared. What if we get off and can't ever get back again? Life is so competitive.'

Bharat: 'So... are you free?'

Sanjay: 'I think we are.'

Bharat peered at him: 'Ok. Can you really let go of any of your cravings, *at will? Only then are you truly free.* Anything. Ciggies, chocos, meat…'

Reena: 'Oh no, uncle!'

Bharat: 'Serious. Your invasive mobiles…'

There was a big chorus of NOs, as well as aaarghs and Ooohs.

Bharat stood up and poured himself some tea from a flask. 'To be free and in control, you need real detachment. Gradually, you will drop these ruinous addictions on your own.'

Mohan: 'But uncle – we *can't* do this "real detachment" thing! Why this restlessness, all these cravings? Why do we lack this control?'

'There are techniques to observe yourself with detachment, like a third party. Then you can watch how your restlessness, these cravings rise and die away – effortlessly – as if these don't touch the *real you*. This is the first step towards control.'

Shanta: 'But can our cravings really die away?'

Bharat: 'Certainly. But many intellectuals and scientists believe that the human race has no need for such modest living ; that we will find super foods and unlock extraordinary inventions which will answer all our cravings.'

Sachin posed: 'Yes Baba, people like Jeremy Rifkin who speaks of an incredible third industrial revolution. You agree?'

Bharat threw a fond look at his son. 'No, because these intellectuals don't endorse living in balance with natural law. The "internet of things; sharing economy" etc are all repackaged concepts which end up supporting something as devious and anti nature as the Chinese OBOR project.'

Bharat got up and started flexing his arms and legs, 'Under Natural Law, there is a typical balancing out. Animals don't overeat or kill senselessly, right? They eat just what they need, always staying in balance. Some species hoard only for the lean months *when there is no food to be had*. Conversely, humans produce many times more than what they need. Yet we hoard and waste huge amounts of our resources. Free will; doing as we please? Even so nations are in conflict over resources; there is mass starvation; droughts in the most advanced countries.'

Shanta: 'Uncle, what is this Natural Law? The people who talk about this in the West... in their worldview, existence is like – unaware; has no consciousness of its own.'

Reena: 'I agree with them. Life is chaotic and has no inherent awareness.'

Bharat crossed his fingers, 'Disagree. Life *is* conscious. In natural law as I have observed, existence *is conscious* and *always* in balance. It functions in a detached manner like a master Computer program. So you will find calamities which even the best scientific brains and machines cannot predict or anticipate, though they are usually rationalized in hindsight.

'This is "intelligent Life" balancing out all excesses. If we are not living in balanced moderation then we will have "corrections" which no super inventions can solve. You screw up one end, another end will tilt and balance out.

'When some super brains believe that they can always manipulate with nothing to stop them – then something massive will have to give. Today, wars are practically an act of nature to perform this balancing out, because we screwed up that nature.'

Bima was getting restless, so Leela left the scene to take him on a long walk. When she returned, the session had progressed further.

Bharat: 'From childhood we heard that if you did wrong, the law caught up with you, or fate did, or someone... the Hero fixed you up in the climax. Right?'

There was a joint 'Right!' exclamation.

'Now, one obvious fact can no longer be hidden: There are so many public examples of people, from commoners to top politicians; people who have indulged in exactly what they wanted by unethical means, enjoyed all the goodies of life, lived life till a ripe old age and then passed away without any apparent justice catching up with them. All playing almighty Gods.'

Mohan: 'Maybe these folks suffered inwardly .'

'Wishful thinking. Most of our politicians and crooks look radiant.'

The students laughed and clapped in agreement.

'So if this is the reality, then any person or group can leverage enormous power without being impeded; can wreck this planet by nuclear strikes, biological warfare, pogroms. All doomsday predictions look possible.'

Bharat took a deep breath. 'So... is this the final reality? Or, is there a catch?'

Mohan: 'There's no catch, uncle. This is life, short-lived and painful to be in.'

Bharat: 'I believe that existence, what I call natural law or others call the impersonal reality, will restore balance.'

Mohan: 'Don't agree.' He looked at Sachin, who smiled wryly.

Bharat nodded. 'Ok, observe what happens when you also manipulate. Don't make – "I did this, so I will suffer that" kind of stupid deductions. Let's say you pay your grocer just Rs three less and he does not notice. You keep quiet and get away. Maybe weeks later when you are rushing around, you forget to collect your balance from a bus conductor till it is too late. Maybe Rs three, maybe more. Sometimes it happens on a much bigger and different scale. Normally you never connect the two things because it is illogical, yes?

'Or you bully a friend or your domestic help, someone who is not in a position to fight you. You are simply being righteous. Many of us do this all the time, getting things done by hustling around, seen as a virtue today. We programme our minds to forget these as "small things". Then one day we get forced to accept a very painful situation imposed on us by our seniors, a powerful authority, a mob… whatever. We come home devastated and remonstrate: "Why did this have to happen to me! Life is so unfair."

'Take my word for it, almost one hundred per cent people don't or cannot make any connect between the many petty acts they do and forget – and this. If you have control, then you can quieten your mind and observe. The connect will come out with pin pointed certainty.'

Mohan: 'Uncle, does this have to do with a so-called God keeping balance?'

Bharat turned to him: 'Don't bring in any God concept. This method is true only when each one of you has experienced this balancing out *personally* as a certainty. Test it again and again. Silent observation with awareness. There are many paths.'

Mohan: 'But uncle, we have booked our meditation slot twenty years from now.'

Sachin quipped: 'Baba, we are still kids. *Jhatka lagne do*… then we'll sit cross legged.'

Bharat laughed heartily: 'That's why I enjoy being with you all. To sum up: Either *Jugaad*. Any means is OK. Or each of you observes that there is indeed a boundless existential web which relentlessly records the smallest acts; which has infinite consciousness and which keeps *auto balance* as a Master Program. Natural law. The game of life is to be aware of what is right and act in sync accordingly.'

Reena: 'Your right can be my wrong.'

Bharat: '*Every action which is as per natural law; which is in sync with the rhythm of life is right, is moral and will provide insight. Your right cannot be my wrong. Never.* You cannot prove this in scientific terms as yet. Science takes time to validate or explain phenomena, but does so unfailingly.'

They all looked around sheepishly.

'I know you're not convinced. Who wants to sit and observe when there is so much going around? But…'

Firdaus entered the clearing on a bicycle with a message for Bharat, whose mobile had been switched off. Bharat got up in the same motion and wore his shoes as he kept talking. Then he turned to the students and said, 'Got to go.'

Long after the many high fives, goodbyes and youthful jostling got over, Sachin and Leela found themselves returning home.

Sachin's eyes were twinkling, 'We love these rare sessions. Some of us don't agree with what Baba says, and this is what he likes. He says he too needs to refresh himself without being pedantic. Otherwise you know that he hardly talks, and wants us to find our own way.'

Then he added gravely, mimicking his father, 'Be aware. Be responsible Lishi.'

Leela pulled his ears playfully as they walked on, but her mind went back immediately to Mahakaal. She had heard almost the same words, but indicated with tremendous insight in the Buxa reserve. But this string session was different. Had her rationalist brother Bharat now become faith driven?

TWENTY FOUR

An hour later, the media team managed to meet Bharat at the Medical Centre after their conducted tour of the complex was over. He welcomed them with tea and exchanged pleasantries, but he declined to speak on what he had written over twenty five years ago. He encouraged the scribes to go around town and draw their own conclusions and emphasized that there were many sensitized people in active public life in India, who were doing similar work in health and education as had been done here.

The journalists were disappointed, but they tried their last shot at a quote. Would Bharat confirm that Prithak Ghati was designed for survival after a nuclear attack? Bharat's response was that the town was meant to survive under *any* circumstances. He would not provide any bytes about getting nuked, so peace. Then he did a Namaste and turned away.

The media team spent their time well in town, seeing the layout and facilities and talking to various residents. The drivers and journalists used the public toilets several times and came away with grudging admiration. A few were state-of-the-art toilets that did not use water and had a very low-cost replaceable cartridge. The local inventor had been able to test this model here after having faced a decade of opposition from Plumbers Unions when he worked in the USA. Now he had patented this bio-degradable cartridge for rural Indian use.

For passing truckers and visitors, these public toilets were pay and use. The urine was processed and used as liquid fertilizer, and the night soil was carefully treated and used in the fields. They even had a witty name for this manure: "Sun-dash". This project was often mentioned to lampoon Bharat's belief that 'wastage of resources' was criminal for humans who only passed through earth as custodians and not owners.

These units were maintained 24x7 by a volunteer group led by a formidable matron: Heerabai. She stood out as an imposing figure, with a huge, well-oiled staff in one hand and a gun slung around her waist! This was to deal with the drunks who sometimes passed through the town. It was a stun gun designed by PC Hindre, with a license to boot. With her typical no-nonsense rural Maharashtrian earthliness, she would put the fear of God into the most hardboiled offenders such as seasoned truck drivers.

The media men found Heerabai, together with the toilets, a befitting subject for a good story. They learnt that after a couple of early stand-offs when Heerabai had bashed up a group of drivers single-handedly, the volunteer group and Prithak Ghati's reputation had spread among the truckers and regular travellers like wildfire.

The toilets remained sparkling clean.

Aman from News Max declared aloud that to size up the potential of the many 'eccentrics' in town, one would need to spend at least a week in PG. What cemented that perception was their meeting with the redoubtable Dr Manchanda, who had earned herself the nickname Dr Mancrop. She was a retired doctor of great International fame and eccentricity. The Journalists had already been briefed that after losing her family in an accident, she had retired and put all her money and energies into this Centre. She was a confirmed atheist.

Dr Manchanda took them on a guided tour of the Integrated Medical Centre, explaining the treatments on offer. They also met a few scientists. She said, 'We use cutting edge treatments to deal with illnesses which arise from stressful living in today's world. For example in our urban Research Lab, we have turned stem cells into brain tissue or large Organoids. These facilitate testing new therapies, such as replacing Dopamirangic neurons which have died in advanced Parkinson's patients.'

While the reporters took notes dutifully, they had no warning about Dr Mancrop's outlandish views. Once she sat facing the camera, she abruptly switched tracks. She was sure that the human race as a species was cultivated and grown as a 'crop' for consumption by invisible superior species that people called 'Gods'. Just like humans grew vegetables and reared animals for consumption, the Gods grew humans and consumed their energy via astral straws throughout the normal human life span. They would 'replant' life in the human embryo at the moment of conception by an undetectable process. Souls were reborn or 'recycled' to be born again for tastier consumption.

When there were small feasts in 'Godland', the host Gods had the ability to screen what was the best 'fresh' human soul-food available anywhere on the planet at that moment, and they would pull the plug immediately! So one could suddenly have a head-on accident afflicting a family returning from a marriage, where the deaths would be instantly triggered after matching the 'karmic' records for such a family. When these souls were released in absolute panic from their bodies, they tasted like chickens that were slaughtered by halal for chicken tikka!

The journos lost their poise for a moment before they warmed up to these 'dynamite' quotes.

If a single 'God' needed a shot of instant energy, the karmic graphs of the entire mankind were scanned right away. Maybe a child would die in a bombing incident or be throttled by suicidal parents or eaten by a leopard – so many choices! And each choice, each illness has a unique 'damadam' masala flavour, just like when humans choose between different pizza, salad or *chaat* toppings.

Dr Mancrop suddenly turned to Jagan and quipped, 'Sounds perverse, right? But next time you stand at the butchers and pick your tenderloin, or get the small bird slaughtered for that fresh protein boost, sautéed to give a yummy taste, don't ever forget that all of us are also cooped up in invisible cages. We think we are free, but in reality the

"Gods" can pick us up for a similar quick bite at any time. The human body is such a brilliant piece of precision and yet so many of you think this is an accident that we evolved? Everything about life around points to conscious design, and getting "consumed" is of a piece with this.'

She went on to treat the scribes to a sumptuous lunch, but before long her '*bak bak*' got on their nerves.

Her theory could explain *any* phenomenon, especially famines; riots; earthquakes; all mass accidental deaths. There was a Ready Reckoner too for mass ceremonies among the congregation of 'Gods' from time to time. The big fat weddings; festivals of every faith and following; mass seasonal feasts... all these big ticket numbers in the human realm had their counterpart in the 'Gods' world. One boat capsize and two hundred heads were consumed – khallas. Three thousand heads consumed in riots and sectarian violence – like fresh lamb, mass cooked in fiery Mangalore or Chettinad curry! Or thirty thousand dead in volcanic eruptions – like Spit Roasted Spring Lamb in human terms. Earthquakes – like our own Dum Pukht. All instantly consumed as energy boosts in 'Godland' as part of the secret of their energies. Or Bheja fry if you please.

Jagan was giggling, but Dr Mancrop froze him in an angry stare. They all waited till he could control himself and pull a serious expression over his face. Dr Mancrop asked, 'You find this funny, yes? Ok, I invite you all to stay with me in a general hospital for a week – if you can. Just watch what kind of people are brought there and in *what* condition, the unbelievable amount of suffering! Patients who are brought in half dead; limbs cut off from violence; or with excruciatingly painful tumours, congenital diseases; kids – yes innocent kids crying in pain from killer aliments which are certain to take their lives in the long run, except that we doctors fight battles every day against all hope to save them. Then I would like to see you smile if you can. Then tell me if life has any meaning at all. And these imbeciles talk of karma, *punya*, day of reckoning, *Swarga - Narak, Jannat - Dozakh,* all delusions going on for millennia!

'We are grown. We are cultivated. We are harvested! If you have guts, then write about this. I want the world to live with full awareness. Live healthy. Stress free. And duck the plug being pulled without warning. There are ways to do this, because our creators have a great sense of humour too, and they have humoured the human race by allowing a small section in each generation to escape their fate through techniques, to get a promotion and become junior Gods themselves. No more recycling, no rebirths. Join the party!'

The two media men promised to telecast her views and left for their jeeps. Jagan remarked, 'Another ten minutes and… ufff! *Main inkaa bheja fry kar daaltaa.*'

The camera man was still giggling, 'Boss will love this *bheja fry* story.'

The entourage made its way towards the Panchayat Community Hall. Aman turned around and said in an exaggerated filmy way, '*Ab hamaraa kya hoga re* – what will happen to us?' and doubled over with laughter.

TWENTY FIVE

Leela realized that a feeling of stress was building up inside her again. First the visit from the Press people, which was exactly what she had come here to avoid. Then Bharat's 'string' session which had deeply disturbed her. She was hoping to talk to him about Mahakaal, the codes and her alienation, but this had not happened till date.

After a long time her mind went back to Aditya. She had last heard that he was soon joining a Trans Himalaya (TH) scientific expedition. Till now, every time she thought of him, she would try to transplant this memory with some other thought. Today, all the chapters of their life together flashed through her mind. She ached for his presence right now. Eventually it was MK's visage that worked as a soothing balm, calming her.

She occupied herself by visiting the local seed bank which had been set up by a famous seed expert from Orissa. For Prithak Ghati, their seed bank was the real key to sustainable agro ecological farming which had never let them down. Birbal Kaka also took her to see another novelty: a conservatory for seven humped A2 Indian cow breeds.

Leela found it remarkable that despite such a unique mix of people with diverse opinions, the residents had adopted a low profile and a peaceful existence. But now, the town had the devil sitting on its shoulders. After the recent financial scams, an unknown source had begun a relentless internet campaign to highlight Bharat's lone ranger writings and public campaigns from over two decades ago. This had brought PG into focus again.

Leela had read the three unpublished articles posted by the anonymous blogger in 2015, and now she followed the repost of some more of Bharat's old articles with renewed interest.

In 'The Ghost of Malthus', Bharat had spelt out his basic belief that the earth could comfortably sustain a healthy balance catering only to finite needs and no more; *that its carrying capacity was NOT limitless.* Any attempt to extract more would come with major environmental and other costs.

'The issue is man's desire to acquire more as an insurance against the insecurities of life and to hide his terrifying existential loneliness. Peel away, and what you find is the constant inner awareness of a finite life and impending death, and a clock ticking away. You defy this fear by conquering, overeating, hoarding, pillaging, contorting the reality around.

'Massive state and consumer spending to drive consumption based growth is a long-term disaster model, which promotes artificial stimuli to boost unlimited desires, rather than living responsibly in balance or correcting by fasting as all other species do. Politicians shall always plump for such irresponsible "growth" models, mainly for the economic loot they can extract therefrom. Witness the frantic lobbying for electoral tickets and cabinet berths in India by unscrupulous people and even criminals, and how they are promoted by all parties.'

Bharat had written for a return to a system where governments could not manipulate money supply and print notes at will, nor tamper with lending or borrowing rates. He had advocated slowing down; getting out of the consumptive spiral; decongesting life.

Leela recalled another strident article by Bharat against pseudo secularism, but he had ended that article on a provocative note: 'Today's burgeoning Hindutva forces have reduced our great Sanatana Dharma to an emaciated mimicry of the very theocratic religions which they fulminate against. The British left over seventy years ago, so how long will these forces blame them for today's rot? How about settling today's caste divisiveness? Where are their correctives; the self discipline; setting

161

their own house in order?'

Comments from several readers blasted Bharat saying that if his immature ranting was to be heeded, much of India's population would end up committing suicide. Trolls lost no time in labelling Bharat as a 'cave man' – 'Jurassic thinker' – 'Neo Luddite'. One critic titled his piece on Bharat: 'India's Rip Van Winkle from Fukouka land'. Bharat responded by saying that if each generation passed the growing burden to the next, with no one wanting to face the truth, a suicidal catastrophe was anyway imminent. He said: 'Just live in balance with mother earth and see. She will return the bounty to you manifold.'

With a jolt, Leela realized that Bharat's words echoed what Mahakaal had told her in the forest: 'When everyone feels personally responsible for the trees and every living species around, the air you breathe, the way your home is shaped or harmonized with nature; when you have embraced the earth around as yours without the need to put up a fence; when you progress from personal property to a flowing benevolence: only then inner peace would lead to an outer peace which will abide.'

TWENTY SIX

Aweek after the visit of the media folk, the first part of the documentary was telecast. Though there was plenty of masala in the sub-stories on Dr Mancrop, the toilets and Heerabai, the main focus in the article and documentary series was about Prithak Ghati and Bharat. It was a TV-Print series, and the first article too appeared in the magazine Pinnacle.

Suddenly, all of Bharat's earlier published views captured the imagination of a large section of the urban public, and the three 'radical' articles posted in 2015 became almost viral. People across the country informed their friends via the social media about the existence of a person who had never sought attention for his work, and had always been a non-partisan thinker and doer far ahead of his times. Despite many setbacks and against steep odds, here was a man and a village town holding strong. They had embraced every modern invention and scientific advance which added value to balanced living. They had created a private village-town that paid taxes to the government but raised its own resources to prosper.

Curious urbanites started pouring into Prithak Ghati. When Leela came here from the Kumbh Mela, she never imagined that she would be almost trapped in the town and its new public profile. Bharat had been promising Leela each day that they would lounge around like old times but the sudden onrush of events and visitors took away his time. Leela could sense that he was slightly unsettled by all this.

Two days after that first telecast, Leela and Sachin lunched at an ex-Air Force Officer Mahadevan's eatery. This was a favourite haunt for the town residents and even for people who dropped in from bigger towns in South Central Maharashtra.

After a sumptuous meal, they decided to walk home the long way. When they had wandered out of the village boundaries, Sachin noticed a group of men making measurements and taking photos. He nudged Leela and said that these men worked for a local politician, Sardar Mane, who was behind the move to create a new road through Prithak Ghati as per a proposed Development Plan. It was in reality a move to harass the Panchayat.

As they passed the group, they heard a few cat calls and whistles. Bima started barking but Sachin advised restraint. 'Ignore.'

Leela protested, 'But how can they do this? I thought your Panch had got a court order?'

Sachin shook his head. 'No one gives a damn here. We are trying to fix this ourselves. The Panch wants Baba to call his friend in the Mantralaya Mumbai.'

Leela grimaced, 'So Bhai does ask for help.'

Sachin stopped. 'Hellooooo! He needs to do that all the time, Lishi, all the time. What did you think? Baba is Batman? He always tells us that without the goodwill of his loyal friends, we would have no peace, only fire-fighting.'

Right then an old Maruti car was passing by, with luggage piled in the hold. It screeched to a halt in front of the men taking measurements. A pot bellied old man stalked out and let loose with the most offensive load of abuse that Leela had heard in a long while. To her utter surprise, instead of collaring him, the young survey team literally took to their heels and vanished in their jeeps within seconds. The old man got back into his car and drove away.

'Now what was *that!*' exclaimed Leela.

'THAT is one of our most famous residents: Machenda. Ex-Trade Union Leader and Baba's loyal supporter. More about him when we get home.'

Then Sachin turned to her with a sense of urgency, 'This morning

Baba forgot to give you an important update. Some Intelligence Officers have been trying to track you in Pune. Baba got word from Anu Dida, because these officers even landed up in Dehradun.'

Leela's nostrils flared in anger, 'That's exactly why I am here incognito. Why can't they leave me alone?'

'Not just that, these fellows have been badgering Mada and Rajen Dadu too. I heard even your neighbours and friends were questioned. What's the deal? The same missing old man?'

'Yes, partly that, but I'd rather not talk about it for now. Someday soon I'll let you know at one go.'

'Ok chill for now. You need a mood booster. We'll meet Rudy (Rudolph). He's been asking for you, and he's the best man to tell you about Machenda.'

At Rudolph's home, they got talking again. Yes, he had come back to India to experience PG, solely due to an invitation from his ex-employee, Machen Ghosh. Rudolph conceded that he had yet to completely abandon his hardcore non-vegetarian German diet, but his many ailments had almost vanished after he put his faith in Bharat's prescriptions.

The topic drifted back to Machen Ghosh who was Rudolph's most favourite personality. When he worked under Rudolph, Machen (Makhonlal) Ghosh picked up a smattering of German and often used this when Rudolph was out of earshot. One of his favourite phrases which he barked to push all and sundry was *'Machen Sie schnell.'* (Speed it up!). He pronounced Machen as Makhon, and could not get it right despite being corrected many times. So people started calling him Machen Ghosh. The name stuck.

When a situation would get out of hand during work, Rudolph would exclaim: *'Scheisse!'* (shit) Machen would immediately add: *'Khaisse'* (damn it) in an aside in his native Bangaal dialect. Or he would spin quasi German-Bengali rhymes:

A TRYST WITH MAHAKAAL

'Plötzlich mache Ami phis phis,
Ich liebe dich.

'Suddenly, I whispered, shh shh,

I love you.'

Rudolph eventually grew to love Machen and his mad ways. To celebrate their friendship, he invited the Ghosh couple to a tiger safari in Bandhavgarh. Despite mortified requests from Machen, Rudolph decided to break free from the forest guide and independently wander around looking for tigers and other 'desirables' in the thick forest. When the tigers proved elusive, several rounds of *'Scheisse'* and *'Khaisse'* followed.

Then a huge tiger suddenly appeared out of thin air right on their path and roared loudly.

Rudolph crouched in the bushes and let out a trembling whisper: *'Achtung'.*

Machen immediately whispered back: *'Nein Sir. Baghatung!'*

While Leela and Sachin almost died laughing, Bima was getting restless so they had to bid goodbye.

Once they had reached home, Sachin regaled her with more jokes about the redoubtable Machenda, to which even Bharat added a few. As it turned out, this would be the last occasion in a long while that the family would sit together and celebrate life in such a carefree manner.

Sensing Bharat's receptive mood, Leela took him aside just before retiring for the day. In one uninterrupted session, she told him the details about her entire experience during the last few months, starting with her break-up with Aditya and ending with her stay with Mahakaal.

Bharat listened without a word. When her narration got over, all he said was that she should take complete rest here and meditate on these events. The insights to unravel her dilemmas would manifest in due course.

TWENTY SEVEN

Neither Bharat nor Leela could have ever imagined how Prithak Ghati and he would gradually be pulled centerstage to unwittingly become the fulcrum of a simmering civil unrest. There was an enormous public interest in the decades old articles written by Bharat following the documentary telecast. Seizing this opportunity, his 'admirer' immediately posted another highly contentious piece. About eighteen years ago, Bharat had emerged from his silence to post this singular article to a local newspaper.

When faced with ruthless political forces who continued to exploit the citizens with the State Machinery at their disposal, Bharat had detailed a desperate agitation to counter this oppression down to the last 'T', with multiple options at each stage if something did not play out as planned. He had stressed that such an agitation needed tact, a high degree of thrift and thorough coordination between the common protestors and a battery of dedicated lawyers, media and press people who were willing to help the cause. The effectiveness of such movements would rest on the tenacity of its leaders. His admirer had added Bharat's warning that these methods were to be used *only* when all other means to stop the loot in 'Independent' India had failed.

When he wrote these moves, the trigger had been a situation in Pune when all political forces had combined to shunt out an incorruptible crusading bureaucrat named Arun Bhatia in 1999. Bharat had initially sent this to '*Rashtriya Doot*' but they refused to publish it. Quite clearly someone had kept a copy which his modern admirer had acquired.

Now, hundreds of small support groups sprang up within a week across the country, all linked via the social media, to follow Bharat's 'instructions' *but with their own spin on it.* There had anyway been a groundswell of simmering discontent in many pockets in the nation. Now it burst into the open. The ruling forces everywhere were caught off guard.

As things stood, the present regime had relentlessly pushed for even greater statist control over the economy and populace. The people assigned to implement government schemes were usually the same cynical lot who had sprouted like weeds under the previous corrupt regimes. Even well meaning initiatives were invariably stymied.

It was against this backdrop that the protest movements were initiated by educated youth who were fed up with false promises of jobs and the lack of options to enjoy a stress-free existence. These protestors were not leftists, Gandhians or new-age green activists, but ordinary middle class people who now closed ranks with the lower income groups and the unorganized sector for a do-or-die battle with the polities.

Prithak Ghati was hit by an onslaught of visitors. Leela found her peace vitiated. The town residents too were alarmed. The Panch issued a dictum that day passes were needed to enter and stay in the town, to protect the ecology.

Typically, the political parties in Maharashtra announced that all Indians had the birthright to enter or pass through the town. This had the opposite effect. Young people everywhere protested this harassment of a small community. Many wrote that they would gladly pay a small access fee and book their visit, to keep Prithak Ghati in top shape.

Initially, the mainstream political forces dismissed the whole affair as a passing fad. But they woke up when some of the protests to combat state oppression started pinching. There was the 'No Tax' method, where large numbers of aggrieved citizens in low governance areas stopped paying all taxes; in fact anything which fed the government coffers. The protesting citizens pointed to the pathetic public healthcare systems; abysmal public school standards; power and water shortages;

corrupted police and lack of security; distributing freebies at public expense – so what were they paying taxes for? Contributing the same money to collective community set ups would tackle such lacunae far better.

Another idea had been to boycott all those huge public-private projects which were rip-offs due to the opaque manner in which they had been awarded to Corporate cronies as a quid pro quo for electoral funding. These business houses were now exposed for having secured windfall concessions at the cost of the public, with the state and Central Governments running up massive deficits and mortgaging the future of the coming generations to finance such projects. The protesters demanded that each such project be renegotiated even if they had been signed or launched already.

The response from the ruling coalitions' to these initial public protests was immediate and brutal. In several cases as in the mining industries, the entrenched mafia and their muscle power was put to use to terrify the protestors. This led to a calibrated response from the protesting groups. If the state governments did not desist from reigning in the mafia, such diversionary tactics would make them run a 'negative vote' NOTA (None of the above) campaign against candidates of the guilty political parties.

The governments did not take the threat seriously, but had to wake up to a new reality soon. A vigorous online social media campaign was run by the citizens groups that had networked across India, advocating 'zero' or NOTA vote in some state elections. These proved to be a resounding success, astounding even those who had launched these initiatives. The disparate movement now started acquiring a Pan - Indian character.

Needless to say, this did not make some people happy. A small group sat informally over drinks at the India Global Centre in New Delhi. A Triad was formed comprising of three people who were fundamentally opposed to everything that Bharat stood for: Prabhat Aiyer, Sobha Singh Gujral and R. Subramaniam, three powerful figures from the 'Deep State' faction within the ruling alliance. They would now onwards watch every move from Prithak Ghati and Bharat's supporters.

A thoroughly disillusioned public demanded that all politicians take an oath on the immediate implementation of a charter of demands, of which the first two were: comprehensive Police reforms, and clearance of all pending court cases within a strict time-frame as a part of sweeping judicial reforms. All citizens were asked to report if any politician or bureaucrat demanded or secured favours. Spy-cam sales went through the roof, which helped in pinning down offenders. An open threat was issued that if the political and executive class did not respond, the agitation would be scaled up manifold.

The political parties lambasted these demands as utopian when straitjacketed into unrealistic timeframes, but the protesters persisted with their charter of demands, adding a new set each week.

The local state governments or district level bodies initially had success in curbing these protests by a combination of arrests, hefty fines, threats and outsourced muscle power. However, the net was soon bombarded by gruesome pictures of the government's brutal tactics, as well as the opposition's complicity. If some of the initial protestors were 'broken' while in custody, ten more were willing to take their place but the resolve stayed put. No brushing under the carpet with appointment of committees headed by retired judges or senior bureaucrats. The full details of action taken had to be put in the public domain – Now! Verification would follow.

Prabhat Aiyer soon nudged his contacts in the media. The TV channels were promptly packed with famous experts and opinion makers of all hues decrying these nihilistic movements, and of course Bharat as their irresponsible Godfather in hiding. They ran him down in every conceivable way: via expert discussions, print media, public speeches, and pamphlets in universities where he had suddenly become popular. This did not stop the fascination of youth groups with Bharat bhai. Prithak Ghati was flooded by youngsters seeking Bharat's blessings and asking him to go public and take a clear stand. The sale of daily visitors' passes went through the roof and there were week-long waiting lists.

Leela was appalled by this turn of events and retreated into her shell again, thirsting for Mahakaal's comforting presence. She could see that Bharat too was flustered by the manner in which *his old action plans were often being altered to suit a different class of vested interests.*

The ruling party and the opposition forces soon realized that they could not pretend that Bharat Biswas did not exist. The strategy to neutralize him was informally discussed by the Triad. They proposed to somehow bring him onto a media show and then browbeat or shame him through a battery of experts. As a parallel strategy, SS Gujral had emissaries sent to Bharat with the message that as a true nationalistic Indian, he should come forth and cooperate with them. They could work together to make India a better country. Or in case he had outgrown what he had written in his youth, all he had to do was issue a disclaimer.

Bharat refused. He said that his mission was to build a frugal town which lived as per 'natural law' and could withstand any disaster. While he stood by all that he had said or written many years ago, he had neither the time nor inclination to guide such movements, or appear on TV shows.

Immediately the various political parties went to town crowing that the anarchic protesters should dump the views of such a coward who did not wish to stand by them.

For a while there was indeed a pause in the protests. The ruling polities grabbed this pause and had interparty talks to discuss how to tide over this 'pain in the neck.' Most opined that this was a minor passing fad that would soon blow over, like many previous movements. This was a movement with a non-existent leader who declined to lead.

Why give him importance? Once people got tired of being sent to jail, or experiencing shortages etc, the fad would melt away. So it was best to use drastic measures only when needed, to bring these novice protestors to their knees.

One senior politician and his cousin in the intelligence department dug out the details of Bharat's interaction with the Maoists in Kalasa and later in PG. They passed a complete information package to R. Subramaniam, who instinctively now knew how to deal with Bharat at any critical point in the coming months.

TWENTY EIGHT

While the Triad was at work on their strategies, another 'Triad' made the nation gasp. The evening news was flashing the sensational arrest of the three individuals who were uploading Bharat's articles, along with their own comments. Bharat was himself shocked to know their identities since the three persons were the unlikeliest of allies, and he had known them distantly long ago.

Radhika was a lady now staying in a senior citizen's home. She was a spinster and a one-time communist from Kerala who had competed twice against Bharat on quiz shows during her college days. She had become completely disillusioned after a long stay in China on a deputed tour to study how Chinese communism had created an economic miracle. She found out for herself about the cronyism and typical corruption there. After her arrest she confessed to the police that Bharat had been prescient in his projections a few decades ago, and that these needed to be highlighted.

Dr Misra was just as non-typical. A reputed doctor, he had been Bharat's teacher in medical college for a while. He had renounced worldly life and now lived in Pithoragarh, where he spent much of his time in meditative practices. Even so, he had been tracking Bharat's life and stated that he had received 'instructions' during his meditation to bring Bharat's name back to public memory.

It was the third member, DCP Ahire, who had actually introduced the first two to each other. He was a highly decorated police officer who had resigned some years ago after a controversial case. Coincidentally, he had earlier investigated Urvashi's death near Kalasa. After retirement he had run into Dr Misra and become his follower. He already knew

Radhika and that she was net savvy. He had sourced Bharat's earlier articles and Radhika had created a blog to upload the same. Any questions from readers were answered by the trio by a neat division regarding who would answer what.

All three were released on bail since the judge found no ground for detention. A case for sedition was not admissible anyway. They had not directed the readers to follow Bharat's earlier dictums. It was a simple case of uploading and clarifying the present applications for Bharat's views, which had anyway tallied with the present reality in society with unbelievable accuracy.

The government filed an appeal in the High Court, but privately they were shell shocked. Dr Misra was singularly respected in Govt. circles and DCP Ahire's family had an early association with the Hindu Mahasabha. How could 'one of their own' direct a campaign to support an anarchist?

The same morning, Bharat received a call from his mother in Dehradun. Shivdadu wasn't well at all. Bharat immediately decided to visit them, which would also give him some time away from all the commotion around Prithak Ghati. He was in Pune airport, waiting to catch his flight, when he saw the news on TV about the court verdict. He called up Leela and told her to be a bit careful during her walks, lest she run into media people.

Once Bharat reached the farm in Dehradun, both his mother Anu and Shiv started agonizing about the fact that Leela had vanished again. He learnt that the SIT was still looking for the old man who had saved Leela, because they suspected this entity was a cover for an anti national spy gang that had kept her in custody. Maybe she was with this gang again? The Biswas family had denied this in one voice, saying that Leela was given to major mood swings and often took off on long treks to undisclosed locations. Leela's Lawyer too had assured the SIT of the same, but inwardly the family was worried about her. Bharat tried to reassure Anu without revealing much.

After stabilizing Shiv, Bharat met his childhood friend and son of another INA soldier, Avinash, who had also settled nearby in Dehradun. He was a small-scale Industrialist who had even served as a state minister before withdrawing from politics. The sudden interest in Bharat's views had fired him up no end.

Avinash insisted that Bharat drive back with him to Delhi. He himself had some work there, so he could drop Bharat at a friend's place near the IGI airport for the night.

They drove into Delhi via NH 58 and snaked around the ISBT (Inter State Bus Terminus), past Kashmiri Gate and on to Bahadur Shah Zafar Marg. Bharat noticed that many people were walking in big groups towards the city centre. This was a working day so he wondered why there were such unusual crowds. Avinash cryptically remarked that these could be people attending a protest rally at the Ramlila Maidan.

A little later, Bharat noticed that they were being tailed by two cars, one of which was certainly a police vehicle. He turned to Avinash, '*Kya Avi*? Either you have an escort car since you are an ex-VIP, or are we under surveillance? Or is it just me?'

'No idea, Boss. They could also be heading for the rally,' said Avinash.

'Doesn't look like it. They had ample scope to overtake us, but they are sticking on behind us.'

Avinash shrugged and asked the driver to speed it up. Bharat noticed some nervous energy in his friend. However, as soon as the car reached the crossing of the Ramlila Maidan and Gandhi Ghat, it took a right turn towards the rally.

After another three hundred meters, the car was flagged to a side. Avinash showed some papers to the Security personnel and requested the Sub-Inspector (SI) to lower his head. They had a very short whispered talk. All Bharat could hear was, '*Theek hai Sir. Aapki Zimmedari.* That's your responsibility.'

Then the SI glanced at Bharat and saluted, '*Jai Hind Sir. Akkha force aapke saath hain.*' The car leaped forward and was quickly guided to a special lane meant only for VVIPs.

Bharat realized at last that something was happening to a plan. 'Avi, *kya hain*? I thought you had some work, but looks like you are attending this rally. Now don't tell me…'

And then he stopped short.

The car was speeding towards the dais and Bharat could now clearly see the huge 'DETOX INDIA' banners all around. All these posters had his name and face prominently displayed. By the time he turned back to Avinash, the car had come to a screeching halt near the huge dais. While a speech was in progress, a number of people and security men came running and surrounded them.

Avinash took Bharat's hands in his own. His face was stricken with anxiety and guilt, 'I know you'll never forgive me for this.'

Bharat was calm in his response, 'Banners with my picture? What's happening? Just tell me.'

Avinash's voice broke, 'We had been planning this Chintan Rally for quite some time. We wanted to bring you from Prithak Ghati anyway, but when I heard that you were coming to Dehradun… Yaar, I stuck my neck out and promised to bring you here. We got the banners done overnight. You can abuse me yaar, but… but Brijesh was confident he would manage…'

Bharat was still looking confounded. 'Brijesh? He's here? *Arre, saaf saaf bol!*'

There were people knocking at the car door and on the glass. The driver had unlocked the car and now a posse of strangers and security people were urging Bharat to come out. One of them even opened the door, but Bharat firmly closed it again, sending the people outside into a state of panic. He turned to Avinash, 'Have I been co-opted into something I don't know of? Is that it? Tell me.'

'Boss, what could I do? With Shiv uncle's health condition and your running around, this was the last thing I could talk of.'

'But on the phone? Or even when we started this morning? Damn it, you are still not lifting the curtain!' Bharat's voice now had a faint trace of exasperation.

'Because if we had told you, we were sure you would say NO... that's why I...'

'You are right. I will say no to anything you have put me into without my consent.'

The door was suddenly yanked open and a booming voice grabbed Bharat's attention, 'Oi Bharat! *Kutte, kamine, Khuda ka tattoo... Oi Johnny bahar nikal!'*

Before Bharat could even get in a word, Brijesh, one of his closest friends from his IIT Kanpur days had literally lifted him out of the car and swept him into a bear hug. Bharat hugged the giant back with equal affection, seeing his very dear friend after almost seven years. Brijesh along with Srinivasan, Rajshekhar and Avinash were the core members of the online advisory forum that had helped Bharat when he first came to Prithak Ghati.

Brijesh now whispered into his ear, 'Boss, *Johnny ke jigar ke jalle, zara mundi phirke tho dekh, tera Baap khara hai.* Boss, it's your time at last.' Then he stepped back and did a high five with a despondent Avinash, 'Avi, you really managed. Unbelievable!'

'Naa yaar, I cheated him,' replied Avinash with a crestfallen look.

'Bullshit.' Brijesh turned to face Bharat, '*Chal, tu mujhe galiyaan de de. Jitne chahe.* We have been really zonked up with this campaign, and our hero – *behenchod tu* Johnny – playing truant? Just look around, how many of our gang are here...*kahan kahan se aaye hain hum...dekh, mundi ghumaa!'*

Bharat looked around and saw at least half a dozen faces from his college days crowding around him. They were all slapping his back, pumping their fists and greeting him ad lib. Rajshekar Rao was the loudest, 'Maan! I was visiting, and we all had our feet on the campaign trail. When Avi told me of your Doon visit, I told him, do whateverrrrr needed…'

'Kaise bhi ho – haath pair baandh ke, jhooth bol ke, just get Johnny here,' Brijesh quipped in, *'Baaki main dekhtaa hoon…yaar?'*

Bharat had turned to get back inside the car. Avinash stood in his way, 'Sorry *yaar. Maafi.'*

Bharat found the car door locked. He started walking away from the dais towards the main road. The security, volunteers, his friends all went into a tizzy. Brijesh ran after him and held him back. 'Boss, Whyyyyy? You're not the coward they accuse you to be. We know that.'

'Because I'm not the hero you all want me to be. This is not my way.'

'Baarat, just look.' Srinivasan spoke with his quaint accent, 'There are no political party people here among us. Not one. Just as you always wanted. But there are thousands of desperate, disillusioned, fucked up Junta out there. They believe in you.'

'No they don't. I'm only their latest fix – their puff for today. This is still a mass living in denial. They don't have it in them to correct course. I'm not their leader.'

Brijesh suddenly picked Bharat up on his powerful shoulders and ran towards the dais. He had barely struggled up two steps when a huge cheer went up. The moderate crowd spotted the unthinkable – that Bharat was making a first-time appearance.

Avinash hissed out an alarm, 'Brij, you can't take him like this. Please!'

As soon as Bharat was released on the steps to the podium, he patted both Avinash and Brijesh and started climbing down. Srinivasan tried to hold him back and beseeched him in a quivering voice, 'Baarat don't do this maan. When you had a problem – ANY problem – we all got together, fought together, bailed you out. Time after time.'

'Never forgotten. Take my life for it, Srini. But this public platform is not mine.'

'Ok, *toh yeh* platform *hamara hain – yes?* But can't you say a few words in support?'

'I won't argue. But this movement is not …'

Rajshekar held Bharat firmly by his shoulders, 'Ok go. But take a look around at our fucked up janta, like us. Imagine *you* are out there… desperate… looking for some hope… some way out…'

Brij exploded, 'What go! What the fuck… *Behenchod tu…*'

Avinash restrained him. Bharat took a deep breath and took one step down. The people around on the dais, the crowd, sensed that something was going on which was not scripted. The noise suddenly came down a notch.

Bharat looked around at their faces. How could this be his platform?

He took another step down. Brij and Srinivasan were smashing their fists in exasperation, while Avinash held them back to make way. They sat down on the steps. The DIG Police (VIP security) was seen coming hurriedly with some papers in his hand.

Suddenly, Bharat jerked back. Something had caught his eye. He traced his gaze back in the same line. Then he became transfixed.

A man covered in a robe was standing there in the crowd. He was a hundred metres away, but Bharat already knew who he was.

As if in confirmation, the man raised his hand in a gesture of blessing.

Bharat knew the sign. All else stood still.

TWENTY NINE

He swivelled around and in one swift move he was already on the dais and walking towards the mikes. The nonplussed Brij broke into a huge grin and ran to overtake Bharat and introduce him. The media personnel just under the dais in the press enclosure were now all falling over each other to get a vantage position and better coverage.

The man in the robe fixed Bharat in a gaze. Even at this distance, Bharat felt it go into his very being. He smiled and lifted his hand to request silence.

'Namaskar. This will be my first, and perhaps last, public appearance,' Bharat paused and continued, 'I am no leader. No politician.'

There was a sudden silence. Only the distant sound of traffic could be heard.

'All I can say is: You can choose to revitalize our great country. By living differently. More than ever before, this is needed now, when we have such hopelessness around.

'You want it all now! Like the generations before you also did. But are you ready for change? I say – No! Not one bit. You all are *not* willing to really, *really* change yourself.

'Till you can't change things in your body and mind, in your immediate environment which is an extension of that you – nothing will change.

'You live in filthy, enervating cities and even the successful among you do nothing to change this. Can you stop spitting on the roads for even one day? No. Instead, you spit, pee and throw rubbish around; buy multiple vehicles and clog up the roads; screw up the environment

180

around you. Why blame your rulers? How many of you have initiated do-or-die movements to change the very quality of life around you?'

The audience was stunned. The people had only heard politicians speak of promises or criticize other politicians. Here was someone who was actually telling them where *they* had gone wrong. There was a single clap and then an uproar! The people loved what they heard. Thunderous applause followed.

Bharat raised his hands and continued, 'You need to make that change happen in your own lives, starting from home. First rule: be nobody's slave. And equally important: never ever make others a slave to you. Not your mothers, wives, husbands, children, workers – no one. Live and let live. Nobody has the right to your life. A single life – your life – is sacred and supreme over any collective. *No state, panchayat, or government can ever abrogate that.*

'Remember the horrors of the Emergency? 1977? Sardar Swaran Singh said that the "Rights of Society must prevail over any Individual". This remains the basic impulse for your current regime, no different at the root from all previous regimes.

'Here you are, demanding an end to dominant state rule, and yet you happily sleep when thousands of tribals are ruined forever. Why? Because the politicians promise you energy and water, never mind if innumerable native forest dwellers are thrown out of their centuries old hearth again and again since 1947.

'Way back in 1948, Jawaharlal Nehru said, "If you are to suffer, you should suffer in the interest of the country." Whom was he addressing? The hapless villagers who were to be displaced by Hirakud Dam. Then followed Harsud, Bargi, Kutku Dams; Upper Kolab Project; Salandi; Machkund; Jalsindhi – so many more. *Kyon*, does anyone here even remember these names? *Nahin naa?* Have any of you gone and slept on the cold floor in those doomed habitats, knowing you would be thrown out the very next day... again and again? Who cares? You need the power in all of your devices at all times, the water in your taps, and even for your swimming pools.

'So, man uses man. *You* use the weak de facto and close your eyes. And now stand here clamouring for change.

'I'm pro development, but *not* with attrition – not with man versus man as the ONLY way of going forward.'

The applause that followed indicated the mood of the people. They were in. They liked what they heard and wanted more.

Bharat raised two fingers. 'Second rule: While you should never *initiate* violence against others, it is your sacred right to act in self-defence – even proactively, if someone announces that your life can be taken over for the "greater good".

'I say again that *gheraos* and pickets are acts of violence. Fast unto death is an act of violence, where you commit the violence on yourself and blackmail others. This is legitimate only when you act in self-defence, with no other choice.

'You have a contract with some people who say that they will work for you. Just imagine, instead of abiding by this contract they cheat you, bully you, extort your money, and make any and every demand on your life in the name of the public. That "Someone" is any political party or entity who changes labels, slogans, manifestos – but always demands the right to dictate how you will run your life. And that public is *you*.

'If you don't accept, they can jail you or even kill you. *You* have empowered and financed them, given this right to them for over seventy years. So, now they will never stop running your lives. NEVER, no matter what their label or banner or who they are.'

The crowd roared in agreement.

'So what's the road map ahead? Let us go step by step and explore what can be done. *Theek hai?*'

An overwhelming *'Haaan'* rose from the crowd. Many more had flocked to the Rally by now, and the numbers had swelled rapidly.

'First is absolute and total self-discipline. There are drills to achieve this. Form silent self-help groups with self-reliance and discipline as a must.

'Second is acquiring the ability to live with minimal needs and treating luxuries as occasional picnics. At a moment's notice, learn to live out of a suitcase with a few shirts and trousers, a shared cycle or opting for bus travel. Pool in for a support fund. You need to have the *dum* to stay like a *sadhu*. Then these despots cannot touch you or break you so easily.

'Keep these two steps in mind: Self-Discipline and Minimal Living. I will talk about the third step a little later.

'So, you really want change? Now? *Dum hai?*'

There was a massive roar. The media persons who were telecasting this live scanned the vibrant crowds with the cameras.

'Say yes now and forget by tomorrow?'

A big 'NOOOOOO' followed.

'You want change – from being ruled to self-rule; self reliance?'

'Yeeeesssss!'

'When you are fully ready with complete self-discipline and the ability to live frugally, *only then* comes step three. No screaming, hooting, candlelight processions and pressing LIKE buttons and signature campaigns. Get real. All governments want to play God, extract, rule you, and control you in the name of a larger good. They will say that after five years, ten years or more, results will come! And you are willing to be fooled. *Baas, aur nahi?*'

'*Aur nahin!*' roared back the crowd. Bharat could see even the DIG shouting as hard as the others.

'Step Three: Starve your oppressors. They live like leeches on your

183

blood. Find your own ways to starve them. Your rulers and oppressors have initiated, I repeat – initiated, thousands of projects in your name by printing notes, *by borrowing and indebting you or your next generations forever.* And then they loot, extract, siphon off from the same projects. Now – you have the right to self-defence, yes?'

'YES!'

'Compel them to show completely transparent expenditure and progress reports on electronic boards in every town which can be cross-checked by your own vigilance teams. Not like some "Fund and Reform Tracker" controlled and compiled by the government. These vigilance teams should be from the public and changed every month to avoid reverse corruption and infiltration by the corrupt forces. Identify the culprits. Boycott them socially, as well as their goods. Do everything in your power.

'If someone takes money from you and does not deliver the goods, you can penalize that person. Tell me which top accused politicians have been convicted *and* actually served jail sentences *long term?*

'NONE! NO ONE!'

'Support people who pledge their life only to their motherland and do not take refuge behind hundreds of complicated economic dictums, which are all meant to fool you. Indians are geniuses at creativity and adapting to any reality, only if they are left free to develop their lives within safety and discipline. DISCIPLINE – never, ever forget that word.

'So Step four: Find completely new "soldiers" from within, armed with a single agenda – mother India. No fake patriotism please. This is all about love for the soil; for every form of life around your villages or your neighbourhood. If you can't respect and love this, there is no patriotism.

'For starters: Insist on a reformed police force with multiple checks as per Chanakya's policies, a force which is incorruptible.'

There was cynical laughter from members of the crowd, while some even patted and pulled at the police constables on duty in jest.

'I can see some of you laughing, but it can be made to happen.

'Then... a judicial system, where major reforms are needed. Thousands of new courts must be established by law to dispense justice in a completely revamped system and binding time frame. This includes a multi pronged vigilance set up at the Mohalla – village – town – city level, where the smallest civic complaint is assuredly resolved. This has to be monitored by your people, a watchdog keeping all governments on their toes.

'Lastly, supporting an army which is sworn to the motherland, and ruthless in defending the idea of *Bharat Varsha* as a way of life – the land of a million paths.

'Start with this much now, with self-control and de-addiction. *ALL addictions please!* Sugar, drug dependence, meat, 5G networks with unlimited data – *inke chungal se nikalne kaa himmat hai?*'

The boisterous crowd quietened down a bit and a muffled 'YES' followed.

Bharat looked at the bewildered faces and said, '*Nahin hai?* I know. *Aapko lagega:* Why this discipline? *Kyo jaroori hai bhai?* It is important because you need to have control over body and mind, instead of the helpless addicts which many of you have become. Addiction to the mobile, to TV, to drink, tobacco, sugar, popping pills and killing your gut – and don't forget that the gut is the second brain. Yes I repeat – refined sugar, meat, pharma induced drug dependence; many more...

'For real change you should be able switch on and off at will from consuming all this.

'For instance, if I told you that the cost and ability to grow food for you is impacted by your meat and livestock consumption – will you reduce your intake? No. You will ask what has my meat eating got to do with getting a job or putting bread on the table? None of you are ready yet. Habits, addictions run very deep. No one wants change there. Unless you are willing to live in real moderation, there is no hope.'

The crowd was attentive, but some of them were getting restive and looking around. Bharat could see them exchanging quick comments with each other. Some shoulders started to droop.

'Just think. Today you stand here, angry and cheated by the polity; demanding jobs; education; better health security and so on. Forty years ago, to give a rough example, even then the demand was the same "We want all this – NOW". *No basic self correction was attempted.* Only *Now – Now.*

'Today you have grown to many times that number, and demand the same – NOW. The politicians and economists talk about super foods; super inventions which will solve all your problems, but how many talk of living in balance with mother earth; in moderation? How will they sell their goods; how can they continue to play God unless they have not made you an addict and redefined what are the necessities of life?

'So don't blame only your leaders like the previous generations. *Don't tag my ideas or old action plans to your addictions, living in denial while seeking a panacea.'*

The entire audience broke into loud applause again.

'Many *buddhijeevis* will sell you quick fixes. But for real change, you need discipline first and discipline last – because – *because the world of nature too runs in a magical sequence which is disciplined. Your body, your heart, your inner organs, nervous system, all these run in perfect discipline like a perfected machine. What you need is the same discipline applied to daily life, to human action.*

'So many of you, living in polluted cities, are unable to fight this invisible enemy called inflation where food output cannot match demand, where you are encouraged to be extravagant and not austere;

to be gluttonous. Our unsustainable population growth has fed these industries. So more meat; more pressure on the land; more food – no matter how it is produced; more oil and energy needs... You wonder why prices are so high and ever new health problems are appearing every day?

'They have sold you these lies, hooked you on to these deadly habits; to dictums that without expensive medical processes and checkups, one cannot have a healthy body. And you have willingly swallowed this dope for decades, forgetting our own traditions of balance and medicine. Urban living throws these up, and then you need dollops of urban medicine to solve them.'

Brijesh and Rajshekhar looked at each other, the smiles wiped off their faces. The crowd had gone silent. Bharat surveyed them for a moment and continued in the same vein.

'Go home and think of a *test case situation:* Ok I love meat, but am I addicted? Can I stop it, or eat meat in real moderation *only* when my body needs protein, which I cannot get from a nutrition deficient vegetarian option because the soil quality has been ruined overtime? Can I start using my feet instead of driving my car to travel even 200 metres?

'In short, this will be a period of severe abstinence to cleanse the system, where you support each other and enable thousands of value added "earth saving" inventions to gradually emerge from free enterprise and such balanced, natural living.'

The crowd was now uneasy. There was applause but the noise was considerably low. A group of young people in front were vigorously nodding their heads but Bharat could see many, mostly middle-aged citizens who have families to look after, looking almost crushed.

He stood with his feet slightly apart and hands open in front of him. The crowd was nonetheless listening to him and trying to absorb his words. This was still a crowd that was looking for solutions.

Bharat smiled. 'What is so impossible about this? You want self-help groups to create a new order, but can't tolerate such inner discipline? Then go on with what you are doing, because there is no hope. You will always be crushed like you are being crushed right now.

'One last alert: In the aftermath of any war with our many external enemies, don't panic. Operate in such self-help groups, conserving and making judicious use of water; treating the ill, infirm and injured; rebuilding from almost scratch.

'Avoid politics of any colour. Avoid every known political or associated volunteer groups, because all these have hidden agendas. Even the shadow has to be washed away. Only motherland matters.

'There will be a war unlike any that you have ever known or seen. We have to win that war, within and without. You will be in shock, but how to face it and overcome is in your hands. From now, the countdown is on.

'I wish you well. I am already doing my karma in Prithak Ghati. I cannot do yours.

'Jai Hind.'

THIRTY

'Self Goal! Bloody asshole. Fucked himself royally!' R.Subramaniam remarked, as he raised a toast to his friends at the IGC. They had just finished watching the live feed from the Chintan rally on a big screen. They had been on edge right through Bharat's talk, but now the Triad sat back relaxed.

'Babua konphoojd hai yaar. Amateur *saala.* Imagine, telling the public to alter their diet for real change! Ha, ha, ha, *maja aa gaya* – and we were worrying.' Gujral rolled his eyes as he savoured his whisky.

Aiyer concurred, 'Boss, this guy has ended by giving *gaalis* to the janta. Honest chap, whatever you might say. And no tact. You could see the public already in "flight" mode. Give up their mutton, chicken... sugar? Bloody hell, sugar!'

Gujral was stumped by the look on Subramaniam's face. 'What Subi? Worry lines again?'

Subramaniam silently looked from Gujral to Aiyer and around the room, where several others were also commenting on Bharat's speech and ridiculing it. 'Let's wait before we toast this moment. The way the game has played out so far, every time we counted him out, this Bharat and his damn Pagla Ghati have bounced back even stronger. The stars are with him, and the Janata is *paagal* anyway. You never know, some may even go with these strictures.'

Gujral banged the table with full force. 'Never! No way. Diet and food are major hook-ups which even the toughest cookies can't pole vault.'

Subramaniam was drumming his fingers. 'I would wait and watch.

They may not change diet, but the disruptions could go on.'

'That's Ok, Boss. Patience as usual. They will go *thanda* in due course. This Bharat chap has read out the Commando Manifesto at the high school Induction Party. Ta ta.'

In Pune, Mada too had just finished watching the same feed along with two friends, who were laughing and lampooning Bharat. The General got up abruptly, excused himself and went into his personal study. His friends sensed he wanted *Ekaant* and left.

Mada remained sitting there in silence for an hour, with his chin resting on his stick.

A block away, Rajen shook his head in frustration. He had interrupted an important meeting and everyone had watched the live feed. He turned to the others and said, 'The face of today's India – misguided genius – my own nephew talking through his hat. *Apni* Janata and discipline?! Wrong number. *Ab tho iskaa patta kat gaya. Kahan iskaa* Prithak Ghati – *Kahan* India. If only life was so simple.'

Bharat turned sharply and strode away. The crowd was initially silent. He stopped at the edge of the dais and looked at them. Then the crowd started applauding again.

The man in the robe was no longer to be seen.

Bharat had almost reached the car when Srinivasan came running, 'Wait boss. We'll drop you.' He looked over his shoulder as a big assortment of media crews were scuffling with the police cordon to head this way. Bharat could see the DIG issuing instructions to his men. He too was someone Bharat had known earlier.

DIG Shafaat Qureshi joined them and pressed Bharat's hand.. 'Now move. Next time I can't guarantee that the media will not squeeze you.'

The driver was already in place along with Avinash. Bharat leaned out and said, 'That's OK. There will never be a next time.'

'Want to bet?' retorted Shafaat, 'You've just stepped in. No turning back – *naa mumkin.*'

'I've just stepped into the car. And it takes me in only one direction.' Bharat patted Shafaat, 'Take care Shafi.'

The car started off. Bharat was still leaning out, since he could see that Brij and Rajshekar were waving at him and indicating in sign language that they would connect later via their mobiles.

They soon reached the Rajghat junction again. Avinash turned, '*Yaar, mujhe maafi de de.* I shouldn't have lied to you.'

Bharat patted his friend on his forearm, '*Nahin Yaar.* You had no choice. You were meant to bring me here.'

'Huh? *Nahi nahi*, I said I'll bell the cat, so…'

Bharat laughed merrily, 'Actually you never belled me. You were belled by the Dead Ghost and you never came to know.'

'*Kya bol raha hai Yaar?* What Ghost?'

'You won't understand. Just relax and enjoy the drive.'

'Huh?'

Bharat turned Avinash's face away. Srinivasan had changed Bharat's travel plans in the light of his speech at the rally. They got him a last minute ticket to Pune by the late evening flight, so he was driven directly to the airport. The two police cars were in tow. A couple of press cars had tailed them, but the heavy traffic ensured that Bharat could not be tracked.

DIG Qureshi had arranged with the airport security that Bharat could dodge the waiting media and enter from a side gate. Bharat got off with his small luggage. He paused and looked at Avinash. 'Keep in touch with Ma and Shivdadu. They will be really happy.'

Avinash embraced him and started weeping, startling a few

onlookers who pointed at Bharat and started taking snaps with their mobiles. In a few minutes, these would be circulated on the social media.

Bharat whispered in Avinash's ears, 'Don't worry *yaar*. I am not upset. Take care because the times I spoke of are very near. Bye – till our next embrace.'

Avinash wiped his eyes and stood watching till Bharat proceeded to the check-in counter. By now more and more people had recognized him, and the response was electric. A number of passengers standing in the security queue greeted him warmly and offered to make way for him, only to be stumped by a middle aged bespectacled flyer who turned and snapped, 'Please follow the queue. There is no separate line for health freaks as yet.'

That set the tone. The whispers slowly grew in volume and turned into an irate buzz. While the Officials handling Security saluted him, a young group of flyers hooted provocatively on the sidelines. A large number of people came up to congratulate him and shake his hands, while many tried to touch his feet.

At the same time there were offensive comments of all kinds from the mostly middle aged trendy flyers, who made loud talk to ensure that Bharat heard them all, without looking at him in the eye.

Another younger lot made exaggerated gestures, dropping their burger packing and cream tart foils into a bin close to Bharat, while adding to the barrage of ad lib comments: 'No addictions. Discipline – abstinence – *Detox shuru!*'

'Oye, I'm for change, gave up my steaks from today.'

'I told you; I *told you* long ago, this guy was just hot air. Happy now?'

'Bloody Phussss! Latest namunaa of *bakchodi* bullshit!'

'Budget balanced at last. No sugar; no chicken; no pills...'

'Shut up yaar. No 5G, no milk? Mamaaa!'

'Incorruptible Mama log! In India? *Bhadwa sala*!'

A couple of young men stepped away from the jostling group and approached Bharat. When he looked up, they muttered 'Sorry Sir' to him, only to be subjected to catcalls and jeers, 'Oye Detox chaatu! So all the magic Gyan of your Guru is stored in his gut and ass? Go-go-go and lick away!'

Some passengers stepped in angrily and loudly upbraided the irreverent youth. Just when these two groups were heading for an ugly brawl, a large number of senior Air Force Officers in Uniform who were flying to Pune came and stood in front of Bharat. They saluted him in unison. One of them glared at the jeering group of motley flyers and announced in a booming voice, 'Sir, count us in as new soldiers for Mother India. We can start by cleaning up the noise pollution here right away.'

Bharat only shook his head, smiled and folded his hands in a grateful Namaste, but the imposing presence of the Officers ensured that the lounge returned to 'whisper mode' till boarding was announced.

THIRTY ONE

In Prithak Ghati, Leela had watched almost the whole event with unmitigated shock on Sachin's mobile. He had been alerted by Avinash and within seconds he was sharing the 'live coverage' with Leela. As Bharat left the dais and Brij took over, the live feed shifted to a screaming anchor. Sachin punched in the air, 'Avi uncle's a genius. Baba did it! Did it!'

'You mean *that* Avinash? He was such a softie. Can't be!'

'It's him, Lishi. But shit! We missed out on seeing such a *dhamaal* on the big screen – *kyaaa...*'

'I almost missed it too.' said Leela, 'I never ever thought that I'd see Bhai in form after so many years. But asking the janata to abstain from non veg was a real killjoy for them...'

'That's typical Baba – testing resolve. Remember the "doing without mobiles" thing?'

Leela nodded, 'But you really made my day.'

Sachin widened his eyes and smiled wickedly, 'Then you do something to make my day.'

'Ok, tell me, *kya hukum hain?*' asked Leela with a wide grin, '*Sahi sahi Maangnaa.*'

Sachin looked around and outside the room like a conspirator. Then he put his finger on his lips, requesting for caution. He tiptoed from the living room and an amused Leela almost danced on her toes to follow her nephew. To her surprise, he passed through the corridor and very gently opened a small door which led to Bharat's room. Leela paused and made a face. She whispered, 'Nah! You're being real naughty.'

Sachin responded with an urgent whisper, '*Aree, baad mein chance kahan milega.* Now cooooome.'

'What chance?'

'Don't argue. Kaushalya Maushi keeps tabs. No one's allowed. Come.'

Leela entered the room. It was the same kind of Spartan room she had seen Bharat inhabit all his life: sleeping on the floor; very few fixtures; a medical kit at the ready; his favourite musical instruments in a corner.

Her attention was drawn to a scraping sound from Sachin. He pushed away the *dhurrie* that covered a slab of lime and mortar. She whispered, 'What are you doing?'

Sachin did not pay heed, but after feeling his way around the slab in the dim light, he motioned to her. Then he came close and whispered in her ear, 'There is an underground chamber here.'

Leela jerked back and whispered incredulously, 'Underground?'

'Yes. I came to know by accident. I'll tell you later. Maushi knows, so I'll keep watch outside. You go down.'

'But why me? *You* come with me.'

'Nooo! Right now they are all looking at the repeat telecast of Baba's speech on their TV, so Maushi won't come here for a while. Just goooo.'

Before Leela could react, Sachin was out of the room in a flash. Initially she could not figure out how to shift or open the slab. After a few attempts, she was able to give a slight jerk and slide it open without a sound. As soon as she released it, the platform started closing again. So she tried a second time, and this time it opened at least three feet, almost half the size of Bharat's bed which lay parallel to this mechanism. When she had opened it fully, there was a tiny clicking sound and a light came on in the underground space.

Leela descended by a fairly comfortable block of stairs to a carpeted floor, whereas there was no carpet in any other part of the estate. The left wall had a big circuit board. Facing her directly was a door and the right wall was all metal cladding.

She gently opened the door. Again, another light came on automatically and the entry light switched off. The room had an odd shape. She looked around and found that on her right was a cabin which had walls with the same metal cladding. There was a double-walled glass panel with some kind of a security system. She peeped in through the glass and found herself looking at several sealed alternators that were all connected to a strange device situated on a platform. There was another futuristic looking generator below this assembly. All these coupled devices were running silently.

Leela mumbled to herself, 'What on earth is this? Really strange.'

On her left was a study. She located Bharat's audio system with his stacked music library. There was a simple desk and chair, an old laptop as well as a host of in-use files. On the other side were two open bookshelves with many of his medical case studies and assorted books. One steel cupboard was tagged with 'Design and structure', 'Invention and ideation', 'Organic living designs' and so on. The keys to the cupboard were hanging in place.

There was a wooden cupboard at the end of the room which she found locked. Behind it was a small curtained space in the corner. A single person could barely walk through at a time. She did that and turned.

There was a framed, welcoming quote which she remembered from her childhood: 'A revolutionary should die unnamed, unheard & unlamented.' In this section there were hundreds of pictures, often as paintings, some of which she recognized as heroes whom Shivdadu and Saraswati had introduced to her during her childhood.

She found photos of musicians and unheralded scientists, most of whom she would not know but for the tags. There were also paintings of old sages and medical men all along the wall. Each one was spotlessly clean and very well maintained.

There was also a small altar. She had never known Bharat to be a God worshipping, ritualistic person. Her brother dug spirituality but not organized religion.

Right in the centre of the altar, occupying pride of place, was a big framed photo flanked by several other photos. All these were covered with a fine muslin cloth.

She gently pulled the cloth away and froze. A huge shock went through her body and she turned pale.

The centre photo was actually a painting. Mahakaal's smiling face looked into her eyes. He seemed as alive as if she had met him a moment ago.

Leela slumped down and clutched the framed painting. Who had made this? It was much more accurate than the police painting which was a take-off on the Subhas Bose based 'Gumnami Baba'.

There were eight other smaller paintings – four on each side of the main painting. All had been done by Bharat and signed in a corner. To think that Bhai even had a talent for painting! They depicted the man in various situations and age profiles... a bare-chested mendicant; a Sufi saint in some small shrine...

When she looked minutely, she could sense that though there were slight differences in each, there was no mistaking that the subject was the same.

What was going on? What did Bhai have to do with any of these other lookalikes? Did Mahakaal and Bhai know each other? Then why had Bhai kept silent when she spoke to him about MK? Her mind was numbed by the questions.

Her eyes returned to the main painting. It seemed to be alive. She touched it and started crying. It was only after a while that she heard Sachin's frantic whisper as if from another planet, 'Lishi, come faaaast!'

She put back the muslin cloth carefully over the row of paintings. Then she wedged her way back through the narrow access and pulled the curtain back.

Closing the main door behind her, she hastened back up the stairs. She was pulled up by Sachin, who shut the slab while admonishing her in a furious whisper, 'What were you doing so…'

Then he noticed the tears in her eyes, and the look on his face changed to a deep concern. 'The repeat of Baba's speech must be over. Hurry, I think Maushi is coming.'

They quickly exited the room, shut the adjoining door and ran tiptoe to the main entry. Leela walked to her room. Sachin saw Kaushalya entering Bharat's room, and then he hastened to join Leela.

'Phew! Hope she doesn't suspect. Maushi is verrrrry sharp. Lishi…?'

Leela was still in a trance. She was barely aware of Sachin's existence at her elbow. She entered the room and sat down on the bed without putting on the light. Sachin opened his mouth to speak, thought the better for it and then plonked down on a cane chair outside the room. But his eyes remained alert to any movement from her.

She had never lost her sense of balance even when she had been chased through the forest. But now, the more she thought about what she had just seen, the more she was sucked deeper into a turmoil which she had never experienced before. The overpowering feeling was that of having been let down by her dearest brother. Despite knowing what she was going through, why had he kept silent about the fact that he knew about Mahakaal, more so when the rest of the world had concluded that MK was a figment of her distraught mind?

And why would Bharat want to keep this as such a guarded

secret, so much so that a well-planned basement was there to house these paintings and God knows what else? What were all those drawings about? Why were other persons resembling MK also figuring in that series? She asked herself: *'Had MK been here? Did Sachin know? Why did Sachin bring her to the basement?'*

She awoke from her reverie with a start. Where was Sachin? Then she recalled that he had followed her to the bed. As she got up, she could feel how tense her body had become.

Sachin entered the room at the same time. 'You Ok?'

'Sachin, I...'

'What happened? I was really scared. You were trembling.'

Leela smiled weakly and pulled Sachin down to sit next to her. 'I'm sorry love.'

'No sorry. You were crying – *you!*'

'Why? Can't I cry?'

'No. You're the strong one.'

Leela took a deep breath. 'I'll tell you what happened, but first I need to know. Why did you take me there? You wanted me to go in. Why not yourself?'

'No Lishi, not me. He can't trust me enough.'

'How's that?'

'I discovered it by accident. After that I have been to his room many times, but it was impossible to tell that there was a chamber below. No windows; no ventilator. God knows what's there? Now you tell me.'

'But you never tried to find out?'

'From outside, yes. I did try. Found nothing. But...'

'Yes?'

'If he doesn't want me to know, why should I bother? It hurts me even now.'

'Then why did you tell me? Or show me this hideout?'

'You're different, Lishi. You can break all rules. Baba loves you more than himself.'

'I'm not sure if he will forgive me for being there. He never told me about it either, just like you. This was a mistake. I shouldn't have gone down.'

'But what did you see there?'

Leela took a deep breath again and closed her eyes. Sachin waited with bated breath, but no words came forth. Minutes passed.

Sachin could not sit still, and started tapping a rhythm on his knees. Then he burst forth, 'Lishi?'

Leela opened her eyes. She was looking lost again. 'Sach, ninety-nine percent of what was there was the usual: books, music, files with medical cases, design concepts, some relics from his activist days... and...'

Sachin asked impatiently, 'Tell me the one per cent that zapped you.'

Leela looked at Sachin for a long time, and then she stretched out and tousled his curly hair lovingly. 'Yes, I will finally, but...'

'But not now! Whyyyy?'

'Before I do that, I need to confront Bhai, because what I found also concerns me.'

'You?'

'Yes, that's my shock. You can't even guess, so I beg you, I really beg you to have some patience. I promise I will tell you, but *after* Bhai explains just what is going on.'

Sachin looked at her, up at the ceiling and then banged the bed with his palm in a display of rare anger.

'You too? Why can't you trust me?'

'Why can't you press a 200 kg weight right away? Why? Because you have to train your body to handle this. You saw how I took it.'

Sachin slumped down at her feet and put his head on her lap. '*Maafi*. This is one code I can't imagine. If it can crash you, it must be awesome.'

'For once I agree with this much abused word – awesome. I can't imagine what and why Bhai is hiding under his feet. So shall we both wait?'

'Yeah. We'll checkmate him together.'

'When is he due?'

'No idea. The Panch are waiting for him too.'

'But where is he right now? Don't these people know?'

Sachin rolled his eyes and started whirling like a madman. Leela burst into laughter, and that is how Kaushalya found them when she announced dinner.

THIRTY TWO

Meanwhile, after landing in Pune, Bharat followed DIG Qureshi's parting instructions to avoid the huge press presence there. Pune was a small airport, and being an Air Force Base at the same time, the security set-up was stringent. So an Air Force car picked up Bharat from the tarmac itself and drove off with him. It made a halt for a few seconds behind a shielded security cabin, where Bharat was quickly transferred to a private car, while a second person dressed in near identical clothes took his place. The media personnel chased the Air Force car, while the private car with Bharat took a different route to the Bengaluru highway.

Bharat looked around. Apart from the driver, there were two other people in this car. Umesh was known to him as a social worker close to Srinivasan. The lady, Tanvi, was introduced to him as a media consultant who was helping the fledgling Detox movement.

Tanvi said she had a few questions for him while they were on the road. 'Fire away', said Bharat.

Tanvi started off by asking him to expound his views about politics and politicians. Bharat repeated that no political entity in India held out hope for the future. They all lived opposed to natural law, so they never adopted steps which would make the masses live in moderation. These were desperate times, when people in many interior pockets had been left to their own devices to work almost like a parallel administration. This is why people were refusing to pay taxes.

Tanvi mentioned the common accusation against him was that such movements were anarchic and would bring even what little existing civic administration was there to a grinding halt. Bharat agreed that these movements had borrowed only limited parts that suited their needs from his earlier thinking. Prithak Ghati's experience could not be applied verbatim elsewhere. PG had been extremely lucky in having secured help from his friends, without which their whole progress could have collapsed. Then the Panchayat was atypical in many ways. But while he did not feel responsible for the present situation, he would not step in to suggest course corrections. People had to stumble and rise again in order to find their own way.

However, Bharat reiterated that while people could stop financing their own looters, most important was to prepare for rebuilding from scratch after a war involving a HEMP or chemical attack. This was almost inevitable.

Tanvi prodded him: Were his fears of a war with China unfounded? Bharat was quick to point out that he had nothing against the Chinese as a people. In fact there were regular Chinese delegations of yoga enthusiasts who visited Prithak Ghati twice a year. He had great regard for their emphasis on self reliance, sense of discipline and political shrewdness.

But as a nation, the Chinese polity had played havoc with nature on an unprecedented scale, far more than India. It had manipulated its citizens lives, which had left millions dead during their reform movements. This was a nation which had the highest levels of corruption among its top officials and communist party bigwigs. It condoned and protected terrorists in Pakistan, and was now ensnaring many smaller nations into debt traps. Witness how they took possession of Hambantota Port by sucking Sri Lanka into indebtedness. War was the only way for all these totalitarian powers to stave off domestic unrest.

But war or not, living in balance with nature was the way he had found best. So many innovators were providing Prithak Ghati with options which made life better. Every new invention or idea either improved health or living essentials, not just cosmetic comforts.

Umesh asked, 'But won't returning to products with long shelf life slow down growth for many enterprises and create unemployment?'

Bharat answered, 'Yes, possibly in the short run. But this is exactly the poison of the demand concepts. Create and feed ever growing and changing consumer demand. Fast turnovers; booming exports. Quick firing economic growth models lasting a few years at best... all assuming that the raw material is available forever, and that the waste can be perpetually recycled or dumped somewhere without damaging the environment irrevocably. And yet each generation screams: "Why should *we* practice prudence and pay for our elders mistakes? We want it all now."'

Tanvi quizzed him, 'Sir, you are seen as anti development; anti science...'

Bharat shrugged. 'Please note: In PG among other things our scientist doctors are treating neurodegenerative diseases in advanced stages; Parkinson's, Alzheimer's and so on – often with pioneering genetic therapies from their urban Labs. This is pro science – yes? But even for them, this genetic stuff is only an interim, emergency measure. Our scientists admit that they need to use technology to solve the health problems that such a technology driven world is throwing up. Do we have to 'fix' our brains to adjust to this technological society? Your futurists have no real answers. *Is this development?*

'So, balanced living remains our focus. This is the essential way people remain healthy here because they are at peace with their drug free lives.'

Tanvi asked him, 'Do you think your views will be embraced by many enthusiasts?'

'No.'

'No?'

'No. I talked about spitting, littering and peeing. Tell me, why this continues everywhere – and will continue. The Govt. can impose fines on you, but some other violation will emerge. Why? Because you don't see the cities and streets as your property; nor the farmlands; nor the forests... Yet, mark my words, when from birth you lie on this earth; on the paths in the dhool (dust); dirty yourself in the fields and play in the forests as a child; eat and enjoy the earth's bounty as fruits of worship; *and then stand up to nurture and defend this land as your own – this* is patriotism and not just "Pakistan bashing" on the net. Our children have been given such a raw deal and "must do" goals. Everything except mother earth. *This* is the patriotism we need, and change will come.'

'Sir, Sir! No leader will waste time with such change. Where do parents have the time?'

'So there you are. Today I made a test poser about abstaining from certain foods, and you saw the response, yes? The addictions worldwide run so deep that beyond pressing Likes and signing online petitions, large numbers will not cleanse themselves. Instead, they will be promised another hundred "brilliant" solutions by the politico-intellectual lobbies. Except in small pockets, most will go on doing what they want.'

'Doesn't that make you a pessimist?'

'Not at all. I am a realist, only doing my work, not directing some people's movement. It is always small, motivated groups which are in the forefront of change. Only they matter to me, none else.'

'Doesn't it bother you that the entire political class is so much against you?'

'Ask them why. What have I done? This whole thing was sparked off by non-partisan, desperate people. I had no role. No role whatsoever.'

'But they want you to give a statement disowning what you said earlier.'

'Why should I? I stand by what I said and did over two decades ago, and events have borne this out fully. I have been trying in a small way to create a frugal community, and I'm blessed that over seven thousand people feel the same and act on it. No government can take that away.'

'But Sir, what about the civil disobedience? Do you support this in today's times too? This is almost Gandhian...'

Bharat slapped his forehead lightly in a mock show of exasperation, 'You didn't do your homework. Firstly, modern civil disobedience predates Mohandas Gandhi by almost a century, and has had many other practitioners. Secondly, anybody who is familiar with my early writings knows that I have been intractably opposed to Gandhian thought, though his principal role in bringing awareness of the freedom movement into every remote household is indisputable.'

'But in today's age — a tax boycott...'

'Ok, let someone else suggest a better, more efficient way of self-defence, of starving your tormentors. Desperate times — desperate measures. The polity will not allow you to contest effectively. If you win as an independent, you either join their ways and forget about making changes, or are dog housed. The bureaucracy can smell a real reformist miles away, and will cut him down unless he or she "cooperates". So what do we do? Get raped again and again? Join a class war? Tell me another way to stop this "slaughter".'

'Slaughter? But this is a free country!'

'Free to vote but not to recall? To empower but not to truly monitor? Why are we discussing this? You, you should know all this as a journalist, or are you worried that the embedded media will hound you?'

'Sir, I am not worried. Actually, yes I am, for you, for Prithak Ghati.'

'Yes, we live on borrowed time. I know they will bring us down, but by then we, these seven thousand odd undaunted citizens, will have been burnt into the public consciousness. War is a great leveller, and the country may remember at least one building block after the horror and pain have faded out.'

'Sir, on this no one agrees with you. They all think you have a war phobia and are driving people into a cult thing.'

'I drive no one. Please go on dancing away in Neroland. What are seven thousand people in a nation of over 1.3 billion? Stick to your prognosis and outlook that all is manageable on the borders, and within. Your call. Let us be.'

The car had already entered Prithak Ghati between Bharat's frequent naps and conversations with Tanvi and Umesh. Bharat could immediately sense that the mood in the town had changed. There were many more people huddled in small animated groups. No one noticed Bharat's entry in this nondescript private car.

Once he reached the Habitat, Bharat went straight to the common kitchen to grab a quick bite. He was surprised to find that both Sachin and Leela were missing. Then he went to his room. As soon as he put on the light, he knew someone had entered his 'vault'. Everything was in order, but as a rule, when he slid back the platform, he always put a tiny part of the bed cover inside the joint. Today, this was hanging free, and he never made such an error.

He was walking out to talk to Kaushalya when he noticed a figure sitting in the darkness.

Leela rose into view as the room's light spilled onto her face. Bharat knew at once that she had been 'there'. The dried tears, tormented face and searing reproachful look said it all. He could guess who had allowed Leela access, but this did not matter anymore.

Leela did not speak a word, but her tears were forming again.

He silently pulled her into a hug. She tried to shake him off with a 'No, no...', but her shoulders sagged as she started sobbing. Bharat caressed her head and patted her back till her pent up emotions had been released.

'Trust me, Lili, you will know all the whys and why nots till now...

As it is, I have spoken more since you came than the last ten years put together. A few days more of ventilating, this much I owe you.'

'Bhai, you did the unthinkable in Delhi, but this too begs questions.'

'If I said that what you saw down there – *and* all these days in Prithak Ghati – *and* what I did in Delhi; that these are all connected, you wouldn't understand. Come in anyway.'

Both sat on the low bed, with their backs to the underground entrance, their feet spread out on the floor. Bharat turned to Leela. 'I intended this earlier... that I will take you on a long journey. We will start now, and I will go on over the next days till this journey ends.'

'Your journey?'

'*His* journey. With us as blessed witnesses – to the great journey of the veiled warrior who appeared and vanished again like a firefly. My *Anaam Sant – perhaps your Mahakaal.*'

There was a faint sound. Bharat held a warning finger to his lips, tiptoed to the door and flung it open. Sachin stood there looking like an errant child caught in the act.

Bharat unexpectedly turned stern. 'Sachin! This is not for you, and when it is, I'll... '

Sachin immediately turned back and started dragging himself away. Leela ran after him and held his arm. He had unshed tears in his eyes. Leela's heart went out to this lonely, motherless boy.

Bharat called out to her, 'Lili, I'll freshen up. Five minutes.'

Sachin mumbled, 'Leave me alone.'

'I'm sure there are very good reasons why Bhai kept things from me and you,' whispered Leela.

'Don't console me. It's all about trusting.'

Leela kissed Sachin on his forehead, '*Naa re*. If he could risk hurting me so much by guarding his secrets from *me*, and I am a hard nut, I think he has very good reasons to exclude you. You respect his judgment, yes?'

Sachin nodded silently.

Leela smiled and tousled his hair. 'Then await the light.'

Sachin whispered in a small voice, 'Lishi. Don't ever go away.'

Leela held him close for a long time. As he ambled away, Leela turned back to see that Bharat was already waiting. She grabbed his arm. 'You're tired. We can continue tomorrow.'

'Ok, at the crack of dawn. Can you be up?' Bharat's eyes were twinkling.

They went in again. Bharat leaned back on his bed, while Leela sat on one of the cane chairs.

'Did Sachin show you?'

'Yes, but he said he had never gone down, and that he had discovered the chamber long back.'

'That I know,' said Bharat. He opened his eyes and peered at Leela, 'Did you see it all?'

Leela nodded very faintly, but Bharat missed the gesture. He asked again, 'Yes? Did you?'

'What do you mean by "see it all"? I looked around, saw that generator thing... Oh! What *is* that?'

There was a long pause. Then Bharat leaned forward conspiratorially. 'PG is powered by three such Generator assemblies. Presently confidential.'

'The entire town?' Leela asked incredulously.

'Yup. The Indian inventor died recently after a lifetime of opposition to his ideas and this invention.'

'My God! But when did this get here?'

'Installed two months ago. Will go public when these perform flawlessly and perpetually for at least six months... Tell you more later, Ok?'

Leela let her breath out impatiently. 'And the sketches?'

Bharat's eyes were closing. He was soon fast asleep. Leela turned off the light and went to her room.

She pondered: Here was a town struggling to keep a wonderful way of life alive, and she was distressed about some unknown figure who nobody believed existed. Was he omnipresent in Prithak Ghati too?

Mahakaal had now moved closer to her again with his enduring mystery.

It was at least an hour before sleep came.

PART THREE

MAHAKAAL - THE ESSENCE

THIRTY THREE

Dawn and a pregnant silence brought Leela back to life. She put on her yoga pants and her favourite cream coloured cotton jacket and sauntered out of the room. Bharat was waiting for her and she followed him to a small lawn behind his room, surrounded by flowering trees and a hedge. There was a wooden platform below a frangipani tree with two mats. Bharat had arranged a tray too with a small solar-operated hybrid stove, a case with tea leaves, cups and a small glass kettle. He sat cross-legged on one mat and indicated the other to her. She followed his lead and tried to concentrate on her breath as she lost herself in thoughts that finally gave way to emptiness.

After a while, Leela came out of her reverie and brewed their favourite jasmine tea.

Bharat's eyes were still closed as he started speaking. His voice sounded far away, matter-of-fact but gradually it became suffused with deep feeling.

'My first encounter with Santji was very ordinary. Not like yours with Mahakaal, which was full of drama and media attention.

'One day I got an emergency call from Shivdadu. He had an old INA colleague who was ill in Kanpur. Remember Hrishi Da? Hrishikesh Bhattacharya?'

'Oh, you mean the sports Instructor you used to tell me stories about?'

'Correct. When he was taken ill at Kanpur station and hospitalized, I got involved.'

'How's that?'

'I was studying in the IIT in the same city. On Shivdadu's

bidding I went and looked after Hrishida. After three days, when he was discharged, he requested me to accompany him to Ayodhya. I was curious as to how a no-nonsense person like him had suddenly turned religious, but I went along anyway.

'Even there, his behaviour struck me as odd. He asked me to escort him to a particular lane, and then insisted on carrying on by himself. He wanted me to come back to the same spot after a couple of hours to pick him up. I offered to support him further, but he was resolute in his refusal.

'He painfully walked into another lane with a walking stick for support, and then disappeared. When I returned to the spot after the promised two hours, I found the old man waiting there, but looking changed and fired with energy.'

'After doing what?' said Leela.

Bharat frowned at Leela's impatience. She silently folded her hands in a rueful manner. Bharat took a sip of the fragrant tea and continued, 'Hrishida repeated the same routine twice within the next one year, and each time I took him to Ayodhya. On his third visit, he was struggling to even stand properly. This time he suddenly changed his routine. He took me to an enclosure in the compound of an old temple, Lucknowa Hata. This was the first time he mentioned that he had a Guru who was extremely choosy about who enters his space. Hrishida grabbed my hand and made me swear that I would tell no one about this address, and that he had taken his Guru's express permission to bring me to this compound. He had made this trip only to ensure that I was introduced to this Guru directly. I asked him why he wanted to introduce me, but he did not answer.'

Bharat continued, 'We were allowed in by an old lady who looked me up and down. A mattress was laid along a wall in the arched enclosure, covered with white bed covers. I was asked to sit there while Hrishida struggled on his walking stick towards a corner and sat on a chair that the old lady had placed for him outside a room.

'I was sitting at quite a distance and all I could see was Hrishida joining his hands, offering *pronams* to someone in that room. I was puzzled. Why was his Guru not calling him in? It was quite warm and Hrishida was a sick man. And even in the day, there were plenty of mosquitoes.

'Meanwhile, the old lady brought us tea and snacks. I could see Hrishida point towards me and say something, but I could not hear the person whom he was talking to. It was too far away.

'After about half an hour, Hrishida beckoned to me to come forward. I went and stood there in front of a door which was open, but a thick cinnamon coloured curtain blocked the view of the interiors. Hrishida said in broken Hindi, "*Yehi hai* Bharat, *jinke baare mein maine aapko bataya tha. Shiv kaa potaa.* You know I have already cleared this boy's visit with Pobitroda."

'Then there was silence.'

'Silence?' said Leela, 'No one responded?'

'No one. I got the instinctive feeling that I was being scrutinized from behind that curtain. Then Hrishida requested me to go back to the mattress. I walked away, but I still recall that for no apparent reason I had goose pimples all over my body. Hrishida soon got up with much effort and indicated that we were to leave. So I asked him about the introduction. He smiled and said that it was done.

'But his last injunction was the strangest; that I was to come back here in exactly two months. In case he himself was not available, I would have to come alone. Again, the strict instruction was not to talk about this to anyone, or else the way in for me would be barred forever. Further, I was told that it was his Guru who would always direct any talk, not me.

'A month later, we heard that Hrishida had passed away peacefully in his sleep. He had earlier written to Shivdadu thanking him for the help provided, and that I should follow his advice.

'When the time came, I found myself in Ayodhya, and the suspense started at the station itself. I hailed a rickshaw and when I mentioned the address, the rickshaw driver took a good look at me and said: "So you are going to the *Pardeh Wale Baba*?" I learnt that this was some strange Baba who was never seen by anyone and who always spoke from behind a curtain.'

'Hang on,' said Leela, 'Which year was this?'

'1980. A summer evening. It was very hot. When I knocked on the door, the same old lady behind the door first asked me to identify myself. As instructed earlier by Hrishida, I put a chit with my name under the door. Then the door creaked open a bit and she peeped at me. I was let in and the door was locked immediately. It was back to the same mattress for me, while the lady went to a tiny shed to resume her cooking.

'I got up and strolled around, taking a closer look at that room. It was a part of a large run down hall and I could actually walk around it. That's when I got a real shock. The room had two windows which were sealed off by thick cardboard painted in black and nailed into the wooden frames from outside to prevent the slightest light from entering inside. How could he survive this? In that extreme heat or cold with severe power outages... how?

'The old lady came back after a while and motioned to me to sit down on the chair. As if on cue, the door to the room opened from within. There was the same cinnamon-coloured curtain separating the outside world from the inhabitant. The booming voice which addressed me in Hindi sounded like that of an Army Commandant, "Shivprasad *ke pote* – Bharat?"

'My hair was almost standing on its end, but I managed to mumble a "Namaste". Then I told him that Shivdadu had never mentioned anything about him so far. He answered, "I knew him in 1944 when he fought during our advance into Nagaland. But that was before I became a Sanyasi. He doesn't know my present *identity*."

'Lili, those days I loved getting into a tautological discussion like this potential one on "identity", but I noticed that something strange was happening. There was such power and positive radiation in that voice, it was almost hypnotic. I kept quiet.

'The voice continued, "Hrishi lived a life celebrating Jai Hind till his last breath, much like Shiv is doing even now."

'I thought I heard a sigh. There was a brief silence. Then he asked, "You want to work only as a Civil Engineer or do you want to study medicine as well? Or will you formally study Economics now?"

'I was stunned. Till then, I had not spoken to anyone about my interest in studying Medicine or Economics. I could not afford the same and had given up all thoughts regarding this till my engineering course was over. How could a man holed up in a remote place know all this including the choices facing me?

'At that time I answered, "I wish I could do both, but I have no idea how."

'"You will have to create your own opportunity. *Ekla cholo re.*"

'When he uttered the last three words, it was with a perfect Bengali pronunciation. I pondered: was he a Bengali? Then why did he speak only in Hindi? I did not ask him anything and just replied, "Yes Baba."

'"I am no Baba. You can call me Anaam Sant – Santji." The voice stopped speaking for a moment before continuing, "In medicine or in civil engineering, you will need a thorough knowledge of our own medicinal traditions as well as many classical building practices in such a vast country, many of which can be adopted."

'I thought to myself: God! Is this another ritualistic Baba selling me spurious "non scientific" ideas as alternative medicine? So I asked, "Our medical traditions and building practices – in preference to?"'

'The voice came as a whiplash, "Is that what I said? Or suggested?"

'"No Santji."

"'Then retain focus! Acquire thorough knowledge about the *real* functioning of the human body; learn which medical traditions understand the integration of the various layers of human existence and help maintain balance. You are quite ignorant."

'I slowly got into a discussion about medicine, healing systems and so on. After hardly twenty minutes or so, maybe more because I never looked at my watch, I was so astonished by his unbelievable knowledge of all these systems of treatment that the wind was out of my sails for good! I mean he would just touch on any one medicinal system – ANY – and describe its theory and practice with such astounding detail and mastery, such precision that... I felt like a pygmy in front of a mammoth giant.

'As the talk switched to other topics, my self-allotted one hour had long gone by. I had lost all sense of time. From civil engineering, latest construction technology, road building, various dam construction methods and their maintenance; to nuclear plants; to dockyards; to simple dwellings in an organic habitat... each subject was expounded with stunning mastery, micro detailing and... *and a complete lack of arrogance*. Here was an unknown and mysterious Sadhu behind a curtain who was opening my mind to an energy and sense of life which I had never known to exist till then.

'In the meantime, the old lady, whom he addressed as Jagadamba, had even cooked a meal at Santji's behest. When I commented on her wonderful gastronomical skills, the topic turned to cooking and food. Santji reeled off first hand anecdotes of meals he had enjoyed from all over Europe, China, Russia, Burma and Vietnam. All these stories were interspersed with details about each tradition and how they had evolved. In many cases he even pointed out Indian influences. He remarked that our ignorance was the result of a systematic effort by the white man and their Brown Sahib cohorts to distort the history books and obliterate these facts overtime.

'Then suddenly he stopped and said, "It is time for my *Sadhana*.

218

I will retire now."

By that time, slowly I had observed a change in myself. I realized that I did not want to leave at all. And I had already been there for almost six hours.

'I said, "Santji, I feel blessed to have been with you, that you allowed me this time. Can I come again?"

'Santji replied gravely, "Note two things. First, write to my disciple Dr Mishra here. Jagadamba will give you his postal address. I will let you know when you may come. Second and more important. Not a word about me or your visit is to be discussed with anyone. If you do, I will know."

'I made bold to ask, "When I go back, should I not tell even Shivdadu about you?"

'"You will not tell anyone about me. Anyone. This is an oath which you will take."

'I offered my *pronams* to him. The old lady gave me a Faizabad address on a chit and impassively let me out. The door closed again.

It was pitch dark outside, around 2 am. There were no people on the streets, and no street lights either. It was ghostly and really unbelievable that a strange person of such phenomenal abilities was sitting in this dingy place incognito. Who was he before he renounced his previous identity? How did he know Shivdadu? The questions crowded my mind.

'I somehow found a Dharamshala at that unearthly hour in Ayodhya, but I could not sleep. I had known sadhus who could predict your past and also had powers of clairvoyance. Both Sarasdida and Shivdadu had trained me not to be overawed by this. They always said that this was a low level *siddhi*, and had little to do with true self-realization. But this evening was nothing like what I had ever... *ever* experienced. There was no way he could be called a typical sadhu. This was just one part of the real person, but again – who was he? How did he land up here, in this dusty town in Uttar Pradesh?

'I kept thinking: Why the curtain? And that sealed-off dark room? Was he a so-called truly realized soul, the likes of whom I had never met till then?

'The "whys" were never ending.'

'Halt!' said Leela, as Bharat opened his eyes. She had been listening mesmerized the whole time. 'What is the connection between this Sant you met and MK? Three of your sketches resemble the man I met. Is my "Mahakaal" the same as your Santji?'

'Let's go back to the house,' said Bharat. The sun had risen some time ago and the rays now caressed them through the leaves.

He picked up the mats and continued, 'Lili, I have no notion as to how Santji could also be your MK, but please hold your horses. If you will keep questioning at each step, I can't relate it all in a flow.'

Leela clamped her hand across her mouth. They sat down on the cane chairs in the verandah. Firdaus brought them fresh cups of tea. Sachin was not up as yet. For a while, both remained silent.

'After my third visit, I had already heard the whispered local belief that this was Subhas Bose living undercover. It defied all logic. Why would Netaji be in "hiding" in this nondescript place? This was totally out of character. But all the whys in my mind dissolved in his presence.'

Leela whispered, 'Same with me.'

Bharat continued, 'Anyway, after a month or so I wrote to that Faizabad address, asking Santji if I could come on a particular day. Almost three weeks later, I got a reply via postcard signed in Hindi, blessing me and stating that I could "go ahead with my plans". So my second visit came about. A third followed. Then there was a gap when he fell and broke his femur bone and was not in a position to grant me such sessions. Apart from this gap, my visits went on fairly regularly and continued right till July 1985, when Santji told me not to come again.'

'How many times did you go there?' asked Leela.

'I think ten times. In hindsight, I was incredibly lucky because most of his followers from Bengal visited him ten times in twelve years.' Bharat paused and then added, 'Coincidentally, this period also tallied with the turbulence in my relationship with Urvi, till the point when she vanished from my life.'

'Did these two experiences impact each other?' asked Leela.

'Maybe so. She could sense that I was no longer the same. It was like Urvi could not log in to me anymore, because the password had changed.'

'You never told her about Santji?' asked Leela.

'Lili, if this man told you not to speak about him to anyone, that NO jumped at you if even a small thought arose to do this. No to even Ma, Shivdadu or Sarasdida. Don't forget: I had taken an oath.'

'It was NO about telling me later, when I was an adult.' said Leela with a smile.

'Yes, you too. The idea to share this with you later came up more than once, and I watched it getting shot down. Maybe at that point Santji was like a father I never had.'

'Was there ever any hint as to who he was?'

'Never any direct hint, but on rare occasions when we discussed India's pre-independence history... then he would let fly with utterances like: "When this body met..."'

Leela jerked back. 'This body? Meaning?'

'He said it in Hindi: "Yeh shareer" – This body. That is how Santji referred to himself – in the third person – "this body met Hitler"... or...don't interrupt ... "when Maulana Azad said this"...or "got a box of cigars from Mussolini..."'

Leela jumped up. 'Whattttt?! You mean he actually uttered these names as if he had met them?'

'Sit down. You forget that by then I had heard rumours from

locals about Santji actually being Subhas Bose. Of course it produced a tremendous feeling of excitement in me, but...'

'But?'

'Everytime I visited him, I lost the focus to ask if he was Netaji, even if I had resolved to do so. I was overwhelmed by the sheer affection which this person showered on me.'

'You never saw him even once?'

'I'll come to that soon. On one of my visits I had carried four LPs for him: bhajans by Dilip Kumar Roy and sitar LP's by Ravi Shankar and Vilayat Khan.'

'He even had a system to play vinyls?'

'I suppose so, but this happened at a different location. After his fall, he had recovered very slowly to progress to a wheelchair. By Oct 1982 he had been shifted from Ayodhya to Ram Bhavan in Faizabad by his physician Dr Mishra. Santji's health had deteriorated a lot and his meals too were coming from Dr Mishra's household.

'In Ram Bhavan there was a two room segment where he stayed. An outer room was separated from his own room by a grilled window between the rooms. I sat next to this window whenever I went to meet him. It had the same heavy curtain, and Santji would be seated on the other side.'

'What kind of a house was this? Was it also in a temple compound?'

'No, it was in fact an outhouse at the back of a bungalow. No one could see it from the main road. The most amazing part was that this outhouse flanked the Dogra Regiment's compound and had a common wall cordoned off by barbed wire fencing. How such a secretive person could stay right next to an army property; this remains a real mystery for me.'

Leela sat up. 'Bhai, you were talking about the LPs you were carrying.

'Yes. I had forgotten about these LPs, when he gently asked if I had got them. So I apologized and started to search in my baggage in the darkness.'

'Huh?'

'There was a power failure. Normally there was a candle and matches on my side, or Jagadamba (Saraswati Devi) would come with a lit candle.

'It was pitch dark and very quiet. I suspect Saraswati Devi was not around. So I found the LPs and passed them to him from under the curtain through a gap in the grill. What I experienced next is burned into my memory forever.'

Bharat took a pause, while Leela hung on to her breath.

'There was no sound of any light switch or device being turned on. Two completely focused glows, like beams of light, *slowly* appeared across the curtain. They moved from left to right, as if reading the sleeve notes on the LPs. Actually these were more like minute dots of light clustered together, like we see animated beams in films today – but *not* a lamp or torchlight.

'To confirm my thoughts, Santji said: "There are nice photos in the artwork. And... and such profound Ragas. Some of my favourites."'

Bharat continued in a tight voice, 'I could not speak. The two beams were coming from Santji, *exactly where his eyes would be*. Then they faded away. *Note – faded away. Not switched off.*

'Then he asked me to sing one of his favourite bhajans.'

'He knew that you sang too?'

'He knew everything. Some of my best moments with him were spent in discussing music. So I sang like never before, and I heard him cry on the other side. It was this Bengali folk song...'

'He – *he* cried?'

Bharat looked sternly at Leela. 'What did you think? Such people

223

cannot cry? They only produce ash or rosogullas, or jump up and down on podiums to initiate you into enlightenment?

'He told me once: when we live in this gross body, it will suffer like all others. Suffering via the five senses is inescapable – and Santji suffered immensely throughout his life.'

Leela raised herself to look into Bharat's eyes, 'So you never saw him?'

'I haven't finished the saga,' Bharat said, his hands on his knees, 'However, I better get going now. Let's continue tonight.'

The hens were already clucking and a variety of bird calls filled the air.

As Bharat glanced towards the gate, he paused in an odd manner. Leela sensed that something was amiss. She looked up. There were at least four cars with Press people and OB vans waiting. No wonder the dogs were barking now.

'My day just got longer,' said Bharat.

'You won't relish this.'

'Not one bit.'

'Why did you have to go on stage to speak, even if Avi had diverted you there?'

Bharat looked at Leela squarely and replied, 'Because "he" was there.'

Leela could not speak for a while and then she let out a hoarse whisper, 'Whatttt?!'

'Yes Lili. Right there in that crowd. He signalled silently that I should not step away.'

'This Baba had passed away in 1985, so how could he be there?'

Bharat tapped Leela's forehead playfully, 'I'll explain that later when we continue.'

THIRTY FOUR

At that time nobody had any inkling about the media frenzy which was about to be unleashed. The previous day's rally had lit the fire. The breakfast news that morning carried excerpts of Bharat's speech and the surreptitious interview in the car. The fire now threatened to become an inferno.

The edited snippets were lampooned by several political heavyweights and intellectuals. But this had the opposite effect. More and more people came to know about Prithak Ghati, the unique Panchayat and Bharat and swayed towards him. The Political Class was furious that this small-time civil engineer and 'village' doctor could dare to ask people to boycott political parties and effectively call them rapists. But to their chagrin, even the repeated highlighting of Bharat's comments criticizing the public at large did not swing the opinion against him. In swiftly growing numbers, there was self-introspection and appreciation for a person who had spoken the blunt truth, who was pro-technology and yet proposed that a major self correction be performed by the present generation. The only points on which most people were divided were on his diet standpoint and his earlier prediction of a war involving China and Pakistan. Bharat was faulted for having a war phobia, and for 'pushing' a small village-town of seven thousand people into believing such a remote possibility.

There was certainly a major pause in the momentum. A sizeable number of people stopped following Bharat or Prithak Ghati and dropped out of the Detox movement, but many more people were fired up to join the stir as new enthusiasts for Mother India. However, Bharat's Detox India campaigner friends had no pointer as to what to do next. For them, 'self discipline' and de-addiction was no plan of action at all.

Sensing this opening, several TV channels and online forums brought in a range of experts to prove how idiotic and farfetched was this de-addiction mode, when people needed economic betterment. Bharat had no solutions to provide except so called discipline. And his war mongering was ridiculous, at a time when the relationship with China was on the mend. Ergo, Bharat's opinion in general too counted for nothing.

The relentless coverage following Bharat's shock public appearance started rapidly tapering off. It was all happening exactly as predicted by R. Subramaniam. The strategic game players from the political arena seemed to have stalled the Detox movement at last.

When Bharat emerged from the farm he was besieged by some media personnel, but he firmly refused to comment. He needed to speak to the Panch, who along with Heli Sir, Dr Mancrop and many others were waiting at the community hall. Everyone was worried about the aftermath of this sudden national attention.

The impassive members of the Panch called for a town meeting the next day. Bharat left the Hall and hopped onto a mobike to attend to a patient sixty km away.

It was night when he returned home. Leela was in her room revising her notes on MK when she was called for an early dinner. Bharat told them that just one day of public attention was already weighing on his nerves, and yet he knew this was to be his karma.

'Why is it your karma?' asked Sachin, scowling when he got no reply.

'Let's have a cookout,' said Bharat, changing the subject.

The men folk got the fire ready in the area allocated for bonfires outside. A wholesome *Khichuri* and a Bengali style *Labra Torkari* or mixed vegetable was the menu. Leela baked the home made papads and Sachin roasted some potatoes. They all ate outside under the stars on banana leaves.

'This is heaven,' sighed Leela.

Everyone soon retired for the day, including Sachin. Some late night movie started running on the small TV in the workers cottages. Sachin's room was soon dark.

Leela slowly reclined on the mat, her cheek cupped in her palm. 'Tell me Bhai – did you finally see him?'

'Well yes. This was in July 1985, when I sat across the curtain talking to Santji. My last visit.'

Bharat paused to recollect, while Leela waited impatiently.

'On one of my previous trips Santji had been discussing music with me, and how *alaps* actually evolved from mantra chanting. He had shown me how to chant AUM properly so that it would release curative energies and resonate the pineal gland, lifting me to a higher consciousness. During my last visit, he introduced me to the seven *beej* mantras. I still practice these and several kriyas, just as he had taught me.'

Bharat leaned back on the wooden platform. 'These mantras and discussions were meant to prepare me for a future full of setbacks and whatever else life could throw at me. *Santji stressed that the real contributors to the human civilization would always work behind the scenes, and would never get known, or at best remain little known.*

'He said, "Just look at how women have silently sustained life. They are the real all-round creators, managing a daily punishing work schedule like a smooth multi-geared power structure. It is because of them that the world is still afloat."'

Leela looked up puzzled. 'What was the context for all this talk?'

Bharat shrugged, 'I think by inference, Urvi, though I never talked about her. Through his "second sight", he knew about the struggle that Urvi was going through. That day I had gone to Faizabad after wrangling with her over her poor time management. So Santji scolded me and pulled at this string. That's how the subject of women came up.'

'Wait a minute,' Leela made him halt the narration, 'Your String

227

exercise…'

'Is not mine. This is what Santji would do effortlessly all the time, pull at any string within the fabric of *any* topic, and gradually trace back clinically, till each time the same axiomatic truths of life stood waiting for me to reaffirm. That day he used this string and talked about women working silently, unrewarded and yet sustaining life as we know it – and finally affirming karma.

'Karma Lili – the key. He said reincarnation was an intrinsic, essential aspect of karma. He also believed that the human being was a direct creation, and did not evolve via the evolutionary ladder from other species. Nor did he accept that all men are created equal.

'When I argued that all this was unscientific, he pulled me up. He said: "I warn you to forget all this imposed western educational brainwashing, these hackneyed notions of what is unscientific. Later you will have no choice but to accept reincarnation and karma as stark truths. This is action – reaction, exactly and unfailingly squaring out in life, whether in this one or another."'

Leela frowned and inclined her head.

'Santji continued: "Understand karma. Having been born as a human being, automatically you are driven by a karmic seed in your DNA, the DNA which merges every time into the soul's infinite memory at death as a carryover. Through thousands of births, all your habits which you now keep repeating are indicative of karmic arrears stored in your karmic seed. These tendencies will *never* leave you unless you face them like a man and overcome them by human action."'

Bharat paused and continued, 'I recall replying in dejection: "Why is humanity born into such karmic debt, even if self-created, of which it has no real awareness?"

'Santji replied softly: "Man initially was in a state of eternal equipoise and at peace with his being. Then, *he or she wanted to expand, to experience the limits of this individuality.* Consequently he started his karmic journey, accumulating more and more diverse experiences during successive lives in his DNA, in one spiral after another. He *willingly* created his own web and lost himself in that web, right up to today's complex and technology driven world. But in his deepest recesses, he senses his original *paramanand* (blissful) state of equilibrium. He searches desperately for a way to return to that blissful state. This is what you are doing, cleansing your karmic debt to have the *real yo*u emerge.'"

Leela could not restrain herself. 'Bhai, have you changed your ideas about afterlife? Can't imagine that you listened to such tired clichés about karma without a murmur.'

Bharat replied easily, 'We are already at a stage today where physicists from the Max Planck Institutes in Germany agree that when the body dies, the brain "uploads" its Data in the "spiritual" quantum field. Our consciousness lives on. These scientists say that in the quantum world...'

Leela made a face. 'Frankly, this is over the top for me. Hope it's not some *Bakwaas* pseudo science. But yes, I concede that after deriding astrology as a superstition, I came across the controversial new science of astrobiology triggered by Michel Gauquelin who found that typical human personalities and the position of the planets at birth *are* intimately related *and* confirmed by statistical evidence. But Bhai, does science itself also talk about afterlife; about character traits or unexplained memories becoming a part of a "carry over" DNA?'

Bharat slapped his index finger on his palm, 'You should look up the research from Dr Stuart Hameroff and Physicist Roger Penrose, who found via their quantum theory of consciousness that our so called "souls" are contained inside protein based structures called microtubules which live within our brain cells and which carry quantum information stored at a sub-atomic level. When a person dies, this quantum information is released from the microtubules into the universe and can exist indefinitely as this "soul". They say that these "souls" could have existed since the very beginning of time itself.

'Tell me, are we closer now? Karmic seed and quantum information? Isn't this only a short step from what Santji said about afterlife? In fact to my mind this appears inspired from Advaita. I told you already that science always validates, but it could take time – yes?'

Leela took a long breath and shrugged, 'Speculative stuff. You sound like a New Age Guru.'

Bharat sighed and closed his eyes, 'Ok, but hear Santji out. He said, "Remember the saying: Pulled down by habit? Negative desires and habits impact you much more, because it is like being helplessly adrift on a river with a strong current flowing *downstream*, pulled by the gravitational forces and thrown on any bank. Eventually you remain stuck in the muck, life after life. To break free, you need to summon your life force and pull yourself up to the positive plane; to travel upstream.

'Santji told me fondly: "For now, *you* strive to create small enclaves in as many pockets in the country as you can, where man can break free and realize his immense capabilities. The Divine Mother will look after you."'

Bharat clenched his fists and took a deep breath. 'At that moment, a great surge arose within me, that my life's mission was now reconfirmed. And then it happened.'

Leela thumped her hand on the bed, 'What happened?'

Bharat leaned back against the wall with his eyes closed. 'Till then I had been unaware that there was a strong breeze blowing outside. Since no one ever came at night to this part of the compound, the windows to the section where guests like me sat had been left partly open to provide relief from the searing heat. This was July and the rains had not yet arrived in North India.

'Suddenly a gust of air blew the curtain to one side. Lili, I saw him. He was speaking with his eyes closed, and as the waving curtain brushed past his face, his eyes opened.' Bharat paused for a long time and then continued dreamily, 'I can never forget. *Never.* There was such a strong – actually I don't have a word for it – *such an ethereal glow in those eyes*, I was forced to close my own eyes because I could not withstand that luminosity. No exaggeration.'

'And then?'

'That visage was gone in an instant, as the curtain returned to its resting place. He continued telling me small details about how these village set-ups should be structured, but my consciousness was drunk with his eyes, that gaze.

'Then abruptly he said that it was time for him to retire for his meditation. It was already unusually late. I got up and wanted to know if I could come again in two months. Instead, I heard his last words in that Faizabad home: "Don't come here again. Wait for my contact. Have faith... I am always with you."'

Brother and sister sat silently for a while. Leela whispered, 'What did he look like?'

Bharat did not reply immediately. His eyes closed again. 'An aged person with a much younger face. Bald. Fair. But that gaze... it penetrated you.'

'Did he really resemble Subhas Bose?'

'Can't say one hundred percent. I never saw Netaji alive pre-1945. That was before I was born. I only saw his photos, and a few film clips. But yes, the parting in his teeth, the jaw and head structure... yes there was great resemblance, though he had a white beard. Even in that one glimpse, I saw that there were several *Panjikas (Bengali Astronomical almanac)* behind him, though he always spoke in Hindi and English to me. He knew Bengali for sure.'

Leela was still bursting with questions but Bharat got up, indicating that the session was over. It was already late. Leela motioned that she wanted to sit for a while under the stars. She lingered there in silence, still enveloped by 'his' eyes – 'that luminous gaze which penetrated and enthralled you'.

THIRTY FIVE

The morning saw the whole town moving to the Chaupal (Community Centre) for the meeting. Leela attended it as a guest, wearing her dark glasses and a long scarf. It took just thirty minutes to decide their future. PC Uncle and then Machenda stood on the raised platform and emotionally upbraided Bharat in strong terms. In his past years, he had been evicted four times from different locations, and so many of his evictors had regretted and joined him here. How could Bharat even think that this town would not defend him? They would fight any force which targeted their pioneer to the last man.'

Bharat wanted to reply but the residents refused to listen to him: 'We have heard you for over ten years. Now you hear us.'

Especially vocal were the displaced labour and farm worker class who had come here from remote places. These were all locations where Bharat had worked earlier on corruption ridden projects and left in disgust, from Lalmatiya and Jogikhura in erstwhile undivided Bihar (present Jharkhand), to Chikapur, Koraput and Bolangir in Orissa, and even Sarguja in Chattisgarh. They had faced this kind of outside pressure for generations, and were willing to face it again. But this time they would not yield.

One resident added that now the cyber world was besieged by professional trollers who worked for the very forces who were opposed to Bharat. Prithak Ghati needed real help to counter such insidious strategies to run them down.

Sachin stood up and proclaimed, 'I can handle it.' Bharat and Leela pulled him down, but he stood up again in a determined manner. Amidst wild clapping, Birbal Kaka declared that they would find a professional group from among their well-wishers to counter the misinformation campaign.

He said, 'This is actually our moment of glory. Many others want to try our ways in their environment, without politicians and money lenders meddling in the process.'

Once the meeting was over, residents were willing to talk to the media. They expressed distrust for all political groups and their affiliates who promised change through short-cut economic measures. 'We don't need such people – get off our backs' was Heli Sir's refrain, seconded by the migrant labour who were rooted and happy to be in Prithak Ghati.

Sachin was missing through the day, busy with school work. When he joined them for dinner, he was distinctly off-colour. A soft flute recital was playing in the background. Sachin got up and switched it off. After a while Bharat quietly turned it on again. Immediately Sachin announced in a solemn voice, 'Eating is a process of meditation and needs no distractions.'

Leela and Sonichari started giggling. Sachin first asked what was so funny and then he took his half-eaten plate with him and stomped off to his room.

Both Bharat and Leela sensed that the boy was feeling bottled up. They coaxed him into joining them for a walk. Sachin was now peaceful and one with the night. The soft orchestra from the small crickets was often drowned by the sporadic cannon fire from the giant crickets. Fireflies would appear and disappear into the void, adding colour and mystery to the darkness. The neutered street dogs would often walk with them silently and step away when their territory was over and the next dog kingdom announced itself through their advance scout's barking.

It was close to New Moon. Many other people were taking a stroll too. By amazing discipline, no one stopped to ask Bharat questions but only waved and walked on, knowing that he needed his peace.

After some time they reached a crest overlooking a stream that danced over and around the ragged rocks. Bharat was humming a refrain. He looked at Leela and Sachin sitting together in the darkness and then sang a soft 'nom tom' prayer in the raga Kaushiki. The quietude was overwhelming.

When they reached home, it was close to midnight. Sachin was half asleep and went to his room. Leela was still full of questions about Netaji's probable afterlife. Bharat wanted to call it a day, but Leela cajoled him into having a 'mini' discussion before retiring. She made her way to the lawn again and Bharat soon joined her with a pot of jasmine tea.

Leela took off immediately. 'I kept thinking about Santji's looks the whole day. I also checked on the net. On one hand Gumnami Baba had appeared to others as a faqir or a monk. Like you, those few who actually saw him also claimed that he resembled Netaji.

'Then there are photos from the Tashkent meeting of our then Prime Minister Lal Bahadur Shastri with Pakistan's President Ayub Khan in 1966, which supposedly show Netaji present there in disguise. How? No answer.'

Bharat smiled and inclined his head, 'Santji told me he had several body doubles who could stand in for him at any time.'

Leela was taken back. 'A sadhu having body doubles?! Then what about a mysterious man shown in a film during the Paris peace talks between the Vietcong and the USA Officials in 1969? It is alleged that this was Netaji incognito and that he played a vital, behind the scene role during those negotiations. This can't be a body double, so how can he be your Santji? In all these cases, the looks don't match 100% with Netaji Subhas Bose. Neither is there any conclusive data to back any of these claims.'

Bharat quipped, 'Firstly, leading handwriting experts have verified that Santji's handwriting matched that of Subhas Bose. And conclusive data? I told you earlier, there are strong vested interests who don't want such data to come out even now. Instead, they have abetted the creation of a so-called "Netaji Cottage Industry" to muddy the waters.'

Leela sighed and nodded, 'I know what you mean. I read up the wildest stories about Netaji's fate on Sachin's PC yesterday.' She drew lines on the floor for emphasis as she continued, 'Died after a plane crash; exterminated in a Gulag; hanged in an abandoned London gallows; shot by the Japs on order; shot by the Americans; becoming one of the many Babas – these are some typical fancy stories which are floating on the social media. These Babas include your Santji aka Gumnami Baba. There is also time pass speculation that he did a deal with the Govt. to protect his family abroad.'

Bharat tapped her on her shoulder, 'About the last story you mentioned, there are some people who believe that this "Netaji's wife and daughter in Germany" narrative was a part of a deeper conspiracy. This controversy is in the public domain. There have even been past legal cases and a pending one in Alipur Court Kolkata challenging the veracity of this family's claimed relationship with Netaji. But if Santji had done a deal with the Govt to protect this family in Germany – damn it, in that case why were security agencies always looking for him while he lived a destitute undercover life? Wait till I tell you about it.'

Leela continued in a troubled voice. 'What a complicated mystery! Bhai, I came here from Kumbh, not knowing that I would be enveloped by a way of life which I guess is inspired by Santji's thoughts. But I keep musing over why MK gave me this task of digging up the past.'

Bharat tapped the floor for emphasis, 'Without having entered this cesspool, how would you ever comprehend Lord Macaulay and learn how the British distorted our history, including the Subhas Bose story? The British had unparalleled guile. Came here as a trading company as the world's first multinational, and ended up rewriting our history and ruling us by using our own people. And maybe they still do.'

Leela looked up in surprise, 'Still do?'

Bharat nodded, 'Do you doubt it? This is a country full of Trojans. The British outsourced their rule post 1947 via as yet undisclosed arrangements, and MK gave you one such key: to investigate the secret T.O.P documents, *which every patriotic Indian must demand as a birthright.* And you became aware of other such dubious issues too: The fog over Article 147 of the Constitution; the 'War Criminal Act'...'

'But Bhai, what on earth could I have done with any leads about these murky issues?'

'Though you reached a dead end with those leads, your digging brought you here. Right?'

Leela shrugged and threw her head back.

Bharat continued, 'Pull the string. What more did you find out? That for a few decades after we became a Dominion in 1947, we had the best chance to stand up and demand to know the truth about our terms of Independence; about Subhas Bose's fate; the hidden INA massacres; what really did Article 147 of the Constitution mean – *and I emphasize that most of these are intertwined.* Did we do that? No.

'It is the British system, their laws, their falsified Indian History, that we have imbibed in schools and colleges to this day. I would say that even now, many Indians feel inferior to their counterparts in the Western nations. This acute lack of self-esteem had been challenged by Netaji, who was successful in breaking that stranglehold of the British. So our native leaders, the Brown Sahibs, blacked him out and ensured that the emerging *"other India"* was stillborn. MK's riddles opened you up to all this.'

Leela cut in, 'But I wonder why the Government threw such a fit when Mada and Baba mentioned MK's codes?'

'Lili, if India is still constitutionally bound by secret treaties, which government has the guts to open such a Pandora's box?'

'That's all idle talk! Fact is, secrecy is leading to all these conjectures getting wind. The ruling governments have been able to perpetuate this secrecy because the so-called followers of Netaji, many members of Subhas Bose's family, self-professed experts... the whole lot are often fighting among themselves to restore the honour of this man whom we found so convenient to forget. There is no united pressure group.'

'True. The demand for de-classification of the secret intelligence files about Subhas Bose or Gumnami Baba utterly lacks nationwide presence. People don't give a damn,' said Bharat.

Leela poured herself the last residue of the tea. 'But Bhai , I wonder why would Netaji, if he was alive, have waged war against the USA *in Vietnam?* Does this agree with you? In college you would speak glowingly about USA...'

'Yes, I did because that country *initially* upheld individual rights and rejected collectivism. Even then, they had to live down two of the worst injustices ever committed: exterminating the native Indian tribes and later building their wealth through slave labour.'

Leela queried, 'And you think that USA managed to live these injustices down?'

'Absolutely not! Particularly post World War II, they have always supported totalitarian states, fascists and puppet regimes. *This is why Santji spoke of having waged war against them.'*

Leela protested, 'But it all sounds so bizarre. First, Netaji become your Santji and lives in India. And next he fights against the USA in Vietnam?'

Bharat caressed her hair in a fond gesture of blessing. Then he stepped back and said, 'Tomorrow. His journey.'

He turned away and disappeared in the darkness.

THIRTY SIX

Bima woke her up the next morning, whining to be let out. Leela took a quick bath and then prepared some herbal tea. She knew Bharat would be deep in his meditation now. He had trained himself to sleep for five hours and wanted to reduce this to three. Santji had told him that with practice and yogic discipline, three hours was sufficient.

Leela carried the tea pot with two cups to the enclosed garden. Bharat looked tired as he came out of his meditative state. Sipping his tea, he remarked, 'I could not meditate properly today. Here am I, flustered due to just one incident of public exposure, and when you know what this man went through...?'

Leela sat cross legged on the wooden platform as Bharat eased into his narrative. 'Santji was known to most followers as Bhagwanji. After he supposedly passed away on 16 Sept 1985...'

Leela frowned, 'Supposedly? What does that mean?'

Bharat pursed his lips and said, 'Well, the records show that he was cremated. But there are other versions, all unsubstantiated. One: that he went away somewhere, and a different person was cremated in controversial circumstances in Faizabad. Two – Santji had several body doubles, and one of them died and not Santji. There was no death certificate and so on. Yet another belief is that by a special yogic process called Kaya Kalpa, he left behind his mortal body and entered a new one – now don't ask silly questions which I can't answer.'

Bharat paused while Leela opened and closed her mouth in protest, 'Anyway, sometime later a local newspaper called *Naye Log* published a report on a "Gumnami Baba", which was the first time this name was used for Santji. This was followed by the *Northern India Patrika* which started a print series. Both reports claimed that Gumnami Baba was Netaji Subhas Bose. I also came across unconfirmed accounts of Santji's first presence in India in the early 1950s as a Sanyasi in Rijor in Uttar Pradesh. It appears he came from Nepal, where he had reached from Siberia via Mongolia through the Mansarovar region.'

'Was he behind a curtain from day one?'

'No, initially he met people openly, till someone suspected him to be Subhas Bose. Later he left India and re entered again from Nepal in the mid 1950's. *From this point onwards he was behind a curtain.* He became known as Bhagwanji to a few followers in Lucknow, where the widowed Saraswati Devi joined him as a domestic help along with her child.

'Anyway, in Lucknow, Santji ran into trouble with the house owner over rent default and had to leave without his belongings. This kind of abrupt exit recurred three more times till 1985.'

'Why so?'

'Each time he had to decamp at the last moment to evade the clutches of undercover security personnel who were looking for him everywhere. Please note that Intelligence Officers were snooping on Subhas Bose's family members in India till at least 1968. *So our rulers were aware that he was alive somewhere.* Santji said he was a hunted man, and he knew he could be captured and secretly exterminated! That is why his secret abodes were selected by his trusted followers very carefully, that too only after he personally approved of the locations. Also keep in mind that the followers who carried out Santji's orders often comprised former members of the INA who had known Subhas Bose personally.'

'But why would Netaji hide from some Security Forces? This was his own country after all. On the other hand, if Santji was *not* Netaji, was he some fugitive criminal?'

'Just pull the string and see. If this was Netaji, to quote British secret documents, he was the "only civilian Renegade of importance" for the British who was not caught, a man whom the MI6 had a carte blanche to kill. From the 1950's till even today, if such a man emerged in public or was apprehended, the Allies would demand that he should be tried for War Crimes. Don't forget that in January 1971, the Indian Govt had signed into perpetuity, the "UNO Convention for non applicability of statutory limitations to war and crimes against humanity." Why? Which revolutionary from India was still on the run, who had committed war crimes against the Allied Forces – and who was expected to be caught and prosecuted?'

'You mean this was signed into perpetuity keeping Subhas Bose in mind?!'

'You figure. Now, if there was a demand that this missing person, Subhas Bose, was to be handed over to the Allies, specifically Britain and USA, against whom he had waged war officially – was India at that time strong enough to resist? We were in a pathetic economic condition, almost at the mercy of the super powers for aid. And if India was starved and bullied to hand him over, and we refused because the public outcry would make it impossible for any elected Indian Govt to do this, imagine the sheer agony the wider populace would suffer due to this.

'So Santji said: "It is not in the nation's interest that I come out now." *He had to bide his time; wage an underground war. And note: the Provisional Govt of Free India under Subhas Bose never surrendered to the Allies – only a section of the INA surrendered to them – never forget that. That Govt only declared Cease Fire.*'

Leela sighed and nodded several times. Then she looked up. 'And what if Santji was not Netaji? Why would he keep moving to dodge some security forces?'

'Does not fit, right? There were VIP's who would visit Santji in that Army Cantonment compound behind his Ram Bhavan abode at midnight, which in itself is a mystery. Which absconding common criminal would have such a privilege?'

'And the nation never learnt of it?' Leela shook her head in disbelief. 'Ok continue.'

'Then in 1958, after he had to leave Lucknow, for the next six to seven months, Santji together with Saraswati Devi, her old father and her child stayed in a ruined Shiv temple on the banks of the Gomti River near Neemsar.'

Leela's eyes widened, 'How did they survive?'

'They survived from day to day, often depending on alms, till they again shifted to Neemsar proper and stayed in a Dharamshala. Picture this in your mind. If Bhagwanji aka Santji was indeed Subhas Bose, the man who crossed the oceans in a daring submarine transfer and enabled the raising of India's first flag of freedom on Indian soil in Moirang — the leader who really brought freedom to our country — *this* man was reduced to begging for alms at that stage. Imagine! Just feel the sheer injustice of it all.'

Leela could not respond. Her eyes were brimming with tears.

Bharat continued softly, 'In 1958, they moved to an old temple complex in Neemsar. Now there are pictures of his pit stop homes on the net. You simply cannot imagine how he could have stayed in such run down spaces swarming with insects and reptiles — a man who said that he had moved with some of the biggest names in the world. You can visualize what kind of equanimity he must have had.'

Bharat looked at Leela for a reaction, but her eyes remained closed. Her knitted brow and the deep sighs told him that she was standing on the banks of the Gomti River and witnessing a family of three begging for alms along with a man who himself said that he had travelled over continents during his quest to free his motherland.

'It was in Neemsar that he was "rediscovered" by several key members of Subhas Bose's erstwhile inner secret circle, mostly from Kolkata. These included the INA's former Secret service agent Pobitro

Mohan Roy, legendary lady freedom fighter Leela Roy; politician Samar Guha who fought for Subhas Bose's cause all his life... and so on. The Kolkata group set up an informal arrangement with utmost secrecy to keep on meeting him and carrying out his instructions.'

Leela shook her head, 'Bhai, do you *really* believe that a daredevil like Subhas Bose was hiding after abandoning his oath taken in October 1943 that he would work to preserve India's freedom? Impossible.'

Bharat shook his index finger at Leela, 'See, *this was simply tact — not hiding*. Netaji needed to survive and play his moves on the world's chessboard. This was a world which was and is still ruled by powers that saw him as *the* fugitive enemy No 1. Increasing facts are coming out that he continued to guide a major range of activities while remaining underground.'

'Still iffy. Ok... back to the pit stops for Santji.'

Bharat poured another cup of tea and continued: 'Then... in July 1964, Santji left Neemsar for Darshan Nagar, Faizabad,'

Leela waved her hands, 'Wait. Please tell me — how did he move about incognito with his belongings? How could a man without any money survive? Who paid for his rent, his food or other expenses? Sorry, but it all sounds so impossible to...'

'One by one, Lili. It was often Subhas Bose's Kolkata based followers who procured these personal possessions on Santji's express instructions *because they all believed he was Subhas Bose*. They also organized the repeated shifting of the many trunks which contained Santji's growing belongings over these three decades, and which were later found in 1985 at Ram Bhavan Faizabad after his purported death.

'By the time I met him in Ayodhya he had been through several such transfers, each time because the local public had become too inquisitive about the 'Sadhu who was never seen'. Fortunately, by 1976 he had solid local support because all his physicians such as Dr T Banerjee and the civil surgeon Dr RP Mishra had become his trusted disciples.'

'Dr Mishra? The person whose address was given to you after your first visit?'

'Exactly. By the time Santji had shifted to his last pit stop at Ram Bhavan in Faizabad. he was completely dependent on Dr Mishra.'

'Bhai, how could a person with no means travel from Siberia? Just think. And then Mongolia, Mansarovar...'

'Well, there is a theory that Stalin kept him in safe custody in the Urals in a gulag or even a dacha. Santji himself told me once in passing that he had spent a long time in a gulag,' Bharat marked the air with a quote-unquote sign, 'as a "protected" guest of that country. Possibly he had solid backing in Russia, as opposed to the well known story of Subhas Bose being killed in Siberia. No proof though. And regarding his return to India via China...'

'When was that?'

'He never provided dates. But he mentioned that he was a guest of Mao Zedong, for whom he used a code name – Tungabhadra. So he *did* have some support base in China too.'

'Bhai, a Swami walking through Mongolia, living as a guest in Siberia, talking to Mao... how do you swallow this? If indeed this was Subhas Bose, how does he become a Santji who does *tantra sadhana* and so on in secrecy?'

Bharat lifted an eyebrow and a faint trace of irritation appeared for a moment. Then he took a deep breath and continued, 'Despite the handwriting match, you and many others doubt Gumnami Baba aka Santji was Netaji. Why? One major viewpoint is that it was entirely out of character for a such a lion hearted patriot to live in secrecy, when he knew that India was still suffering.

'Firstly Netaji was always, I repeat, *always* driven by a spiritual core. Apart from his journey to the Himalayas during his youth, just a few people are aware of his *Diksha* by famed Tantrik Master, Barada Charan Mazumdar. Fewer still know of his visits to other tantric masters. So *Sadhana* did not happen suddenly. He was always a practitioner of tantra yoga. If indeed he was Santji, he had acquired great powers while undertaking Tantrik Sadhanas in secrecy. I suspect that is why he lived in a darkened room for some time.

'Do you all know what this means, this formal initiation into the Sanyasi Order? *What is renounced; what are the rules governing your conduct and so on?* No you don't!

'Santji told me repeatedly that he was metamorphosed during his epic journey from Siberia to Mansarovar in Tibet, when he stumbled into the astral realm of a place known as *Siddhashram*. This is revered since ages as a mythical conclave where supposedly souls of the highest spiritual power live and meditate. It was here that he really learnt his future path. As a renunciate *Sanyasi,* he had to be dead to his past. No family, no ties – nothing. Yet at the same time as a *Yoddha (warrior) sanyasi* he was to continue his activities in the phenomenal world with great tact and caution.

'Netaji, according to eye witnesses during the INA days, never stopped his *sadhana* even at the height of battle; not even during that submarine journey. So, if he was Santji, being underground for *Tantra Sadhana* was understandable and perfectly logical.'

Leela nodded gravely. 'I had no idea about this aspect.'

'If he was Netaji – IF – then questions arise. Did he go back and forth between Russia and China? No real data. Did he finally leave Russia for good after Stalin's death and proceed to China to bide his time? Again a blank. Meanwhile, the successive Indian Govts kept brainwashing generations that he *did* expire in 1945 in that fake plane crash.

'One theory doing the rounds is that the British possibly persuaded Stalin, who was their war ally, to eliminate him.'

Leela immediately objected, 'This is just speculation!'

'True. Then why did this man leave China for India? Who initially helped him make that journey? Again, we draw a blank. But I repeat: it is at Siddhashram that Santji realized his Karmic path.'

'And what was that?'

'He was to deliver a cathartic solution to eradicate the horrors we live in. *Being mandated for such a mission*, he had received cumulative energy from the spiritual entities in Siddhashram, and he would take it to a logical end. If you question the fundamentals of this, it will defy logic and sound surreal.'

'I really don't understand.'

'Through my own meditation, this is what I could glimpse: This mission had been assigned to Santji...'

'By whom?'

Bharat smiled and shook his head, 'If I start answering your "by whom", it will soon lead to a dead end or sound trite.'

'Bhai, the minute your narrative slips into this esoteric territory of karma, souls, reincarnation, destiny and so on, even at the risk of being slotted as a brainwashed modern Indian, I'd like to call the bluff,' said Leela looking troubled and flustered, 'Much of this sounds right out of the modern Hindutva brigade archives, exactly the kind of drivel from the dark ages which earlier provided fodder for the Islamist and European invasions. And I just can't believe that even you of all people entertain this fatalism, this supernatural stuff.'

Bharat reacted calmly, 'I will answer you on this count later , but for now let me stick to Santji's timeline.'

Leela made a face, 'Yes, we have digressed from how Santji survived in India.'

Bharat nodded, 'Well, he survived while always keeping his dignity intact. Though many influential people including Chief Ministers of UP visited him secretly, he consistently avoided taking favours from them.

'Now there were three groups from Kolkata sworn to his protection. It was these small groups with limited means who looked after his rent. When such help was not available, he had to vacate due to non-payment of rent.

'Ditto his food and other expenses. On very rare occasions he lived well, paying for his expenses with fresh currency notes; smoking the best cigarettes. But most of the time he lived through long periods of destitution that we cannot even imagine. He survived on ash and wild plants while in Neemsar.'

Leela gaped at Bharat, 'Eating ash?'

'Yes. I also learnt from Dr Mishra that the interiors in his room were very damp and the roof was often leaking. His bed and clothes remained wet for days. Despite such miserable conditions, he rarely complained except in a few letters to his closest followers.'

There was a long pause. While Leela was thinking about the desperate conditions in which Santji had stayed, she spilt the tea in her absent mindedness. She composed herself and continued, 'Bhai, did he stay inside for almost thirty years – in various shades of darkness?'

'No. He went out at times. We don't know where, when or why. Still a major mystery. But now researchers show circumstantial evidence which bolsters his assertion, that he played a behind-the-scenes pivotal role during the Vietnam War and subsequent Peace Accord negotiations.'

Leela's eyes widened, 'Same as I found on the net?'

'Yes. There are uncorroborated photos. But the various foreign nations and governments are not releasing their relevant secret files, not when *our* own official Indian Intelligence records are not allowed to see light. And you talk of conjecture?'

'Unbelievable!'

'Yes, incredible. You know, he is also rumoured to have been involved in the Bangladesh war.'

'Stop! Now this is starting to sound sooo far-fetched. This is like a supernatural dimension affixed by fanatical followers. A aged, meditative person doing all this...'

'I can tell you that Santji was as profound in his silences as the most radiant saint, and yet he was completely focused on accomplishing practical missions in this dark world. He often told me that he never wanted this. *For him it had been a spiritual life desired, but a warrior's agenda granted.*'

'Bhai, tell me about...'

'Lili, there is more to come about seeing him again.'

Leela sank back and closed her eyes. They sat quietly immersed in their own worlds for a while. Dawn was about to break. The milk collection van was yet to come. Ganapati, the local flute player who heralded each morning by playing his folk tunes, had not made his appearance on the streets as yet.

THIRTY SEVEN

Bharat continued in a solemn tone, 'After Santji's departure in 1985, it took me quite a while to get used to his absence. Then around 1986, there was a spirited effort by some of Santji's followers to legally protect his belongings, which led to these being sealed in the UP government treasury. Subsequently the matter was no more in the public mind till almost fourteen years later.

'I completed my MBBS and then my economics course while working in Kumaon, as Santji had forecast. After that I started work on my targeted rural projects. Each time I faced problems, mostly with the corrupt politicians and bureaucracy.'

Leela asked, 'I suppose even then there was no important update on this Gumnami Baba issue?'

'True. But his followers kept up the pressure on the successive Central Governments through legal petitions inquiring into the fate of Subhas Bose. Many of the same followers were in touch with Santji till 1985, like me.

'Anyway, I loved my stay near Kalasa and was at peace with myself. The Western Ghats are magical, and especially that area is inspiring. Then Urvi appeared out of nowhere.'

He stopped talking. His chest heaved a few times and then he resumed, 'Those years till 2002 were really wonderful, but after she was gone, after that... no meditation or pep talks could lift me out of a pit. Lata Maushi... that is PC Hindre's wonderful wife took Sachin under her care.'

Leela peered at him. Bharat's tone had changed again.

He continued, 'Then Sarasdida passed away too. I asked myself: What is this so-called Karmic Law which ends up celebrating pain? Why does it dog me all the time?

'Then... then I met him again.'

'Who? Santji? But you just said that he was known to have passed away in 1985?' Leela asked urgently.

'That's what I knew too. I had gone to Pithoragarh in Uttaranchal to help a group to set up a self reliant village. While I was there, I took a solo trip to Munsiari to relive my hiking days. I was carrying two bottles of rum. I planned to drink while strolling around in the jungle,' said Bharat in a contrite tone.

Then he smiled to himself and continued, 'One morning, as I climbed to an old vantage point, I was suddenly alerted by a figure. A bearded man was sitting there on a rock. He looked in his early sixties. Balding, wearing dark glasses. He was looking in my direction.

'I felt I knew this person, It was a strange feeling. Then he took off his dark glasses and I was dumbstruck. He had a strong resemblance with Santji.

'Can't be!'

'There were subtle differences, but it was when he spoke that I froze.'

While Bharat paused, Leela prodded him, 'What did he say?'

'He stated something with specific, *exact* pauses and intonations which astounded me. "Remember, I am forever by your side. Have faith... I am always with you."

'These were the same words said in parting by Santji, the same voice, the same intonation and even the same pause after the word "*FAITH*". On one hand, this man appeared to be younger, though with a similar facial structure. But the voice was the same and the parting in the teeth was there too. There was no mistake about it.'

249

'Bhai, you're hallucinating! This could be a coincidence.'

'Just listen. While I could scarcely breathe, the man continued: "You have lost your way. For nineteen years and forty-nine days now, I have watched over you. Your wife went as per her own created karma. Why do you abandon yours?"'

'My God!' whispered Leela.

'Then I just sank to the ground.'

Bharat stretched and rotated his neck, with his eyes closed. Leela reckoned that he was dwelling over that past chapter when Urvashi's body was recovered burnt and mutilated, as the final signature to her goodbye letter.

He sat down on the grass. Leela joined him there as he continued, 'The man caressed my head, which was resting against his waist. After a while, I can't say how long, he goaded me gently to get up. We walked to the very edge of the spur. The sun was partly hidden by a cloud formation which was now slowly yielding to the soft amber light. Then he spoke again.

'"As long as your wife was there, you mingled with her on the physical plane. You called it love. But I had told you earlier – the inner door to true love will open *only* in that moment when you finally shed the downward pull for the physical. Gradually the flame for Kama goes out and the light for true love is to be lit. Two wicks, but the oil is the same. In *that* light of love, you are lit up to your highest potential. Remember my words?"'

Bharat continued, 'I was again baffled. Indeed, these were the exact words which he had uttered when I had once come to him after my on-off tussle with Urvi at that time. How could *this* man know it all?

'I only nodded silently. Then he beckoned towards the sunlit peaks, "Now look at this horizon, the promise and fulfilment playing out on these peaks every day."'

'We sat looking at the sunrise. It was like any other that I had seen from the same spot, but this time something was happening within me. An acceptance, a great emotion was rising. I could see that the man too was going through some deep experience. He looked dreamily ahead and spoke softly, "You must realize the core fact of life. Till one has not truly let go of everything – *everything,* or conversely till one has not been rejected or abandoned, till then it is impossible to know what true love is."

'"Remember what I told you about my journey from Siberia to Mansarovar, and finally back to India? The path was frozen even over the water bodies. If I had walked upright, the ice could have yielded. So inch by inch, I had to lug my body forward in a prone posture to avoid detection by any soldiers on either side of the border."

'"Then I stood there all alone, the wind sweeping my battered body. I had finally sighted my land, my beloved."'

Bharat took a long breath, 'The man stopped speaking. He was overcome by emotion. After an almost interminable silence, he continued, "For so many years I stood alone at unknown Horizons: exiled; abandoned by all; a man with no nationality – my name crossed out of the human register. I looked wistfully in the direction of the far away land which is my sacred God. Only *then* I realized how desperately I could love. How unfortunate was I that I had never realized the true essence of this soil while I dwelled upon it. It was only when I was forced to stay away that I..."'

Bharat's eyes were filled with tears. 'And then I saw that he was weeping profusely. My tears were of release, his were those of pure love and benediction. The silence that enveloped us was soothing beyond words.

'I gazed at his face. How could this man seemingly have a younger body, and yet speak and behave exactly as Santji, in fact even know the precise, most private moments spent between me and Santji? It defied all logic and understanding.

'Then he turned to me and smiled, "You doubt, yes?"'

'I shook my head, "No, I don't understand."'

'He continued affectionately, "I came because you forgot your dharma. You must learn to laugh in this dark world and spread that laughter, without letting go of your community building objectives. But you will also need the controlled aggression of a warrior."'

'I was still in a daze, "Are you the same person I met over nineteen years ago? How? Tell me, how?"'

'He said, "Just perceive me within you. And heed my words: From now on you will be a mother to your child."'

'I had closed my eyes for a long while. Suddenly I felt alone. When I looked up again, he was gone, and I never heard him move away.'

Once again Bharat paused, but Leela burst out, 'Honestly, this seems sooo implausible! On one hand, just hearing his traumatic words breaks my heart. But... but how can a man who passed away in 1985, and even if he had gone somewhere else, *even* then, how does he come back younger? You can't even call it a case of transmigration. This man is surely a clone or a body double of Santji that you spoke about earlier.

'Secondly... I can't take this karma thing at all. It is a never ending *katha*, an endless tale! You work out some negatives from your past account, and your present circumstances literally make you commit several others. That Urvi had to die like that! Just look at the completely *senseless* ways in which countless people are said to suffer due to this karma thing. Even the ability to remember the karmic reasons as to why such suffering hits you is blocked off. Squaring accounts – huh!'

Bharat replied calmly, 'It's simple. What you sow, you reap. There is no free ride; no jugaad. Working out past karma in this life is an opportunity and not a punishment.'

Leela retorted in an exasperated tone, 'It all looks so perverse to me, to explain away all the suffering around by this karmic bond.'

Bharat held firm, 'You have to learn to still your mind to observe the action-reaction thing working out...'

Leela was fuming now, 'And I can't believe that Santji is the same as your latest saviour from Munsiari, let alone Mahakaal. This is delusional!'

'What I just described is no miracle, only a deliberate manifestation from another dimension of existence in our own. This is as real as you and I. Science cannot corroborate this as yet – because humanity is not matured for it.'

'Sorry, I don't buy this!'

Bharat spread his hands out, 'Ok, on one hand you probe the depths of the oceans, or take off into space exploration in special gear, vessels and aircraft to probe unknown realities. And you do all this *only after intensive training.* Yes?

'Yes, but so what?

'But you don't even once want to train your mind to acquire the *inner* competence needed to experience *how* other layers of reality manifest in our phenomenal world... *all the time*? Instead, you dismiss all such experiences as paranormal and demand that the unbounded existence should stand in your 'logical' court to prove itself? This is pathetic!'

'I will only go by evidence...'

'Life is still a work in progress in many layered dimensions. Our evidence based life is only ONE among them. One can never realize the ultimate truth through intellect alone.'

Leela looked away, her jaws working furiously. Bharat waited for her tempest to subside. After a while she turned to face him again. 'Was that the last time when this person appeared before you, till this rally in Delhi?'

'No, he came once more in between, when Prithak Ghati was threatened with closure. There was this clash going on between the Panch and some poor Muslims who had been instigated. At around the same time, some Maoists wanted to extract tax from us. Then Santji appeared at the gate after dark and I almost jumped out of my skin. I brought him quickly to this room.'

'Did he look the same as in 2003?'

'The voice was still the same, but there was no beard. He wore thick rimmed glasses and even looked a tad taller. But he pulled me up severely. He said that I was *not* asserting myself.

'I told him that I was happy with what I was doing. But he stressed that it was also my Dharma to defend against any negative forces which wanted to destroy the flowering of human potential.'

'Did you do that?'

Bharat replied, 'Well, we did stand our ground, both with the local politicians and the Maoists. But this time Lili, the rattled forces are too big, and I have never taken such a public stand earlier.'

Leela nodded vigorously, 'This time it is pointless to assert yourself. People are clutching at anything to save them from the terrible hell which they themselves have created. They will never change and will vent their frustration on you for their miseries. Why should you take a public stand in a drama where they want to be fooled?'

Bharat glanced at her sharply, 'Say that again?'

'You mean "they want to be fooled"?'

'That was one of Santji's typical refrains – "you people *want* to be fooled all the time."'

Leela got up in excitement. 'Unbelievable! MK also said this several times and I picked it up from him. Oh, by the way, what did this person in Munsiari want to be called?'

Bharat laughed aloud. 'He did not want to be called.'

'But then... how did you address him?'

'When I called him Santji, he said: "That identity is over. I have now evolved from being a Pilgrim and a poor faqir to hibernating in Shiva's force field. Later I may be assigned Mahakaal's role by the Divine Mother."'

Leela shook her head in bemusement several times. 'Right now, I am worried about you. This Munsiari man is right. These negative forces will devour you, and you have done little about it.'

Bharat got up and looked out of the window. Then he yawned lazily and stretched himself. 'Right now I will live today, this day, to the full. Come now, I have to run along. Sonichari will call for breakfast very soon.'

THIRTY EIGHT

They were soon savouring their breakfast of *poha*, flattened rice cooked with vegetables from the farm. Bharat overheard the farm hands talking in strained whispers about some news on TV, but there was a strict rule not to eat and talk at the same time.

Sensing the mood, Bharat asked Sonichari to speak up. There had been major incidents of communal rioting the previous night in Assam and Bengal, and down south in Mangalore and Aurangabad. The army and RAF (Rapid Action Force) had been called out. The central government suspected that this was a planned outbreak triggered by sleeper cells of divisive forces at work. The RAF had to open fire and several rioters had been killed and injured.

After breakfast, Leela remembered her promise to Sachin. She asked him to come in an hour, so that they could start on their long awaited session. He happily skipped away.

She sat down to update her notes about the entire Santji saga, right up to the Munsiari Avatar. Her heart said that they were the same person, *but all this defied logic by a huge distance for her*. How did a grounded person such as Bharat talk now like a devout? Maybe this is how she appeared to others when she tried to convince people that Mahakaal had been real? Could she not encounter life's truths in a simple form, shorn of such complications? She remembered how she had been attracted to Buddhism at one point precisely for this reason.

While she mused, the next hour went by almost in a flash. Sachin duly came in and sprawled on the mat. Leela looked at him with a solemn face and put her finger on her lips. He immediately mimicked her gesture, but Leela scolded, 'This is dead serious.'

Sachin frowned as Leela continued, 'I am learning new facts every day with Bhai. Normally I would wait till it is over before I speak a word, but since you have to attend college soon, I will push the first pawn today itself. But I warn you, most of this is strictly confidential. What is not, I'll indicate.'

'Is there a lot of data coming up?' asked Sachin.

'Yes, but I'll only tell you the highlights,' said Leela, 'You will *not* fill in the gaps with your imagination or interpretation.'

Sachin's eyes were twinkling. 'Can I share?'

Leela's eyes flashed, 'I thought I just said – strictly confidential?'

They stared at each other. Then Sachin slumped back on the bed. 'OK, shoot.'

For the next two hours, Leela gave Sachin a gist of what it was all about, and even referred to her notes to be correct. She emphasized that there was a great deal that needed to be corroborated. All through her talk, Sachin listened without a single word or interruption, while his hands kept making sketch after sketch.

At one point, Leela paused. Sachin had stopped sketching. Tears had slowly formed in his eyes and had started rolling down, and he did not even attempt to wipe them away. This happened when Leela described how this old man had dragged himself over frozen glaciers on his chest, avoiding detection by the armed border guards as well as the danger from hidden crevasses, and had wept when he stood alone on Indian soil – a forgotten fugitive who was a living dead. Then she realized that she too had been crying. Both of them had been transported to the unknown spot where a man had wept on being reunited with his beloved motherland.

Sachin whispered, 'Lishi.'

She looked up at him and smiled weakly. The house was now almost empty and silent. The workers were away and the women were at their respective chores, or looking after the small children. Bima was still sleeping after his morning run.

'Lishi, tell me. Was this man whom Baba met in Faizabad, could he really be Netaji Subhas Bose?'

Leela turned her palms up in a question. 'You just heard that his handwriting matches that of Netaji.'

'Maybe he was a body double who could replicate Netaji's handwriting... '

'Sach, no imposter, body double or planted person could know such intimate details.'

Sachin stared at the floor for a long time, his jaws working furiously. Then he muttered, 'Our generation never had a real hero to fire our daily lives. All straw men or Bollywood fakes. And all this time, such an incredible person had lived and been denied? Lishi, give us heroes like this and we can really change the world around us.'

He continued in a strained voice, 'We happily celebrate Children's day, Gandhi Jayanti and so on, while the man who really dared without compromising had to suffer like this? Eating ash, living in such poverty and agony? ... We deserve our present fate. We love to be fooled by the popular stereotypes.'

'You know, this was one of Santji's favourite quips,' said Leela, 'You people want to be fooled.'

'He said that?'

'Yes. Often.'

'But the person you met in Buxa, or the one whom Baba met in Munsiari, how could they be Netaji? That is impossible. A man over hundred years — what would be his age?'

'MK looked around sixty years, but yes, Subhas Bose would logically be over 120 years of age today if he was around.'

'But that's a deal breaker! How can…'

'I know this sounds crazy, but Bhai is not done yet, and already I've heard many things which defy logic.'

Sachin looked away, his jaws still working, 'The mainstream Indian polity still denies Netaji his pivotal contribution, right? They also denied Bagha Jatin, Madan Lal Dhingra, Vasudev Phadke, Rashbehari Bose… so many about whom we never read anything in school.'

Leela's eyes widened, 'Where did you pick this up?'

Sachin tapped his chest for emphasis. '*We* are the scavengers on the net. And you were denying me this knowledge, like our teachers?'

Leela held Sachin by the shoulders. 'First you need to get real tough. As MK would say – become iron-willed.'

'Lishi, my hero is Baba, but he just wants to do his thing and does not mind if he gets crushed while doing so. It stumps me good. Why can't he turn around and fight?'

The sudden sound of a distant explosion brought their talk to an abrupt halt. Firdaus came running within minutes. An old closed jeep with tinted glasses had been blown up near a public toilet, perhaps by a remote device. This was the first ever act of major violence inside the town and the impact was electric. It was soon discovered that Bharat had travelled in the jeep and got off impromptu near the dense jungle ten km earlier to attend to a sick tribal. Luckily, even the jeep owner had stepped out for a pee.

It took an hour for a police team to arrive. They initially suspected Maoists, though there was no thread to connect them. They soon changed their line of investigation and rounded up the heads of four Muslim families in town, including Firdaus. Bharat was furious, but the police contended that this could very well be the fallout of the abattoir case three years ago. At that time, it had been proved that the Sardar Mane faction had instigated some Muslim families to act against the

Panchayat and Bharat.

The entire town rallied to a man behind the four families as the most nationalistic citizens here. The counter charge against the police was led by the dramatic entry of Machenda, who had recently returned from his Char Dham Yatra. With his acerbic tongue and quaint mix of several lingos, his quotes became an instant hit. 'Have you guys come to see a Lungi dance? The bombers are in the jungle and you are shooting off your mouths here? You Bloody Chutiya Sulphide idiots!' followed by more unprintable abuse.

After perfunctory questioning the men were released to tumultuous cheers, but the police said they now had orders to provide an armed escort for Bharat, even if he did not want this. They could not take the blame if something happened to him. This Security Gunman would join duty in a day or two.

Bharat returned with Firdaus, who wept when he embraced his grandchildren and the farm workers. Sachin issued a smart military salute to Bharat and said, 'Baba, your orders are awaited. We want to do our bit for the motherland.'

Bharat burst out laughing. 'My orders right now are to start going to bed early and getting up early to steel body and mind.'

Sachin grimaced, 'Baba, I'm serious about you taking us seriously. They tried to kill you.'

Bharat looked at Leela and back to his son. 'Take *us* seriously? Who's us?'

'Us is our generation. As a nation, we're in a dangerous crash mode, and the hard disk seems headed for the junk-house. Let us help.'

Dinner was a silent affair, with Bharat looking quite tired again. But when they were cleaning up, Sachin asked, 'Baba, want the headlines?'

Bharat surprisingly shrugged and nodded.

Sachin took off. 'The situation in Bangladesh is starting to mimic

Pakistan. There have been a growing chain of attacks by Jihadi groups against ruling party members, minorities and even members of the intelligentsia. Similar attacks have started impacting the border areas of West Bengal too. There are security warnings of more turbulence to follow.'

Bharat dried his hands and sat down on his easy chair with his eyes closed. Leela tried to silently shoo Sachin away, but the boy would not be denied. He continued, 'Also Baba, the reported cases of people, especially children, dying from a new unidentified virus has globally reached epidemic proportions. I found a common factor: that all the affected countries are fed by rivers originating in the Tibetan Plateau.'

Sachin stopped reading from his mobile phone. Till then they all had a serious, strained look on their faces as each news item increased the sense of foreboding. But now they heard a humming sound. Someone was singing through closed lips. It was Bharat.

Sachin protested, 'Baba, does this attack and the dark news fire your energy or what?'

'Bhai, what *is* this?' chided Leela.

Bharat stopped humming. He took a deep breath and said, 'I *do* feel gutted inside on hearing all this. But see: We just had a great meal. The air is scented with the many plants giving off their offerings to life. Bima is still playing out there with the farm children without a care in the world, and yet instead of being grateful that we're alive, we allow this moment to be coloured by the distant drums.'

He smiled softly and looked at Leela. 'HE would say, and I quote: "In the coming days during our sternest battles, only those will survive who can embrace nature; who can look at themselves as nature's children and play life's game. More than all your stupendous scientific progress, if you cannot lose yourself for a while in the simple flowers around you, their beauty, their aura and their celebration of life – then you are already

261

dead."'

Sachin had been listening with his eyes shining. Then he opened up, 'Baba, who is this that you quote?'

Before Bharat could react, Leela quipped, 'From what you quoted, I have been dead for a while.'

Sachin started speaking at the same time as Leela, 'You're not telling – who was it that...'

'Sachin wait! Bhai, you've taken today's attack on you so lightly,' said Leela angrily, 'You could have been there in the jeep.'

'But I was not. Somebody watches over me,' replied Bharat with his usual disarming smile.

'That "somebody" you quote may have warned you to become vigilant... now don't interrupt. I haven't finished. The communal madness around; this bomb blast which happened here today; children dying like ants from some river borne or air-borne virus, maybe even created by man... Bhai, this is all so morbid. And you talk of playing games; smelling flowers?'

'I can smell spilt coffee.' Sachin shouted.

Firdaus exclaimed and ran towards the kitchen, looking angrily at his wife, who bit her tongue and followed.

Bharat nonchalantly went on. 'The quote is not over. It says: "If you can feel the bird's song with your heart, if you can merge with the wind rustling in the trees, if you can laugh aloud in your solitude, only then you will avoid becoming a hardened machine. If you cannot play with yourself, you cannot progress. When all these inhibitions have crept in due to our "civilized" life, we have ended up throttling and killing our ability to play with ourselves; our very divine abilities. They are there as your playmates. Release them."'

The words wafted into the air, like a piece of inspired music. The silence that crept into their living moments was too delicate to breach.

Leela spoke after a long time. 'Bhai, I can't see these playmates, nor release them.'

'These words came to me right now with the tide of memory, as if I had just heard them on the spur facing the Himalayan peaks in Munsiari. Later that night, when I went back to the same spot to relive these words again, the pain slowly left me. And I saw Urvi.'

Firdaus came in with the coffee. Sachin could no longer curb his anguish and burst out, 'You saw Ma – meaning?'

Bharat answered easily, 'Yes. But not like I'm seeing you now.'

'Then?'

Bharat continued, 'The moon was not full and a really thick cloud layer had formed. I entered the forest without turning on my torch, while I kept chanting a Mantra which someone had taught me earlier.

'Then I stood still, as I got an eerie feeling. Tiny dots of light gathered, like many fireflies or glow worms getting together. Slowly, they took a shape. My instincts were then so strong, I was one hundred percent sure whose shape it was. I could even see very clearly that she was smiling. But I never saw Urvi again.'

Bharat got up abruptly, the coffee cup in his hand, and proceeded to his room.

There was a numbed silence. Then Leela walked over to Sachin, who buried his face in her shawl. Suddenly, in a painful flash, Aditya's absence hit her at that very moment. She sat down slowly and drew Sachin's head over her shoulders, but the tears were her own admission that she herself had forgotten how to play.

THIRTY NINE

Leela awoke much earlier than usual. It was still dark. She went towards Bharat's room and saw that he was coming in from the forest with a large collection of freshly fallen, fragrant white *Shiuli* flowers with their orange hearts. He nodded, and she followed him into his room. The trap-door to the basement was already open. She accompanied him there.

This time she could see many more things in Bharat's *Dhyana* chamber with a relaxed mind. In the section where the images of spiritual thinkers, scientists and freedom fighters were aligned, she realized that many of them were still unknown to her.

Bharat was occupied with laying out the flowers in front of his inner shrine. There was a big board on a wall near his desk: "Santji's Favourites". Here, he had pinned up various starred poems and quotations. Leela could recognize one written by John H. Aughey, but the others were mostly quatrains from Omar Khayyam.

There was the Door to which I found no Key:

There was the Veil through which I might not see:

Some little talk awhile of ME and THEE

There seemed — and then no more of THEE and ME.'

A little below this poem, a vital quote caught her eye: *'If we are to escape the catastrophes that have ended earlier civilizations, we must learn that Man cannot live by Science and intellect alone. The Wild World IS the Human World.*

'Having evolved in it for millions and millions of centuries, we are not so far removed by a clothing of civilization. It is packed in our genes. In fact, the more power driven, complex and delicate our civilization becomes, the more the likelihood arises that a collapse will bring us back to wilderness. There is in wilderness a natural

wisdom that shapes all earth's experiments with life.' (Charles A. Lindbergh)

Leela followed this quote down to the next one from Santji: *'Democracy can function only in a disciplined population. Undisciplined Democracy is nothing but mobocracy or factionalism. It is synonymous with Demonscracy.'*

Bharat had stuck a note just below it: 'Shaktibahini needed but not happening'.

At the bottom of the roll she found Bharat had framed yet another string of Omar Khayyam quatrains which she skipped till the last set:

'With Earth's first Clay They did the Last Man's knead,

And then of the Last Harvest sow'd the Seed:

Yea, the first Morning of Creation wrote

What the Last Dawn of Reckoning shall read.'

Destiny again?! She sat quietly for a while and then moved on to the section with the photos, trying to regain her positivity from these inspiring personalities.

Bharat was applying fresh sandalwood paste on Santji's feet in the large photo. He turned to Leela and said, 'I keep introducing these framed images one by one to Sachin, his friends and the farm children. Remember Dida and Dadu would do this, or even Ma?'

Leela's eyes lit up. 'Of course, but why don't you do this on a wider canvas? None of today's children know about Panini, Suśruta, Charaka, King Lalitaditya and so on... so many of these lives you have highlighted here.'

Bharat paused before he replied with a heavy voice, 'But I don't want to.'

'Why not? I think this is where you erred. You did not try to reach out.'

'What's the point? I tried in the past. Most people love saying "How inspiring" and then going back to doing what they do every day

265

out of habit. That's why I kept Santji to myself... Damn it, why should I reach out?'

'Why did *he*?'

Bharat stared at Leela, and she returned his gaze with even greater intensity. He mumbled, 'He what?'

Leela did not shift her look. 'When you were walking on that spur with a bottle in your hand, why did *he* bother to come to you? He could have also thought: "This condemned chap will go back to his drinking habit." But no. Whoever he was, he came. For you.'

When Bharat did not answer, she continued, 'There are many such YOUs and many such MEs. Who need to know. Need that one spark, one finger held out to hold. The majority of people in India don't know any of these inspiring personalities you have adorning your wall. Even I don't know so many as yet.'

Bharat kept silent for a while, his jaws working. Then he shook his head. 'I withdrew from the public forums because I realized that all my knowledge was useless – *useless*! Unless a community like this could survive or even flourish, what use was all this gyan? But now...'

Bharat paused again. Leela waited for a few seconds and then she prodded him, 'But now what?'

'Santji appears at that rally. Why? Does he want me to reach out to people now? But why me alone?'

'Alone? Shivdadu, Sarasdida, Anumashi – they all taught us and many other children. Likewise, what about your admirers who put your experiment with life on the net? That's why it circulated and inspired so many – this small socio-economic miracle which you made possible.'

'Not me. It was this extraordinary Panchayat led by Birbal Kaka. They took the risks. Anyone can have ideas, but you need men of courage to put them into practice.'

'Ok, so go ahead and tell people about them.'

266

'Agreed, but even this plan was inspired by Santji.'

'By him?'

'You bet. He had outlined small living units for a national model of sustainable living. All my projects, from the earliest till now, had his words as a source of inspiration.'

'Did he describe a national model to couple with your micro plan working here?'

'Not really. In his plan, the government only had the role of a supervisor. Each person was free to grow to the best of his abilities and aptitude. No reservations please!'

Leela sat upright. 'You mean this was said by Santji pre-1985?'

'Yup. He said that government had no business manipulating the economy.'

'Isn't that a real bombshell? How on earth can this be Subhas Bose, the man who envisioned the Planning Commission?'

'Lili, Santji had experienced how the gulags ran in Siberia. He told me that when he actually saw the horrors of communism in Soviet Russia and China, he had to correct himself big time. He even predicted that communism would be eradicated forever: "Will be buried 3000 fathoms deep, never to surface again."'

Leela was still excited. 'Just imagine, even today there is not one top leader who speaks of a "hands off" policy in socialist India.'

'Correct. On this point alone, he stands apart from all mainstream political opinion in today's India. Don't forget that when he spoke about minimal Government to me, it was hardly fashionable. He was prophetic.'

Leela's fingers were conducting a staccato dance. 'You know what Bhai? I discovered that many communists are now finding virtues in Netaji and admitting to their past mistake in assessing him. But the same chaps are shooting down the Gumnami Baba angle, proclaiming this is a fake story and can't be linked to Netaji.'

Bharat grimaced. 'They have no choice. Firstly, there is the popular story of Netaji being imprisoned in Siberia and killed there. The Commies were defensive anyway. But now, the word has spread through the social media that Bhagwanji aka Santji condemned Communism. Now, which Commie will like this?'

Leela nodded gravely. Then she observed, 'So how come you have written against the Left movement all your life, yet you often ended up supporting the causes raised by the same Leftists?'

Bharat did not back off. 'I have supported *anyone* who has had false charges slapped on them or who has been held without trial for years. You deny the unorganized sector their very right to exist, you throw them out of their habitat time and again with hardly any meaningful compensation – do you wonder why they fall into the ultra Left anti-national trap? '

Leela protested, 'But you have given shelter and even contributed money to fight the cases of some victims who later joined these ultras.'

Bharat leaned forward, 'Such deprived victims fall prey to any power centre that promises them justice through violent means. But once they take up the gun, these foreign funded Red power blocs end up controlling them. The inner politics of these Maoist movements is even more ruthless and authoritarian than the feudal powers that they oppose.

'I have fought for the oppressed victims. I tried my best to prevent them from taking up a gun and getting slaughtered later, caught between the powerful landowner-police nexus, and the countervailing ultra left armed groups.'

Leela inclined her head to one side and asked, 'Ok, conversely do you think the present ruling polity really champions the cause of your Gumnami Baba?'

'Eyewash. Firstly, never forget that *Santji was opposed to aligning with any and all political outfits.* But you know why this misconception? Apparently RSS Guru Golwalkar had known and eulogized Santji too, addressing him as Vijayanand.'

Leela shouted, 'Nooo!'

Bharat replied calmly, 'Yes dear sister.'

'But the records before 1945 show that Subhas Bose had been opposed to the Hindu Mahasabha and all communal forces.'

'Correct. At that stage, Subhas Bose's men *did* go around breaking up the Hindu Mahasabha meetings. His credo was: Observe your personal faith at home and discharge your duties according to Rule of Law. No communal politics!'

Leela raised an eyebrow. 'Despite this, why do some Netaji researchers think Santji would find favour with today's ruling party?'

'I'll tell you. Some of Santji's utterances as transcribed by his faithful followers have been collated in a little known Bengali Book titled *"Oi Mohamanob Ashe"*. One of his quotes in this book is that he would prove that the Taj Mahal, Fatehpur Sikri and the Red Fort were all Hindu Palaces. See the problem?'

Leela's mouth fell open. 'No wonder many Netaji fans think that Santji could never have been Subhas Bose!'

'But believing that the Taj Mahal was a Hindu monument does not make him a Hindutva follower at all. *He was his own man.* The present polity is only trying to usurp Netaji's legacy, while Mohandas Gandhi remains their preferred currency. Typically opportunistic!'

Leela was still sceptical. 'All this sounds like plenty of conjecture by believers: Maybe this, maybe that; *maybe* Santji was Netaji and was released from a Russian Gulag; *maybe* he was Mao's guest in China; *maybe* he crossed over to India and made his life changing pit-stop in the Himalayas – I forget the place...'

'Siddhashram. Could also be in the Ural Altai Mountains, or even the Mongolian Altai, where secret ageless societies have been rumoured to exist for a long time.'

Leela asserted, 'Another contentious *maybe*: that Santji had a soft corner for RSS Gurus. On this count too, I doubt that Santji was Subhas Bose.'

Bharat started pacing the room in slow steps. 'No maybe here. He had the courage to admit that his views had radically changed. He admired the general RSS cadre, having personally observed that they worked silently for the motherland and didn't expect anything in return. *But he had reservations about RSS leaders who had tasted political power.*'

Leela shook her head, 'I can't accept all this offhand because...'

'I now know that over fifty years ago he had predicted the eventual ascendancy of radical Islam. He wanted no minority appeasement, only an even handed state policy. This has nothing to do with his having turned communal.'

'So Santji made two predictions: death of Communism and rise of militant Islam.'

'Many more. In India, there is a lot of similarity between communism and Islamo-fascism: No belief in nationalistic patriotism; bumping off those who do not agree with them; plumping for totalitarian set ups... Santji foresaw all this and warned me against both credos.'

'If he really predicted this in the 1960s, it is amazing foresight.'

Bharat shook his head. 'Now, the same Santji spoke of the State having the sole function of defence and upholding the law of the land: Protecting its citizens; foiling attempts by anyone from breaking the laws or circumventing them to unfair advantage. Punishment for any such crime: DEATH!'

'No! Nooo!' This time it was a real shriek. Leela paled and vigorously shook her head in disagreement.

'I was waiting for this typical reaction,' said Bharat impassively, 'Yes, Santji did say that the flat punishment for breaking *any* law would be the death penalty.'

'I refuse to believe this.'

'Lili, I found it hard to swallow it too. Till now it sticks in my throat. But for him, this was essential in the initial years of a nation. You saw his quote here, right?'

Bharat walked to the scroll and read out loudly, *Democracy can function only in a disciplined population. Undisciplined Democracy is nothing but mobocracy or factionalism. It is synonymous with Demonscracy.* 'For him, respect for the individual life and rights had to be established by iron law.'

Leela was silent. Then she mumbled to herself, 'Mahakaal was not like that. He was so affectionate.'

Bharat emphasized his point, 'The Santji whom I knew was affectionate too. But he spoke of a no man's land perhaps across the Pamirs between Russia and China, where he had secretly established the social structure he had in mind. He said this land had the death penalty but it needed to be used just a couple of times, that too only in its initial years.'

Leela countered him immediately. 'But here you are trying to experiment with a model town with no punitive steps, nothing to protect your residents.'

Bharat mused over Leela's charge and then replied, 'It did set me thinking. Can't man live without such iron laws and enforcement? But yes, Santji's transformation *was* remarkable. From being a left oriented politician, if indeed he was Netaji, this man had turned full circle and advocated "each according to his own ability" as a fundamental necessity.'

Leela smiled, 'That was your lone ranger line in the College days.'

'Nah, this one from Santji has a crucial difference. He said: "No tax. You earn what you can or want, but you *voluntarily* give much or almost all of your earning to the local governing unit."'

Leela was flummoxed. 'This sounds so unrealistic. Hell, who would agree to do this today?'

'Yes, he eulogized the Joint family. He thought that his kind of social order would be like a large loving joint family, where you are free, but you *willingly* support the child and the elders, like the families of yore.'

Leela's face lit up. 'So did you reach somewhere on this score?'

'I made bold to ask him: how can this be possible? We have long outgrown the joint family structure. But he said that it would come back after a massive catharsis hits India. This time it would evolve in a new, renewed form.

'I thought: another idealistic utopia? I gradually learnt that Santji had a very clear vision about education, the village unit, technology, all co-existing with nature. A sort of complete individual freedom revelling in harmony with a cooperative family. I believed it was impossible.

'But when I tried to follow a bit of this idea here, to my great surprise, something worked. The houses and plots in Prithak Ghati were designed in such a way that while you had privacy, you often had to cross another's property to access your space. The patterns were always inclusive, never separate.

'Initially numerous residents, both old and young, rejected the idea. Many left Prithak Ghati. But one by one, most of them returned here after months and even years.'

Leela had been listening patiently. 'I'm curious. It can't be that simple.'

'Here they had tasted the actual love of living in a society in sync with nature. They missed this deeply in the cities. In PG, the better placed residents are genuinely happy backslapping with the labour from many impoverished corners of India.'

Leela nodded. 'I saw that during my walks. Infectious! But this is not Singapore. Why do you think your model worked in a country where people are not punished for indiscipline?'

Bharat replied, 'Why? Most people here have voluntarily followed our rules, because they *treasure* this seamless bonding with fellow human beings and nature. The taste of success achieved without manipulating anyone, brings about such a blessed fellow feeling. That's why our residents, affluent or otherwise, donate unsparingly to all our causes. You can really experience Santji's dream about a so-called collective soul here.'

'I fear for you,' said Leela shaking her head, 'Bhai, I can't see the present ambitious Indian middle class accept even a minute of such discipline or austerity. These agitations...'

'Right. Those who come here are either unorganized labour who exemplify austerity, or urbanites who are sick of chasing attachments.'

'Then why this huge Halo for you? This public frenzy?'

Bharat grew serious. 'Desperation. They dug up my old writings about how to deal with political scoundrels who take turns to rape the country relentlessly. *Chanakya Neeti.* Starve them of resources; choke off their blood supply. *This* is what people are willing to try, but they will not sign on austerity measures and self discipline beyond a point.'

Leela kept waving her index finger in disagreement, 'I bet you, the political class will rough it out and outlast this agitation. This is their expertise, honed over generations.'

'True, but right now the financial losses are starting to bite, and with many ex-servicemen from the defence forces joining the agitation, they are worried.'

They now heard Ganapati pass the streets playing his soft flute, saying adieu to the stillness of the night and gathering its energy into an invocation for the day poised to emerge.

Bharat got up and beckoned at Leela to follow him. They emerged from the basement and left after securing the slab. Bharat guided Leela into the adjoining forest.

FORTY

They walked in silence for a while. Bharat moved with practiced ease, while Leela held his hand to avoid stumbling in the dark. The path became steep after a while. Leela found herself on a crest overlooking the Habitat. There was a light burning in Sachin's room. He usually attended to his most important tasks at dawn.

They parked themselves on a rough hewn bench. Ganapati's flute could still be heard very faintly. Bharat looked up and continued slowly from where he had left. 'You are worried about me, this agitation, the urban mess — yes? The sad part is that there are many brilliant minds around but no guts to admit that we goofed up royally. The whole economic drive to achieve growth rates *at any cost* has been criminal. Anyway, who's listening?'

Leela shuffled her feet uneasily. 'So would you say that the way ahead is the return to a joint family thing?'

'This marriage of free enterprise to the joint family has to evolve organically, but really, what made things work here was this unique Panchayat.'

'But I recall you would write strongly against Panchayats?'

'I still hold to that. Many, perhaps most panchayats are quasi-control centres: feudal, often caste-driven; landed dominant classes and ruling lobbies dictating every step for the community. That's what I say again.

'But what happened here is that for many years there was a violent feud between Birbal Kaka's family and other families. Kaka himself had gone away to Jalgaon to escape his father's dominance. Then almost his entire family and cousins were killed in a highway accident while returning from a marriage. The complete landed assets came to Kaka by inheritance. So when he returned here, he told the community not to stay in a well. He started encouraging outsiders to settle, but only those who would provide value addition. That's when Shivanna told Kaka about me.'

Bharat waved his hand in a wide arc. 'Birbal Kaka got exposed to the outside world, especially the Internet, when he was in exile. He was a visionary and put his vast inherited resources and acumen on the line. Many locals were against our ideas, but Kaka had his way. As the results trickled in, the Panchayat too joined the ride. Then some of my college friends sponsored one scheme or the other as a start-up, factoring in an initial incubation period between five to ten years.'

Leela asked, 'Who decided... I mean did the Panchayat decide who all can settle here?'

'No, in most cases it was Birbal Kaka who chose each settler carefully and he rarely went wrong.'

'But how do they get to stay legally?'

Bharat explained, 'It works like this. The Panchayat (Panch) has designed a framework for legally leasing out land to outsiders, where they make their small homes. Sometimes a nominal rent serves as instalments towards long lease.'

'Ahaa. But how did they enforce compliance with your civic rules?'

'Initially a major problem area. Quite a few residents turned hostile after settling in, despite signing that they would obey all community rules. Typically, they wanted to do their own things but Kaka called their bluff. He invoked the agreements, which decreed that anyone breaking the rules would have his power or water supply choked off.'

'Incredible! Was this choking off really done?'

Bharat nodded gravely, 'Yes it was. Water is a critical resource and no one here can bugger up our planned reserves. So, in this remote village town, we already had local stakeholders getting together and negotiating their own agreement, including rules about water use enforced by punishment, and Lin Ostrom got a Nobel honouring her research into the same premises. Amazing.

'For example you can't install a borewell without an inspection from the Panch. One resident fought the Panch, installed a solar-driven pump to extract as much water as he wanted, and lived as a cut-off from our power grid. But his crop selection and cultivation ended in two years of failure, and then his solar battery set-up was giving constant problems. He finally came around. But yes, we've often had problems.'

Leela queried, 'What's so different in what your resident farmers do?'

'Under the broader agroecological farming, some use the "platform and trench" method of irrigation: No ploughing except initially, so as to retain earthworms and weeds which are both blessings; using biological pest control –these are following the Umbergaon model. Some try "Cowism"; a few others the "Subhash Palekar natural farming" model, using a culture of Micro Organisms. They avoid flooding the fields, the key being simply moisture. There are many claims and counter claims, but Birbal Kaka never allows misleading contentions about agro output to gain currency.

'So this resident who defied the Panch; he tried his mainstream ideas by using chemical farming and flooding his fields which eventually failed, while his neighbours were growing bumper crops. They have all learnt through failure; sometimes for years.'

Leela asked, 'All this in PG? I mean, do you have the resources such as plenty of land for so much of experimentation? And how does your Panchayat help?'

'For agricultural practices, many neighbouring villages have followed suit. And help from the Panch? They marry online info from the farming sector think-tanks with astro-meteorology, and we have never gone wrong.'

'Astrology? *You* and astrology?' exclaimed Leela in an appalled tone.

'This was an ancient Indian practice that had almost disappeared. I was inspired by physicist-meteorologist Dr P.R. Pisharoty to put it to full use. Appaji, an elderly farmer, and his daughter always check on animal, plant and insect behaviour. Invariably, they can detect warning signals for errant rains or disease which the computer analyses could not anticipate. There are astrological calculations too. At one time I would deride these. Now no more.'

Leela rolled her eyes and let out her pent up breath, 'Bhai, you really have changed so much that...'

'You feel contempt? Non-scientific nonsense? Every lesson I learnt in life is from the Bengali dictum: *"Jeta ghote, shetao bote"*. What happens – *is*. Why, you were quoting Gauquelin and Astrobiology. So pray, why not astro-meteorology? A different astro?'

Bharat was chuckling as he continued, 'I myself had campaigned against homeopathy while in Medical College. Used Placebos, conducted double blind tests... all that. Now, apart from humans, I have cured more serious cases with animals via homeopathy than I can count. The creatures never knew a Dr Bharat Biswas would be coming with some sweet pills – yes?

'It simply works. Just forget the theory! Someday science will certainly develop the instruments to find really how these things work. Science always works, albeit it needs time to validate. Right now it is the classic case of saying that what you speak in Greek is untrue because it doesn't make sense in Chinese.'

'Ahem. Ahemmmmm! Bhai, wonders don't cease with you.'

'Lili, there has never been a smooth ride here. I recall Santji's quote: "Zeus, who guided men to think, has laid down that wisdom

277

comes alone through suffering." That's for me too.'

Leela was looking at him with shining eyes. 'I love quotes.'

'Want another? I saw you looking at this quote from John H. Aughey in the basement:

"This is one of the sad conditions of life,

that experience is not transmissible

No man will learn from the sufferings of another

He must suffer himself."

'And then… Lili!'

Bharat knelt down and held Leela gently by her shoulders. Sudden tears were streaming down her face, while she stared vacantly into the distance.

Bharat waited for a long while till she calmed down. Then she whispered, 'Aditya suffered all his life from his burden. But I never learnt what that meant till I suffered myself. Now I know what you and he have endured, maybe only a little bit.'

Bharat gathered her into a warm hug and kept stroking her head. Then he asserted, 'Santji made me practice ways to still the mind. You must learn this discipline.'

They sat in silence for a long time with their eyes closed. Leela composed herself and tried to bring her mind to bear on what Bharat was saying.

'Santji said: "Controlling the mind; making it pinpointed like a magnet fixed to a core – *this is discipline*. There are four phases to this process. If you have complete mastery, you can wilfully focus your mind in *any* direction with equanimity. Those sadhus and faqirs who are really focused in this manner never break the spiritual laws."'

Leela spoke in a pained voice, 'Why don't all these Holy men use their so called powers to solve our suffering, especially economic ones?'

278

Bharat replied, '*Because they exist under spiritual laws whereby they cannot interfere and take over our karma,* though some do this willingly and suffer for it.'

He held out his fingers in a *Buddhi Mudra*. 'So how to attain such composure; to overcome suffering? Santji asked me to concentrate on certain mantras. I had to repeat these with the same *exact* modulation, same volume, day after day.'

He paused and then uttered the AUM mantra very slowly three times in a drawn out manner, vibrating the ending MMM sound prominently. 'For this to be effective, your body has to be cleansed; your gut freed of toxins which can clog your ability to be truly aware. Slowly, very slowly, with practice, this creates a vibration within you, till from head to foot you are filled with the same vibration. Then you can "witness" something, the matching Divine energy (Ishta Devata) manifesting in front of you. This is how Ragas manifest for true devotees.'

Leela whispered cautiously, 'Isn't this like the Photosounder Program or Cymatics, where any sound can be converted to its visual twin?'

'No. That software program is like playing a Raga on a synthesizer. Technically correct, but the inner subtle vibrations, the srutis are not captured, which the Mantras alone can evoke, with the human body as the medium.'

There was a pause in the narration. Then Bharat spread his palms outwards and brought them in to rest on his heart. 'Santji said: "As you are filled with the mantra vibration, you *witness* that energy field. It takes a form, a shape. You become one with it. You merge into yourself."

'This is a sadhana which stills the mind, in fact the essence of our Marga Sangeet. This I will teach you.'

Leela was staring into the distance. Bharat stopped speaking. They sat in complete quietude, merged into the forest and the immensity of the night leaving the sky. Leela felt the presence of Mahakaal around her more than ever before, as several forest flower scents enveloped her. She noticed that even Bharat was breathing very slowly with his eyes closed, taking in the pure air in deep inhalations.

They slowly walked back to the Habitat and returned to the worship room below. Bharat lit a small incense stick and sat back against the wall. The first birds and forest life had already started stirring.

Leela looked at Bharat and sighed sadly. 'You speak of natural law. Karmic law. I learnt that life is essentially one of suffering, because one learns personally only through suffering. That's what you said, right?

'Bhai, I want to ask: Why are we programmed to suffer through so many countless rebirths, instead of getting it right in the first instance? What on earth are these invisible disciplinary laws that binds us at our births, secrets which even your exalted Rishis cannot name? Like this constantly going back to the idea of sacrifice, or being sacrificed? This seemed to be a refrain in Santji's or sometimes even MK's talks: to sacrifice lives.

'Just think of all the pain that parents go through to bring up their children, so that any time — *any time* they can just be wretched away forever? Run over by a drunken trucker on a highway; pulled out of a car, raped and killed during mass madness — just like that! A Rockefeller being speared to death and eaten in Indonesia — just like that? Countless deaths which carry no meaning. Except this karmic reason you talk about, that this *had* to happen due to interwoven, self-created destiny from some previous time, or even due to actions from this lifetime, and that your great Yogis cannot really interfere? What is the point of it all?'

Bharat replied, 'Being sacrificed? I'll tell you what Santji once said, even though it's not exactly in this context. This was about Goddess Kali being an *ultimate* force field, a metaphor for the vast swathes of energy pulsating in the Black holes in the Universe; those dark energies which impact us — a scientific phenomenon.

'Now keep aside the imagery of Goddess Kali for a moment.

Think of her as an embodiment of this primal dark energy; the core of the conscious universe.'

Leela looked up.

'Santji said Ma Kali always gives birth to the phenomenal world – that's us. She, that is this core conscious energy, procreates only to devour her (its) own creation later, to produce a better strain. So – being sacrificed? Please contemplate how this works.

'Santji explained: "Ma Kali is *that* aspect of the life force that is revolution, which brings about real change in our world. That is why in every era, this primal energy force aka Ma Kali has given birth to her selected revolutionary children, only to take them back later as sacrifices on her own pedestal. In her incarnation as Revolution, the conscious energy force *(Ma Kali) uses her own children as offerings at each step of the revolution to regenerate things, to change the order of things.* That is how the human civilization has revitalized itself during different stages of her hoary past."'

Leela whispered, 'Magical words.'

'"Which child of hers she will anoint with *Sindoor* and invoke the sacred Mantras to accept as sacrifice; this "decision", this push and pull of her enormous energy fields, this is her mojo. See our history, when the fire of revolution spread in those golden days. This Kali," said Santji, "is *his* mother who directs him. She is Time's time, a Black energy that can swallow as well as direct time. There is no power in the Universe that can counter this primal energy force."'

Leela's lips barely moved in shaping her response, 'So profound. Really.'

She retreated into herself. There were a couple of night birds jostling for territory just above their heads. Gradually, they too fell silent.

Suddenly Leela opened her eyes and exclaimed, 'Isn't this concept somewhat resonating with what Dr Mancrop says, though in a perverse manner?'

Bharat was taken aback. 'What a coincidence! I too just remembered Dr Mancrop's last stellar performance about her "humans being harvested" theory. This was when Gen. Ponappa ran into her during his visit here.'

Leela said eagerly, 'That's what I wanted to know. How did Pony uncle know that you had some link with Santji or Gumnami Baba?'

Bharat shrugged. 'No idea. That day, he and Chitra Mashi were relishing their visit to PG. Now, Dr Mancrop's thesis with allusions to famines, wars, accidents... you know how she presents her idea. This had Pony uncle in splits.

'In one unguarded moment I remarked: "I can't really agree with all this conjecture but I have heard something similar". Dr Mancrop pounced on me: "Bharat, what's this? You have been sitting here quietly. Please tell us."'

Bharat continued, 'So I quoted the Ma Kali devouring her own children postulate which I had heard from Santji. Exactly as you heard it now. Suddenly Pony Uncle's boisterous mood swung the other way: "Whom are you quoting?" I replied: "My Manas Guru." He got even more flustered: "Is he from Uttar Pradesh?" I was unsuspecting, so I said: "Yes! But what does..."'

'His voice became a command: "Was this Guru from Faizabad, someone you never saw?"'

Leela's shock was immediate. 'What?'

Bharat continued, 'I was so taken aback that I only mechanically echoed: "How do you know that...?"'

'Pony Uncle got up and pointed his stick at me, "You will drown and take the others down with you!"'

Bharat clenched his fists and shook them in the air, 'You know he is like this when he gets into one of his fighting moods. He shouted: "You were the great free spirit spokesman – and now? Now you speak for a Guru who wants control over literature; supports the death penalty..."'

'I replied politely: "Sir, what *is* this?" But he continued firing: "The Guru who wants you to give him blood and he will give you freedom – kya – should I speak more?"'

'My God!' exclaimed Leela.

'At that very moment Chitra Auntie took hold of Pony Uncle by his shoulders and fixed him in an angry stare. She said: "We are leaving. NOW."'

'This is a huge mystery for me. How did Pony Uncle know anything about me and Santji, or even Faizabad and any Subhas Bose angle? Since this happened around 2014, I thought maybe he had read something about the Gumnami Baba story on the media.'

Leela asserted, 'He presumed you had brainwashed me about Gumnami Baba.'

'He will never believe in Babas. No paranormal stuff; no yogic kriyas or siddhis.'

They heard the sound of barking. Bima and his doggie gang were up and about, because some people seemed to be at the door at this unusual hour. Bharat turned and said, 'It is the PG vigilance squad doing their surprise inspection for the EMP Drill.'

Leela looked at her watch, 'At this hour?'

Bharat nodded. 'When something like a HEMP attack does happen, what is certain is that there will be no warning. So our ladies team has the right to go at any time from home to home to check if all the critical devices are unplugged and shielded. Anyone found wanting is fined and warned that henceforth they will not get any community help for living in PG.'

'Bhai, in short, what is this HEMP thing?'

'In short, High Altitude EMP (Electromagnetic Pulse). It is released by a HEMP device; a nuclear warhead detonated tens to

283

hundreds of kilometres above the Earth's surface. There are many variants, but the enemy does this to cripple a wide area without people dying instantly, like from conventional bombing. Power lines; electronics are all busted. I won't go into it now.'

'But you would never be a target for a HEMP or a chemical attack. It's too much!'

Bharat smiled, 'Lili, The peak fields in an EMP have a horseshoe like shape or spread. If we are very unlucky, we will get disabled in case Pune is targeted and we fall in that horseshoe spread. The Sukhoi squadrons are based there; so many defence establishments. So there is a top threat perception. And we *have* to survive any HEMP attack if PG is to serve as a Sanctuary for the multitudes of terrified people who need a hearth to remain alive.

'In fact, after years of having failed to persuade others, some village-towns between PG and Pune have started imitating our model for emergency survival mode. The current war talk on the media did the trick. You can walk into town a bit later with Sachin and see the rest of the Drill at work.'

Leela sighed and threw her hands up. Bharat gave her a warm hug. Bima's barking was getting more insistent. 'I guess you're feeling closeted again. Why don't you connect?'

Leela shook her head sadly, 'No matter what strictures I put, the minute I message any friend or co-worker that I am here, my peace will be blown. But yes, I'll be discreet and connect... Bimaaa!'

Bharat smiled, 'Hurry, or your child will tear the door apart.'

Leela rushed up with an 'Ohhhh'. Bharat came to the altar and closed his eyes. He touched Santji's pictures, took the main one to his head and drank in a long deep breath. He was ready for the day.

FORTY ONE

It was time to switch on her mobile. Leela called her Lawyer and allowed her to divulge her location in PG to selected people.

Her phone rang in an hour. It was Anu Mashi, so she took the call. Anu expressed her immense relief and joy that she was with Bharat. Leela could hear Shivdadu prompt something. Anu disclosed to her that Aditya's Trans Himalaya (TH) scientific expedition had taken off a few weeks ago. His mother Gayatri had called recently, asking for Leela urgently. Should they alert Gayatri to contact her now? Leela consented at once.

Right then Sachin burst into the room. 'Lishi, do you know…?' He stopped short on finding her on a call. Leela signalled to him to wait. He made an impatient face and left, leaving his laptop behind. He mimed with his hands that she could use it.

Leela could sense a certain finality in Anu's sadness. 'Lili, we fear for Bharat after that jeep blast. Baba keeps repeating: "we never fought for this India". What the British torture could not do, today's horrors have done. He just wants to go.'

Using Sachin's laptop, she checked on her emails. Then she tried to call Mada and Rajen, but both their mobiles were switched off. So she sent them voice messages that she had been with Bharat all these days and would be returning soon to Pune. She also added that they should not call her back or bother Bharat. She would connect again.

An hour past breakfast and her phone buzzed again. This time it was Gayatri with news that completely jolted her. Aditya had vanished from the main Trans Himalayan (TH) Expedition camp with some Tibetan Monk! It was still a mystery how this monk could have convinced Adi to drop out of such a high profile expedition. It was being speculated that the monk had brought Aditya some new inputs about his "missing" Buddha Artefact.

The TH Headquarters from Chandigarh had sent his last known coordinates to the Indian Army. He had been declared an absconder and was expected to be apprehended soon and brought back to Headquarters (HQ) to be debriefed and to face charges.

Leela whispered, 'Ma, I pray that he is brought back safely.'

There was only a painful silence from Gayatri's end. Leela bade her a feeble goodbye.

After the call, her mind went blank. Aditya, her dearest love, was now a fugitive. One of the most disciplined persons she had ever known had broken a strict expedition code and vanished in the Himalayas. She knew that once he was apprehended and brought back, it could mark the end of his career as an archaeologist, apart from the public humiliation.

She *had* to meet Aditya, if only to admit her error. She was certain that he still loved her. She would bring him to PG and start a new life here. They could contribute so much to the children from poor families who had never known any education in their lives.

There was an urgent knock at the door. Sachin rushed in and braked to a halt on seeing her wet eyes. 'Should I come later?'

'No, sit. Sorry I forgot to call you back.'

Leela threw her hair back and composed herself. 'Shall we continue our session?'

Sachin immediately sat down at her feet, notepad and pen ready. Leela started off where she had left.

Two hours later, she was done, exhausted by her effort. Once again, both pondered over what could have been.

Sachin spoke with a sense of disbelief, 'Lishi, I just cannot understand how a person whose age does not match or who does not even look exactly the same, can have anything to do with Netaji. Whether it's the person Baba met in Munsiari or you encountered near Buxa Forest Reserve.'

'I don't understand either. In my case I have never met Santji, so Mahakaal is a fresh entity for me. But he knew every intimate detail of my life.'

Sachin looked suitably unimpressed. 'This is something a number of ESP gifted and clairvoyant people are known to do adeptly. They can reel off all details about your past, and often your future.'

The repeated honking of cars interrupted their talk. Sachin looked out. A number of press cars had suddenly arrived, and one of them had hit another while reversing. The two drivers were shouting at each other. Sachin turned back and said, 'I forgot to tell you the breaking news. See these chaps outside? Baba is back in the limelight, and this time his stock has gone through the roof.'

Leela looked at Sachin with a cynical smile on her face.

'This morning Chinese troops launched heavy firing on the Gilgit border, and that's a first in decades. They claim they are protecting their project, the OBOR corridor in Gilgit and Balochistan through to the Gwadar port, which they accuse India of wanting to destroy. Baba's warnings about a two front war being sparked from Gilgit Baltistan has zoomed back to the top.'

'But why should one act of border firing bring about such renewed attention for Bhai?'

'It's a full chain. In Bangladesh, the "back to our culture" movement there is fighting the jihadi forces and the latter have pushed the violence over our borders. Then India has turned the screws on Pakistan via her declared resolve to renegotiate the Indus Water treaty. So Pakistan threatens war. And now this escalated tension over the

Chinese OBOR mega project running through our land, which they possess illegally.

'Moreover, India's underbelly has been bored by hundreds of sleeper cells, both jihadi and Red Brigade. They are all waiting for the signal to launch an all-out war, which is just a call away. Baba had predicted all this.'

Sachin opened a news summary on his phone: *'Slowly, a probable war scenario is starting to look real. Hundreds of non-political self-help volunteer groups have sprung up everywhere in cooperation with ex-army men. They are also distributing home-made EMP survival kits in some urban pockets.*

'Meanwhile, the "no tax" movement is still going strong. Many thousands of women from rural India are networked and are standing up against the Panchayats and local politicians who have not delivered on their promises. They have posters of Bharat Biswas and Prithak Ghati at their protest sites.'

Puran Singh also came in. 'In many towns residents have started storing cereals, medications, candles. There is panic. Politicians are demanding Bhaiyya's arrest for creating a war drama.'

Bharat returned just after sunset. He had received SOS calls from Brijesh, Srinivasan and the entire 'Detox India' campaign group. They were requesting him to stand by what he had written earlier. It was now or never. They all wanted Bharat to get involved.

Several TV Hosts and channels had been requesting him for interviews on exclusive shows. Top politicians had sent him feelers through emissaries with an open cheque to join their ranks. But one public appearance at a mass gathering was enough for him.

An hour after dinner, there was a knock on his door. It was Leela, looking fresh but with a tinge of sadness. 'I have unsettling news coming in about Adi, but that's for later. Bhai, there's an almost regular presence of the press here. It has become impossible for me to go out freely.'

Bharat gave her a huge childlike smile. His eyes were twinkling, as if he was about to spill some secret. '*Chalo*, let's go out now.'

'Now? Where?'

'I'll take Puran's mobike. We both wear helmets anyway, so no identification issues.'

'But where?'

'Till wherever we want to drive and stop – and then start again. Talk, or just walk in silence.'

Leela jumped up and down like a schoolgirl. 'Just give me a minute to gear up.'

FORTY TWO

Bharat wheeled out the bike and they were off. They passed several herbal gardens, the strong fragrances heightening their sense of being one with nature.

It was a crescent moon. They reached the top of a hillock from where the town could be seen with its twinkling lights below. For many kilometres beyond, there was only darkness. Bharat headed for a makeshift bench under a huge tree which had bent awkwardly from its trunk and jutted out into the valley below. Once again the strong smell of some aromatic plants wafted around. They unwound in silence, drinking in the tranquil atmosphere in a restful stupor.

'This is one of my favourite spots where I come even in the day, especially when I want to remember what Prithak Ghati first looked like – and its spread now,' said Bharat looking dreamily at the valley.

Then he continued after a pause, 'Tell me the news about Adi.'

Leela's lips started quivering. 'Bhai... the man has abandoned his Trans Himalayan expedition and vanished with a Tibetan Monk.' She paused to control herself, 'Gayatri Ma thinks it is the same old curse, some clues about his missing Buddha Image. I don't want to dwell on it right now.'

'But this is terrible, I mean about Adi.'

Leela cleared her throat and looked up. 'Let's talk about PG down there. Santji's ideas live in it.'

Bharat waited till she had composed herself. Then he sighed and continued, 'Not all of Santji's ideas have been followed here. For instance, I couldn't do much about his "Shakti Vahini" concept – some sort of moral cum military force drawn from the youth which would produce future leaders...'

Leela raised her eyebrows. 'Govt backed?'

'Yes of course.'

Leela asked, 'Frankly, how does this gel with his thinking that the youth must focus on higher studies?'

'This Vahini (force) was to be recruited from youth other than those students who had the aptitude for higher studies. On this score, he stands vindicated today. Just see the specimens of spurious, undisciplined youngsters projected as our future leaders.

'Santji said: "Place noble real-life examples before the youth, with no trace of man's debased tendencies. They will be inspired to lift themselves to a higher plane."'

'I can't agree. It is almost impossible to correct serious behavioural flaws in today's generation. Such idealism doesn't always work,' said Leela emphatically.

'Depends. I agree that students are always vulnerable to manipulation via their baser instincts, but this is true even for the general public.'

Bharat stopped and stretched out his arm with four fingers spread out, 'Santji spoke of four behavioural rules.'

'Axioms?'

'Correct. The negative forces control the masses at large by exploiting these fundamental truths.

'Rule number one: *Public memory is proverbially short.*

'Rule number two: *Public will come to believe anything that will be constantly and repeatedly propagated to them for a long time.*

'Rule number three: *Normally, the public is incapable of remaining at a high pitch for a long time.* Just observe today's youth when they are agitated; how fast their attention can be diverted.

'Rule number four: *The majority are gullible and can be used in any way or for any purpose by such negative forces. The public loses interest in anything which is long protracted.* So, the manipulative politicians love it when the youth are caught up with this daily need for new fixes and issues to occupy the mind. It suits their scheming ways.'

Leela affirmed, 'I get the drift, Bhai.'

'This manipulation started from Day one. Even now 15th August 1947 is celebrated as Independence Day without any correction in our History Books, whereas we actually got a servile Dominion Status on that date, after millions of deaths during the partition.

'In 1960, looking back, Nehru openly stated why they agreed to the British Partition formula, and I quote him: "The truth is that we were tired men, and we were getting on in years too. Few of us could stand the prospects of going to prison again – and if we had stood for a united India as we wished it, prison obviously awaited us.*"'

Leela nodded, 'I know. Even Sachin knows this quote.'

Bharat sighed, 'Generations accepted this monstrosity saying: Let's not live in the past. Almost all the fearless fighters who fought the British remain absent from our History books for seven decades now. The education syllabi have been dominated by intellectuals who think patriotism in the name of "Mother India" is a bourgeois degradation, outmoded and infantile.

'Remember college? If someone rarely came wearing a Dhoti to the classes, they were mocked at – this is what I saw again and again. This is what Lord Macaulay's British education has done to us. Try teaching anything with the Hinduism tag in schools, and you are stymied by the "communal" flag. This is the Commie manipulation at work.'

* Leonard Mosley, The Last Days of the British Raj (Publisher: Weidenfeld and Nicolson; First American Edition edition (1961)

'Fully agree. I experienced the same in college.'

'These intelligentsia run around raising flags for rebels in Namibia and Nicaragua, but can't revere our own freedom fighters. Such worthies don't utter a word if our soldiers die while fighting enemies, but they rise in great protest if people are dying in Kosovo, or when insurgents are eliminated within India. And our present politicians distract public attention by selling jingoistic capsules and fanciful economic dreams. They exploit these four rules with great expertise.'

Leela protested, 'But why should it boil down to a "pseudo-secular versus casteist-communal" kind of choice for us Indians, where the latter includes almost all parties? Are these our only options? Santji's and your idea of patriotism as a love affair with the earth around you has been completely hijacked. What a degenerate state of affairs.'

Bharat nodded in agreement, 'Yes, this scenario needs to transform urgently.'

Leela was still irate. 'Why can't people organize themselves and act to change things? It beats me.'

Bharat rested his head on his palm and closed his eyes, imitating a sleep mode, 'Santji said we are still sleeping, because we love living in self-delusion. The moment we are awakened, we will be forced to stand up and join in relentless work to change matters from the roots. So we want to avoid that and keep sleeping.

'He said, "When our people don't want to awaken and correct their lives by an act of cleansing, they will be awakened by a hammer blow". I had always deduced the hammer blow to mean a catastrophic war.'

Leela changed tracks. 'Bhai, I remember once when I asked Mahakaal what was his occupation, he told me jovially that he was a firefly.'

Bharat's eyebrows shot up. 'Even Santji used the same term for himself. He said that as a firefly he had a duty to perform; to be seen somewhere, to vanish, then again become visible elsewhere.'

'But Bhai? A firefly inflicting a hammer blow?'

Bharat guffawed, 'Maybe an army of giant fireflies, each the size of a skyscraper? Joking, but suppose I tell you that once I saw a cluster of UFOs near Kongka La, Ladakh for a few minutes? They were in a perfect formation and behaving exactly like fireflies: glowing; vanishing and suddenly showing up again elsewhere in that clear sky. Who knows how Santji will show up again? He had promised that he would manifest after "it was enacted."'

'What was enacted?'

'A war. He repeatedly said that no one need believe him. We should validate our beliefs from real life happenings. But he had hinted at terrible times.'

'Such as?'

'He spoke of a war which would be more devastating than anything in the last 700 years. He warned: store up rice and other cereals, all essentials necessary for keeping alive for at least two to three years.'

'Years?!'

'Yes, years. He said a day will come when no food will be available anywhere, and this stored stock will sustain life. Ditto water. We should recharge underground aquifers, make water distribution lists as per household numbers – why? *Because the entire water of the city would become polluted. Tap water would be useless!*'

'Bhai, are you telling me that you prepared for such a war, all because he provided this hint – without any time frame? PG is not a city.'

'No, because I myself reasoned that such a war would be thrust on India. I had urban plans to prepare for such a scenario. But Santji said very clearly that it is only in the rural areas that we could survive and rise again. That is why I worked only in the countryside.'

'In 2003, did he speak about such a war?'

'No, but he urged me to develop small-town hamlets, despite my previous failures. And then Prithak Ghati happened. But even when he came here, Santji told me: "I ask no one to join in my terrible *Yagna* (ritual), because I know no one will be ready to leap into these fires to revive the motherland."

'So Lili, right now, large numbers of aspirational Indians are partying. They want to only eat, to get, to receive. So be it. What will happen, will happen.'

There was a long silence, as they looked at the town sleeping like a real living being below them; throbbing, revitalizing. They were surrounded by the occasional fireflies, rustle of nocturnal creatures and the heavenly aroma of native fauna releasing their fragrance. The war scenario seemed very far away, perhaps on some distant planet.

Finally Bharat got to his feet and walked to the mobike. Leela followed. He paused and looked around, 'It is so peaceful. Starting the bike now ...'

Leela nodded and whispered, 'Let's just push it till the top of the pass.'

'Clutch and brake – *chalo.*'

They took their time to slowly push the bike to the top of the steep winding path, and then paused to catch their breath. Bharat got on and motioned to her to seat herself. But suddenly he stood still and held out his hand in a warning gesture. Leela froze without a murmur.

Bharat parked the mobike on one side and signalled to Leela to follow him. He whispered, 'Don't make the slightest sound. Something is out there.'

Leela followed him very slowly, almost tiptoeing through the dense growth. This side of the hill was densely forested, but Bharat seemed to know the way. Leela stumbled several times and steadied herself with Bharat's help, who was climbing with practiced ease. Each time Bharat squeezed her hand as a warning sign, they made a halt.

Finally, they reached the top. After a few minutes, Bharat's distraction revealed itself. When they looked very carefully towards the opposite hill almost a half km away, they could see a long, snaking file of people moving silently in the dim moonlight. Bharat looked carefully through his field glasses which he always carried. Then he warned under his breath, 'Ominous.'

'What ominous?'

Bharat quietly handed her the glasses fitted with night vision. It was indeed a chilling sight. These were armed men and women on some mission. They emerged from the forest in groups of twenty and quickly crossed over to the other hill before the next 'sub squad' revealed itself.

There was a jeep stationed at one end of the pass which used its blinkers as a signal to another mobike, which was positioned about 150 meters below them. The biker also seemed to be a lookout man and was flashing torch signals to another person who was hardly 80 meters from Bharat at the crest of the road.

Bharat lowered his face to Leela and whispered, 'Sheer luck. If I had started my bike, these chaps would have melted into the forest and we would never know about them.'

Leela spoke into his ear. 'But who are they?'

'Reds. Maoist ultras. They had last used this route almost ten years ago when several encounters happened. This is just before I came here.'

Bharat took the field glasses and looked again. 'This is their largest Company file I've ever seen.'

After about twenty minutes, the 'mini' army vanished. The lookout man, positioned just below Bharat, pulled out another mobike from the bushes. He glided down to the bottom of the valley with the engine switched off, to join the second bike. A mini Truck emerged from the forest. Both the mobikes were quickly loaded into it and covered with sugarcane. The truck started and noisily ascended till it rounded Bharat and Leela and descended towards the bypass around the town.

They now heard the jeep start on the other hill. Slowly, very slowly it reversed and climbed the opposite pass till it vanished from their view.

Bharat waited for another ten minutes before he motioned to Leela to follow him. Once again, he squeezed her hand for caution. Leela whispered, 'Now what?'

'They usually always position a couple of foot soldiers at vantage points all night when they have such mass movement. Best is for us to exit silently.'

Once they reached home, Bharat parked the mobike and hesitated for a moment before going towards his room. The farm dogs came up to welcome them and then went back to their slumber. A couple of small snakes slithered past.

Leela was still tense. 'Now what will you do? File a report?'

'If I do, they will immediately try to implicate me to divert attention from the agitations.'

'But if you don't report and there is trouble, they could still create problems for you.'

Bharat pondered and replied slowly, 'There has been no record of any Maoist activity near our region for many years. But now, with such a huge rank and file from the PLGA (People's Liberation Guerrilla Army) on the move, they are onto some operation ordered by their CMC (Central Military Committee). I only hope this is not another of my predictions coming true, that of sleeper cells attacking urban regions as a dry run for their D day.'

There was silence for a while as Leela ran a furious mental search. All her Defence contacts were either through Mada or Rajen. She knew Bharat would not want to contact them either. Then the same face flashed in Bharat's and her mind at the same time, and they exclaimed together, 'Gen. Ponappa!'

'But after his last visit here…' said Bharat.

'We need to find out why he got mad at you. But he is the right person to contact.'

'I'll not risk calling him. Our mobile numbers are probably under surveillance anyway.'

'Bhai, I had promised talk to him after meeting you. Let's plug this together.'

'Tomorrow? We can leave at dawn. Send Pony uncle a message from Firdaus's phone. If he doesn't respond, I'll call him from another number. But…'

'But what?'

'It's Sachin's last weekend, so we should get back by evening.'

'Of course. I really forgot.'

Leela smiled and mumbled a '*shubhratri*'. They retired for the night, but questions kept crowding her mind. Bharat met someone who stayed behind a curtain till 1985; then ran into another person in 2003 who literally carried on interacting with him exactly from where he had parted from Santji, and yet this person looked younger. Then the gentle Mahakaal whom she met, and who looked almost the same as the faked sketch based on Subhas Bose…

Were they all different people or the same person in different surreal appearances? And why was this mystery pulling her in? Why did Mahakaal appear to her in Kumbh? Were Bharat and she under some spell?

As soon as the last thought crossed her mind, she chuckled and laughed at herself. But of course there was no spell! Bharat had his feet solidly on the ground. She was equally confident of herself, but she had to see to the end of this mystery. Her last thought before sleep descended on her was the long file of young men and women marching to some mission. It was ominous.

FORTY THREE

Firdaus received a message from Gen. Arjun Ponappa, stating that he was looking forward to their visit. They left very early as planned. Both Bharat and Leela dozed off during the journey and were alerted once the car entered the outskirts of Pune.

As was his wont, Gen. Ponappa was waiting at the gate. He embraced Bharat warmly without any trace of rancour. His Bengali wife Chitra emerged with her beatific smile and held Leela in a long hug. They followed Arjun into the living room.

Leela began impatiently, 'Pony uncle, I would have come earlier...'

Chitra stopped her, 'Lili, first have *naashta* right away. You've had a long drive.'

The others got seated for breakfast while Bharat took his time looking around at the spartan yet beautifully decorated space. Arjun tracked him with his eyebrow delicately raised.

As Leela described their experience and the accidental sighting of the Maoist 'Company' the previous night, the mood turned a tad serious. Gen. Ponappa kept tucking into his neer dosas, but his eyes were alert.

Once she had finished speaking, the General motioned for silence. He looked at his watch and said, 'If you had reported this to the police, either way your goose would have been cooked, given the situation you both are in today. So I'll do the needful, while keeping you both out of it.'

Once breakfast was over, they shifted back to the living room. Arjun entered his study and locked the door behind him. Leela and Chitra continued their talk on animal care and help for the aged. Bharat buried himself in an article on the Indus Water Treaty and the OBOR corridor which was now occupying the top Defence brass.

Arjun was soon back. 'I have news coming in that Insurgents have already launched an attack an hour ago.'

'Where?' asked Bharat, looking up from the magazine.

'This is over a hundred kilometres away near Kolhapur, so this couldn't be the "Company" you had spotted.'

Bharat sat up. 'Kolhapur? But that is nowhere near their strongholds.'

'They have attacked the local armoury and police station, using the latest weaponry and even mortars. Encounter is still going on.'

There was a brief pause as everyone seemed to be taken aback. Leela contended, 'But Maoists don't conduct urban operations of this scale.'

'Scale? This is their seventh attack since dawn.' said the General emphatically.

'Oh God!' exclaimed Leela.

'This is war, just as Bharat had forecast. They've launched attacks all over the country, spreading both east and west from their central corridor. Sringeri, Thiruvananthapuram, Jabalpur, Agra Cant, Bhilai, Raipur and counting. Our C-60 commandos have been alerted to find the Maoist consolidated "Company" near your area.'

Arjun performed a regulation salute. 'Bharat, your predictions... I salute you.'

'Sir, that was over twenty-five years ago. I did not time it for now.' said Bharat.

'All the more remarkable. The top guns who mattered ran you down about the Maoist threat. Ditto about EMP. I've been shouting from the rooftops for a compulsory drill as prep against an EMP or chemical attack. Having seen Prithak Ghati, I never imagined this could be done in today's India – and here you made it possible.' Arjun waved his pipe in the air. 'Ok...topic change now. Tiger, beer as usual?'

Leela was amused to find Bharat nodding, 'Sir, Beer *chalega*.'

The men raised a toast. Arjun exclaimed, 'To you Bharat, your dream and what you made possible.'

'Sir, to your health and fighting spirit. Actually, I did little.'

Arjun leaned forward. 'You know Tiger, I'm not one for humility.'

Bharat nodded in disagreement. 'Sir, without our unique Panchayat; the many people who joined us; friends from my college days who are our bulwark... my ideas would mean nothing. I've failed so often. Without...'

Arjun's eyes narrowed, as his voice went a tad higher. 'Without your Guru's guidance you would be nothing?'

'Babloo!' scolded Chitra in a stern tone.

'Now, did I say something offensive?' said Gen. Ponappa with a smile, as he turned to face Leela, 'In any case we had agreed to talk after you met your Bhai and asked him about... you know what.'

Leela nodded silently. Chitra got up. 'You'll have to excuse me. I want to get lunch ready in time. You have a long drive back before it gets dark.'

Leela turned back to face Arjun. 'So Uncle, I've spoken to Bhai. I'm loaded. Shoot.'

Arjun took a big swig at his beer. 'Lili, I remain concerned about your encounter with this man in the forest. Let's get to the point. Who is he?'

Leela inclined her head. 'I don't know.'

Arjun turned to Bharat, 'Lili says you never ever spoke to her about this character, this Baba from Faizabad. Yes?'

'True,' answered Bharat, 'I told her about him for the first time only during her present visit.'

'This is the first mystery. How did Lili zero in on just *that* painting of this Baba? He died in 1985, so…'

'Correction!' interrupted Bharat, 'Santji purportedly died.'

'Who is this Santji?'

'That's how I addressed him. Now Sir – there was no Death Certificate. No one saw the face *both* just before *and* after death, except the chief Surgeon (Late) Dr Mishra, who was silent on what actually happened,' Bharat gestured with his hands, 'There are followers who believe that he changed his abode through a Yogic process, leaving behind his mortal body and entering a new one. Or that a body double died, and was cremated.'

Arjun scowled at Bharat. The ridges on his forehead stood out. 'Ok, I accept only for argument's sake that the Baba faked his death for unknown reasons and got away by some jadu – some magic! There are many more stories of Netaji being alive today, each one more bizarre than the other. So, would Lili be one of the lucky few to have seen him?'

"The person I met did not look over sixty, maybe even younger.' said Leela.

'Then how do you explain that your saviour resembles that photoshopped sketch?'

'But Mahakaal did resemble Netaji's sketch! How, I can't explain.'

Arjun peered at her, 'Bhagwanji was eighty-eight when he died or went away. Gumnami Baba is a journalist's name tag for Bhagwanji. There are other names too, including both Bharat's Santji (Anaam Sant) and your Mahakaal. Are all these guys emerging from the dead?'

'How do you know these details?' asked Bharat.

Arjun said emphatically, 'I've made it my mission to find out about your Gumnami Baba. Because I can't believe that you both have *de facto* joined the "Netaji Cottage Industry" on an issue milked by every variety of lunatics, politicians, lazy armchair experts and their ilk.'

'I deny this,' retorted Leela.

'Sir, that's an assumption I can't tick either,' responded Bharat.

Arjun paused to take a whiff at his pipe. 'Ok Bharat. It seems this Baba – he is your Guide. So you have seen him?'

'Yes Sir.'

Arjun looked from Bharat to Leela, his jaws working. The sounds from the kitchen had come to a halt. There was a short, uneasy silence.

'I am presuming that you met this Baba till 1985?'

'Yes Sir. Ten times in five years.'

'Are you sure the *same* person spoke to you every time from behind the curtain, and not some body-double?'

'The voice sounded the same.'

'Now we're getting somewhere. So you saw him ten times?'

'No – only once for a few seconds.'

'Oh? So was he or was he not?'

'Who?'

'Netaji Subhas Bose?'

'Too fleeting to be one hundred per cent sure. But yes, there was much resemblance.'

'Only much? Did he resemble that sketch?'

Bharat thought gravely for a while and added, 'As I said, it was too fleeting. But the eyes were – I can't describe it – different from any sketch or old photo I had seen.'

'Explain that.'

'The eyes had an overwhelming glow. One couldn't look for long.'

'So then? What *was* the resemblance!'

'Basic features. Jaw structure. Forehead. Cleft in the front teeth.'

'He still had his front teeth intact?'

Bharat smiled and nodded. 'Looks like Sir.'

Arjun leaned back and grimaced, his hand with the pipe beating a steady rhythm on his knee. Then he spoke slowly with emphasis, 'Then why don't you admit that you met Netaji and Lili met some perfect clone?'

Bharat said evenly, 'I can't compare with any previous sighting of Netaji pre-1945, since I was not even born then. Santji never said he was Netaji, though he provided all the dots to conclude that he was Subhas Bose.'

Arjun opened another beer and poured it for Bharat and himself. Chitra came in silently with a huge bowl of mulberries, and returned to the kitchen. Bharat made an eye gesture to Leela, who signalled she was ready. Then he turned to face Arjun.

'Sir, I have a question. In fact both of us do.'

Gen. Ponappa nodded impassively, as Leela leaned forward to take some mulberries. Bharat posited, 'Sir, something about Santji being my guide rankles with you deeply.'

Arjun's look hardened, 'It does. Because I can see a total mismatch between what you both stand for – and what this person advocated or did from behind the veil.'

'Uncle, please spell it out,' said Leela.

'The fact is: what Netaji or this Santji said makes him *my* man, a soldier's dream for a true leader. But how does he become *your* kind of man beats me. This is someone who wants death penalty for *all* offences. You steal a pen – shot! You take or give a bribe – shot! Bharat, is this your man?'

Bharat reacted calmly, 'I'll respond after you're done.'

Arjun turned to Leela, 'This Baba spoke of the slaughter of a buffalo by his cook. Lili, the animal rights activist, is this your hero?'

Leela countered and matched Arjun's voice with her combative tone, 'How would *you* know, sitting here on your grand sofa, what Santji said?'

An amused smile appeared on Arjun's face, as he kept tapping his pipe on his knee. He was beginning to enjoy this sparring. 'I have checked with several people who spoke to him across that same curtain. There is either evidence or sworn testimony that right from RSS Guru Golwalkar – to one of our past Presidents, they all met this undercover man. Come on, tell me why?'

Arjun looked at his audience, but no one replied, while he kept hitting his closed right fist into his open left palm. 'I have also relied on the gospel for the Kolkata-based followers of Gumnami Baba: this Bengali compilation of his sayings, "*Oi Mohamanab Ashe*", meaning "The Superman Comes" or something to that effect. Chitra translated it for me.'

'Ahaa!' exclaimed Leela as she let out her pent up breath, 'Bhai told me about this book just the other day.'

Arjun held out both his index fingers for emphasis, 'The work is hagiographical – completely! Repetitive, mystifying. *Maybe deliberately so.* Full of complexities with deeper meaning which can tax a normal reader. And yet, it has all the info which you would need to profile this Baba.'

'But Sir, how did you hear about this obscure book?' said Bharat, 'Even we haven't read it so far.'

Before Arjun could reply, Chitra appeared again with a grim look on her face. 'Why not? With so much sacrifice by your INA elders, why no interest in this persona?'

Leela turned to Chitra, 'Mashi, all that my INA elders taught me only brought me into endless conflict with life as it is. I did not want to know about some hidden chapter that could not be rolled back.'

'And now you do – or no?'

'It all changed after I met Mahakaal. He silently made me realize that I just cannot run away from it. I had to be a warrior.'

'Says who?' boomed Arjun, 'That you *had* to be a warrior? Whose warrior? Under whose command?'

'Nobody's command. I will remain a warrior to my own cause.'

'Rubbish! You are already under a spell, to be a sacrificial offering to someone else's cause. Bharat, you too.'

'In what way, Sir?' queried Bharat.

'To explain your "being under a spell", I will need to quote the man. He made these utterances in his fullest senses. This Baba's Doctors had confirmed that he was perfectly sane – in fact having exceptional mental skills.'

Bharat asserted, 'Agreed. I myself learnt not to judge such a *siddha purush* by normal standards, including his mood swings between various Tantrik sadhanas. For me, his sayings emanated from an awe-inspiring intellect.'

Arjun continued, 'Firstly, I presume that your Santji was Netaji Subhas Bose.'

'If you believe that, you might know why the veil was there; why the Hitler stigma dogged him...'

'I know. Even today Netaji is unfairly stigmatized for shaking Hitler's hand, but this was a top shot strategy in my book. It was war. End of ethics. Enemy's enemy – *my ally for now, solely* to free my motherland from a diabolical Ruler of equal criminality.'

Leela cut him short, 'Please get to the point and stop boring us!

Prove how we are under a spell.'

Chitra peeped out and flashed a thumbs up sign. Arjun recovered his wits and smiled at her indulgently. 'Ok, straight on. This great man, who after the Siberian Gulag and God alone knows what else he endured, *comes back to India betrayed by all and blacked out of history by an ungrateful people*. He stays on for almost another thirty years, yes?'

Leela riposted immediately, 'Objection again! Netaji in Siberia and his later life is still unproven. But you think that because he stayed incognito in India – that he was a coward?'

'Never. Maybe there was some strategy in all this. He himself talks about splitting the Communist nations; playing his chess moves in South East Asia; working on a unique global plan. Sounds incredible enough, but often his pronouncements have been vindicated by the passage of time.

'I also read about his supposed role in the Vietnam war in outmanoeuvring the Americans – Ok, don't interrupt – it is speculation but this too *can* explain his remaining undercover,' submitted Arjun. Then he thumped his knee forcefully, 'But what is indisputable is – *he decided not to come out from his seclusion*. Debate over.'

Leela kept quiet, while Bharat nodded.

Gen. Ponappa continued, 'So, he does not come out – by choice. And then a fanatically devoted, tiny band of bravehearts mainly from Bengal locate him as a Bhagwanji in UP and serve him for their entire lifetimes through immense hardships. By now he sets up some sort of secret mission, and a few followers are co-opted into this. *For them, he IS Netaji Subhas Bose – yes?* They keep up his supply lines and do whatever is asked of them. The man lives out his life with the help of people who are for all purposes sacrificial offerings. Why?'

'Sir, every leader has devouts or soldiers who die for a cause. What is Santji's crime?'

'Bharat, we soldiers breathe sacrifice for the nation and Netaji is my ideal as a leader. Right from the Indian Legion in Germany, to the galvanized INA fighters – they all sacrificed themselves for this man who had put his own life on the line. But damn it, as Santji he has his Ma Kali demanding sacrifices for all kinds of esoteric causes, often for his strange activities outside our country.'

Bharat shook his head sadly, 'Sir, this is a man who entered the ring of fire alone. He became the fire *and* the firefighter. If bringing him a few music records and other such offerings is sacrifice, then I'm honoured. He never insisted. Anyone could have walked away, but they made his cause their own.'

Arjun slammed his fist on the hand rest, 'That's exactly my point, the spell cast by this man! One by one, his followers have all passed away, often enduring great suffering, waiting for his promised reappearance. Sacrificial Offerings – all. You both are next.'

Bharat merely smiled, but Leela snapped, 'Nonsense!'

Arjun's tone now turned injurious. 'Can you deny that ever since he departed in 1985, things have slipped almost beyond repair in today's hell all around you? And still we swallow this bunkum that he will return soon to harness his great powers and save the country?'

Leela countered, 'Why is he such a hero to you, if you are so agitated about him using people as sacrificial fodder?'

'The fact is that the mission this Baba wanted to bring to fruition is one which both of you have fought against, at least in part.'

'I don't accept that,' replied Bharat quietly.

'Not me either,' added Leela.

Arjun got up and pulled out a bound book from his shelf. 'This "*Oi Mahamanab Ashe*" is written by one Charnik, a pseudonym for some of the Baba's followers who were people of impeccable character. These writers would be petrified of even changing a word of what the Baba said, such was his influence over them. The spell – remember that.'

'Hang on,' said Leela, 'What is in this book that proves your point? Bhai told me that it was a faithful record of Santji's sayings to his followers, which was even approved by him?'

'Lili dear, he talks of the future society which he wants to shape. With whose help? Some volunteer army he calls the "Shakti Vahini" – a State within a State.'

Leela turned to Bharat in excitement, 'You were talking about this last night?'

As Bharat nodded, Arjun continued, 'See what is clearly written here. Death penalty for the smallest crime. I see little difference between the powers which are to be vested in this Vahini and those with the initial squads set up by the Chinese Communists.' Arjun paused to find a page and then resumed, 'Except for gainfully employed people and students, he proposed to send back all other city inhabitants to their villages by force, and he termed them as..,' Arjun struggled with the Bengali, 'all *phajeel faltu* (flippant, worthless) people.'

Leela suppressed a giggle, while Bharat kept a straight face.

Arjun tapped the table for attention. 'He wanted all unemployed youth between seventeen to forty years of age to be enlisted in the Army Corps. But no minorities allowed in this mission activity for at least three years. Only Bengali Hindus. Yes, I can hear today's Hindutva forces cheering.'

Bharat and Leela exchanged glances, while Arjun carried on, 'There is more. I quote: "Only Kali worshipping real Bengali warriors, whatever that means, have to be settled on all of Bengal's hilly border regions – AND – and all non-Bengalis already settled there have to be made to vanish 100%."'

Leela made a face in protest and wanted to speak, but Arjun's steamroller went on. '"All tasteless literature, culture, arts etc to be thrown out and all similar endeavours to be ruthlessly controlled" – sounds familiar Bharat?'

'Uncle, I need a word in,' protested Leela.

'I'm not done yet. You know, there's so much in this same tract, especially about ensuring quality higher education AND discipline AND dredging rivers AND creating crop buffers – above all about the marriage of discipline and democracy that I *fully* agree with. But – and this is a big BUT, this doesn't erase the fact that "it's my way or the highway" for him, and to get onto that highway, your Kali worshipping Guide always *demands* sacrifices.'

Arjun squatted down in front of Bharat and looked at him in the eye, 'Tell me, man to man, you champion of freedom and individual rights... Can you live with this?'

'No.'

Arjun's eyes widened. 'No? Then how is he your Guide?'

'Sir, for one he never ever said anything in this vein to me. Secondly, what appears so parochial to you must have a context.'

'Context? Isn't that damned clear?'

'Santji was the most egalitarian human being I have ever known,' replied Bharat calmly as Arjun sank back in his sofa with an impatient look, 'If he has implied "cleansing of so and so people", or not enlisting minorities... this *has* to have a context. In fact, regarding clearing out Bengal's border areas, his quoted words from the 1960's have proved prophetic, right? Look at the alarming levels of infiltration and regular violence in those same regions today.'

Leela too turned combative, 'Uncle, ahimsa or universal love doesn't wash in real life, not when there are forces who claim the right to kill you.'

Bharat pressed on, 'Santji thought the idea of Universal love is fake. He said that when you love your habitat on mother earth: you love the world, not vice versa. I repeat, every sentence that you quoted has a exact context and an intended time for manifestation.'

Arjun held up a single finger, requesting for silence. He was staring at Bharat. 'Now wait a minute. A short while ago you said: "He *is* still my Guide". Did I miss the tense?'

Bharat smiled, 'Sir, you heard me right. He appeared to guide me three more times.'

Chitra emerged from the kitchen and was listening intently. 'He met you recently? The same Baba?'

Bharat nodded silently, but Arjun would have none of it. 'What? Behind another curtain?'

'No Sir, in the open,' Bharat's rejoinder was on an even keel.

'Seriously? You saw him properly at last – a 120 years plus person?'

Bharat took a deep breath and spoke with his eyes initially closed, 'No Sir, I saw a human being who looked maybe over sixty, but nevertheless, for me he was the same person.'

Arjun stood up. He was bristling with anger. 'You both have lost your marbles! If you have been meeting a sixty-year-old person, he simply cannot be the Gumnami Baba from Faizabad!'

'Sir, he is,' replied Bharat in his typical soft tone, 'He knows every exact detail of all our previous talks. I repeat – *EXACT*. Right up to his last talk with me in July 1985, including my handing over four LPs during a power failure at that time. I can't explain this rationally, but he is he.'

Arjun's rage boiled over, 'Who knows, maybe you were nailed by some fucking black magic that a soldier like me doesn't understand.'

'Babloo!' scolded Chitra.

Bharat raised his voice. 'Sir. My Guide was a beacon in the darkness when I was lost. Mine was no encounter with a black magic man. Where is the question of sacrifice?'

'I'm told a person never knows he or she is under a spell, until it breaks.'

Leela protested, 'There is *no* spell for me either. I cannot imagine that someone so life giving as Mahakaal could cast spells,' Leela paused before adding, 'You know, recently I made this dash to the Kumbh Mela, just guided by my gut feeling.'

Arjun's forehead wrinkled again and his lips curved downwards, 'I heard that. I wondered: Leela and Kumbh Mela?'

'And see, just when I least expected it,' said Leela after a dramatic pause, 'I saw him there.'

'What?!' Both Arjun and Chitra exclaimed together.

'He was far away in the crowds. When I reached the spot where I saw him, he was gone. But I was so reassured that he was real, that he was not a hallucination as the SIT probe team and psychiatrists were trying to make out...'

'Are you sure this was the same man?' asked Arjun.

'One hundred percent. He turned and blessed me from far, and then he disappeared. I came to Bhai directly from there.'

Bharat spoke with measured emphasis, 'Sir, you had accosted me a few years ago about my Ma Kali quote on sacrifice. Now you have made a thorough study on Santji. So what did you think of his talks about energy and creation, of his "Ma Kali" being an allegorical force field beyond time?'

Arjun waved his pipe from side to side, 'I neither understand nor care for such esoteric stuff.'

Chitra quipped sweetly, 'My Babloo is somewhat puerile about spiritual matters. All his world views, his opinionating, is at the analytical level.'

Bharat raised his voice and said forcefully, 'If so, let me say that you have understood *nothing* about my guide. You only read his outer layer. For knowing him, you need to open up, surrender your...'

'Surrender?! And me? Bunkum! I don't *have* to swallow this nonsense,' said the General gruffly, 'A person aged 120 plus becomes sixty. Or maybe people morph into others like Hollywood sci-fi stuff? What crap is this? I can't put a finger as yet on what shithole you *bhai behen* have stepped into. I'm damned that such sensitized, educated types like you could even entertain such lunatic ideas. Get this straight: Netaji is long dead and gone and some other body doubles are playing games. Why don't these Babas come to me?'

'Netaji comes to me sometimes in my dreams,' said Chitra.

'I haven't had that good fortune till now,' said Arjun wryly, 'I am not checkmated on this as yet. I repeat: the man chose not to come out. This book as well as his close followers claim that he is alive, in deep *sadhana* in the Himalayas; that he will soon harness his stupendous powers for India. Yes? And all of a sudden he starts giving *darshan* to you both? What an absurdity!'

Then he turned to Leela. 'Gen. Mahadev Sir told me this Mahakaal gave you some leads to awaken you. To link your present to a past you refused to get into. Well… you look darned wide awake to me.'

'I'm getting there uncle,' Leela replied with a wide smile.

'Wasting time! No more mad missions like trying to find out the link between the hidden documents and the Bose mystery,' Arjun waved his arms around. 'We have border trouble. Maoist insurgents are sensing the edifice is ripe for the picking, so they test ground by attacking urban targets today. Our economy is stuttering. I'm told this is jobless growth. *Aise mein* who will cast a vote for digging the secret T.O.P files or codes – or even Netaji's fate?'

'Uncle, you urge us to drop it all?'

'But this is not for you. Right now, give your all for securing your many infirm elders who will be gutted by a war more than the others. You have a great example right in front of your nose. Bharat and his Ghati; damn I keep forgetting the name.'

313

'Prithak Ghati.'

'With your rebellious zeal, join a cause like this. I second Bharat's war perception. Our forces have been preparing for a two front war for long. But you civilians are hopelessly undercooked.'

Arjun turned to Bharat, 'Bharat, your Santji inspired you to develop this Ghati – sorry Prithak Ghati. That's a great story. But it's a story that shouldn't devour its orator. No Gods sipping our astral energy during sleep... oh that Dr Mancrop was great fun!'

The bell rang. Firdaus had returned with his purchases. Chitra immediately signalled lunch.

Leela stretched herself, 'Uncle, my heart tells me that Mahakaal will show me the way.'

Arjun stood up and slapped his forehead in exasperation, 'Your Mahakaal needs to show you some *akal*. God, you're still blindsided! Ok, truce for now, but I'll be on the button to finish this duel.'

Lili exchanged high fives with him while Chitra made a face and shook her head.

Lunch was served.

Later they were seen off graciously, though Arjun hardly spoke. He embraced both Bharat and Leela and held them close for long, while his face had a pained, set expression. He caressed and patted Leela's head in a tender, fatherly gesture that left Chitra teary-eyed.

Once everyone was seated in the car, Arjun leaned close to Bharat, while his tone remained grave. 'Why don't you work out something for Lili to do instead of chasing a chimera? Leave this mystery to me. You can bet that I'll unravel this one, if it's the last thing in life that I do.'

The car eased away. As it turned the bend, Leela could still see the forlorn couple standing at the gate, waiting till they were completely out of sight.

FORTY FOUR

They drove on silently for over an hour. Leela wanted to talk, but Bharat whispered in Bengali, 'Don't talk about last night till we're home.' And then he added, 'Now you know why I never discussed "him" in public.'

Leela nodded silently, but after a while she could not hold back any more. She muttered, 'Pony Uncle thinks that I am possessed.'

Bharat opened his eyes and looked her up and down. She slapped his knee playfully and said, 'Serious. Is MK some version of Netaji defying all laws of reality? Am I infatuated with him?'

'Only you can answer that.'

'For me, Mahakaal was this loving realized soul who mostly conveyed silently. Is this really the same person who demands death sentence, accepts buffalo slaughter, wants to control our tastes? I can't believe it. I can't!'

'Lili, firstly you have to meditate on his words and him. I repeat, all that you heard needs a context to be understood. I have both faith and trust in Santji – that's it. Do you?'

'But MK sits on my mind all the time. I have no peace of mind.'

'That's not trust. He could be some "morphed" version of Netaji, or a different person, but why should he be a load on your mind? If Mahakaal lit a lamp, go ahead and spread that glow and don't brood.'

'I want to ask him if he is really a death sentence votary for everything.'

'I repeat: this *is* becoming an obsession for you now.'

Leela suddenly grabbed Bharat's hand. 'Say that again?'

'Say what?'

'What you just said, the last part?'

'Becoming an obsession?'

'Bhai, this is the word I dread so much. This is Adi revisited for me. We parted because he was obsessed with a missing image.'

'Aren't you too?'

Leela stopped speaking. Her eyes were closed, but she was breathing heavily. Slowly, she released Bharat's hand and slid back in her seat with her head thrown back. She remained silent for the rest of the journey.

They made a halt at a roadside restaurant. This eatery seemed to be very popular, with an assortment of locals, travellers and even tourists taking a quick bite and moving on. Some of them looked at Bharat and whispered to each other: 'Is this that chap?'

Right then, the local bulletin came up on the TV hanging over the cash counter. The news was electric. After suffering shock and losses due to the countrywide Maoist attacks, the Government announced a major success. Based on intelligence reports, crack C-60 commandos had cornered and killed over twenty Maoist ultras in a forest about fifty km from Prithak Ghati. The remaining ultras had escaped into the jungle, but the commandos were in hot pursuit.

Someone from the visitors erupted with hoots of glee, and many others joined the clapping. A large group of youngsters had come in on their mobikes and stopped to listen to the news. One of them now shouted in a threatening voice, 'You mother fuckers! You're cheering for a staged encounter?'

There was a short stunned silence. Then a man seated in another large group retorted, 'Tears for traitors? Terrorists, Maoists; wipe these bastards out.'

Within a few minutes, the situation developed into an ugly brawl. The restaurant owner and his staff stepped in to restore order. Firdaus whispered to Bharat, and they quickly made an exit after depositing cash at the counter. When they were driving off, they could hear the sound of glass shattering and ladies screaming.

Just when the car was about to enter Prithak Ghati, Bharat got a call from the police on his mobile. A prowl car had reached the restaurant and detained some of those involved in the brawl. There was a CCTV installed in the eatery, and the footage had revealed Bharat as well as Leela. Now they requested Bharat to testify as a witness by coming to the *thana*. At the same time, Leela got frantic messages from friends. They had seen a motivated news flash on TV: '*Left supporters clash with Desh-Bhakts. Bharat and Leela Biswas escape injury.*'

Leela showed the text messages on her mobile to Bharat who nodded gravely. 'If we become defensive, we get pulled in anyway. Santji was right. I should not have left it so late to take a stand.'

Leela realized that it was time for her to leave PG for now. This Cafe fight clip was going viral already. The police and media personnel were sure to hound her in no time.

She shared her decision with Bharat. He sighed, 'Your choice. Let's do a wrap up tonight. You can always come back when the heat is off.'

Leela replied, 'I don't want any wrap up. Can I spend my last night in PG in your basement shrine? In silence?'

'Anything for you Lili. I know many of your questions remain pending. Tonight I will at least clear the first one – in silence.

When Bharat and Leela dispersed after dinner, they saw Sachin packing his things and supplies for hostel. They noticed that he had put a lock on one of his drawers. What was he being secretive about?

Bharat remarked tongue in cheek, 'I hope he's not under some spell.' Leela smiled and walked away.

An hour later, when Leela descended to the basement in her night clothes, she could see that Bharat had prepared well for her final evening here. There were mattresses, dhurries and cushions laid out on the floor, with soft vocal music to go with it.

She turned to Bharat and wanted to speak, but he signalled to her that she must maintain discipline and keep her silence.

There was no talk. Bharat released the pause button for the music to flow. Leela had her eyes closed. Bharat too was lost in thought, with his eyes fixed on the low ceiling.

After over an hour the music track ran out. Bharat got up and bade her farewell, as he ambled up to take care of Bima who had been whining. Leela continued to sit in silence, while Mahakaal looked down at her from the large photo-painting in Bharat's shrine.

Later she walked slowly over the entire room, soaking up the energies and even sitting on the same chair where 'Santji' had sat when he had visited Bharat last in this very room. She found that Bharat had left a small oil lamp burning in front of the photo of a Native American. The name was written by hand: Chief Young Joseph of Lower Nez Perce ('Thunder travelling over the Mountains') – legendary Native American Resistance fighter.

Bharat had stuck a note below it. 'Your question was: Why did Santji conduct campaigns outside India, such as standing with the Vietnamese people against the Americans?'

This was Bharat's parting stimulant for her.

The write-up below the photo read: November 1876. Chief Young Joseph's speech addressed to the USA Commission of General O.O. Howard at Lapwai, when the European Settlers schemed to take over his tribe's sacred land at Wallowa Valley, biting the very hand that had nourished them.

The Creative Power, when he made the earth, made no marks, no lines of division or separation on it, and that it should be allowed to remain as then made... He (Chief Young Joseph) was made of the earth and grew up on its bosom. The earth, as his mother and nurse, was sacred to his affections, too sacred to be valued by or sold for silver and gold. He could not consent to sever his affections from the land that bore him. He was content to live upon such fruits as the Creative Power placed within and upon it, and unwilling to barter these and his free habits away for the new modes of life proposed by The USA Commission. Moreover, the earth carried chieftainship (responsibility), and therefore to part with the earth would be to part with himself or with his self control.'*

'Chief Joseph's wars against the predatory Settlers, a superior and much larger military force, became a part of heroic folklore in the chequered History of the USA. After his imprisonment, he said, '*We only ask an even chance to live as other men live. Let me be a free man — free to travel, free to stop, free to work, free to trade where I choose, free to choose my own teachers, free to follow the religion of my fathers, free to think and talk and act for myself — and I will obey every law, or submit to the penalty.*'

Leela had goose pimples. What stirring words! This man had spoken not just for his tribe, but for all the native tribes, all dispossessed people anywhere in the world. There was such a stark parallel with India's history at its core.

Santji's words about love for one's roots and mother earth as real patriotism came alive for her with renewed meaning. Netaji had fought for man's freedom and dignity against the same forces, traversing continents and standing with oppressed people, all the while remaining meditative and centred. Bharat had done the same all his life in his own way.

* (Massacre of the Mountains by J.P. Dunn Page 548-549)

Her own task was cut out.

She had now left the mystery around the Codes behind her. These had enabled her to look back at a past from which she could learn and reconcile her present. All that remained in her mind was a blinding faith that she would meet Mahakaal again and resolve her queries, whether in the human realm or in some 'Siddhashram'.

PART FOUR

PRĀPTI

FORTY FIVE

L eela awoke at dawn in the basement feeling completely refreshed. It was time to bid this inspiring space goodbye. She touched the flame from the oil lamp in front of Mahakaal's sketch to her forehead and sprinted up the stairs.

As she emerged from Bharat's room, she heard a high pitched anchor's voice from the worker's TV announcing that Indian and Chinese troops had exchanged fire again on the Gilgit and Arunachal borders. It was of a piece with the latest headlines – the *growing fear of war with China*.

Sometime after breakfast, Bharat, Firdaus and Leela recorded their statements about the Cafe violence with the police. Once they returned, Sachin and she left together with Puran Singh for Mumbai and Pune respectively.

Within a few hours, some press people were again back at the gate. Bharat had recently spoken to a reporter about his old prediction regarding the likelihood of water riots breaking out in urban centres. Uncannily, Hyderabad had a major clash that morning between people who had queued up overnight to fetch water from tankers. At some places the clashes had even taken on a communal hue. The army and RAF had to be summoned to stage a flag march. Similar riots had occurred in Jamshedpur, followed by some satellite regions of Delhi.

Water riots and escalating border tensions – Bharat's decades old predictions were again in the spotlight.

The Media teams who landed in Prithak Ghati were initially disappointed to find that Bharat was unwilling to add a word to all that he had said earlier. But his silence was soon breached. A brilliant young reporter, Amit Kulkarni, who was known to Bharat and who had been the first person to write about Prithak Ghati, had vanished mysteriously while on duty three days ago. He had lately made explosive revelations about Public Sector Banks (PSBs) being arm-twisted to release huge loans to many big business houses.

Before he could reveal more, he was 'taken care of.' News came in that afternoon that Amit's body had been found buried in a jungle, after an unknown person tipped off the police and the press.

Bharat broke his silence. He declared that Amit had run a relentless campaign against the big-time defaulters and this is why he had been silenced. He recalled the murder of journalist Umesh Dobhal by the liquor mafia in the Garhwal Hills during his Kumaon stay in 1989, and said that nothing had changed in thirty years. It was pointless to expect *any* government to recover such outstanding debts because most Governments were hand-in-glove with those business houses who had funded their electoral spending, in a direct trade off involving this loot of public money. This was a typical aspect of cronyism.

He stood by what he had recommended long ago – launch aggressive campaigns for recovery of loans linked to NPAs (Non performing assets); put the public-private infrastructure projects floated by the Govt and these entities on hold, till the earlier public loans were cleared. These projects were being built with moneys from Public Sector Banks (PSBs). which had been coerced into releasing such massive crony loans.

Bharat pointed out that all scheduled commercial banks (SCBs) had written off Rs 225,180 crores cumulatively in the five-year period ending March 2016, and the bulk of these write-offs had been primarily in the large corporate accounts. The NPA linked outstanding loans from Public Sector Banks had now ballooned to 895,601 crores a year ago. Despite this, there was no public campaign against such loot of public money.

The accused corporate houses primed their media favourites

to come out blazing against Bharat, the Detox movement and other motley groups leading the disparate campaigns. Every aspect of his past was smeared with exaggerated vulgarity: his phase of alcoholism and the death of his wife; being driven away from village to village due to his 'non-adjusting' nature and so on. It was repeatedly mentioned that success of any kind in Prithak Ghati did not count at all for the national scene. Insinuating that honourable business Establishments had plotted a murder, whereas they were all committed to repaying such loans to the banks, was in very poor taste.

The focus was thus shifted from water wars and a dead journalist to Bharat. Hardly any show bothered to talk to the many faces who had worked with him and had become his hard-core followers.

Scuffles broke out between public activists and politicians as well as business magnates during sensational studio debates. There were protest marches targeting many corporate offices. Stocks collapsed and wholesale commodity prices soared with the fear that the government would tighten lending norms from PSBs. Hundreds of farmers organizations from all over the country got together to fight such loot and joined forces with the Detox movement for a 'cleansing' of Mother India.

Reporters were sent to interview Mada, who had just recovered from a long bout of illness. In an interview which shocked his close army friends and political contacts, he bluntly conceded that he and his generation had let the nation down. A true nationhood which had emerged as a possibility between the 1920s and 1940s had been buried under private ambitions and greed, and subsequent generations had looked the other way. He said he had differed with Bharat all his life, but he felt no shame in admitting now that his grandnephew was advocating a roadmap to sanity.

FORTY SIX

Leela resumed her routine in Pune, but she missed Prithak Ghati, more so after going through yet another grilling by the Pune Police about her absence. She also had to answer unending questions from the media, neighbours and friends. Many of her contacts urged her to join the movement to take her cousin Bharat's views forward. This was hot right now!

Very few people showed any understanding about her wish to distance herself from activism. She wanted to connect with Aditya again, but he was still untraceable in the Himalayas. In the midst of all this hullaballoo, Leela continued to coach her domestic help Asha's three children after school, helping with their lessons, paying their school fees and supplying their books and uniforms. She disabled her door-bell and disconnected the landline. Her mobile remained on silent mode.

After a particularly exasperating day Leela switched on the television for a change. The news was dominated by the announcement of a High Profile Summit Meeting in Beijing between the Indian PM and the Chinese President. This had been preceded by heavy exchange of fire between Chinese and Indian Troops several times on both the eastern *and* western borders with China. There had been other irritants too. China had been accused of diverting waters from the Tibetan rivers flowing into India. As a counter, India had threatened a blockade of Chinese ships through Indian waters. *War looked imminent.*

Leela felt uneasy. Aditya was still missing near the same borders. She listened keenly.

This emergency Summit was scheduled to take place soon, dispensing with plenty of protocol and the usual months of preparation.

Both leaders were being congratulated for their pragmatism and commitment to 'world peace'.

Now even Pakistan's new hardline government had welcomed this Summit move, despite being embroiled in a simmering feud with India over fresh terrorist attacks on Indian targets. Since Pakistan's pugnacious demeanour had crossed all limits, India had immediately rescinded the IWT (Indus Water Treaty) under International Law; an unfair Treaty which gave just 19.48% of the total waters of the six rivers Indus System to India. Now Pakistan threatened to go to war against India on this issue.

It was China that had prodded Pakistan to support the Beijing Peace Summit. This was because the mammoth Bunji dam in the disputed Gilgit Baltistan region in Pakistan was being financed and built by China under their OBOR project and this dam was certain to be impacted by India's decision to revoke the IWT treaty.

Then there was 'breaking news' about a sudden, simultaneous outbreak of violence in ten major refugee camps in Bathindi near Jammu, where refugees had killed their guards and escaped towards the Himalayan border. It was being speculated that foreign forces had planted their agents among these refugees to create unrest.

Leela sighed and switched the TV off. Shortly afterwards, she got a call from Arjun Ponappa that he was going alone to Prithak Ghati for a visit, so would she be interested in joining him? DCP Ahire was also going to be there, and the sizeable ex-servicemen population in the village town had arranged an informal talk on the looming war scenario.

She baulked. More theories of how to kill people and devastate lands? She excused herself by saying that presently she was a bit 'under the weather' and would rather meet him here in Pune when he was back. She could feel Pony Uncle's disappointment, but no morbid war talk for her.

FORTY SEVEN

Gen. Ponappa and ex-DCP Ahire had a great time going around Prithak Ghati with cafeteria owner Mahadevan's son, Karuna, who worked for a defence think-tank. Bharat was expected to join later after attending to a medical case.

Karuna was the local head of TAES (The Territorial Army of ex-Servicemen). This was an intermediate set up between a Territorial Army (TA) and the regular Forces. The TAES officially recruited only ex-servicemen to form a vast countrywide network which tackled multiple fronts, from flood control to counter insurgency to even civic order a la cantonment living. Arjun Ponappa had been instrumental in getting it funded by the Govt. before his retirement.

After his talk, Arjun took questions about the situation on the Indian borders, given his well-known stance of preparing India for a two front war. The talk had started with the reasons for Prithak Ghati having opted for an 'Insurance model' against an EMP attack.

Arjun was winding up his session. 'We have talked about the EMP specific defence shield adopted in PG, which is now promoted by TAES all over India. But the civilians here have requested for a few relevant highlights so that they understand the possible war scenario. We'll discuss that now.

'As things stand, slowly but surely, the Chinese have encircled us. They have a naval base in Sri Lanka; control the Kyauk Pyu Port in Myanmar; prod Nepal to cock a snook at us; dock their Subs (submarines) in Chittagong. They manipulate the waters from Tibet's rivers flowing into our North East by pasting floods and then droughts on our population. And now they threaten us about our IWT (Indus water treaty) dispute with the Pakistanis. Don't ever forget that de facto this will be China's war. Pakistan is almost China's vassal state.'

Karuna remarked, 'Sir, in fact China's PLAN (People's Liberation Army Navy) is soon doing an elaborate exercise with the Pakistan Navy in the Arabian Sea right up our alley, using the Gwadar port as base. They have their Subs docking in Djibouti and also Hambantota Port in Sri Lanka around the same time. Earlier, the Chinese needed two to three days to enter our waters via the Malacca straits and the Bali Sea. This allowed us reasonable response time. But if they are based next door even temporarily... cause for concern.'

Arjun nodded, 'True. Till recently their Achilles Heel was that most of their international trade was via this Malacca Straits route through Indian waters. Now with the "One Belt One Road" (OBOR) and Gwadar port commissioned, they intend to get around that. It is only a forty-eight hour goods dispatch time from Gwadar to the Chinese Mainland via high-speed rail transit connecting to the Khunjareb pass and Karakoram highway. To rub it in, they have illegally run the route through disputed land – our Indian land.'

He tapped the table for emphasis, '*Keep in mind that one key to such a conflict this time will be the Naval war.* This could be India's decisive weapon – blocking off the Chinese supplies by sea, which they can't yet make up via this land route through Gwadar and the Karakoram network. That could cripple their economy in a protracted stand-off.

'The more we delay facing these realities and putting the Dragon in place via a bloody nose, the more they will tighten the noose till the battle is virtually in their pocket. That they will try to make us bend or break is a 100% certainty. I am damned if we give in – yes?'

There were roars of '*Bharat Mata ki jai! Jaan haazir hai* Sir!'

DCP Ahire was munching a *paan*. He said, 'So you all think that this joint Pak-China front will not hit us with a conventional Offensive?'

Karuna turned to him, 'Sir, we believe that the time for

329

conventional warfare is nearly gone. Satellites (Sats) are today the vital aids which can determine a war's outcome.'

Arjun tapped the table with his baton. 'The Chinese have around 200 Sats which can all be put to military use. *Officially* we have less than twenty military Sats. With such limited Sats at hand, our IASC (Indian Aerospace Command) prioritizes which Pakistani and Chinese nuclear missile bases to cover via Satellite surveillance: all their nuclear tipped ICBMs (Inter Continental Ballistic Missiles) and the CJ-10 GLCMs (Ground Launched Cruize Missiles) and so on.

'The enemy are also tracking info about our Satellites' Orbit and flyover schedules. Any ASAT (Anti-satellite) Weapons attack by China can be deflected if we keep varying our Satellites' tasking and orbits to make them unpredictable. But when the nuclear threat makes our satellites focus *only* on the specific Chinese and Pakistani nuclear bases, *our satellite orbit becomes predictable*. Then China could use their laser technology or ASAT missiles to permanently damage or blind our Sats.'

Karuna stressed, 'Ahire Sir, once we lose our Satellite cover, our ACCC (Artillery Combat Command and Control System) and CIDSS (Command Information Decision Support System) will be partially blinded. They won't have real-time Satellite feeds to warn us about incoming missile and air strikes. We could be potentially decimated in just one night of warfare.'

Heli Sir turned back to Gen Ponappa, 'In that case Sir... What do you propose?'

Arjun replied, 'In a *quid pro quo,* we should ready our Agni V 5000 km range ballistic missiles to take out as many Chinese satellites. We must commission our own ASAT system to terminate these Chinese Sats at different orbits at any point of time.'

DCP Ahire cut in bluntly, 'Sorry, with due respect Sir, we aren't prepared for a war with China, let alone a two front war – and that's the truth. This is not 1971, not even Kargil, and I say this as a *deshbhakt* like any of you here.'

Arjun's eyebrows shot up and there was a sudden silence in the room.

'Sir, firstly our Govt and all Govts in the past have hardly trained the civilian population for such a war. In Russia over 40 million people regularly participate in civil defence training programs. Here they don't even sound sirens to prepare us for what to do during an air raid. All I hear is: *'Pakistan ko uraa do! Cheen ki le lo*! Makes me mad!

'On the military front, we need 45 squadrons to take on Pakistan and China together. Despite the Rafales coming in, we still have 33 – a major gap. Artillery is not modernized anywhere near our needs; spares and ammunition shortages are often cited, and the disparity between our naval assets and the Chinese is even more massive. I repeat that the Spares picture is alarming. Sir?'

Arjun stared at DCP Ahire, who kept munching his paan. Then he spoke, 'We will still fight as a professional force with what we have, and do what is needed to crush the enemy.'

Ahire shook his head, '100% agreed Sir, and no one is questioning that we are the best, having fought so often in the past with a hand tied – *majboori*. My brother died in action during the Kargil war. But Sir, we have not addressed our critical weaknesses. We can't mobilize our main battle tanks on the fronts with China with speed. For example our solitary Shyok-Leh Road is crammed with vehicles, while the Chinese can come streaming into India from Aksai Chin in full strength in their T 99A MBT's (Main battle tanks) via superb flat roads to all the critical points on the border. Aren't these valid concerns?'

Arjun nodded gravely. 'On this point, I agree.'

Ahire continued in his critical tone, 'Sir, I have also followed how the indigenous induction process for military hardware is often goofed up. In fact Defence procurements have become cash cows.'

Arjun said, 'Yes, these issues do plague us. But we are presently focused on our enemy's weaknesses. The fact is that the Pakistani and Chinese leaders are in reality running a Fiefdom. In China the top Politburo bosses live like kings and are far removed from the common man. Many of their generals have unproven skills in combat, but wield enormous influence due to their affiliations in the Communist Party. This is what gives us a handle.'

DCP Ahire would not let go, 'Sir, your words could be a fit with the Indian situation. How many of our own field Commanders have...'

This time Arjun cut him to size, 'In which bloody world are you living?'

Ahire's face went red. At that very moment Bharat entered the room and sat down next to him. He pressed Ahire's arm, signalling restraint, while Arjun continued, 'In both these countries their defence top brass have fattened themselves on a massive military-Industrial complex and are thoroughly corrupt. But they are useful to the top political hierarchy to control their country. I repeat — *to control their own country*. They have a stranglehold on the media broadcasts during any conflict.

'In China, should this media control get exposed by adverse ground realities during a real war, rest assured that we will see a revolt. There is massive discontent in that country, and the common man there knows that a parallel privileged universe exists for these corrupt Communist Party Officials and Military higher ups. Sir, do you see this happening in India?'

Ahire opened his mouth to speak, but typically Arjun went on, 'The answer is — no way. We will win this war, even if we go down to the last man — and no, this is *not* bravado. We have well thought out strategies which I cannot disclose. We will bring the heat right into their bedroom. You may see a split in the CPC (Communist Party of China) and in China, when we make the attrition bite and this becomes known to *their* public.'

Ahire turned to Bharat and ignored Arjun. He asked, 'We started our discussion with the EMP threat and Prithak Ghati. *You* are the man with the vision.'

Bharat requested Arjun, 'Sir, only a short word from me.'

Arjun was still smarting after having been tripped in full flow, but he regained his composure and waved Bharat on.

'Sir, more than twenty-five years ago, I had sent a plan to the government: Ministry of Defence, MEA, and the PMO. This was about preparation and damage control following an EMP attack on India. I got an acknowledgement from all three — and nothing further. I gave Karuna the same plan and he gave it a modern shape.'

Karuna put his hands up. 'It is Bharat Bhai's plan in essence.'

'Cut out the credits. Bharat *ko baadme* Black forest cake *khilaayenge,*' Arjun's rasping comment evoked a great deal of mirth and even Ahire put his thumbs up in approval.

Karuna continued, 'Sir, only highlights. After being hit by an EMP attack, the critical sectors to be immediately revived are transport, especially railways, and of course power. So Bharat Bhai had proposed that an EMP "hardened" (protected) chopper fleet to be raised, to fly transformers non-stop to replace the destroyed ones to help revive critical power systems. Next, "hardening" electronics on all the railway traffic control centres etc, to ensure that our power plants are fed with the essential supplies to keep them running. The Power Companies must create a big inventory of spare parts, so that they can be functional in quick time.'

Ahire asked, 'What about gas pipelines? Many of our cities have gas, so...'

Bharat took a deep breath and said nothing, so Karuna took over, 'That was Bharat Bhai's first suggestion: to use natural gas powered pumps in the natural-gas pipeline systems, so that if and when the electric grid collapses, at least natural gas continues to be available.'

Both Ahire and Arjun exclaimed, 'Excellent!'

'But no one bothered to respond from the Govt,' complained Heli Sir.

'Karuna, send me a copy of your detailed plan. I'll meet the Minister and even write to the PM. If there is no response, they will hear my barrage on the media.'

Arjun looked at his watch and got up. '*Chalo*, let's lunch, or I'll get late. I have a scheduled visit to check Bharat's Habitat, to see how the government security has sanitized it after the jeep blast here. And Bharat, for now I want Dr Mancrop as company. Bharat Biswas, Black Forest cake and Bheja Fry... ha, ha, ha! Vitamin B.'

They were still laughing when Madhavan welcomed them into his cafeteria. There was a clean subsidized section for the worker class, and Arjun insisted on sitting there and back slapping with many labourers who were having their *thalis*.

Dr Mancrop came in to a rousing welcome. As soon as she shook hands and seated herself, Arjun roared, 'What do you say Madam? Will your Harvester "Gods" want to "pluck" us in fermented form, dying months after a Chinese HEMP? That's "Chinicure", like the dish "Colombian cure" – right?'

In the midst of vibrant laughter, Dr Mancrop nodded gravely, 'Yes I know that one. But I see you soldiers, and especially you Sir, being harvested differently on the battlefront.'

Arjun pulled a straight face, 'And what might that be Doctor?'

Dr Mancrop shook her head from side to side and tut-tutted, 'Why, you should know from your wife, Chitra Didi. Last time you were here, she gave us the demo for your harvesting. Remember?'

Arjun's eyes bulged out, 'No Madam.'

Dr Mancrop licked her lips and crooned, 'It's called "*Chêpa Shũtki*". (Pressed dried fish.)

FORTY EIGHT

General Ponappa's good mood from the Prithak Ghati visit did not last even a week. He called Bharat late one night and warned him that a major action plan was being worked out by an inner section of the polity to neutralize him for good. The General asked him to remain extremely alert and keep only trusted people around him at all times. Bharat typically dismissed the warning, only to hear an angry expletive from Arjun.

As an aftermath to the local water riots, citizen groups were protesting the fact that many state governments were encouraging water guzzling crops, mammoth residential building projects with multiple swimming pools, water parks, etc. The central and state Govts had countered this by expediting the much touted river linking project to solve India's water crisis. As luck would have it, a sting operation unearthed the fact that the massive public loans for this project had been granted by PSB's to entities which were in reality shell companies controlled by business houses who were already known defaulters of public loans.

Public anger boiled over. Some corporate heads escaped abroad in quick succession for urgent medical treatment. Cases were registered and summons issued, all to no avail. Star lawyers argued that their clients were in no position to travel back to India. The other named corporate houses issued press statements that they had nothing to do with these shell companies.

There was a spontaneous resurgence of groups which fused their activities with the Detox movement. They demanded that the revenue gap be met by recovering all public loans stuck in NPA's, and by getting back the stupendous amounts siphoned out of the country right under the government's nose. Why should the Indian public continue to feed such loot?

It was during this phase of ongoing turbulence that Sachin uploaded 'The Mahakaal Story', an animated film which broke the Gumnami Baba saga and the immediate relevance of his views to a large young populace. This video about the 'Yodha Sanyasi' became viral on the net. With his skills, Sachin managed to cover up his cyber tracks immaculately.

The video ended by saying that independent of who 'Gumnami Baba' actually was, all the past political regimes including the present government had persisted with a cover-up in hiding Subhas Bose's fate from the masses.

This single upload morphed into a thousand variations and impacted receptive minds more than all the previous pro Subhas Bose agitations put together. Leela was stunned when she got this video as a Whatsapp forward from a friend gushing over it. She immediately called Sachin up in college.

'I have not leaked anything to my friends,' remarked Sachin, 'Nor did I mention any of Baba's and your personal experiences with Santji's clones and so on. More people need to know about Netaji Subhas Bose's probable afterlife. That's all.'

Bharat took the shock of his son's precocious involvement in the MK mystery in his stride. When Leela called him on Firdaus's phone, he remarked, 'Don't feel guilty. Sach is too free spirited to be influenced by what we say. I didn't know he was working on this, but all I can say is – Good job, son.'

Although he advised Leela to relax, Bharat himself did not have opportunity to sit back and unwind. The Triad of P. Aiyer, S.S. Gujral and R. Subramaniam ensured that he was arrested on charges of defamation, albeit a bit late, for his statement damning the corporate houses after Amit Kulkarni's body was found. He was also charged with incitement to destroy public property.

While in jail, Bharat was first administered sophisticated doses of physical and mental torture during interrogation sessions. These were just at the threshold of excruciating pain while not being fatal. When he refused to take back his words or apologise publicly, he was attacked by planted goons during a lunch recess. Luckily, some other prisoners shielded him. Someone was able to send out word and the physical torture stopped, albeit temporarily.

His legal counsel and the Detox India friends launched a frenzied effort to have him freed and were finally able to get a bail hearing after a painful week. The judge was unable to accept even one strand of the 'so-called' evidence from the Public Prosecutor that Bharat had *directly* incited people to destroy property.

In scathing remarks buttressing her judgement, the presiding judge noted that to blame Bharat Biswas for the various anarchic movements was to simply shift the blame for the grave acts of mismanagement which the Executive had committed. Even in his solitary Public speech or his media pronouncements later, Bharat had insisted on self-discipline first, before agitating against the Executive in any manner. He had never associated himself with any of the violent agitations across the country.

The judge prefaced her judgement with the following comments: 'When legally elected people's representatives condone jammed Parliament sessions; when ruling parties moralize and yet give many electoral tickets to known criminals; Bharat Biswas and Prithak Ghati have served as a beacon to the nation and inspired such awareness campaigns and agitations.' She ruled that Bharat was definitely not a dangerous criminal and should be immediately released on bail.

To the dismay of the Triad, Bharat's release galvanized the diverse agitations even further, despite his remaining aloof from them. He repeated that no government is better than its people. He said, 'There is still time to reclaim your sanity. Form intelligent, non-wasteful centres of living. Slow down. Let the earth recover.'

FORTY NINE

Leela still had to sort out her Official matters. After a couple of days, she proceeded to Bengal to attend her court case verdict.

The accused in the riverine attack were acquitted by the district court in Siliguri in the case charging them with murderous assault with intent to kill Leela in the forest. As they had already served six months imprisonment, they were said to have done their time for 'simple harassment' and were free to go. The State's argument that the accused would have killed Leela if an old man had not saved her was rejected as unfounded, because the old man story was seen to be a figment of Leela's imagination. The government counsel said they would consider appealing in a higher court after studying the judgment.

Leela avoided all questions from reporters outside the district court and the jeering from her attackers' supporters and returned to Pune. Her mobile lay in silent mode and she did not take any calls. Mada sent a text message asking her to cheer up, and that he would suggest a better private lawyer to argue her appeal. She did not respond. Rajen dropped in but she forbade him from discussing either Mahakaal or the case. Leela could feel his pain as a father, but the chasm between them was too much to bridge now.

The neighbours rang her bell at all hours to express sympathy and cheer her up, but this had the opposite effect, especially after some of them suggested intake of anti-depressants or consulting a good psychiatrist.

She tried to sidestep her alienation by adopting a punishing work schedule; criss-crossing between the old age homes that she had established and preparing them to be as self-sufficient as possible. It was Gen. Ponappa who had forewarned her that a sudden war could erupt any time. So she also set up a team for EMP checks and drills. Housewives, professors, students, daily wagers; all joined her after their working hours for augmenting such drills.

But she realized that she wanted to go back to Prithak Ghati soon for a weekend. It was pulling her. She did not want to stress Bima with the long journey for such a short trip, so she planned to leave him with Rajen. Then she called up Sachin, who was delighted with the idea. She would meet him at the Volvo stand in Pune on Friday evening for a weekend getaway to PG. He could return to college by Sunday night.

At this juncture, Bharat got a surprise visit late at night from the local strongman Sardar Mane. The car had no official flag and Bharat's assigned personal guard Jayesh let the visitors in after verifying that Mane was there with a 'guest'. Bharat recognized R. Subramaniam immediately and welcomed him cordially.

They met in Bharat's room. No witnesses were allowed. Bharat's farmhands did not even learn that such a Politician was in their habitat.

Bharat brewed some coffee himself and R. Subramaniam was happy to savour a cup. After the first sip he remarked, 'Arabica? From General Ponappa's coffee estate I presume?' From that one loaded comment, Bharat knew something was cooking.

While making some polite talk about Prithak Ghati and its many initiatives, R. Subramaniam (Subi) was also looking around the room and especially at Bharat's mattress on the floor. His derision was all too apparent. 'Bharatji, picture perfect for the kind of person you are. Mane took me secretly around town for over two hours. Fantastic. Really, I mean it. So far away from civilization, and still what a set-up!'

Then he leaned across the small bamboo table and raised his coffee cup as a toast to Bharat. 'I'll come to the point. We understand your situation. All this agitation business in your name. You did not light the fire. Yet, as a person of *ideeels*,' Subi stretched the word "ideal" with sarcasm, 'you, Bharat Biswas, can't disown what you wrote eons ago, nor get away from these stupid agitations which use what suits them from your progressive ideas.'

Bharat smiled, 'That's a bit of a surprise. You find something progressive in my ideas?'

'Of course!' Subi clapped his hands together, while Mane grinned foolishly in tandem. 'We see you as one of *our own* people, a real *desh bhakt*. That's why I'm here. Such positive synergies. We want you to work with us, shoulder to shoulder, to build the kind of nation we have in mind. Why waste away in this remote village? We can work out a common minimum program to implement many of your ideas on a national scale.'

As if on cue, Mane interjected, 'Bharatji, you will never get an opportunity like this. Not only will this entire region get to see unprecedented *pragati*, but this progress will spread far and wide. Just imagine the whole country having a development plan based on your ideas. On the other hand, agar *isko nahi apnaya tho...*,' he paused to let the threat sink in, '*tho sabka ghaata, khaas kar aapka. Yeh dimaag mein daal lijiye.* '(Declining this offer means everyone's loss, especially yours; so get that straight.)

He stopped speaking with a single gesture from Subi, who now leaned forward again, 'Think it over. I repeat: We can work out a common minimum program. I will lobby this with the government. Think positive.'

Bharat kept listening quietly and finally asked, 'Is that it, why you are here?'

Subi's eyes narrowed, while he continued with a smile pasted on his face, 'Yes, that's the basic thrust. But you will need to stop, and I mean STOP, condoning the anti-national acts of all these agitators, this targeting of so many of our public interest mega projects. Even indirectly. And as our natural ally, you can't continue to tell people not to support any political party, to make us some kind of a pariah. We will not tolerate this anymore.'

There was a short silence. Then Bharat leaned back. 'Since you speak about your basic thrust, I'll reemphasize *my* basic truths.'

Subi's smile was gone.

'Firstly,' said Bharat, 'my practice of Dharma is *Sanatana*, yours is transient, *anitya*. I look at a flowering of human potential through rigorous discipline of mind and body; *you seek to control the same. This* is your basic drive. Nor is this any different at the root from all previous regimes.'

'Secondly, we are not natural allies at all, and will never be one. You still embrace socialism and shoot down free enterprise. Where is your nationwide effort to reward competence in morally upright people from the very roots, by giving them electoral tickets or executive leadership? You often stick to the tainted scum who ensure an electoral win by any means. You also knowingly implement your many mega schemes through the unchanging, corrupted bureaucracy, and then wonder why failure dogs you?'

Subi's eyes had narrowed till they were almost shut. He uttered a single word with disdain, 'So?'

'So I suppose you don't need us in your drive. But we don't need you either, because you have nothing to offer us.'

'What? Bharatji, *yeh kya bakwaas...*' Mane exploded, only to be silenced by a look from Subi, who turned to Bharat.

'We have nothing to offer? *We?!*'

'That's right. What do you produce? What is your value added? Zero.'

Subi allowed his chin to drop down slowly till it rested on his chest, while he squinted up at Bharat through his glasses. The malevolence was

341

now out in the open.

'You push deals — exercising the perpetual commanding heights of state monopoly; the same license-permit raj in another "crony" wrapping? This is Governance; your right as the ruling polity? And for this, the people have to be grateful to you, to vote you to power? Why? Because there is no credible opposition, or none that is allowed to sprout?

'You can't even get the basic functions of governance in place, the legal system to protect citizens from crimes and threats to their possessions; protection from the Big Brother, from you. Neither safe roads, nor a really accessible judicial or penal system, nor police reforms. Why are these fundamentals of a civilized society only yours to manipulate, but never ours as a given?

Subi whipped back, 'Bharatji, fact is that you are inflexible. Not open minded, nor aware of what it takes to govern such a complex nation. Most people don't share your perception at all. We have done more work than all the previous governments put together.'

'Debatable. On one hand I honestly congratulate the Govt for acting decisively to fulfill its political manifesto, which has gone side by side with this event management, this headline grabbing projection which your particular faction does better than most others. You *are* doing more work, yes. But it is top-down economic sops which burden future generations under a mountain of debt, while you continue to seek control over us, to play God.'

Subi exploded, 'What faction! You cannot deny us, the elected Govt, the right to legislate. The people of India have given us that right.'

'By all means do so. But I would rather prepare many small conclaves to aid in the reconstruction of India after any war ruination.'

Subi started laughing. 'Bharatji, at least on this point, no one agrees with you. We are close to a real settlement with China, and then Pakistan will have to fall in line too. This is your war phobia, plain and simple.'

Bharat folded his hands in a namaste. 'Go ahead. Preach the good times. Keep on top dressing the economy and make our problems go away. You have many great minds on your side, no sarcasm intended. Why waste time on a Bharat Biswas and our Prithak Ghati?'

Mane could not believe that Bharat was declining the offer of a lifetime. 'Bharatji, *aapkaa dimaag kharab ho gaya hai*. You have lost your mind.'

R. Subramaniam took a deep breath. 'Ok. Think it over properly before declining. Accept this offer, and see how the country prospers.'

'Sir, get off our backs and see how this country flowers.'

Subi got to his feet. He took his time to blow into his glasses and polish them with Bharat's table cloth. Then he stretched out and shook hands with Bharat. 'I think you know *exactly* what you are doing – and the consequences. We didn't want to lose you. Now take care of your health. Good luck.'

Bharat shook hands silently. They walked out towards the exit. The dogs were suddenly barking their heads off, as they sensed aggression in the visitors.

Mane warned, 'They are barking a lot. Do something or I know how to shut them up.'

Subi pulled him away. Bharat's security guard Jayesh escorted them to the car. Puran Singh and Shivanna came running and saw a black car leaving. Bharat asked them to go back to sleep and explained he had a sudden visitor.

This was the final discord. For the cabal, a man who refused to play along; who continued to inspire countless individuals to stand up to the Big State had to go.

The countdown began.

FIFTY

The next evening Leela and Sachin laughed and chatted during their journey to PG. The unpolluted air lifted Leela's spirits. However, when it was approaching dusk, she got a distressing call from Gayatri. While Aditya had been finally apprehended and was being kept under detention, an avalanche had struck the Trans Himalaya (TH) expedition camp. There was no further update as yet.

Leela's heart sank with this news, but seeing the way the stoic Gayatri was taking it, she steadied her mind and said goodbye. She kept the news from Sachin.

They took a rickshaw home from the bus stand. The driver told them that most of the farm workers in town were away attending a night long folk festival with their families.

They found the homestead was eerily quiet. As Bharat was nowhere to be seen, Sachin went straight to his room saying he was ready to drop dead. Leela too was fatigued by the constant running around following her return to Pune. She went to sleep as soon as she hit the bed, hoping for a session with Bharat again the next morning.

Bharat returned home late that night. He knew that Leela and Sachin were there because he saw their footwear on the verandah. He didn't want to wake them up and went to his room. But surprisingly, sleep wouldn't come. He was drowning in an emotion he could not quite fathom.

It was well past midnight when Bharat had the urge to come out and meditate. He went to the enclosed garden and sat on his mat in silence.

A little while later Leela woke up with a heightened sense of unease. Switching on her phone, she saw that it was 3 am. Surprisingly, there was no network.

Sleep refused to come. Her worries about Aditya being hit by an avalanche clouded her mind again.

She put on her slippers and went out. There was a light under Bharat's door, so she knocked. The door was actually open but he wasn't inside. She immediately thought of the enclosed garden.

Bharat was in a deep meditative spell when he felt a presence. The forest 'spoke' to him: 'It is time to leave.'

Suddenly tears formed in his eyes. There was no one to be seen.

While walking towards the garden, Leela thought she could see a faint glow. She stood behind the hedge and peeped in. She was able to locate Bharat in the darkness. Was he talking to a small tree or perhaps to himself? She heard him bid farewell to this hazy tree outline, which was like a misty radiance merging into the forest.

Just when she wanted to move in and question Bharat, three men barged into the compound. What were they doing here at this unearthly hour?

FIFTY ONE

Leela hastened into the enclosed garden. It was Bharat's personal security guard, Jayesh, along with two other security personnel including a village guard known to Bharat for many years. Bharat was quite startled to see them and Leela at the same time. Jayesh reported that they had just got wind of a plan to attack Bharat. A Maoist squad was about to strike here to kill him and his family. They must leave immediately for a safe haven till security forces arrived to evacuate them.

Bharat remonstrated that he would rather call someone from the TAES personnel in town, many of whom would be at home. The residents who lived closer by did not have access to firearms. His guards agreed reluctantly, but asked him to hurry as they took up positions.

Bharat dashed inside his room and was baffled to find that both the landline as well as the mobile services were inoperative. The farmhands were expected only in the morning, and his solitary neighbour Mr Weiz was away too. Since this Habitat was in one secluded part of town, it would take at least twenty minutes of driving down the bends to reach Heli Sir or some other ex servicemen, and the 'ambush' warning had already been sounded.

Jayesh was by now frantic and insisted that they should not waste a single moment. He had received this Grade A alert when his mobile was still getting network fifteen minutes ago, so they were already vulnerable. Would Bharatji expose his son and sister to such a danger? They *had* to leave now.

Leela woke Sachin up and picked up the rucksacks both had carried in just a few hours ago. Then they scampered through the forest led by Jayesh while the other two guards stayed back, ostensibly to divert

346

the attackers. Loud voices could be heard at a distance. The attackers must have discovered their escape.

Bharat brushed against a tree laden with bells which gave off a series of chimes, startling Leela and Sachin. There were other chimes from a distance that echoed this. 'Don't make any sound, Sir,' hissed Jayesh.

It was the dark forest for Leela again. Now they were fearful of danger lurking behind any tree or bush, but this was the same majestic nature which they loved during their daily walks. Leela's mind was racing furiously. She had just decided to join her brother for good. Why this wretched twist in her narrative?

They reached the deserted banks of the river. The waning crescent moon was partly obscured by clouds, but they could see the boat that was always anchored there. Bharat helped Leela and Sachin get on first and then he himself stepped in along with Jayesh. They took up the oars without saying a word and rowed furiously to reach the opposite bank.

Leela was in a trance, as she clutched Bharat's arm. Boats had been a constant connecting thread between Bharat and her right from their childhood, when they made paper boats and pushed them into small streams. Where would this boat take them?

For a while, it was only a lost sister and her brother holding hands, afloat in a boat on that river, forsaken by a world they had wanted to love and cherish.

Sachin drew Leela's attention to something. She peered in that direction in the semi darkness. She could see some men waiting on the other bank. Jayesh waved at them, and they waved back.

As the boat reached the shore, they were helped out by these men. Leela was still holding on to Bharat's arm. Jayesh motioned to Bharat to follow them.

Bharat whispered, *'Arre* Jayesh, who are these men? All in plainclothes?'

'Sir, no tension. These are our people. Just follow us.'

Sachin was feeling uneasy. 'Baba, just check if your mobile is working. Or ask one of these men. We can still call PC Uncle or Heli Sir.'

Bharat took out his mobile, and in that very moment, one of the men seized his arm and tore the mobile out of Bharat's startled hands. Bharat raised his voice, 'Jayesh, *yeh kya hai!* Who are...'

All at once an SUV appeared afar on the rough jungle path and sped towards them at tremendous speed.

One of the men grabbed Bharat from behind, while another one tried to slip a cloak over his head. The third man drew a gun and shouted, 'Come now, or we will fire.'

Leela heard Sachin scream in pain. She whipped around to find that Jayesh had caught the boy in a stranglehold and was trying to drag him towards a jeep which had appeared from the undergrowth. There were two other men inside who had now taken up positions. They were the same unknown security man and the village guard who had accompanied Jayesh earlier.

It was an elaborate trap.

Leela dived at Jayesh's legs. As he fell over, he lost his grip on Sachin.

The SUV screeched to a halt and two men came out firing at the Jeep. The men in the jeep returned fire. Leela distinctly heard a man scream in pain, while the others shouted at Jayesh to hurry. The SUV started again and raced down the river bank towards Leela and Sachin.

Leela heard Heli Sir shout from the SUV, 'Run to us! Nowwww!'

But Leela could not think of moving away, while Bharat was being dragged to the jeep almost twenty meters away. She ran towards him, despite desperate shouts from the SUV. Sachin followed her. The attackers had taken more hits and the men were scrambling to take Bharat with them, while firing at the SUV.

Bharat suddenly lifted one of his captors and flung him to the ground. The other man tried to hit him, but Bharat clung to him and turned the man around to use him as a shield from the gunmen rushing at him. He uttered a desperate cry, 'Lili – runnn! Sach...go...go ...goooo!'

The SUV now overtook Leela and Sachin and blocked them from the firing. Mahadevan ducked and hauled a shouting Sachin into the rear, while Heli Sir was able to catch Leela's arm in a firm grip. He roared angrily, 'Inside!'

The SUV was being driven by an unknown man in army fatigues.

But Leela could not bear to see Bharat being left alone. 'Leave me! Bhaiiii!'

'Liliiii... get away! Now!'

One of the men hit Bharat with the butt of his firearm. As he fell, Leela was grabbed again by both Mahadevan and Heli Sir. They succeeded in hauling her into the SUV.

Now Bharat was being used as a shield, as the attackers dragged him swiftly into their jeep, which was revving and ready to go.

The jeep was getting away. Then a grenade exploded a short distance away and the shrapnel hit Heli Sir and the army man, who uttered an expletive but kept driving.

Heli Sir put his foot on the brake. 'Take cover, Mohsin!'

Another grenade exploded, just as a bleeding Capt. Mohsin veered the jeep away into the forest. Leela was hysterical.

Mahadevan turned Leela's tearful face towards him. 'There will be more of them out there, and will take us out, Sachin included, understand?! We can't go after them... low on ammo and firepower.'

'How did you know we're here?' Sachin was trembling out of nervous tension.

The SUV revved up again. They heard a mobile ring. The network was back!

While Mahadevan took the call, Heli Sir answered Sachin, 'Mohsin was in his trekking camp when he heard the chimes. That's Bharat Sir's code warning during an emergency. Mohsin has a SatNav and called Maddy on his pair.'

Leela turned to them in anger, 'You people are babbling away. God alone knows what they have done with Bhai by now. Dooo something.'

Heli Sir was breathing heavily, 'I smell a rat. How come both the network and the landline were dead at the same time?'

Mahadevan finished his call and turned to them. 'DIG Deshmukh Sir called. I received orders not to take you guys back to PG now. There could be anything... a trap... an ambush. Leela, did Sachin and you come together last evening?'

Leela was still struggling to free herself from Mahadevan's grip, so Sachin answered, 'Yes uncle.'

'You were tracked, so maybe there's a trap anywhere around. Bastards came for all of you together. We need to get you both out now.'

Leela was frantic, 'No! What about Bhai?'

'Search order for Bharat Sir is already out. But I have to drive you both to Pune. We can't risk... Oh!' Mahadevan jerked back and asked, 'Where is Bharat's official guard, that Jayesh?'

'*He* led us into this trap. Didn't you recognize him, holding Sachin?'

'What?' Heli Sir shouted.

They looked at each other. Mahadevan whispered through his teeth, 'Bastards! Fucking bastards!'

As the SUV sped towards Pune, Leela and Sachin were pressed down onto the floor. Soon, they were joined by an escort car to provide further security.

Once they reached the Bengaluru highway, Heli Sir allowed Leela and Sachin to sit up. Meanwhile, Mahadevan had dressed all wounds as best as he could with the help of his first aid box, but the men needed to go to a proper hospital. He himself had superficial wounds, hence he chose to remain with Leela in the SUV, while Heli Sir and Capt Mohsin got into the other car and headed for the army hospital.

They reached the Police headquarters in Pune in another hour. The press seemed to have been tipped off in advance. As soon as the SUV came to a halt with its smashed windscreen and bullet marks, they were surrounded by a full team of police officers and press people.

In one swift move, Leela darted out towards the Press corps. She shouted at the top of her voice, 'Bharat Biswas has been kidnapped! Maybe they have killed him already.'

The younger media people surrounded her in a jiffy with their mikes and cameras thrust into her face, while the Police jostled to deter them and take Leela away.

'Who is "they", Madam?'

The Police had her in their firm grasp and got into furious scuffles with the Press, but Leela had help from another end. Sachin said in a halting voice, 'My father's security guard... he led us into a trap and...'

In a moment, Sachin too was whisked away.

A long session with the police top Brass followed. After more than an hour, Heli Sir and Capt. Mohsin joined them with their wounds dressed and arms supported in casts. Despite being provided a detailed account of the events from that fateful morning, the senior cops were not satisfied and appeared to be edgy.

Heli Sir confronted them with his no nonsense stance and

demanded an immediate inquiry into how both the mobile network and the landline service had gone dead exactly at the time when Bharat was being led into the trap. This fact, combined with the detail that the government appointed security guard was complicit in the plot against the Biswas family, was evidence enough that the Govt *at some level* could be playing a dirty game.

Mada and Rajen were soon in the picture. They escorted Leela and Sachin out of the Police HQ. While exiting, they profusely thanked the defence personnel from Prithak Ghati for having saved Leela and Sachin at great risk to their lives.

The district Police Chief came up to Leela and managed to take her aside for a moment. He wanted her to admit that Bharat was actually hiding to evade his imminent arrest, since the High Court had just cancelled his bail. So where was he? Leela replied furiously, 'In your bedroom, you bloody fool!' This interlude was captured by a smart reporter and the clip was soon all over the networks.

FIFTY TWO

It was still quite dark inside the dense jungle. Bharat's blindfold had been removed and the wound on his head had been dressed by his kidnappers, who were now seven in number.

Soon a big group of armed young men and women with shrouded faces appeared from nowhere and surrounded him without a word. They tied his hands to a thick chain.

The second group retreated with Bharat deeper into the forest, where a vegetable truck was waiting. Bharat was blindfolded again and hidden behind fruit crates covered with hay. The truck had an Uttarakhand number.

The Afternoon newspapers had banner headlines that Bharat has been kidnapped, and that Leela and Sachin had escaped due to Bharat's valiant tussle with the attackers and rearguard action by his army friends from PG. All the news Channels went wild with speculation, debates and panel discussions. Bharat's Detox friends alleged that a section of the ruling junta and certain business houses were behind the kidnapping, but the authorities swiftly denied the same.

As the news spread, there was an unprecedented public uproar. The Home Ministry released an official statement by midday, claiming that they have 'several leads' and would find Bharat soon. Jayesh was suspected to be an undercover agent from a Maoist organization who had infiltrated the government security network.

Rajen took Leela to her flat, but seeing the crowds and neighbours waiting to get 'latest updates' from her, he asked the driver to reverse the car and proceed to his home.

When they reached there, Mada was waiting for them with Sachin and Bima in tow. The DCP Pune emphasized that given the threat perception to Bharat's kin, it made sense that they stayed together in a protected place like Mada's bungalow. The police flatly refused to allow Leela to go back to her flat all alone. There were also extra police personnel now deputed outside Mada's home, till this crisis was still in play.

The Prithak Ghati residents felt orphaned. The farmhands from Bharat's Habitat who had returned that morning to an empty house were guilt-ridden and in shock. Many residents lamented that the inevitable death blow against their lives had now been struck. Some youth formed groups and launched a search for Bharat in the nearby jungles.

The police team found Bharat's mobile in a smashed condition next to some tyre tracks near the riverbank spot where the incident had happened. They followed the track marks of the jeep till a point where numerous people had disembarked and walked on foot, while the jeep had moved away. One police team tracked the jeep tyre traces till it entered the highway, while a second team followed the footprints for five km. They reached a clearing, where there were bigger tyre marks again. It was evident that a truck had been used, but that was it.

For the next five days, there was no news from the kidnappers. The village guard in PG disappeared before the police could question him. Security forces combed all the Maoist strongholds in Maharashtra, Karnataka, Andhra Pradesh and even Kerala, but their efforts drew a typical blank. All the prominent Maoist groups denied a role in Bharat's kidnapping.

On the sixth day a media leak revealed that it was Bharat's tip off that had led to the successful operation of the C-60 Commandos against the Maoist 'Rudra Company', which is why he had now been kidnapped. Shortly thereafter, a splinter Maoist group released pictures of Bharat in their custody with his mouth taped and sitting against a neutral rocky background. They demanded the release of their leader Coomaru (U. Coomaraswamy) alias K. Ganeshan within seventy-two hours against Bharat's release.

FIFTY THREE

Several Maoist leaders claimed that they learnt of Bharat's 'tipping off' role only now through the media. It was their DKSZC (Dandakaranya Special Zonal Committee) peoples' court which had the right to try Bharat for his crime, but they themselves had no hand in his kidnapping. They alleged that this was a government plot to stigmatize them, and that the splinter group which had owned up to the kidnapping had tacit backing from several state governments.

The media ran profile stories about Coomaru, a well-educated ideologue who had converted many urban youth to the ultra left path. A journalist from Pune had once done an exposé on him, which proved that he had access to major funding provided by his foreign backers. After this journalist was bumped off purportedly at his behest, Coomaru and his deputy Madhava Rao were tracked down and arrested. Gradually, his faction of the Red Brigade lost its clout and was dropped from the Maoist JBOBSZC. (Jharkhand-Bihar-Orissa Special Zonal Committee)

There were protest marches in several cities, demanding urgent government action to locate Bharat. Many citizens, who had been uninvolved in the numerous agitations, now threw in their lot with the Detox movement.

Sachin was mercifully spared the media attention as he was ensconced inside Mada's home, well away from public view. Leela, however, had no time to grieve. She had to constantly interface with bureaucrats tracking the case and the security forces who were trying to find Bharat. Mada and Rajen threw in their weight too, but nothing seemed to move.

Meanwhile, the deadline set by the Maoist group ticked away. One section of the Government said that it would stand firm with 'zero tolerance' and not release Coomaru, while another section was supposedly engaged in 'back room parleys' with Bharat's captors.

Gen. Arjun Ponappa came to Mada's home when Leela was also present and warned them that there was a diabolical agenda regarding Bharat, and they could expect the worst. He suspected that he himself could be under some sort of surveillance ordered by a faction of the 'Deep State', given his proximity to Leela and Bharat.

Bharat's kidnappers managed to dodge all the security dragnets and smuggle him to a hidden area near Someshwar in the greater Himalayas. His captors told him that though the Government was releasing Coomaru in a secret deal, they would conduct his trial anyway.

Bharat was held guilty by a 'People's Court' for having tipped off the Govt. about the Maoist 'Special Rudra Company' near Prithak Ghati. He did not react. Given his heroics during his kidnapping in PG, his legs were always chained to a wooden pillar in a primitive hut, except when he needed to relieve himself under armed escort. But from the small window he could see the Himalayas, and that itself gave him all the solace he needed.

Coomaru was shifted around midnight from the high security prison in Jehanabad to Ranchi. During the journey, he was accompanied by a special squad of sharpshooters.

In a sudden move during transit, he was freed near a forest before reaching Ranchi. The wily leader refused to leave, fearing an encounter, but when he saw trusted faces emerge from the forest, he left with them. As per the secret plan prepared by the Triad, specially chosen security personnel then fired around to create a mock encounter. At the same time, Coomaru's deputy Madhava Rao, who was out on bail, was brought to Palamau.

Within an hour of this 'encounter', P. Aiyer's handpicked government Officials released a media statement that Coomaru had escaped after a major intelligence failure. There had been secret reports that some Maoists had been planning a massive assault on the High Security Prison in Jehanabad even prior to Bharat's kidnapping. Since Coomaru was wanted in a case trial hearing in Ranchi in a few days, the move to shift him had been cleared with this in mind. But with this well planned Maoist attack on the escort convoy, it had become apparent that the tip-off about an impending assault on the Jehanabad Prison was a red herring.

A high-grade alert was declared to apprehend Coomaru, and a massive combing operation was ordered. Many theories started doing the rounds. It was alleged that Bharat's enemies within the Polity had sabotaged his release and facilitated this Maoist attack.

Meanwhile, Coomaru was taken deep inside a forest in Palamau. Exactly at 9.45 pm, a motorcycle arrived there. Madhava Rao, wearing a hood covering his head, stepped off and embraced Coomaru. They congratulated each other. Then, as Coomaru turned to get onto the motorcycle, he was shot in the head at point blank range by Madhava Rao. One of Coomaru's stunned men shot at Madhava, who collapsed on the ground.

A group of crack police commandos now emerged on cue from their entrenched positions and eliminated the entire Dalam in a blaze of fire. Madhava was rushed to hospital in a bleeding but stable condition, since he was wearing a bullet proof jacket and apparel covering his head and ears too. The 'contra' operation was accomplished to perfection, thus completing the first part of the plot schemed by the Triad of Prabhat Aiyer, Sobha Singh Gujral and R.Subramaniam.

The news was broken to the press at 11.30 pm. Bharat's kidnappers soon learnt about this second encounter, and that their leader had been betrayed and eliminated.

FIFTY FOUR

Bharat was sitting on a rock in a meditative posture facing the Himalayas. He had requested for this leeway from his captors and it had been granted. However, his feet remained chained to a massive tree stump. He was still wearing the same white shirt as when he was kidnapped.

His whole life flashed before him in exquisite detail. Yes, he had regrets, that he was not combative enough; that he had almost withdrawn himself from public platforms. He wished he had prepared Sachin in a better manner for the rough road ahead. But Leela: she was there. She would take care of Sachin.

He smiled as he recalled his favourite poem, 'He fell among Thieves' by Sir Henry Newbolt, about the betrayal, capture and execution of Explorer George Hayward in Darkot, Gilgit. The irony was that he would perhaps live out his last hours in a similar manner.

... 'ye have robb'd,' said he

'ye have slaughter'd and made an end,

Take your ill-got plunder, and bury the dead:

What will ye more of your guest and sometime friend?'

'Blood for our blood,' they said.

He laugh'd: 'If one may settle the score for five,

I am ready; but let the reckoning stand till day:

I have loved the sunlight as dearly as any alive.'

'You shall die at dawn,' said they...'

Bharat laughed softly and then uproariously. Gradually the laughter turned to singing, alternated with whispered recitations of the poem.

He remained awake all night meditating and revisiting his life with joy. He saw Shivdadu and Sarasdida toiling in the Bengal farm; his mother combing his curly hair before going to school; Leela trailing his footsteps when she was a little child; Urvashi, tempestuous Urvi and their tranquil days in Kalasa; baby Sachin calling him 'Baba' for the first time; all the smiling faces of the many oppressed souls whom he had resettled in PG and around; and finally Santji, the man who was one with him in every breath, with him always… even now.

It was dawn.

'*...Light on the Laspur hills was broadening fast,*

The blood-red snow-peaks chill'd to a dazzling white;

He turn'd, and saw the golden circle at last,

Cut by the Eastern height.'

Bharat was in a reverie, as he faced the dazzling white Himalayan peaks, and the higher ranges further away which were now blood red and crimson. The mountain air caressed him, and he inhaled this vital energy deeply. He stopped reciting the poem, took his palm to his eyes and kissed his mother's photo which he always carried with him. It also showed Leela standing behind, and had a small comment by Santji at the bottom.

His captors now positioned a teenaged recruit behind him with a gun. This boy had been brought here for training to become a fearless warrior. He had in fact been Bharat's favourite help at the trekking camps, whenever Bharat visited Pithoragarh. His family too had been helped by Bharat in their remote village. However, right now the boy did not know who his target was, since his trainers had put a hooded cape around Bharat's head and shoulders.

It was time. Bharat knew it and was ready.

His eyes were open, looking into the infinite. He wanted to go consciously.

'O glorious Life, Who dwellest in earth and sun,

I have lived, I praise and adore Thee.'

A sword...'

The boy pressed the trigger.

Bharat slumped forward, the crimson spreading fast over the white.

Not one word was spoken by the men, nor did they look at each other. They slowly sauntered away.

The boy knew the job was done. There wasn't any cry though as he had expected. After a while, he slowly edged forward and peered into Bharat's dead face.

A desperate animal howl of pain broke the morning peace.

The boy wept as he walked in a trance after his handlers. Slowly, the wailing sound grew faint and then disappeared.

The hills were quiet again.

'Over the pass the voices one by one

faded, and the hill slept.'

FIFTY FIVE

Ablackbird was hopping around peacefully and pecking at the soil, trying to extract some worms. It had just struck pay dirt when it was chased away by a big magpie. The bigger bird quickly gulped the bonus meal and then hopped onto a shoe. It capered another two steps around the foot attached to the shoe.

Leela did not attempt to chase the bird away. It looked at her with trepidation and then back at the body lying still at her feet. Then it uttered a loud alarm and flew away.

She continued sitting next to Bharat's body, with no show of emotion. Gradually, her pulse slowed down. With each intake of breath, a series of absolutes ran in a looped refrain which took over her thinking process: 'Bhai is gone. Bhai is no more. My dearest brother will never row again. He will never sing again. He will never tousle my hair again.'

She was not aware of what the volunteers around her were saying. Bhai looked so peaceful. In fact he seemed to be smiling.

Would she smile in death too?

The local police arrived and started the process of evacuating Bharat's body after recovering all evidence. One of them gently requested her to make way. It was then that she discovered the photo in Bharat's fist. For the first time, her lips twitched and tears poured down her face. But still she did not utter a sound.

She could not bring herself to call anyone, but she messaged Rajen that Sachin was to be kept away from the TV and his mobile for now and immediately taken to Dehradun. Rajen messaged her back and promised to do this. He showed real sensitivity in adding that he would not call her, but was waiting and making all the arrangements.

As the news was flashed, violent protests broke out in several towns. A slew of personalities including luminaries from the Indian Army started breaking their silence and urged citizens to close ranks and prepare to defend the country from within.

Anu sat next to her altar, her head leaning against the wall, a vacant look on her face. The female members among her neighbours were weeping and beating their chests, but she remained silent.

Shiv suddenly asked for a gun to defend the land, before he retreated into complete silence. Once in a while, his chest heaved with silent tears.

Gayatri immediately rushed down to the farmhouse to take over the daily chores. She was amazed to find that a sizeable Garhwali support group had formed overnight outside Shiv's tiny home to fight this battle to the finish. Thousands of passionate ordinary citizens sought Anu out to share her grief of having lost her only child.

Ganapati had just finished his flute round when he got a message on his mobile. He ran all the way to Rudolph's home. Soon they got into a Scorpio jeep with Bharat's garlanded photo fixed atop. Slowly they went around town, striking a single gong on a big bell.

Everyone knew that this meant the passing away of a resident. The residents who peeped out and saw Bharat's photo fixed on the Scorpio immediately passed the message to their neighbours who lived off the roads.

Within an hour, the entire population of Prithak Ghati knew, including all those who had no access to the local network.

As the moments ticked away, Birbal Kaka staggered to the peepul tree and banged his head repeatedly till blood spurted out. As PC Hindre restrained him, many residents could no longer control their emotions and started weeping.

Mada and Rajen arrived in Dehradun with Sachin to join their kin. From her worship corner, Anu saw Sachin entering their home, looking lost and crushed. She slowly dragged herself to the bewildered young boy and ran her hands over his head, cheeks and chin again and again, as if to feel Bharat's presence in her grandchild. Then she pulled him to her heart and her grief burst forth in a great outburst. The boy too broke down for the first time and wept.

Mada sat with Shiv in a corner. The brothers were holding hands and watching their respective lives flash by in a painful remembrance.

By the time Leela arrived with Bharat's body and a posse of accompanying policemen, the crowd outside had swelled to mammoth proportions. They did not allow a single politician to visit and offer condolences. Though there was some talk of airlifting Bharat's body to Prithak Ghati, the family finally decided to cremate him in Dehradun where his closest kin were based.

Anu and Gayatri embraced Leela and cried, but she was dry eyed. After a while she went in past Shiv and met Sachin for the first time since he had been orphaned. They sat in silence, lost in their own thoughts, while their loved one lay smiling within their sight, merged into that same infinite silence.

Leela could not bear to see Sachin's trembling lips as he fought back his tears. She stretched out and held his hand.

'I can't accept,' muttered Sachin while shaking his head in demur, 'that he *had* to suffer; meet such a fate.'

Leela ran her hand lovingly over Bharat's brow, weeping incoherently, 'See how he is smiling? Embracing destiny... now gone forever.'

The next day Sachin did the *Mukhagni* on his own. As the flames finally died down, one by one the huge crowds and mourning relatives departed, including a sizeable section from Prithak Ghati.

It was past midnight when Sachin joined Leela and the Ponappas, lonely figures that stood there till only the embers remained. Birbal Kaka, Firdaus and Shivanna stood huddled in a corner, waiting to accompany them back to Shiv's home.

A day passed. Then another went by. Slowly, the anger at Bharat's killing started abating. While the agitations continued, a sense of despondency started creeping into some people that they had no escape from their fate. Bharat's friends from the Detox movement desperately needed a new trigger to put the fire back into their efforts, but they had no clue about the way ahead. The Triad were predators who had been guided by a killer instinct honed by generations of career politicians and rulers. This Cabal knew that with Bharat gone, the discordant movements would lose steam.

Arjun declined to make any statement or take any calls about Bharat's killing. In a masterly series of moves, he exposed the Cabal's bloody hands in the public space.

First an anonymous message was released on the social media detailing Prabhat Aiyer's role in procuring the intelligence report, which mentioned that Bharat had informed Gen. Ponappa and thereby the security forces about the 'Rudra Company' Maoist presence near Prithak Ghati.

A video footage then went viral, showing a senior Police Officer meeting Prabhat Aiyer and S.S. Gujral over drinks at the India Global Center. The zoomed in footage showed Aiyer passing him a lavish tourism brochure. The Officer dropped the brochure by mistake and a couple of Official papers with top secret notings could be seen for an instant.

This was followed by the exposure that shortly after this IGC meeting, the same Police Officer had met Madhava Rao in the Ranchi jail. On sustained interrogation, the Officer admitted that he had received a confidential file copy from P. Aiyar about Bharat's disclosures to Gen Ponappa, and shared it as per plan with the Maoist Leader.

While Aiyer and Gujral were busy denying the whole expose as an opposition plot and a conspiracy theory, Arjun delivered his coup de grâce. Following the bomb attack in PG on the jeep earlier, the government had insisted on installing a surveillance camera at the entrance to Bharat's Habitat. Unknown to them, Arjun had taken Sachin's help to install another such camouflaged camera near Bharat's room with an outstanding microphone.

So while the treacherous Jayesh had disabled the first camera before R. Subramaniam and Sardar Mane had dropped in, the entire visit was recorded by the second hidden camera with crystal clear audio. This was released to a prominent news channel by Heli Sir on Arjun's instructions.

Sardar Mane was arrested. The same day R. Subramaniam and P. Aiyer were removed from their dominant positions in the Party, and the PM himself ordered an inquiry. Sobha Singh Gujral resigned on his own and retreated to his farmhouse.

Later, the Triad denied the charges and insisted that this was a doctored footage which anyway proved nothing. But they failed to get their hands on the original footage. Heli Sir asserted that he would present the evidence in court. Arjun had locked away the real thing elsewhere, after making several copies. The fuse had been lit, and the Triad were now dog-housed as marked men. A non-bailable arrest warrant was issued by the Pune court and a distinguished battery of lawyers volunteered to pursue the case and vowed to bring the culprits to justice.

Gen. Ponappa had his plans for them but now he set about

executing his life's final mission to protect the country. During the past seven months, he had been assigning commando teams from the Territorial Army of ex-Servicemen (TAES) to different zones over India. They were now given a clear brief on how to guard the land and its citizens from anti-nationals who could attempt to take over during any war chaos.

As a last move, Arjun now disabled all electronic devices and plastic money and shifted Chitra to a cottage in Kodagu where she could not be tracked. Then he completely vanished, to secretly continue with his activities. Only a few chosen people in the Govt. and the Defence forces, whom he trusted, had a dim idea of his mission. This involved traversing much of the border with Pakistan and China and setting up *a second line of defence manned by TAES personnel.*

FIFTY SIX

Leela went back to Pune a day after the cremation, leaving Sachin in the care of Anu and Gayatri. There was a big board outside her flat with a 'Strictly do not disturb' sign. She wondered which kind soul had done this, but it did help initially. No one rang her bell or offered condolences to her.

But it was too good to last. First the postman, then some college friends, then one by one her neighbours – they all *had* to express their sense of shock.

To deflect from her trauma, she immediately set out on a second marathon tour of all the old age homes, animal shelters and destitute communities which her organisations were supporting. Gen. Ponappa had insisted that she conduct a series of trial runs, shifting all residents to temporary shelters which were equipped as per Bharat's 'survival mode'. As foreseen by Leela, half of the inmates refused to shift from their urban residences, believing Bharat's ideas of a probable war to be a false doomsday prediction. Leela left them to their fate with a heavy heart. She concentrated on the ones that met her halfway.

Since the destitute and animal shelters had no such 'voice' of protest, she had better success in shifting them to the temporary shelters in the countryside run by reliable helpers. In each one of them, Leela ensured that the minimalistic model of survival that Bharat had advocated was put in place.

All machinery was shielded against EMP damage. The members were armed with vegetable seeds; stocks of cereals for at least two years stored with neem preservatives, and all essential medical and survival kits. HAM radio sets, professional walkie talkies, natural cooling devices were all put in place with trained people who could handle them. Bharat had left detailed lists of things that should be part of the survival kits, and she followed this to the minutest detail.

In the midst of all this, Gayatri messaged Leela that most of the TH expedition team including Aditya had survived the avalanche, but they were still stranded on a ridge due to inclement weather. The situation had been complicated by the fact that some militant refugees, who had broken out earlier from their camps near Jammu, had headed through the Kishtwar National Park and run into the stranded TH team. An operation was being planned to apprehend these refugees and also to bring Aditya back to the mainland.

Leela was now seized with an overwhelming, almost insane desire to find Aditya in the Himalayas. There was no knowing how this border tension could play out, after the recent firing in the Gilgit region. Being besieged by some crazed refugees who had escaped was itself fraught with immense danger. If war broke out before Aditya was handed over to the Trans Himalaya (TH) Master Control, it was anybody's guess what his fate would be.

She had to bring him out of it, as an act of atonement on her part. Even if he was officially dismissed for his act of indiscipline, she could always bring him later to Prithak Ghati for a meaningful life together.

To overcome her acute anguish, she travelled to Prithak Ghati for a day. The whole town came as one to hold her hand and assure her of their support. After entering Bharat's homestead, she slowly trudged to the enclosed garden and sat on the mat there, meditating for an hour. She could not bring herself to enter his room. The memories were still too painful for her to bear with. She promised to return again later to keep Bharat's Habitat alive.

The next step was one that again caused her great distress. A strange instinct was telling her to leave Bima with Chitra. She did not want to give him for safe keeping to either Rajen or Mada, who she knew would never move from Pune in a war scenario. So she took Bima to Arjun's home, only to find that he had vanished and that Chitra too was gone. Then she remembered Arjun mentioning some numbers when he had called her last, immediately after Bharat's death. Rummaging through her bag now, she got out her notepad with the hastily written numbers. She confirmed that these were the coordinates for a place in Kodagu.

She gave in to her gut feeling, hired a vehicle and drove through the night to a hamlet in North Kodagu (Coorg) where she knew Chitra was stationed incognito. Though Leela did not divulge her travel plans to Chitra, the lady guessed instinctively that Leela was going on some suicidal mission, or she would never have brought Bima so far for safe custody.

For the next two hours, Chitra held Leela in her arms, shedding tears and pleading with her not to travel anywhere in her present mental state. But it was all to no avail. Leela had decided to act and take life into her hands, as had always been her wont. She would not succumb to Karma and fatalism as her dearest Bhai had done.

Leela looked into Bima's eyes silently, knowing that it could be the last time that she would see him. The dog perhaps knew it too. When Leela turned back in tears to her car, he did not bark or try to pull at her. He lay down there and put his head between his giant paws without a sound. He was crying silently.

All through her long drive back to Pune, Adi's agonized face in parting; Bima's mournful look; Bharat's sleeping face... all these morphed into each other. She would take breaks at unscheduled spots where she let out her pent up emotions in a silent flow of tears, resting her head on the wheel or stepping out and hugging a tree. Each time she was revitalized by her memories of Mahakaal at dawn.

The night passed to morning and calm returned. Now there was only one resolve: 'I am damned if I can't bring Adi back to safety and sanity. I am damned! I am damned!'

As she neared Pune, she turned on the radio. The on-going Joint Naval Exercise between the China's PLAN (People's Liberation Army's Navy) and the Pakistan Navy in the Arabian sea was drawing to a close. But the lead story was still about the upcoming Indo - China Summit in Beijing, and the media had raised expectations about it to a fever pitch. There was much euphoria about an anticipated border settlement with China. The ruling polity too was repeatedly highlighting a large number of deals which were meant to be negotiated and signed between India and China.

After reaching Pune and snatching some sleep, she spent the rest of the day preparing herself for the arduous journey ahead. The next morning she proceeded to Dehradun to meet Gayatri, Shivdadu and Anu Mashi, constantly fighting back the thought that she might not get to see them again. She did not divulge the mission which had started taking shape in her mind. She told them that she would be away for a short trek to regain her sanity.

Sachin stood watching her silently with an occasional scowl crossing his face. Leela had dithered about going ahead when she thought about Sachin, but she reassured herself that he was safe with Anu, and that he was the emotional magnet that would power her resolve to return in one piece from her 'Aditya Mission'.

She used some tact in procuring a copy of the TH expedition route map from Gayatri, as well a hand drawn map prepared by a local Tibetan youth, Tashi, whom both Leela and Gayatri had known for long.

A day later, Leela and Tashi drove down to Manali in a rented car. After releasing the car at Manali, they proceeded on a public bus to Keylong and then Darcha. Tashi told her that though the route through the Shingo La pass was shorter, there would be Army units and BRO (Border Roads Organization) personnel posted there for the Project Vijayak new road being built to Padum. Travellers would be routinely questioned. So they decided to go on a longer route known to Leela, via Bara Lacha pass and the Phirtse La. They would start by going to Zingzingbar, follow the Tsarap river, and then track the Lingti chu stream.

Every step spelt danger, but Mahakaal's parting words continued to spur Leela on: 'It will be a lonely and tortuous path. But always remember that I will be with you. Always.'

FIFTY SEVEN

Three days later, the Indian Prime Minister flew into Beijing with a top level delegation. However, the world attention was riveted on the confrontation between USA and Russia over Ukraine's move to join several SEE (South East Europe) bodies as a prelude to joining the EU. Threats and posturing had raised fears everywhere that things could go out of hand.

When the Beijing summit was at its peak, news came in that a series of explosions had destroyed an important chain of high altitude bridges and even a part of the Bunji dam in the 'Belt' part of the OBOR (One Belt One Road) project in the Gilgit-Baltistan and Baluchistan regions. Pakistan promptly put the blame on a plot hatched by India and executed by insurgent agents from Baluchistan.

This had a catastrophic impact on the talks. The Indian PM emphatically denied that India had any hand in these acts of violence, but the Chinese leadership would not buy this. Abruptly, new and intractable conditions were brought in by China to settle the Border dispute, which no Indian government would ever accept. The Indian leadership felt slighted and left for India one day before the official visit was scheduled to be over.

The Chinese stoutly denied that they had gone back on the unofficial MOU about the border settlement. Instead they stated that these attacks on the OBOR project were a deliberate act of provocation by an aggressive Indian Polity. The Chinese media such as the CCTV and Global Times had only one theme: 'India needs to be taught a lesson and shown its place'.

The Indian team flew into Delhi after 1 am. The PM made a terse statement about the experience in Beijing, but it was apparent that he was still smarting from the turn events had taken there. He announced that he would address a major press conference the same morning, with the External Affairs Minister and Foreign Secretary in attendance.

Day One. 2.33 am. All the aircraft operating in the vicinity of IGI Airport Delhi lost computer control. There was no contact possible with the Air Traffic Control (ATC), which found itself paralyzed with its systems burnt out. Many of the pilots managed to steer their aircraft manually without guidance or GPS, but two pilots failed to do so and crashed, killing all occupants on board.

3.07 am. China issued a warning of her security being breached by Indian forces along the Gilgit tract ceded to them by Pakistan. She had already used her ASAT weaponry to destroy many of India's LEO and GEO satellites in their first strike, following this up with *HEMP attacks on Delhi, Bengaluru and Mumbai to bring India to her knees.* China now also initiated a massive cyber-attack on India's security network, coupled with a major ground offensive launched by Pakistan. India was initially overwhelmed by this twin attack on her first line of defence but soon responded strongly, while preparing her nuclear arsenal.

Meanwhile, in all three affected cities, many patients on life support systems died when their oxygen machines, ventilators and pacemakers got wrecked or stalled during surgeries in the Operation theatres and ICUs. The power grid collapsed. Transformers and generators burnt out from the massive pulse, and many fires were sparked.

The worst case scenario happened to communications, when the Internet disappeared and mobile and landline services were rendered inactive. Night shift workers found the Metro rail services inoperative. ATMs were completely stalled.

A TRYST WITH MAHAKAAL

Within thirty minutes, India had met the two front attacks with its strategic command taking over operations. The PM and the Defence Minister were flown with full air escort to an unknown destination to direct the battle from a 'hardened' Nuclear Bunker. The SPG (Special Protection Group) personnel with FN2000 rifles provided a wartime security cover to the Army Chief, Home Minister etc. Other top personnel in the defence and scientific teams found themselves guarded by SPG squads brandishing Excalibur and Dragunov long barrelled sniper rifles, who arrived in 'hardened' transport and took up positions around all critical installations.

The government tried to turn the blackout to its advantage. The Home Minister reckoned that Social media could spell disaster if there was connectivity, and rumours of nuclear weapons being used would cause mass panic in the major cities of India. The government immediately invoked nationwide orders blackening out all networks and phone lines *in the unaffected cities*. Radio and terrestrial TV broadcasts at regular intervals took over.

Fortunately, no mass cases of violence broke out during the night in the HEMP impacted cities of Delhi, Mumbai or Bengaluru, despite the public realizing that something momentous must have caused this blackout and the dead networks. The little news coming in from the war front was conveyed via portable loudspeakers by Army units patrolling the streets in old diesel jeeps, or on horseback. The same model was put into practice in all other cities too, in order to prepare the public for further shocks in case more HEMP attacks took place.

7 AM. The Prime Minister addressed the nation from his Bunker. In a brief speech, he stressed that India had been betrayed and was under a twin attack forced upon it by an act of well-planned deceit. Despite the initial setbacks due to the surprise element, India was going to take the battle into the enemy camp. He spoke of Dharma and righteous action

374

to force the enemy to regret this reckless act. All citizens had to remain calm and not take the law into their own hands. With folded hands, he sought their support in this darkest hour. While the world community had already been informed, India was not waiting for any succour. She was fighting to win because they were with Dharma, with God.

The PM could not contemplate ordering a counter conventional nuclear strike on either China or Pakistan. This could quickly escalate into an all-out nuclear exchange which would obliterate all three countries. The HEMP strategy had been chosen by the attacking nations with precisely this in mind. While there was no major direct loss of life in the three Indian cities, people would perish slowly when food supplies ran out and disease took over.

So while India showed the intent to prepare her nuclear arsenal, it decided to lull the enemy for the time being by neither using any counter HEMP attack nor ordering an actual nuclear strike which could be tracked by the Pakistani or Chinese Satellites.

Meanwhile, since many of India's satellite systems were destroyed, the Indian Army's Tactical Command, Control, Communications and Information (Tac C3I) System and DIPAC (Defence Imagery Processing and Analysis Centre) pre-warning system were now handicapped for a while. Taking advantage of this weakness, China concentrated on selected missile attacks and air strikes. Their objective was to take out as many Phalcon AEWs (Airborne Early Warning and Control Systems), Rajendra Radars (Slewable Passive Phased Array Radar used for 3-D Target Detection) and Akash SAMs (Surface to Air Missile Defence Systems) as possible, to soften up India's protection for its ground installations and air force. China's ground offensive was imminent.

With daybreak, the realization of being at war on both fronts had reached many people despite the internet and mobile shut down. The digital generation was completely paralyzed. Many youth were seen weeping, clutching their dead cell-phones and scared out of their wits.

The HEMP attacks had tripped all the major national power grids, so there was no power in almost all urban centres, cities and small towns. Irrespective of the government blackout, it became clear that the networks would not sustain anyway on temporary back up power.

As the missile attacks intensified on major Indian cities; with no power or water, with most gadgets, machinery, petrol pumps and transportation rendered inert; terrifying scenes of fear and destruction were witnessed on an unprecedented scale. As Bharat had predicted long ago, several prominent politicians and VIPs soon slipped away from India. The masses desperately tried to get out to the countryside on foot or mechanized transport to survive.

8.32 AM. The Maoist factions and regional jihadi groups launched attacks all over the country in premeditated manoeuvres to seize control of strategic facilities such as armouries and banks, but they found themselves outsmarted by the well-trained squads of TAES personnel who coordinated with the Indian army to protect the country from within.

Soon, Prithak Ghati became an oasis for the desperate hordes that walked huge distances to find succour. Though Pune had not suffered a HEMP attack, people there panicked since they feared that the same fate as nearby Mumbai was about to befall them. Many had heard of Prithak Ghati, so they would do a night halt at the nearest safe pockets and continue their journey at dawn till they hoped to reach PG. This had not been anticipated by the Panchayat. The TAES squads immediately fanned out to restore order in this chaotic situation, but the situation remained very tense and kept getting worse by the hour.

Sowing of vegetable seeds was started immediately, supervised by Birbal Kaka along with his dedicated team of farmhands. The same story was replicated in other such self-reliant pockets all over the country. The political leadership operating from the nuclear bunker issued instructions to the Army and TAES to lend full support to such units and set up as many others as possible, while the Chief of Defence Staff directed the war on both fronts.

With rail and air services at a complete standstill, the PM's War Cabinet realized that the spent nuclear fuel rods in the Nuclear Power plants would soon start melting down when the backup fuel ran out, causing terrible catastrophes. So a small 'hardened' fleet of massive army helicopters started a non-stop series of sorties to deliver more such fuel to keep the Nuclear power plants afloat and safe.

On the western war front, the five main Indian divisions under the 15 Corps, 1 Corps and 11 Corps were all fighting the Pakistani forces with their backs to the wall, since they were without Satellite guidance. In almost all the major sectors, from Ladakh (Kargil) right up to the Barmer and Kutch, the break in logistics initially went against the Indian defences.

But the Indian Army remained confident of containing Pakistan. The strategy was that if the Chinese could be countered and beaten back despite the massive head-start they had managed due to their ASAT assault and the HEMP damage, Pakistan would lose the war of nerves and take major losses in the long run. It was the Chinese who had planned for this war for long, so India focused on using her critical defence resources mainly on the Chinese front.

The Chinese ground Offensive started by 9.43 AM. On the western front, the Chinese Aksai Chin forces with their T 99A and the latest ZTQ-15 MBT's (Main Battle tanks) attempted to cross the Chip Chap River together with their amphibious ZBD - 04 and 05 (Chinese Infantry Fighting Vehicles), backed by 6th Fighter division Sukhoi SU-27 aircraft from the Kashgar airbase.

A TRYST WITH MAHAKAAL

The Indian forces, backed by their MIG 29 and Mirage squadrons, countered in a move along the Shyok River heading north towards the Galwan river section and further North to DBO (Daulat Beg Oldi, Military Base in Ladakh). Further south, the Chinese targeted Indian Brigades along the Chang Chemno River between Kongka La and the logistical pivot at Shyok and tried to cut off all routes and supplies to other Indian brigades deployed between Galwan and Karakoram.

Additionally, in the entire crucial belt between Chushul, Rezang La and Demchok, the Chinese used their control of the mountain passes at Chang, Jara and Charding near Demchok to attack the Indian XIV Corps Brigades.

Day two. DBO was a crucial location in the opening battle. Two Indian reinforced mechanized formations and the 10th Mountain Division were armed with a modest strength of T-90S and T-72M Tanks, counter battery SMERCH MLRS (Multiple Launch Rocket System) and a number of NAMICA (Nag anti-tank Missile Carrier) vehicles. They fought desperately to repel repeated attacks from waves of Chinese tanks backed by Chinese air strafing, as the rival air missions fought brutal dogfights in the skies to prevent each other's ground assets from being destroyed.

119HU fighter helicopter units and Mi-17 choppers using the Indian forward airbases in DBO, Chushul and Thoise conducted both attack missions and dropped supplies during the savage battle. But both these units took heavy losses.

With much of India's Satellite support destroyed, some Indian air squadrons were now using the Soviet GLONASS (Satellite Navigational System) assistance. They were able to snuff out a SAAB 2000 Swedish built AWACS (Airborne Warning and Control System) deployed by Pakistan, but only after losing four of their aircraft in the dogfight. The Indian Sukhois used the same system and destroyed one of China's HQ-

9B interceptor based air defence systems. Nonetheless, the Indian forces took far heavier losses than the enemy.

On the Eastern Front, the PLA (Peoples Liberation Army) 13th Army launched their ground offensive in Arunachal Pradesh. Facing them on several locations between Yumthang Valley and Chumbi valley was the Indian 5th Mountain division and the 23rd Infantry, using Pinaka MBRLs (Multi-Barrel Rocket Launcher), unmanned drones and artillery to ward off the huge threat to the Siliguri corridor. The simultaneous Chinese air assault was countered by the Indian Air Force (IAF) conducting BARCAP (Barrier Combat Air Patrol) operations through their SU-30 and Mig 21 Bison fighter aircraft units from Tezpur and another SU-30 Rhino squadron from Chabua.

The grave threat to the Chumbi Valley and consequently the chances of the Siliguri corridor being overrun were growing by the hour. The brand new Rafale fighters from Hashimara base were immediately pressed into combat. Two unscathed Phalcons from the Kalaikunda base were now joined by the CABS AEW (Centre for Airborne Systems designed Airborne Early Warning Aircraft) from No 51 squadron to provide the 'eyes in the sky' surveillance cover for all the air operations in the Eastern Sector.

Day Three. By now it became clear that the Indian logistical weaknesses were slowly turning the war in China's favour. The CMC (Central Military Commission China) had opted for a top heavy HEMP plus ASAT strategy as their first salvo. Many of India's air bases had already been debilitated by a massive missile barrage from the Chinese D 21 and D 31 ICBM missile launchers, and from Pakistan's Shaheen TELs (Transporter Erector Launcher). While many missiles were destroyed in the air by the Indian Barak-8 interceptor missiles, due to the huge numbers of missiles launched, a few got through and crippled the airbases even deep inside India.

In the next phase which kicked in after the second night, wave after wave of the Chinese J-8 AND J-16 fighters diverted the IAF fighter squadrons and cleared the skies for their J 20 stealth fighters to sneak through and destroy Indian military targets. Exactly at the same time, the Pakistani JF-17 combat aircraft drew away Indian air defence formations, while their Mirage III strike aircraft conducted successful bombing missions on high value targets. India soon started running out of her UAV (Unmanned Aerial Vehicle) assets, the Israeli built Herons, which were shredded while still in the hangers. Without Satellite cover and adequate Radar guided defence batteries, India could not provide an accurate counter to these combined enemy attacks.

By the third day, diplomatic efforts to stop the war had speeded up. USA, France and Russia had ordered their warships to the Indian Ocean and put their armies on alert. But none of the combatants were willing to stop. China and Pakistan knew that the odds were turning in their favour, and the Indians were desperate to retrieve lost ground, or else it would be a replay of the 1962 debacle.

A Chinese mountain division battled its way to Walong in north-east Arunachal, where the Indian 2nd Mountain Division staged a desperate holding operation which they were losing by the hour.

The Chinese 55th and 11th Divisions broke through in Chumbi Valley and worked their way to Kangra La. A second Chinese Division progressed rapidly to Bomdi La - Dirang - Se La Pass along the Dirang River. Their target was Tawang. One more division joined the assault from Gyantse towards Chumbi Valley. They were confronted by three Indian divisions: 23rd infantry plus 2nd, 5th and 71st Mountain divisions, who failed to cut off the Chinese supply lines due to the massive missile barrage, along with an overwhelming number of Chinese air strikes.

The superior Indian air force remained severely handicapped by lack of AWACS (Airborne Warning and Control System), which had either been destroyed or the surviving units had been diverted to meet the threat to South and East India from the seas. Despite this, Indian strike aircraft were able to inflict critical damage on assigned targets in China and Pakistan.

But this did not change the overall trend in the war. With China's backing, Pakistan was on the verge of breaking through to Ludhiana, Chandigarh and Jaipur, which were already looking like bombed out ghost towns. Complete chaos had taken over.

Day four. Leela and Tashi continued to struggle on the treacherous terrain during their long and lonely journey. With many fighter aircraft roaring through the skies, they suspected now that war had broken out.

In the mainland, violence and looting had started in the HEMP hit Indian cities. Kolkata was enduring a terrible bloodbath due to an attempt by jihadi forces to take over control.

Somehow stray pieces of news about the general trend of the war and India's fate had reached sections of the Indian populace, aggravating their panic. However, not too many people knew that the Indians too had inflicted severe damage on Pakistani and Chinese military assets, cities and support systems with their pinpointed missile attacks. Deep penetration Jaguar fighter jets and Mirage aircraft using NGARM missiles had wrecked critical enemy assets deep inside the Chinese mainland and Pakistan, while the supersonic Brahmos missiles had accurately hit military bases and core infrastructure in both countries, creating panic in the enemy camps. *The Junwei- Konjum Communist Party Headquarters in Beijing was shaken and in a bitter internal debate if they should continue the war because the urban Chinese population was now fleeing to the countryside in large numbers.*

But India's biggest worry was on the Naval front. A well-planned Naval operation was carried out by the Chinese submarines which had participated in the Joint exercise with Pakistan and were still on their way back to China when they were ordered into action while just off Indian waters. They made an audacious attack on the Vizag Port and sank two of India's diesel electric Subs and several Delhi and Rajput Class Destroyers. In an immediate response, one of India's new Vishakapatnam Class Stealth Guided Missile Destroyers managed to drop Sonobuoys (Expendable Sonar System dropped from Ships conducting Anti Submarine Warfare) and accurately pin down and destroy one escaping Chinese submarine. But the damage was done. This was the single biggest loss in the Indian Navy's History.

The Chinese had over sixty submarines and a sizeable number of Type 054 Frigates, as well as several PLAN 052C Class Destroyers. Many of these had been boldly patrolling very close to the Malacca Straits choke point, and with the outbreak of hostilities had immediately slipped through to join their already deployed contingent in the Indian Ocean. The Indian Air Force surveillance aircraft from the Andaman and Nicobar base had spotted them. But India could not divert too many aircraft or resources from its frugal Naval strength to take on all of them head on, while the country was taking a pounding on its northern and western borders.

With such a wide disparity in their respective strengths, and with the Pakistan Navy also aggressively joining the war with its five submarines and frigates, India was under attack from all sides.

The COAS (Chief of the Army Staff) India realized that it was time to shift a gear. The PM was consulted in his underground bunker and the moves were greenlighted. Operation OORMI-MANDALA was on.

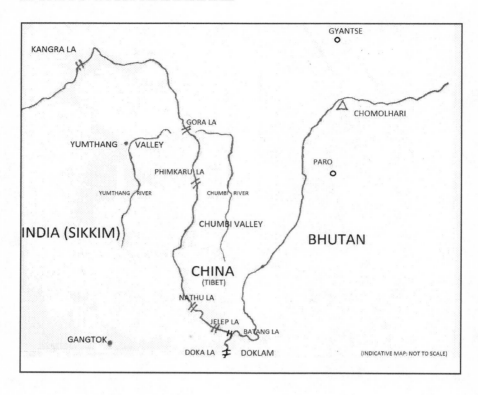

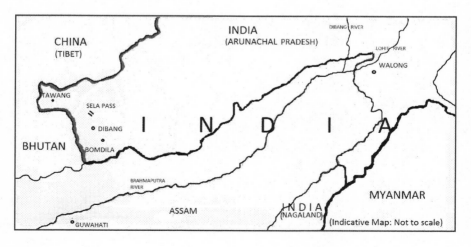

FIFTY EIGHT

It was the sixth day since the war had started. Leela and Tashi had been managing with meagre rations supplied to them by kind villagers on their route. By now they already knew that hostilities had broken out on the border. Some villagers fleeing the war front had passed by and informed them that the army had evacuated all the areas near the front and soon they would be here to sanitize the region and keep the locals out of harm's way. Though this region was remote and not on any logistical route, the PLAAF airborne Corps or even the Pakistani Special Forces could drop their paratroopers here to make a rearguard assault on the Indian Positions.

Leela was now glad that she was carrying a licensed gun gifted to her long ago by Arjun Ponappa. She was dressed in local clothes, with her hair cut short.

They reached a small village inhabited by people of Tibetan stock. The stoic villagers only warned her of troubles ahead. So far the limited news from the war front had been negative, and the rumours said that Indian Forces had suffered reverses almost everywhere and were losing ground.

Leela could not glean any information about the fate of the Trans Himalayan Team or Aditya. But the news from the mainland was even worse. A few locals had come back from cities such as Jalandhar and Chandigarh to shift their elders from this settlement before the hostilities impacted them. They spoke of the chaos and rioting which had taken over many Indian cities, where there was no power and often no water supply. The local governments and TAES teams were struggling to restore order. So they had decided not to shift their elders from here to any city, but only to settlements in valleys around Keylong or Mandi.

Her heart sank. Tashi was still game to take her to the last known camp of the TH team, which was about two days march away. But all the locals were against such a step. Leela told Tashi that she would go ahead alone even if he decided to return to Keylong.

But she had an unthinkable shock in store for her.

Leela had been resting in the stable where the animals provided warmth to the inmates in the room above. She was just coming up to talk to Tashi when Sachin rose into her view from the steep road and collapsed in a heap!

She screamed and ran to him. The other inmates helped her carry him to the warm living quarters.

Five days ago, Sachin had escaped from Dehradun. He had instinctively guessed that Leela was not going on some small trek, but on a journey which could be life-threatening. To confirm his suspicions, he had rummaged through Leela's luggage and found her maps, while she was readying herself for her journey. He could not bear the thought of losing her too.

As soon as the first signs of trouble had broken out, Firdaus had come to say goodbye to Sachin before returning to PG. Under the ruse of seeing him off, Sachin left home in his tracksuit. He picked up a loaded backpack with the copied maps which he had hidden near the gate.

When Sachin did not return, Anu looked around and found a note he had left for her, promising to bring back Leela.

This single act broke the elders' resolve. Shiv had a heart attack and hovered between life and death in the local military hospital. Anu herself was now completely broken. Her son Bharat was no more; Leela had not returned from her 'short trek' while all hell had broken loose here – and now her grandson was gone.

For the first time in her life, Anu turned solely to prayer, while running between the Army hospital treating Shiv and the military authorities who had little time to search for a teenage boy who had decamped.

Sachin had a relatively easy passage to Chandigarh, since rioting had not yet broken out. He had trekked in the Keylong-Manali region with Leela earlier, so he already knew how to approach the Bara Lacha - Phirtse La route. But his journey till Manali and beyond turned out to be a nightmare. By now chaos had begun to impact the region with the complete blackouts. He was assaulted and the little money he was carrying was snatched from him by gangs.

By the time Sachin managed to track down Leela in the Tibetan Dardo settlement, he was looking like a battered ghost from a concentration camp. For Leela, the thought of taking him with her into a Trans-Himalayan war zone was suicidal, but she did not have much choice now. To take him back was also loaded with risk. Besides, he was running a fever.

While Leela dithered, Tashi told her that while he could not promise Sachin safe passage back to Dehradun, at least he could provide him a safety net of sorts in most of the villages around Keylong, since Tashi belonged to the same ethnic stock. But this could change any minute, if the army came by to sanitize the region.

It was a Sunday. Sachin had recovered quite fast after swallowing the antipyretic tablets that Leela had given him. He was resting under a thick blanket.

Leela could not even imagine what was happening to the Biswas family in Dehradun, now that Sachin had vanished. She had no means to inform them that he was now in her custody.

The settlement was almost deserted, since the men had taken their elders and families and already left for Keylong. Only two old ladies

387

and an even older Buddhist monk were still there. Leela herself was now ready to proceed to a point where the TH expedition had a scheduled camp a week ago. This would be the place where Aditya had been kept in custody.

She was resting outside with her eyes closed when she heard a vehicle approaching. This was an absolute rarity in this region. It was an armoured LSV V2 army vehicle which was coming straight towards the settlement.

The monk gestured to her to go inside and keep out of sight, while he would talk to the soldiers.

As she turned to go in, from the corner of her eye she saw Arjun Ponappa step out of the jeep in a local dress. There were also two other commando-like personnel with him, with one more person manning the wheel, who were all dressed in local clothes.

The monk ran forward to talk to them, but Arjun bypassed him with his typical swagger. As he turned the corner, he came face to face with Leela. The huge shock on his face was palpable.

They stood that way for almost a minute. Then a flicker of pain shot through Arjun's rugged face. His chest heaved and he shook his head in reproach twice from side to side, before he opened his arms wide. Leela ran into his embrace and sobbed her heart out.

The two old ladies quickly prepared some salt tea for the visitors. Arjun and his TAES men were going from village to village and setting up Sections (Squads) to confront any enemy attacks. He was deputing TAES commando personnel together with local fighters for each Section. He had learnt of Leela's 'small trek' almost a week ago, but his complete focus was on defending the motherland.

Just a day earlier he had been fortuitously dropped by an Army Chopper on evacuation duty at a point on the incomplete Darcha-Padum link road, where the emergency operation to set up a second line of defence with TAES personnel was in full swing. Now he was on his way to an important rendezvous and didn't have the time to take Leela back to safety.

While they were taking a quick tea break, two more groups of TAES commandos and local fighters arrived along with a FV 180 combat tractor and started setting up their defensive bases. Arjun sternly told Leela that the only option open to her was being put on a Chopper which was shifting stranded infirm elders. Did she know what agony the Biswas family was undergoing due to her repeated acts of foolhardiness?

Arjun was shouting about the madness of her mission when Sachin came out, rubbing his eyes. The General's eyes almost popped out! He put up his hands in the air without a single word and trudged outside the hut.

Using his Satnav phone linked to GLONASS, the General immediately contacted a senior Army Official in Dehradun and asked him to give the news to the Biswas household that both Leela and Sachin were safe. 'As of now', he added tersely. Then he turned to Leela and announced that he had decided to find a good Guru once they were out of the woods.

Leela allowed a smile to cross her face. Arjun's sense of humour had not deserted him even during such trying times. She learnt that there was another reason for his good mood. This was due to some incredible news coming from the war front.

After suffering major reverses during the war till now, when the Chinese and Pakistani armies had been poised to threaten Guwahati, Jaipur and even Delhi, there had been a dramatic reversal in fortunes. Both Japan and Vietnam had indirectly entered the war by allowing the Indian Navy and Air Force a close degree of collaboration as a part of the Operation codenamed Oormi-Mandala.

It had started with a Vietnamese submarine made in the Indian dockyards under the 'Make in India' scheme, which was travelling back from India with an indian crew after retrofitting. Shaurya missiles and a series of the latest Brahmos had wreaked havoc on several cities and ports in the Chinese districts of Guangdong, Fujian and even distant Yunnan.

Within an hour, explosions had rocked a patrolling Japanese warship near the Senkaku Islands. This had been followed by another rocket attack from a private shipping vessel on the Japanese Self-Defence Base on the Island of Yonaguni. China had got a taste of its own medicine, since both these were false flag attacks staged by India with full concurrence of the impacted Nations.

For the record, Japan had angrily blamed China for both the acts, and this had been followed by the destruction of the '*Pier for warships*' on Nanji Island, allegedly by the Japanese Navy as a retaliatory measure. And the real blow came when Japan allowed several Stealth fighters from the Joint Indo-Japanese project to mount sorties from their Kadena and Misawa air bases. These aircraft had fired both Brahmos and Nirbhay missiles adapted for air delivery directly into the heart of Beijing and four other major cities with catastrophic results.

Now both Vietnam and Japan stood with India and a new front had been opened in the east. There was unconfirmed news coming in that missiles had flown into China from Mongolia too!

A third front had been reported on the Afghan - Pakistan border with a similar pattern. Trademark false flag attacks on Afghanistan and explosions near Chabahar Port had been swiftly followed by Indian fighter bombers flying sorties from their Farkhor Airbase from Tajikistan and creating panic in western Pakistan. Indian stealth submarines initially docked at the Chabahar Port had attacked and left Gwadar port in ruins. The battle had been truly joined.

But the most incredible mystery had emerged from China's Western Heartland. Reports had come in of a practically vertical split in the PLA formations along the border of Tibet and Xinjiang with Gansu and Qinghai. No one knew if this was a split in the Chinese army or if the Soviets had entered the war, but the PLA contingents fighting their way into India were now trapped in a pincer movement between Indian forces and 'alien' forces attacking their rear! This was not a part of any strategy.

Above all, suddenly the missile and air attacks from North Tibet had come to a halt. The Indian War Cabinet had no clue as to how this had happened, or if the control over the Chinese strategic nuclear assets, the Nuclear tipped GLCMs with the 2nd Artillery Corps and the Chinese 821 brigade had passed to an unidentified counterforce.

Buoyed by this update, Leela expressed her determination to find Aditya at any cost, but the General would have none of it. There was still a war going on in full swing, and he could not go along with such madness. His companions informed him that the Chinese artillery could be barely eighty 'klicks' (kms) away from this location. And Chinese special forces had been Para dropped just twenty 'klicks' away. While the Indian commandos had captured or killed many of these intruders, there would still be a number of them operating in the region which they now had under their control. Going ahead was a complete no go.

She now started thinking of ways of getting around this quagmire and going ahead. If Arjun's men used force to pull her into the jeep the next morning, she would not give in easily. This was her life and she would live it on her own terms.

The General remained with them for an hour more. As it approached dusk, he instructed his men to bring Leela and Sachin to the pick-up point in an APC (armoured Personnel Carrier) which was due next morning. The soldiers would ensure that she and Sachin reached Dehradun in one piece, but no more acts of madness please.

Arjun left with his men in the jeep. He did not look back even once, though Leela knew that he was in great turmoil over her situation. It was mother India for him first, and Leela had to fall in line.

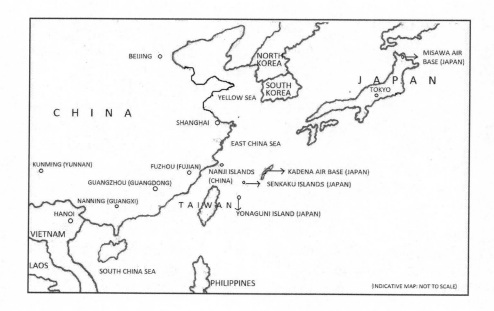

FIFTY NINE

The next morning just before dawn broke, Tashi and Sachin, accompanied by a couple of soldiers, went to fetch water from a stream which was little more than a km away. The TAES commandos and the FV 180 combat tractor were busy fortifying the tiny village and creating bunkers and outposts in a five km radius. The pick-up APC was due in two hours.

Suddenly Leela, who was assisting a Commando in making a bunker under a nearby hillock, was flung to the ground by a sudden pulse of energy. This was the outcome of a misfired HEMP attack from China. Unknown to Leela, this completely destroyed the communication apparatus of the Trans-Himalayan Expedition around sixty kilometres away and cut them off for good from the Monitoring headquarters in Chandigarh. It also crippled all communication equipment in a radius of thirty km.

Leela was unable to move her limbs or think coherently for some time. The Commando was hardier. He pulled her under a small overhanging cliff and told her to stay put while he set out to find Sachin and Tashi and re-establish contact with the commandos in the newly created outposts.

Alone and fatigued in that vast Himalayan Desert, Leela now suffered from a deep sense of guilt. She had set out on a mission of madness to find Aditya, to save him. Instead, here she was, weakened, with hardly any food supplies left, waiting with her heart in her mouth for Sachin, Tashi and now Arjun's men.

But? This 'but' tore at her entrails. How on earth did she give in to Sachin's obstinacy to stay the course with her? Why didn't she immediately return with him to Keylong? Was it her motherly attachment for the boy which had blinded her?

Half an hour passed. Then an hour. Leela tried to calm her mind, but to no avail. But where could they all have gone?

She prayed with tears rolling down her cheeks that the Commando would find Sachin and the others and bring them back. But there was no sign of them.

Yet another hour went by. The Commando had told her not to leave her position under any circumstances, but she could not bear the tension any more. This was wartime, and anything could have happened to them. She decided to look for the missing men.

After a while, she could hear the slow approach of some major human formation from one direction. For Leela, this formation could mean any of the following: The Indian Army or the Chinese or Pakistani paratroopers, who would shoot first and ask questions later.

Just when she was on the verge of turning back, she heard a gunshot. She was close to the ridge top, so she quickly climbed to a position behind a rock face, her gun at the ready.

After a while, she saw a Doe (mother antelope) running frantically and calling out. A little ahead not far from Leela was its baby, a tiny calf. When she got the focus of her field glasses right, Leela could see that the mother already had a small wound on her hind portion. Then she rotated the view and saw a couple of soldiers at a good distance on the opposite part of the valley. They were shaded by some dry bushes. These men were weaving in and out of sight and it was impossible to make out whether they were Indian soldiers or the Chinese.

Yet another shot rang out. They were targeting the calf.

Leela remembered the strict training which she had received long ago from Gen. Arjun Ponappa, that come what may she should not open fire unless in self-defence, and not ever reveal her position in such a situation.

She quickly detached one section of the field glasses and fixed it atop her gun. Now she could see two armed men who were laughing and pressing each other to shoot first. She zoomed in to the maximum. Maybe they were hungry and the antelopes could be their meat rations for a few days.

Leela restrained herself. Surely these men had a right to survive. But they looked quite well-fed. Were these Chinese troops or Pakistani forces or what? She was unable to make out.

A few seconds later, she had no more doubts. One man stepped out in full view and bent down to take proper aim, while two others appeared behind him. These were certainly Chinese paratroopers who were fully secure in the mistaken knowledge that their assault troops had now taken over control of the surrounding region from the Indian forces. The misfired HEMP attack had destroyed their communication links too.

Leela's heart was pounding, as Arjun's training drill kept playing back aloud in her mind, restraining her from revealing her position.

The soldier fired. Immediately, the Doe was spun around by the impact of the bullet on her hind upper leg. But she struggled up and started racing desperately towards the summit.

The man shouted a frustrated abuse. He was pushed aside by another soldier, who now took aim and fired. This missed the calf by a whisker and raised a small cloud of dust in the desert. This time both men shouted in anger and bent down to take careful aim.

Leela threw caution to the winds. Here were well stocked men, professional killers who were enjoying a blood sport as to who could hit pay dirt first and nail an innocent calf.

She trained her sights quickly and fired.

The first soldier was hit somewhere on the shoulder and was knocked back by the impact. Immediately the second man shouted a loud warning and swung around towards Leela while aligning his rifle. But she fired first and found her target. The man slumped down.

Within seconds a posse of paratroopers had appeared from behind the rock face, where they had possibly been taking a bite. They opened up in Leela's direction with their weapons.

Leela took cover behind the rock face, but it was not enough. The men were spreading out in a bid to encircle her position. If she stayed here, she was doomed. There were smaller rocks behind her leading to a summit. She had to make a dash for it.

She fired a couple of rounds while moving. Then she ran for her life towards the summit. Now there were bullets spraying dust and scree all around her.

Just as she almost reached the top, she was slammed to the ground. She knew she had been hit. Her right leg would not move.

The bullets were still flying. She made one major thrust with her able leg and pushed herself over the edge. At that point a second shot slammed into her, fully tilting her over.

She rolled down for a good thirty meters or more and came to a stop, trapped by a bush. For a split second, she saw that the Doe and her calf had crossed into this wide valley and raced far away. The limping Doe was still on her feet.

But when Leela tried to get up, she found she could not move. There was nausea and an urge to throw up. She could feel her strength gradually ebbing away. The troops pursuing her would have her in their sights in no time.

The unending stretch of turquoise above her was reflected in the waters of an exquisite lake a small distance away. Had she been here before?

Her thoughts were suddenly disrupted by the sound of a tremendous burst of firing from far. She could not see any Chinese troops on the summit, so it was not directed at her. After a while she even heard heavy artillery open up.

Her sights were starting to dim. She saw a strange looking Aerial vehicle which suddenly appeared and hovered above her silently for a while – and then it flew away. A little while later she heard the sound of heavy bombardment which shook the ground below her.

After a short gap, there was complete silence. Some mountain eagles were circling over her. She tried to get up, but slumped back in pain. Yes, pain was now entering her world.

Was this the end?

Slowly, through excruciating pain, she set her eyes on the sunlight lighting up the magnificent snow peaks around her. There was no Aditya anywhere and Sachin too was gone.

She wept and raised her voice to utter an imploring cry to the 'heavens' above.

And then through her stupor, she saw them: a long line of strange soldiers marching silently towards her. Why couldn't she hear their footsteps?

She seemed to see Sachin among the first file. The boy was limping while trying to run towards her. How was this possible? Was it Arjun Ponappa behind him?

As they came nearer, a Tata Kestrel FICV appeared from behind the column. It raked up a cloud of dust as it came to a halt near her. As her vision blurred again, she dimly saw a tall figure who alighted from the Kestrel to head the fast approaching column. But why did this figure cast no shadow? Was she hallucinating?

Leela was filled by a new found strength, by a fervent desire to live. But her legs did not support her, and her eyes started closing. Darkness was enveloping her, and the light would break through only with some effort.

Silhouetted by the lambent halo on the snow peaks, a hand descended and held her palm in an invigorating clasp.

And then she heard the majestic voice through the haze:

'*Jago Maa.*' (Mother... awake.)

AUTHOR'S NOTE and ACKNOWLEDGEMENTS

A TRYST WITH MAHAKAAL, (formerly titled Mahakaal - The Ghost who never died), is a parallel narrative to my film screenplay 'QUEST'. As an International film project, QUEST secured a Letter of Intent from India's leading Film Production Company in 2008 but was never turned into celluloid. The leading character in QUEST, Dr Aditya Basu, appears briefly in this book and forms an important link between the two works. The book uses Quest's futuristic backdrop as the setting in which the main protagonists meet their life's challenges, inspired by the words of a mysterious man who never appeared in public for over thirty years and who always spoke from behind a curtain.

It is Anuj Dhar and Chandrachur Ghosh who made me aware of the existence of such a personage, otherwise known as Bhagwanji or Gumnami Baba. What started with references to my granduncle, ex-Foreign Secretary (late) Subimal Dutt's role in the official Netaji Subhas Bose files post 1945, gradually led to a long relationship with this duo spread over fourteen years. They also introduced me to the key people connected with the Bhagwanji saga in Kolkata and Faizabad. My foremost gratitude is to them for being forthcoming for all my questions and concerns.

I remain grateful to Shri Bijoy Nag and the Late Dr RP Mishra who personally gave me several deep insights into Bhagwanji's character. My sincere thanks to Ms Rita Banerjee, the (late) Dulal Nandy, Dr Vishambhar Nath Arora, Nirupam Mishra and Shakti Singh who recounted their experiences to me.

I also thank Dr Madhusudan Pal for regularly interacting with me since 2009 and for his generosity in providing archival references and clarifications whenever I needed them.